The Misadventures of Myndil Plodostirr
In which a beloved missionary encounters heathens, werewolves, murderous faeries, and people who generally dislike him, and he tries to tell everybody about god, only the person whom Myndil thinks is god is not really god, and the abbot does not really like him, and he accidentally causes the Great War...

by: Michelle Franklin

Published by Pendelhaven 2022

Pendelhaven
121 2ieme Bourbonniere
Lachute, Quebec, Canada
J8H 3W7
www.fateofthenorns.com
www.pendelhaven.com

Based on the Fate of the Norns world created by Andrew Valkauskas

Cover artwork by Yulia Novikova

Editing: Ed Greenwood

ISBN 978-1-988051-29-1

Published in Canada
Printed in the USA

RAGNAROK
FATE OF THE NORNS

GRONLAND
SVALBARD
FINNMARK
HALOGALAND
THE NORTH SEA
POHJOLA
TRONDHEIM
JAMTLAND
HORRLAND
ISLANDIA
MIRKVID
HELSINGLAND
KALEVALA
FAROE
SOGN
UPPLAND
THE GREAT SEA
HORALAND
SVEALAND
ROGALAND
ALBA
VESTFOLD
RANRIKE
STRATHCLYDE
IRSE SEA
GOTALAND
NORTHUMBRIA
HIBERNIA
JUTLAND
THE GREAT ISLES
ZERLAND
SKANE
WESSEX
BALTIC SEA
BALTIC TRIBES
FRISIA
SAXONY
WENDLAND
BRITTANY
FRANCIA
BLACK SEA

For Terry Jones,
Whose wit and knowledge is incalculable, whose history lessons always put me under the glamour of discovery, and whose comedic voice, though unjustly muted, will forever be in my ear.
And how in the world did you get in there, man? Do have the decency to clean the canal, if you are going to make house in it.
Comedians, like historians, are never fully housebroken when let out upon the world, and they will bang about and make a noise despite the floggings. When one is both comedically and historically inclined, scribacious habits will follow, a side effect of genius that will not sit still. Knowledge is a tried remedy for pedantically related complaints, but there is no cure for comedy, a condition which afflicts many and is conquered by so few.

For Eric Idle
Suppose you're all right too.

For Sir Terry Pratchett
A damn nuisance to have lost you so soon. Now, whenever I want to ask your advice about something, I have to consult the spices. Salt is always in fashion, but lilac is rarely in bloom.
I did as you said and wrote the ending first.

For the Werewolves of Osraige
Who are responsible for much of this book. Thank you for sending your agents to drop that book at my door. I am indebted to you always.

For Lily
Devotional danglies. May Brigid bless your house always.

For Rebeka
Because thirsty nuns require meaty weremen.

For Brittany
Because boobs will find a way.

For Ed Greenwood
Rather for your beard rather than for you, because I know it is sentient and does all your typing for you.
Outlast the bastards, squelching sounds and all.

For James Kerr
Oh, dread. That stain is never going to come out, said in Kermit voice.

For Andrew Valkauskas
Because you love Myndil so much.

Table of Contents

chapter 1: in which myndil plodostirr happens to the orphanage

Life happened to most people, but Myndil Plodostirr happened to everybody else.

Where other children had grown up with the usual complaints of niggling mothers, wholesome dinners, and work to be done after daily lessons, Myndil was the disposition to like everything and a capacity to like everyone. His mother had died young, and though little was known of Myndil's father, it was certain that he had one: someone had to bring him to the orphanage. All that was known of the Plodostirr parents was that one of them must have been good natured, and the other must have been very quiet, for Myndil had inherited all the friendliness and anxious curiosity from one side of the family, and had been passed over by all the tranquility of the other. He arrived at the orphanage when he was just five years old, and from the moment the Brothers and Sisters came to claim him to the time he had gone to bed, he spoke in eager ramblings, professing his excitement at being in a new home, waving to the man who had left him there with a "He's your problem now. Lord have mercy on you," and altogether expressed a mind and maturity rarely seen in a child of twice his age. The Brothers and Sisters at the orphanage had no fears for Myndil: he had a natural inclination toward exuberance, blamed nobody for their faults, believed everyone commanding themselves with right intentions, and found a comfortable home at the orphanage, a good establishment with right-minded matrons and masters, where Myndil was tricked into an early education and out of physical labour, where his moderate understanding and high glee were wasted on peers who knew no more of kindliness than they did of sharing.

If left to themselves, children have no idea of prejudice when choosing friends, and while each child has their own way, they were all alike in their dislike of Myndil. Orphans usually had nominal friendships: knowing they were going to be adopted and separated from one another, they kept their schoolfellows at a distance, limiting their friendships and rivalries to grades and games. Myndil, however, never maintained the hope of being taken in by another set of parents, his talkativeness and constant need for attention hardly recommended him for adoption, and he therefore decided that he ought to befriend everybody, feeling himself loved enough by the Brothers and Sisters at the orphanage and desirous of sharing their affection with everybody else. He knew he was not well-liked, but had no idea of how much; mantled with childlike innocence, Myndil skipped through childhood and into adolescence without maintaining a single friendship, his incessant questions, tireless parentheticals, and offers to go shares in everything a source of perpetual irritation. He begged to be allowed in every game, would invite himself to every conversation, and would reiterate every story the Brothers and Sisters told them at lessons or at bedtime until he had learned them by rote. He was a great talker for one so young, a font of information about the natural world, a religious scholar who loved discussing gods and heathenry with everyone whether they wanted to hear his views or not, and had learned how to talk his way out of any situation he had got himself into, not from any want to be seditious, but from a genuine desire of wanting to rally every rock and tree and child to his cause. He wielded affability as a weapon and directed it at everyone who approached him, attacking his opponents with warm-heartedness, unabated solicitations, and delirious smiles. The children at the orphanage and the school eventually grew tired of his blathering and contrived to escape whenever Myndil was by, when the Brothers and Sisters were wearied from his conversation, they made the usual excuse of having work to do and fled, and Myndil delighted in it all with a shrug and an "Oh, well," and turned his attention toward his one true friend, the one who would never turn away from him, had heard all his supplications, had borne all his questions with ready forbearance, and had answered all of his prayers.

God, said Myndil, had saved him: he was young when his mother had died, but he had the distinct remembrance of her telling him that God loved him and was watching over him always. This was taken literally, and at a young age, with no companions and a father who was not much for conversation, Myndil began talking to god as though he was a third parent. He asked for guidance after his mother died, told god all his plans and machinations, played games of Three Bowls and Hop-penny with god as an opponent, and while Myndil was delighted to be the fondling of his mother's patron aegis, his father was concerned that Myndil was happier than a child who had lost his mother should be. The boy was smiling, was laughing and tumbling down hills, was reading books out loud and commenting on the passages as though someone were sitting there beside him. At first, his father thought it was a clever coping scheme, an imaginary friend for a grieving child to cling to, but it never ceased: Myndil set a place at the table for god, took baths with god, ran through the meadow and caught frogs at the pond with god, and when this fascination would not go away, Myndil was brought to the one place where he could be with god for as long as he liked.

Myndil was never lonely at the orphanage: between his prayers, his lessons, his chores, and his attention from the Brothers and Sisters, god was an auxiliary to his daily life, and his father, a quiet man with no ability for raising children, was relieved to relinquish Myndil to the care of those who could love and mind him. The Brothers and Sisters were prepared for something very different when Myndil was brought to them, but even though he was young and preoccupied, at five years old he was already his own master: he washed and dressed himself, he brushed his teeth and cleaned his room without being asked, and when he was not in his lessons or saying his prayers, he was talking to god or reading a book aloud for the benefit of the other children though no one asked him to.

Except the occasional rambling whenever he answered a question, Myndil was an exemplary student: he learned all his books, did his assignments and even helped the other children with theirs, became a second to the Brothers and Sisters when asked, and was a model for right scholarly habits. He was eager and busy, always ready to give his opinion, ready to interpret passages, and always answering for everybody else with a fervent, "I know! I know! Ooh, ooh! Pick me! Pick me, please! Please let me answer this one!" He was a peculiar child, acting more like a young boy of fifteen than he was boasting his real age, more knowledgeable and thoughtful than child brought up in an orphanage should be. "How is it, my dear Myndil, that you know so much?" the Brothers and Sisters often said to him, meaning it as a means of praise, but Myndil always replied, "Well, you see, I asked God about it, and he said—" This explanation and all its subsequent variations were endearing at first, but his admissions grew tiresome; he must be telling stories, fabricating these conversations with God as a means of giving credit to unexplainable genius—but for Myndil, God and His Divine Presence could never be explained away. After a while, the Brothers and Sisters laid it down that Myndil was merely a 'good but strange boy who was not altogether as stupid as he looked', and forgave the little excesses of character.

Myndil, however, was firm in his connection with God: god had been his first thought, his first vision, his first word, and being a child of good understanding and few social abilities, he was much more sensible of a higher power than any other child his age was. He spoke to god every evening and often talked himself to sleep, said his morning prayer aloud, that everyone might hear him ask God why there was poverty and starvation in the world, why there had to be raisins in the frumenty, why the gruel had to be so cold and thin, why Maribel liked to pull his hair especially after she had used the same hand to exhume the contents of her nose, and why no one wanted to share his warm milk with him at night, even though his milk had been untouched when he offered it, etc. He was suspiciously unmoved by things that usually frightened children his age: he loved the dark, because it was quiet and he liked to hear the sound of his own voice band between the walls, looked forward to nightmares, because the boggarts would come and play with him there, and enjoyed the company of monsters, especially the ones that corralled in the garden and under the bed. Closet monsters were second rate and did not factor into much of his nightly conversations, but fairies were more talkative, and night-hags at his window listened in amazement at Myndil's ability to charm the dust from the walls merely by talking it off. His ability to communicate improved with age, even if his ramblings remained the same; he reasoned and coaxed without disguise, and he grew up under the glamour of faith, believing everyone to be good, thinking that all god's creatures were divine and ought to be protected—even the dairy cow, who had kicked him a few times, though he had brought her mangolds to eat—and loving a god who neither liked public appearances nor spoke so frequently to anybody else.

Myndil, with all the confusion that adolescence supplies, soon became a young man and began happening to other people, especially those who hated him most. His pleasant character and general goodwill should have recommended him as everybody's firm favourite, but he was always being so wretchedly helpful, so smiling and so musing, never uneasy or irritated, was forever waving or greeting someone or other, was continually offering his blessings and advice without being asked for either, and though he was an agreeable and good-looking young man, his solicitations for everyone's ideas and opinions became insufferable. He was amusing to look at, a blameless boy darting about with benedictions and questions for everyone, but his voice and volubility were a curse, and once Myndil was of age, the Brothers and Sisters deemed it advisable that Myndil should be gone—not got rid of, but moved farther off, somewhere at an abbey, where he might speak to god all day and bother nobody else. It was a hardship deciding where he should go and who should be the one to tell him. He certainly could not be permitted to stay; he was pleasant to children and did not mind their biting and hallooing very much, but he was unfit for teaching, his oration was deplorable at best, and he had better find a new vocation and get permanent home elsewhere. His peers were all moving on, some to towns, some to local villages for apprenticeships, some to other orphanages to be responsible for bringing up others, and Myndil was always seeing them off with indefatigable smiles and frantic waves, crying out, "Goodbye! God go with you, because, you know, he is everywhere, not because he should be always watching you every second, which he is doing anyway, but benevolently—oh, you're already gone. Well, you must be eager to see your new home. I will stay here and wait, in case you should like to come back—God bless you!"

Myndil was twenty-one, and it was time that he should find himself employment, a good situation, one that would cater to his right-minded principles and well-meaning open-heartedness. Farming would not do for him, though he did help the farmers in the summer, nothing in the arts would satisfy one so devoid of creative talent, and while Myndil was proficient in lifting and illumination, physical labour would not exactly suit someone who talked more than worked. The Brothers and Sisters waited eagerly for news of some situation—Brother Vindimir especially, as he had been craving Myndil's room for the last few years and was desperate for the large bed and view of the white tree in the garden—but even with a position in mind for Myndil, the difficulty was in getting him to it. He was so well-settled at the orphanage, being the steward of the library, commander of the byre, and lord of the besom, it seemed a shame to pluck a fixture from its fitting. They thought he might ripen with age and lose some of his cultivated social failings, but at twenty-one years old, Myndil was still making the same blunders as he did when he was ten.

At last, a place for Myndil was found in a neighbouring abbey: it was newly established, and Myndil was thought of as being a possible caretaker of the building and the issuing grounds, and though the position was not what Myndil deserved, it was a something to get him out. Brother Crannach was given the office of breaking it to Myndil. He was a large and loving man, doting and attentive, one who had installed himself as a father figure for the orphans, one who had always been fond of Myndil, thought of him as a son, and was sorry to see him go; like Myndil, Crannach was fond of most people, had a tempered resolve, and had forbearance even for that which distressed him most. He was not one for long and laborious conversation, and when he came to Myndil, to speak to him about what must be, his words and heart began to fail him. He came to Myndil just after breakfast and gestured toward the garden.

"Myndil, son," said Brother Crannach, in a grim tone, taking Myndil by the arm, "'mon, lad. Let's walk fer a bit."

Myndil always listened readily whenever Brother Crannach had anything to say, and he went with him into the garden, where they walked amongst the first of the snowdrop and daffodil, Myndil remarking the how the violets were sure to come out soon, and Brother Crannach meeting his conversation with an "Aye, son," punctuating every phrase.

4

They walked to the far end of the garden and sat on the stone bench, Brother Crannach dreading the coming conversation, and Myndil too busy admiring the first signs of the coming spring.

"It really is a lovely day," Myndil proclaimed, putting his hands beneath the front panel of his scapular. "A bit of a chill in the air, but the sun is out, and everything is beginning to thaw. I will miss the winter, however. I know it can be a difficult for the elderly and infirmed, but there is really nothing better than snow. I love when I can see my breath in the air—I still can—haah, haah—see the way it coils and vanishes—"

"Lad," Crannach began heavily, putting a hand on Myndil's knee.

"Yes, Brother Crannach?"

Myndil gaped with speaking anticipation, and Crannach sighed and stared at the nearby well.

"Do ye ever think o' things, lad?" Crannach began.

"Oh, I know the answer to this one— Yes, I do. I think of many things all the time."

"What Ah meant was, ever think 'o what the world has tae offer?"

"Of course I do," Myndil proclaimed. "I think about it all the time. I think about God and the coming holidays. I think about all the cheeses I haven't yet tried and all the bread that was left over from yesterday that would go along quite well with them. I think about all the eggs I have to take in, because Sister Iarlaith does not like going near the coop—the chickens do peck her a lot— I think about Ozzy and how much he laments his flowerbeds in the winter—"

"Ah meant life beyond the orphanage, son," Brother Crannach interposed. "Ever think about what comes after?"

Myndil pouted in deliberation. "Well, I try not to think about it, because I want to finish my work first and appreciate everything God has given me, but I suppose we all must consider what comes after sometime."

"Aye, that's it, lad," said Brother Crannach, giving him an encouraging pat on the back.

"It is somewhat distressing to think about. I do wonder what the hereafter will be like and if it will be anything like how the Good Book says, with all the clouds and angels and Divine Judgement—but God will be there, and I should very much like to see God. He told me all about it once when I asked. God said there are many pillars and long halls, and that there are pits of fire that smell like brimstone—"

"Aye, that's good, son," said Brother Crannach, petting him, "that's plentae, but Ah meant do ye ever think about leavin' the orphanage and livin' somewheres else?"

Myndil blinked. "No. Should I?"

"Well, yer gettin' aulder, son."

"I am, but I don't know that I can stop aging."

"What Ah mean is," said Brother Crannach, straining under a heavy heart, "lads yer age go off tae make their own wae in the world, to find work and make a life for 'emselves."

"Most do go away," Myndil acknowledged, "but not all. Brother Vindimir is here."

"Aye."

"And you're here."

"Aye."

"And you're older than me."

"Aye, Ah am that, but Ah'm also ordained as a Brother, and Ah've dedicated mah life to carin' for wee-uns and bringin' 'em up by the Grace of God."

"Then that's what I'll do," Myndil proclaimed. "I'll stay here and help you."

There was an awkward pause. "Well—ye see, Myndil-son— Ah want ye tae stay, but there's nae room here for another Brother."

"But I love everything about the orphanage. I love you and all the other Brothers and Sisters and all the children, and I love everyone else who lives with us, like Ozzy the Wight, Mr Dullahan, and the nisser—"

"Aye," said Brother Crannach, turning aside. "Yer not makin' it easae, lad— Mebbe God needs ye elsewhere. There're other orphanages and abbeys what need yer help."

"But I help here," said Myndil, in a softened voice. "And I don't think I am very much in the way. I do all my chores. I love getting up early to the ring the bells and bring in the water, even when the water is cold and it whips me in the face when I put the basin down. I love the garden and sward, and how we are so nestled in here by the sea. I love caring for our animals and looking after the boggarts—"

"Aye, yer a good helper, son, but ye doan't want tae mebbe learn a trade?"

"Should I? Well, I already know how to make tiles and do waddle walls. I don't know that I would be very good at brickmaking. I am useless for masonry, because I talk too much to make the chisel go straight, and I don't think I should make a very good blacksmith either."

"Well, think what else yer good at."

Myndil hummed and considered this. "I'm very good at running away," said he thoughtfully. "I'm also good at being kicked by things."

Brother Crannach must laugh here. "'Mon, Myndil-son. Ah know there's one thing yer good at doin', better 'an anaebodae else, and it's so obvious yer no' thinkin' of it."

"Praying?"

"Talkin'."

"Yes! Talking! Of course! I'm very good at talking, that's true. I didn't think of it."

"Probablae 'cause yer too busae talkin' when ye should be thinkin'."

"Yes, probably, but I do think an awful lot too, only I do much of my thinking by talking things through."

"Aye, lad," Crannach simpered. "As Ah alwaes say: ye've alwaes got yer mind in yer mouth."

"But what can talking do for me? I don't know that there is such a thing as a profession for talking. Well, there are marketmen and traders, and they are very good at selling things, but there is a great deal of shouting in their professions, and my oration is not as good as—"

6

"Communitae outreach." Crannach explained, stabbing a finger at Myndil's chest. "Ah think it'd be a good thing fer a lad like yersel', goin' out and seein' things and makin' friends. Gonnae have tae work on listenin' though."

"I am rather deficient there," Myndil solemnly agreed, "but that's because I compensate so much by talking—but how can I practice outreach?"

"Well, when you go to the abbey and talk tae 'em about a position, ye might—"

"I'm going to an abbey?" said Myndil instantly, his aspect brightening.

"We found ye a place ye might liek, for the communitae outreachin' an' o'."

He told him about the abbey there and about the small farming community attached to it. It was a retired place, quiet and out of the way, in the northwest, green and cool in the summer, white with frost in the winter, and there Myndil could bother every rock and tree, practice his oration to the wind, and talk to as many otherwise solitary parishioners as he liked. He could help the local farms with their harvests, mind the animals and mend fences, tend the garden, help with prayers and ceremonies, and spend his evenings speaking to God within the confines of his own room. Myndil agreed to all this: it was the most natural thing in the world for him to be sent to an abbey, a place where he could command his own time and make friends, but he should miss the orphanage, should miss the Brothers and Sisters, should miss his bed and his pillow—well, he might be allowed to take that with him, he was sure nobody else should want a pillow in the shape of the Good Book, especially one Sister Iarlaith had made for him so long ago—but he would have to say goodbye to everyone who had been so kind to him for the last fifteen years. He was somewhat vexed, as anyone who is being made to leave his home must be, but god would be with him—no one so comforting and so soothing as god.

"I don't know that I like the idea of leaving home so much, though I wonder at how all my peers have done it so easily," said Myndil, in a mindful hue. "It's a wonder that they all did not become Brothers and Sisters—wait!" The sunlight broke through the trees and glanced off Myndil's eyes, bringing a glow to his face. "What if I want to be ordained?"

Brother Crannach seemed hesitant. "Ye want tae be a Brother?"

"Yes! And why shouldn't I? I love God so much and I would be devoting my life to Him and glorifying His Grace—of course, it only makes sense for me to be a member of the laity. If I am ordained at the abbey by the abbot there, I could come back when there is room for another Brother here!"

"Aye, suppose ye could be ordained, aye…" Brother Crannach struggled here: Myndil must go away, but how to make him leave now? It was perfectly natural and unfortunately perfectly legal for one who had grown up under the auspices of god to want to join it. Myndil could not be excluded on the grounds of talkativeness alone; he was irritating at times, but he was well-meaning and would do well for the religion, if he could point his rhetorical assault in the right direction. Myndil would have to govern himself if he wanted to return to the orphanage, would have to learn discipline, and if guided by right-minded and educated people—but how to give Myndil time to cultivate these qualities was the question. How to get Myndil away now? Brother Crannach deliberated—he had it! He continued: "Once yer ordained, ye'll have tae get the abbot's permission to be a Brother here, and bein' ordained might take a while, son. 'Tis no' an overnight thing."

"Oh, I know. I was thinking I could go to the abbey for a year or so, and then I could come back, to visit for holy days, surely, if not to live here. I would like to see you sometimes. I should be very sorry to go and leave you behind, you who have done so much for me and loved me since I was a boy. It would be rude of me to leave forever and never come back to see you again."

"Aye..." was all Brother Crannach's reply, said with eyes low and heart heavy. The pangs of guilt assailed him; it was wrong to send Myndil away under a false pretense, but Myndil must go or he would never learn. Would that he and his rants were not so tiresome to everyone else—he had the warmest heart, but that was not enough to do away with all the little irritations that plagued the orphanage when Myndil was around. He must leave, for the benefit of himself and others, and if he came back a sober and more sensible man, so much the better.

It was decided: Myndil would go to the abbey the following morning, he would be allowed the whole day to say his goodbyes to the inmates, the library, and the cow, he would have his last meal in the orphanage, say his last story to the children, enjoy one last sleep in his own bed, and then would be gone from the place as long as his new superiors at the abbey could keep him. Myndil had his last dinner that evening, said his goodbyes to the kitchen, said he was sorry to leave the bread oven and his frumenty bowl behind but could do without being made to stand in the ewery cabinet for an hour after meals with the plates, drying and drying them again, smoothed out his bedclothes, flumped under the covers, and tucked himself in with a 'goodnight' to all the creeping creatures beyond the sill, a 'sleep tight' to all the fey living in the cracks and closets, and a 'don't let the boggarts bite' to himself as he drew up his blankets, adjusted his sleeping cap, and cuddled with his Good Book pillow under his arm.

His sleeping cap had a smaller version of the Good Book dangling from the end of it, made with felt, crocheted with the phrase GOD LOVES YOU written in the folds. Myndil hoped he would be allowed to take it with him when he went; he would donate it to one of the other children, but it was one of his few possessions, and it meant so much to him, a sentimental piece that revived Sister Iarlaith's tender caresses. A more doting warden could not be found anywhere, and as Myndil held his pillow and eyed the felted one hanging from his cap, his mind harkened back to the two soft immense mounds his face was crushed into every day when Sister Iarlaith had held him against her chest. She was a large and loving woman, one whom Myndil had grown fond of, one who never seemed too busy to read to him or teach him something new, one who always dressed his wounds and combed his hair and pressed his cheek to her ample frame and cooed at him with fat sighs about how good a boy he was and how well he learned his book.

"I don't think they should mind very much if I take my pillow with me," Myndil sighed, reading over the GOD LOVES YOU in the pillow fold to himself. "It doesn't have much value to anyone else, and it was made for me, since I was having difficulty sleeping the first few months when I came

8

here. It seems so far off now, my first night here. Hard to imagine how I was back then."

"Aye, Ah remembeh 'ow yewe woz," said a gravel-choked voice from under the bed. "Fryghtened ov yer own shadow, yewe. Didn't even feel fit ta scare yewe till yewe woz settled in propah."

"I remember the first night you tried to give me nightmares," said Myndil, in a warm accent. "You were so disappointed that I wasn't bothered by you."

"Aye, Ah woz. Thought t'meself, 'Ere this lad's jogged, wot with yewer excytement at meetin' a bogeyman and all." A languorous and wraithlike hand crept out from under the bed. "But we com t'undehstand won anothah, don't we, oveh the years?"

"Yes. I will miss you, Thingunderthebed."

"Aye, and Ah yewe, mah pretteh wan. Though, Ah must say, Ah'm lookin' forward t'fryghtenin' wotever comes in 'ere next. Ah hope it's Brotheh Vindimir, or whateveh t' won's name is."

"Why is that?"

"Because Ah knows 'e wants this room, and though the place belongs t'yewer lord, the bed and the closet are myne."

"He is in for a treat, then," Myndil professed, sinking down between the covers. "Nothing like hearing the demonic murmurs of an otherworldly being to soothe you right to sleep. I will miss it. I wonder if there are similar creatures at the abbey."

"Ah've probableh got a cousin or two down t' way. Ah'll send the werd along and tell'em yewer comin'."

"Thank you, Thingunderthebed. I shall always be grateful for how much you look after my wellbeing."

There was a shrug under the bed frame. "Fryghtenin' wee wans and seein' t' their needs is wot Ah dewe."

A tender sigh here: it seemed like only weeks ago Myndil had his first fright by the resident boggart. There were several creatures that lived in and around the orphanage, nothing very bad, a few wisps, a phuca or two in the warmer months, Ozzy the Wight out in the garden, the nisser in the pantry, and Mr Dullahan running around the gate. Myndil would miss them, even the ones that liked ripping his hems and biting his fingers while he slept. There were a few faeries that tried to lead him astray in the neighbouring forest once or twice, but he passed their schemes off as their way and lamented that there would be no bog-hags at the parish worthy of trying to kill him. God always saved him from a crueler fate, or his Faith did, and while the joke of Myndil talking his fellow inmates into madness was not meant with any seriousness, his ability to ward off the many evils of the world by talking them away extended to all of God's creatures, especially those who had no idea what god was. They listened to Myndil, they heard his supplications and felt his woes, and though they did indulge in a nibble or two now and again, he would be very sorry to leave them.

"Maybe I ought not to go?" said Myndil doubtingly. "If I leave, who will talk to the nisser and make sure he doesn't try to marry our cow? Who will fill the pond for the nixie during the drought season —though he can be a bit conceited and rude sometimes— and who will read to the children when Brother Crannach has fallen asleep on himself after dinner? Perhaps, if I could find a way to stay—"

"You're leaving—I mean, ahem—MYNDIL. YOU MUST LEAVE THIS PLACE. GO OUT FROM HERE AND SEEK THY PURPOSE."

The voice came from somewhere beyond the far wall. Myndil sat up directly.

"Is that you, God?" he asked, glancing about. "I was just about to ask for your guidance. How did you know? Well, I know how you knew, because you are God—but is it really you?"

"YES, IT IS I. ME. Er—I... IT IS GOD, MYNDIL, AND I AM COME TO GIVE YOU COUNSEL."

"Oh, that's so thoughtful of you, because you know I was just thinking—but are you all right, God? You sound a bit different tonight. Are you well?"

"GOD HAS A COLD."

"Oh, I am sorry to hear of it. That is what comes from spending so much time around your children, I expect."

"YOU MUST LEAVE THIS PLACE, AND DEVOTE YOURSELF TO A LIFE IN MY HOLY SERVICE."

"I mean to, God. As I'm sure You already know, I am being sent to an abbey, where I mean to be ordained eventually—"

"AND YOU MUST STAY THERE."

"Oh. Must I?"

"YES." The voice paused. "AND YOU MUST NEVER COME BACK TO THE ORPHANAGE. OR TO THIS ROOM. OR THIS BED."

"That is rather specific for a commandment—"

"GO AND BE A BROTHER, BUT BE A SHEPHERD TO A NEW FLOCK."

"I don't know that I've ever been a shepherd before. Well, I did manage the sheep the one year we had them, but they were very violent and liked eating my hair, and when it came time to shear them, one of them did tear a patch from my robe—"

"MYNDIL."

"Yes, God."

"LISTEN."

"Yes!"

"YOU WILL LEAVE THIS PLACE AND GO OUT, TO KNOW THYSELF AND SHARE MY MESSAGE WITH THE WORLD."

"I will, O Lord!"

"AND DO NOT COME BACK HERE UNTIL YOUR WORK IN GLORIFYING MY GRACE BE DONE."

"I won't!"

"DO YOU UNDERSTAND?"

"I do, O Lord! Praise be to God!"

Snores suddenly billowed up from the blankets, Myndil croosled in his sleep, tootling about becoming a Brother and how God made him promise he would never come back to the orphanage, and Brother Vindimir, satisfied with the charade, stepped away from the wall. He was a tall and thin man, considerate but more practical than most, his features sharp, his long nose large enough to fit through the small hole in the wall.

"He had better not come back," said Vindimir, turning to Brother Crannach behind him. "Fifteen years long years I've been waiting for that room. It should have been mine long ago, but I felt too guilty on his behalf, and I believe I have paid my penance by spending the last long while sharing a room with you. Tomorrow, that bed will be mine at long last."

"Are ye sure ye want it though?" Brother Crannach asked, walking with Vindimir into the main hall. "A boggart lives under it."

"I'll get Iarlaith to get rid of it. You know how she loves those things."

"Aye, she likes anaethin' she can hug too hard." Here was a sly glance.

"You ought to be delighted in that regard. I leave our room for one of my own, and you get to invite her into your bed without my groaning about it. The woman is a tent, practically made for spreading out, and she loves caring for anything that eats well."

Brother Crannach eyed his own round stomach, but his conscience was beginning to weigh on him. "Ah cannae help think tha' askin' him to leave and pretenin' tae be God is o' wrong."

"I agree to a certain extent, and I do feel badly about it sometimes, but he is long past the age of leaving."

"Aye, but ye know how Ah feel about it. Myndil's a bit gentle in the brain, and he doan't deserve tae be tossed out liek he doan't matter tae us."

"He does matter to us considerably," said Vindimir stoutly, "but you know as well as I that there is such a thing as giving too much charity. We cannot coddle him forever."

"He was sent tae us for a reason."

"And so is every child that we care for. We taught him only good things, told him that God loves him, and that he would be blessed in everything as long as he was kind to all of God's creations."

Crannach disliked disingenuousness; he did not wear compunction well, and throughout the evening, he sat in his room alone with his wonderings, staring ruefully at the opposite wall, lamenting over what he had been witness to and hating himself for allowing it. He could not retract what Vindimir had done; he could only repent and hope that God understood that what they did, they did for the peace of the orphanage and the overall good of its inmates, though Crannach and Iarlaith certainly would rather have him stay than submit him to the cruelty of strangers.

Punishment is not always a swift business; alacrity was strangely left out of the Divine Powers when they were giving away from the Celestial Seat, but where Myndil and retribution was concerned, god wasted no time in ruining all Brother Vindimir's happiness. The following morning, as Myndil was packing his things and debating over whether he should carry his Good Book pillow or pat it down into his pack, a letter arrived at the orphanage. It came from the nearby abbey and brought disconcerting and delightful news: the abbot was to visit, to take a perusal of the grounds and draw up plans for a new abbey, one that would annex the orphanage and create a monastic complex, replete with dormitory and attached gardens, where every Brother and Sister and all those who would be a member of the Lord's laity could come and seek refuge from the barbarism and heathenry of the outside world. The abbot would install himself as a permanent fixture in the place within a few days' time, everything was to be under his domain, and all those wishing to be ordained and made Brother or Sister under the sanctity of the Lord's Will should report to him directly.

Vindimir regretted his schemes and hated himself immediately.

"Telt yis," said Crannach, chuckling to himself.

Vindimir read the letter over again, glunched, and began to simmer. "Well, no matter. This news is between us. The abbot will not be here until tomorrow or the day after depending on the roads, and Myndil will be long gone by then. He has already packed his things and is in the front room, having his tea and frumenty. The news won't have reached him, and no one need talk about the abbot being to visit until he is well on his way. Who else knows about this letter?"

Brother Crannach scratched his head. "No one Ah know of."

"Good, and that is the way it will stay until the evening. Why are you smiling?"

"'Cause even if ye keep that letter to yerself, yer gonna have to give up that room to the abbot."

"I don't see that he needs to know about it," said Vindimir sharply. "I'll prepare another room for him, one that doesn't have the bed I've been pining after for the last fifteen years."

This would have succeeded in appeasing the abbot's ideas of a pleasant room; being a man of harsh mien, odd humours, and disagreeable character, thinking there was nothing so nourishing for the soul as a bad night's sleep, the abbot had a horror of large rooms and comfortable beds, both being advertisements for sinful behaviour. Brother Crannach need not have distressed his friend, however; other sounds came to put fear and agitation into Vindimir's heart, making him forget all about the abbot's visit for a while.

"The abbot is coming!"

The cry came from down the hall, the familiar tones of a certain voice being just then particularly unwelcome. Brother Vindimir's shoulders crept up his neck.

"The abbot is coming!" the voice repeated. "Did you hear? Everyone—the abbot! He's coming! And he is bringing the whole abbey with him!"

In a flurry of confusion, Myndil appeared at the end of the hall, bolting out of a cloud of dust, rounding the corner and hastening toward the two Brothers, crying out, "The abbot is coming! Is not that good news? And he's coming tomorrow!"

Vindimir looked all the anger he felt, and Brother Crannach turned aside and laughed into his hands.

"Brother Vindimir, Brother Crannach!" Myndil panted, stopping in front of them. "Did you hear the news? The abbot is coming! And he wants to make an abbey right here! Isn't that wonderful?"

"Wonderful, truly," said Vindimir, with a flat look.

"This is so very exciting! We will have our very own church—not that I do not love the chapel here—and there will be a new dormitory, and everyone will have their very own room. But did you hear—?"

"And how do you know about the abbot's visit? Who spoiled the surprise?" Vindimir demanded, breathing through clenched teeth.

"Sister Iarlaith told me. She saw the letter coming and spoke to the messenger about it and then told everyone else. She's already making up a bed for the abbot and preparing the kitchen for his arrival. She said there is to be no more frumenty whilst the abbot is here, unless it's for the children, and we are to have boiled oats and brined meat excepting holy days. I don't much like fish, but she promised to make dinner plaice or salmon, or even haddock sometimes, which are really the best fish—and she asked me to help her do some of the laundry, sweep the halls, and improve the approach near the front steps, though I don't know that there is much that can be done about it now—but the abbot is coming! Isn't that exciting? And best of all, now that he is coming here, I will not have to go anywhere. I can stay and be ordained right here! Isn't that lovely?"

"Don't think that's what Brother Vindimir would call it, lad," Crannach chuckled.

"I call it injustice," was Vindimir's short answer. He sighed and rubbed his temples. "Very well, but if you will stay here, you will be leaving that room, and I do not care what you have to say about it."

"Well, of course I will have to leave the room. I will have to give it to the abbot, or whoever else wants it, as I've already moved my things out of the way, but I will go anywhere the abbot tells me. I would have given up the room earlier, only I didn't want Thingunderthebed to lament my going. She gets dreadful lonely if I don't talk to myself in my sleep."

Vindimir paused. "You mean you would have moved out of that room at anytime?"

"If someone else wanted the room, of course. The room belongs to the orphanage, not to me, though it has been mine since I got here, but that's only because no one else wanted to share a room with me."

"What Brother Vindimir means to sae, lad," said Crannach, with an sagacious smile, "is since ye'll be movin' into the dormitory, whenever it's up, the rooms in the orphanage are gonnae be kept for those Brothers and Sisters who take care o' the wee-uns."

"Oh. Well, that does make sense-- but you will be kind to the Thingunderthebed, won't you? I know she is shadowy and has spindly fingers and causes nightmares, but she is really a docile creature, and she eats all the cobwebs from the corners while you sleep."

Crannach gave his oath that nothing should happen to the caliginous creature that inhabited the realm under the bed, but Vindimir made no such promise; fifteen years he waited for the best night's sleep the orphanage afforded, and he would not be plagued by night terrors now. He would have Sister Iarliath move the boggart to her own room, where they might enjoy a cuddle and a conversation over who was to govern the more macabre corners of the new abbey.

The orphanage was in a rage of spirits over the arrival of the abbot: everything was to be done by nightfall, the children were to be scrubbed and dressed, the robes abraded and dried, the curtains and carpets let out, the garden pruned and the larder gleaned by Sister Iarliath's skillful hand. Myndil was put to cleaning out the byre and the sty, a task he always disliked on account of the animals being disagreeable when moved during feeding time, the grass in the peristyle was trimmed in favour of the abbot's approval of the proposed grounds for the annex, and Brother Vindimir retired early, to savour that reward so long promised him: the large and comfortable bed.

"At last," said Vindimir, with an amorous sigh, eyeing his prize from the doorway.

The bed sat under a lunar glow, the beams of soft moonlight caressing the covers and browsing the bedclothes. He approached and touched the blanket, his hand grazing the weave, his delight and triumph surmounting him. He removed his shoes and leapt onto the bed, rolling upon and down the length of the blanket with a childlike glee. It was his, the best bed in the orphanage was his at last, and he climbed under the covers, wrapping himself in an impenetrable cloak of wool and linen, and sunk into the mattress, allowing its softness to envelop him in a cubicular cocoon.

He grinned at the ceiling. "It is mine, even if only for one night," he cooed, the blankets swallowing his head at the cheeks, "absolute and paralyzing comfort."

He exhaled and sank farther into the bed. He could hear Myndil struggling in the byre, calling out for the cow to be a very nice girl and go back into her shed without kicking him or he should call the nisser, but his echoing tones in the open air, sounds that would usually be offensive to Brother Vindimir's ear, had no power here; it was all pillows and perfection now.

"I am finally going to get a good night's sleep," he proclaimed, speaking his feelings to the moon, but no sooner had he said it than he heard a scratching sound from below.

Something crept and sniffed, a low sibilation pervaded the room, and Vindimir glanced over the edge of the bed to find a set of spindly fingers glauming at his shoes. They pulled the laces and dragged the shoes under the bed, there was another sniffing sound, and the air began to change and darken.

"Ah, so, yeh've com at last, aye?" a voice under the bed hissed. "The wan what wants the bed. Ah remembeh. What delicious nyghtmares yew shall have…"

Brother Vindimir jolted. "Sister Iarliath!" he called out, rolling to face the door. "Can you come in here, please!"

A heavy plodding came from down the hall, the bedstand and fixtures shook, the windows and drawers rattled as the thundering steps neared, and in a moment, the door was thrown open, and Sister Iarlaith stood on the threshold, her immense chest heaving, her fulsome frame rippling from having barreled down the corridor.

"Wha's tha' noo?" she raled, catching her breath. "Somb'dae call me?"

14

"I called you, Iarlaith," the bed replied.

"Where are ye then? Awll Ah see's the covers." She searched the blankets and found Vindimir's face amongst the folds. "Vindimir? 'Stha' ye then? Wha're ye daein' under o' these blankets?"

He paused. "Trying to sleep."

"Wha's a matter then? Wha're ye shoutin' fae?"

Vindimir eyed the edge of the bed. "The boggart, if you would. It is threatening me. Please take it somewhere else, somewhere it can give delightful nightmares to someone who wants them."

"Oh, aye." Her round cheeks lifted, her smile working to raise up all sides. "'Mon, then, mah wee duck," she crooned, holding her arms out. "Ah'll take ye to mah room. 'S not so comfae as it is here, but Ah have a nice closet ye can clean, lots o' cobwebs for ye to eat. Tha'll be nice, wuntit?"

"Ah lyked the boy," the voice contended, a shadow billowing up from under the bed.

"Aye, we awll like Myndil, doan' t we," said Iarlaith sweetly.

Vindimir tucked his lips into the blanket and said nothing.

"He's a good lad, and he'll no' be leavin' like we thought, so when he's got a new room, Ah'll bring ye over there, so ye can go on plaugin' him how ye awlways dae. Howsat sound, pet?"

The shadows seemed to nod. "That'll do."

The boggart slipped away from the bed and under Sister Iarlaith's large shadow, clinging to the dark folds in her robes, and Iarlaith leaned over the bed, inspecting Vindimir's encasement.

"What're ye daein' in here anaewae?" she asked the blanket log. "Ah thought thess room's gonnae belong to the abbot."

"He can have it tomorrow," Vindimir insisted. "I am only making sure the bed is as comfortable as possible before he moves in."

"Aye, that's good o' ye. Well–" She leaned over and kissed Vindimir's forehead, her heavy breast knocking dangerously together, "–Night, then."

"Mmrnt," the blanket replied, crushed under the weight of a formidable chest.

Iarlaith marched out of the room and closed the door, and the moment Iarlaith reentered the darkened hall, a caliginous hand appeared from below and tapped her on the shoulder.

"He wanted the boy to leave, yewe know," said a faint voice.

"Aye, Ah know," Sister Iarlaith sighed. "Nae bother, Thingunderthebed. No need to dae anaethin' aboot it. God'll punish him right enough." And she strode into her own room with the confidence of a cormorant, her smiles proud and breasts bounding, bringing her new bedfellow to the closet, where there were cobwebs aplenty to be cleaned out.

Myndil was bringing in the piggin from the dairy and just lamenting over the hedging that needed to be mended by the fence when he realized he had no bed to sleep in for the night. He could not very well go back to his room after having given it away, and there was always a table to nest under or a cabinet to slouch in for an evening. Fortunately, however, he need not have troubled himself long about beds; Sister Iarlaith always had a soft place where Myndil could lay his head.

"Thank you for letting me stay here with you for now," said Myndil, smiling up at her. He fruzzled his hair against her chest and nestled between two precarious mounds. "Your chest is very comfortable."

"Aye, yer welcome tae it anaetyme, lad," Sister Iarlaith crooned, petting Myndil's forelock. "'S just like how it was when ye were a wean, mind."

"I remember. It was so lovely when I first came here, sitting in the front room before the fire, resting on your lap. I won't impose upon your hospitality long, I hope. When the new dormitory is up, I shall have a room of my own, and then you and Thingunderthebed can come and visit me. "

The shadow under the bed warbled and made a pleasant slurping sound.

"Ye just close yer eyes noo, Myndil-luv," said Iarlaith. "We've got a long dae ahead th'morra."

She pulled him close against her well-spread frame, tightening her hold at his neck, and Myndil felt his chest crush against her in an excruciating embrace. She shifted against the back of the bed board, and Myndil slipped into her furrows, smothering himself with her overpowering chest.

"I don't know a good deal about the female form," Myndil wrenched, straining for breath, "but are women in general always so comfortable?"

"Aye's tha's us," Sister Iarlaith assured him, "built fer snudgin'."

He rolled to face the window and accidentally lodged himself in a rather warm and heavy vale. "MmfGoonit, Sitr Iarlmmf," said Myndil, his voice muffled by a wall of flesh.

Sister Iarlaith gave his back a hardy pat. "Goodnight, luv."

"Gunirt, thng'ndrthbd."

"Goodnyght, boy," said a quiet voice from below, "All the unpleasant dreams to yewe."

"Gurnnut, God."

GOODNIGHT, said a voice in Myndil's ear.

Whether by fatigue or the want of breathing room, Myndil was snoring into Sister Iarlaith's chest a moment later, and soon other stertorations came to rival his: all was perfectly peaceful in his old room, and the drumbling of Brother Vinidmir rapt in a deep sleep caromed throughout the corridor all night long. He should relish his sleep; it would be the last he would spend in comfort and ease for sometime, and though he did not yet know it, he would soon pay the tax for one night's peace got with disingenuous dealings.

The morning came, and with it came news of the abbot's arrival: he would be at the orphanage early in the evening, expected to have his room and the evening meal prepared, and everyone should be ready to receive him by mid-afternoon. Brother Crannach read to the children and occupied them whilst the rest of the laity fudgeled through their chores: the halls were swept, the gruel was prepared, and anything that could be misconstrued as pleasurable or amusing was whisked away, to be kept for the midnight hours, when watchful eyes should be closed and vigilant minds should be sleeping. There was nothing really evil in or about the orphanage, but the abbot was known for his strict economy and firm character, and would not look kindly on the nisser in the kitchen anymore than he would look favourably on a slice of cake.

Myndil was just finishing helping Ozzy the Wight in the garden when he was told of the news and promised to have all of the chores done before the abbot's arrival. "God," he implored, raising his eyes to the sky, "do you think the abbot will like me?"

There was a pause. Myndil closed his eyes and raised his hands, and there was a hemming sound not far off, as though someone had been nominally listening to him and was only now beginning to pay attention.

"What is that?" said a voice, one familiar to Myndil's ear but unheard by anybody else. "Ahem, hrm—GOD MEANS, IS THAT THEE, MYNDIL, MY SON? WHAT DOST TROUBLE THEE?"

"Oh, hello, God!" Myndil proclaimed, opening his eyes. "I was hoping you would come. I was just saying how I was worried that the abbot wouldn't like me."

"WHY SHOULDST THOU WORRY, MY SON?"

"Well, as I'm sure you must already know, I want to be ordained, to become a Brother and spend a life magnifying God's Grace, but I'm anxious that the abbot might dislike me. What if he says no to my request? I am the oldest orphan that has ever stayed here, and if he refuses my request—"

"HE WILL NOT."

"Oh, he won't? But are you sure, God? Well, of course you are, you are God and you know everything—but can you tell me with certainty that I will be ordained?"

"TO TELL THEE WOULD BE TO REMOVE THY FREE WILL."

"I suppose you're right about that," Myndil nodded. "I cannot make choices if you're going to tell me your plan for me. Well, if you're sure he will—I only I wish I could stop being so anxious about it."

There was the sound of a fleet of currachs docking in the near distance. Myndil looked beyond the front gate, and down the front path, leading across the low tide, a travelling party appeared. "He's coming! Look, God! The abbot is coming!"

"YES, CHILD. I SEE. THE LORD SEES ALL."

"Yes! Only I'm so excited! Oh, I hope he will like me!"

"GO, CHILD, AND LET HIM KNOW THEE."

Myndil was gone, off in a hurry, to trim the moss along the walkway and tell Mr Dullahan to stay away from the front gate, and the voice of god made something of an audible sigh, its disappointment perceptible to no one but the nearby hedge.

"He'scominghe'scominghe'scomingohhe'scoming!" Myndil rattled on, fussing over footstones and dusting the front passage.

After weltering in agony for ten minutes, which seemed like an hour by Myndil's calculation, the abbot was at last arrived. His things were put down at the front gate, the sounds of which summoned everyone within orphanage to the entrance. Many a curious head leant in from the threshold, eyes widened with curiosity, and as the children were lined up and all the Brothers and Sisters took their places, the gate was opened and the abbot walked into the main grounds.

Myndil leapt in ecstasy. "He's here, Brother Crannach! He's here!" said he, in a loud whisper.

"Aye, lad," Brother Crannach laughed, putting a hand on Myndil's shoulder to keep him from jumping.

Though much had been made of the abbot's arrival, and much had been said of his character, he boasted neither presence nor stature. He was not well-looking, his back bent and neck craning, he shuffled along the walk like an old man afraid of the damp, frumpled and stooping, the many wikes and wrines marking out an age far older than he actually was. He gave a disapproving look toward Ozzy, who was putting in the cutting clover, sneered at the orphanage, and upon the whole seemed displeased with the gathering his arrival had excited. He glowered at the flowerbeds, spied the children with affected unconcern, and perused the issuing grounds with as much disapprobation as his jowls commanded. He was a mean little man, stern and unforgiving, a man who said much in the way of reproaches and little in the way of praise. He scowled at everybody, inspected the furnishings of the orphanage with severe condescension, examined everybody's dress with contempt, and was resolved to think the worst of everything that did not immediately agree with his ideas on decorum and devotion. He was onerous and offensive, and when he marched up and down the walk, making rude observations—"Much too fat. This one much too distracting. Sisters ought to be ugly and disgraced to be loved by God. These robes far too expensive. We are made to suffer, not to parade ourselves about. God, these children are sullied. They belong in the sty, not in the learning hall," –the whole of the orphanage was inclined to dislike him—except Myndil, who would like him because of his calumny rather than regardless of it.

The abbot introduced himself to the children, his hands clasped and back bent, his capricious powers all at work: their smiling faces, their laughter, their complacence, their propensity to want to have fun instead of spend their life on their knees thanking God all offended him. He hated flatterers, sweetness, and needless sympathy, liked the silence of the early mornings, liked prayer at all times, and would not endure loud sounds and unwarranted noise of any kind.

Myndil was a walking noise.

The moment Brother Crannach's hand was off his shoulder, Myndil hastened forward and accosted the abbot with a hardy shake of the hand. "Oh, hello!" Myndil cried, jostling the abbot's arm about. "So, you are the new abbot—well, you are the old abbot, but you're new here—I am so very glad to meet you— we all are, I'm sure. I should love to show you the place, though there isn't much to see, I'm afraid. I have only just got in the new waddle wall in the byre, and you won't be very impressed with it, because daub is a bit difficult to mould in colder weather, but the garden is in, and Ozzy did a famous job on the flowers. The bulbs have only just started to come in, and come summer, we should have a pretty rows to look at. You will find the sitting room very comfortable. I put the fire on, dusted the mantelpiece, cleaned the cushions, and aired the carpet this morning. I also made tea—I thought you would be thirsty after coming such a long way—I can bring you to the kitchen, if you like. Sister Iarlaith does an amazing frumenty, but she made gruel for you today, and she really does make the best gruel."

The abbot's lip began to twitch. He hated Myndil immediately.

"Who is in charge of this?" said the abbot, gesturing at Myndil, searching about.

Brother Crannach quietly stepped forward. "Ah'm responsible fer Myndil, abbot."

"Hmph." The abbot waddled toward him and stuck his chin up at him, a pontifical partridge pecking at the heels of a mammoth. "You, oak tree, or whoever you are—who are you?"

"Brother Crannach," said the great oak tree, restraining a laugh.

"Hrm, yes. Of course that's your name. How fitting. And you run this establishment?"

"Well, we 'o dae taegether, 'o the Brothers and Sisters."

"Hrm." The abbot pointed at Myndil. "And what is this?"

"This is Myndil, abbot, a lad we took in fifteen years ago."

Myndil waved and smiled furiously, mouthing with audible breath, "Hello! So excited!"

"It looks grown up enough," the abbot observed, narrowing his gaze. "What is it still doing here?"

"He wants to be a Brother, abbot."

"I want to be a Brother," Myndil repeated, with a bobbling nod.

The abbot winced. "Why does it make so much noise? It hurts my ears unmercifully. It sounds like a braying jackal when it speaks. Lower your voice, boy. We all hear you well enough."

"Yes—only I'm so excited! I was very much looking forward to your coming, and I wanted to talk to you particularly about being ordained—not now, of course, once you've settled and had your tour of the place—and ask you about the materials I would need to study. I learn well, or well enough for someone my age. I'm not so learned as Brother Crannach or Brother Vindimir, but I do know a few languages and the Good Book by rote—but I would like to hear your opinion about my oration, because it I'm not very good at it, and would like to know how to improve and what else you think might be worthwhile to practice."

The abbot wished Myndil would think it worthwhile to practice drowning himself. He snuffed, gave a curt "Ha!" and began walking into the peristyle, bringing the whole orphanage in his train.

"I know I am rather young to decide on ordination," Myndil continued, sidling him, "but I have thought about it, and there is nothing more I would rather do than help the Brothers and Sisters here and glorify God's Grace."

"Then go speak to God about it and go away from me."

"Well, you will be very happy to know that I did speak to God about it," Myndil added, with broad smiles.

Brother Crannach tried to quiet him, reaching forward to put a hand on Myndil's shoulder, but it was too late: the abbot had stopped, offended probably by Myndil's candour and uncommon familiarity, in his making direct answers to the abbot's counsel and subrisive airs in all his replies.

The abbot gave Myndil a hard look, assessing his exultation and raging affability with a flout. "You spoke to God about wanting to be ordained?"

"Oh, yes. I told him I wanted to be ordained, only I was afraid you would refuse me, and God said you wouldn't—"

"Oh, God told you that, did he."

"Yes! God talks to me all the time."

The abbot fleered at him. "And I suppose you think you're a prophet of some kind?"

"Me? Oh, no, God doesn't give me prophecies. I'm sure I shouldn't want to be a prophet, because then I would have to go away," Myndil laughed. "God only gives me advice, and tells me he loves me, and sometimes tells me I should brush my teeth. He does look after my wellbeing, which I'm always grateful for, but God has always been there for me, ever since I was child. He came to speak to me today, when I was feeling anxious about asking you for ordination, and he came the other night, to tell me that I was to leave the orphanage and make sure I give up my bed when I go."

Here Crannach glared Vindimir, and though Vindimir had learned to be satisfied with his japes at the time, the remembrances of an evening spent in the comfort of a large bed hanging over him, he could not be so pleased with himself now.

"You, tree," said the abbot, gesturing to Brother Crannach. "Come. Stand here and tell me: what is the meaning of this? Have you put this boy up to this, all this going on about God visiting him and whatnot?"

"Beggin' yer pardon, abbot," said Crannach, with a nervous laugh. "The lad means no harm. Myndil's a little soft on the inside, but he's good lad, one of the best there is, aye. He minds himsel' and cleans the place and does his chores how he should. He's jus no' cooked through, if ye understand me. He's alwaes been this wae, ever since he came tae us. We just got used tae how he is and liek him fer it."

"We were going to send him to the parish," Brother Vindimir explained, coming forward, "to study for ordination and to be with the community there, but—" He hesitated here, all his compunction returning, "—but we decided that we simply couldn't part with him. Yes, that's it— we could not bear to part with him, and as you were coming to make this place into an abbey, we thought it might be best for him to learn with you here."

"Aye," said Crannach, with an approving nod, "nae sense in sendin' him awae fae his faimlae.

He's happy enough here, and he takes as much good care of all o' us as we did of him when he was a lad."

"Brother Crannach, do you mean it?" Myndil exclaimed, putting a hand over his heart. "I never heard you say so before--but do you really think I'm family? But then we ought to include all our friends, like the nisser, and Ozzy, and surely Thingunderthebed is more my sister—well, she is more of an intimate friend—at least I think she's a she. I'm not exactly sure how that works for bogeyfolk—but can we say God is family too? He's always here, and without him, I never would have come to you—and he really does speak to me, though I think God speaks to everyone who asks him for help."

The abbot waited for Myndil to stop for breath and sighed. "Well, even if the boy is a bit delicate, perhaps he ought to be watched by those who know him. I suppose his ideas are harmless enough, even if his voice is calculated to erode ears."

"Oh. Perhaps it's my natural key that is so irksome? I will try to practice lowering my pitch— LIKE THIS," said Myndil, in a guttural baritone. "HOW IS THAT? IS THAT BETTER? SHOULD I PRACTICE THIS?"

"Mibbe we should let the abbot rest a bit, lad," Crannach implored, putting a hand on Myndil's arm. "He looks a bit tired."

The abbot gaped at the ceiling, silently begging God to give him strength, and tried to refrain from saying how much he regretted having the abbey annexed to such a place. The boy was intolerable! Everything he did and said agitated him: his quick and exaggerated movements were an agony to watch, his inability to follow the natural laws of propriety were unpardonable, and his manner and address was so entirely unmodulated. "Yes, I am tired," said the abbot, sinking under a sigh. "You said there was gruel to eat? I have been fasting since the morning, and I would like something before I take my repose for the evening."

"Aye, Ah've got in oan in the kitchen," said Iarlaith, with fulsome smiles. "Ah also did a bit o' puddin' fer the occasion an' o."

"No, no, no—there cannot be pudding," the abbot snuffed. "God's children cannot be stuffed with sweet things. Those who suffer in the name of God must learn to live on less."

Here the Brothers and Sisters exchanged chary looks.

"Perhaps some tea and broth then?" said Vindimir.

"Much more acceptable." The abbot humphed. "Pudding for a servant of God-- ridiculous!"

"But might not something be made fit for a servant of God, if it is blessed properly and appreciated with God in mind?" said Myndil, in a plaintive voice. "I love Sister Iarlaith's pudding, especially the way she does it with cream and the currants in—"

"You will learn how to do without cream and currents, if you want to be ordained," said the abbot stoutly. "Brothers must understand the value of suffering, if they want to be accepted under the Grace of God."

"Really? But all the Brothers and Sisters here eat the same things that the orphans do, and God doesn't seem to mind it, as long as we say Grace and give what is left over to Brother Crannach. And we have many things richer than puddings besides: on holy days we have butter biscuits, and on birthdays we all have cake, and Brother Crannach is always sure to eat what we don't finish, because waste is ungodly, as he says—"

"Ah'm sure the abbot doesnae want tae hear about o' that, lad," said Brother Crannach hastily. "We oughtta bring him tae his room and help him with his things—"

"I have everything," the abbot insisted, raising a small satchel hanging at his side. "The carpenter will be along in the morning, to take his measurements for the new dormitory, and then I will have my full look of the place. Have someone bring the tea and broth to my room, please."

Each looked to some other, everyone expecting their neighbour to volunteer for the office, but as everyone liked their creams and cakes and would rather not have the abbot make more rules and restrictions, the wave of gathered laity slowly ebbed away, leaving Myndil in the line of archimandral ligation. Brother Crannach moved behind him and held his arms at his sides, in an attempt to save Myndil from himself. It failed horribly.

"Oh, thank you for the hug, Brother Crannach," said Myndil, smiling up at him. "You know how much I love hugs, especially from you, because you are so big and crushing. I'll hug you back, when you let me use my arms again. Anyway, I will get your tea and—why are you shaking your head like that? Is it because you want me to volunteer for the abbot? But you know I would do that already without anybody asking me."

Crannach tried to convey by fervent stares that Myndil really ought to be quiet, but his aspect only spurred Myndil on.

"Should I go and fetch the tea and broth now? No? Is that no I should or a no I shouldn't? So you mean yes, then? Oh, Brother Crannach, how amusing you always are when concerned for me, but I know where the kitchen is, and I'm sure I can do the tea myself. You know I love to help and make myself useful."

Crannach sighed and released Myndil's arms, and Vindimir quietly grumbled that Crannach should have covered Myndil's mouth instead.

"What you need is practice in ritual silence," the abbot suggested. "Nothing half so good for a boy than a lesson in quietness. It teaches them to be mindful and grateful of the gift of speech. A few hours of silence a day will teach you the value of communication without words."

"Oh, I know how to talk without speaking, if that's what you mean. When I am not talking, I am always thinking, which is just talking in my head, though my voice always sounds a bit different in there. But what are the rules for ritual silence? Is it merely a matter of no speaking or may I ask questions? Am I allowed to talk to himself, which I do often, or can I not speak to anyone at all? And am I allowed to think about talking? I hope talking to God is exempt. It ought to be, because He knows what I am thinking anyway. When does the silence end? Does it go by day and night, or by meal, or by—"

"Boy!" the abbot growled, his fists trembling at his sides.

"Yes, abbot?"

The abbot exhaled and adjusted his robes. "What is your name again?"

"Myndil."

"Myndil—"

"Yes?" said Myndil, his eyes sparkling.

"I see now that the only way to get you quiet is to get you gone, so go get me by tea and broth, and a fresh washcloth please." The abbot rested his hand over his eyes. "I am going to need it."

"Are you feeling ill? Did the travel make you unwell? Should I go to the infirmary and fetch you the herbs and salts?"

If the abbot was not ill before, he was now: Myndil was walming his stomach. The boy was a moving headache, a veritable vapour of babeldom, one that spoke with all the force and rapidity of a mallet pounding the nails along a ledge, and the abbot would do much to have his newest disciple ten miles off, far away from any means of communication, tied up in chores and prayers— or tied to a pillory on some distant hill, if nothing else should quiet him.

"Fetch me a cloth and basin, and be quick about it, please," the abbot commanded him.

A gust of wind rippled the drapes, and Myndil was gone, run off in a blaze to the scullery and the kitchen, to do exactly what the abbot asked.

The abbot watched him go with interest. "Is the boy always this obedient?"

"Yes, most of the time," said Vindimir. "He will misconstrue your orders sometimes, but in general, he will do what you say, even if not exactly."

"So if I tell him to spend the whole day studying in his room—"

"Did you want water in the basin?"

Myndil suddenly reappeared, his face flushed, his chest heaving, his nose thrust at the abbot's face.

The abbot started and clutched his chest. "Gah! Good God—do not creep upon me like that. What do you mean, do I want the water in the basin? Of course I want the water in the basin! Where else should you put it?"

"Well," Myndil panted, "I got the basin and the cloth, knowing you would want them for a bath, and then it occurred to me that you would need water, and, of course, you might want hot water, so I would have to put the kettle on—I would be doing it anyway for your tea, but I would need much more water— and then you might be waiting a good while, so should I bring the cloth and basin now and the water later, or should I bring the water in the basin with the cloth all together?"

The abbot turned to Brother Crannach and seemed dispassionate. "Forget I asked for anything and take me to my room, please."

"Aye, just down the hall here, where the children's rooms are," said Crannach, waving Myndil away. "We'll have tae wait till the dormitory's up tae give you a proper room, but this one should suit fer now."

Myndil seemed bewildered. "So, shall I not bring the basin then?"

"Yes, bring it," said Vindimir sharply, "but don't make such a fuss about it. You waste the abbot's time and try his patience. You bring the basin and the cloth. I will boil the water."

"There is no need for that," the abbot contended. "Cold water will do. Hot water in the bath riles the blood and makes the skin feel sensual."

"It does?" Crannach asked, scratching his head. "We use hot water tae scrub the wee-uns, 'cause the dirt won't come aff 'em anae other way."

"For children it is all very well, and in the winter I daresay it is a useful way to keep them warm, but abbots ought to know better than wasting firewood for a bath. I have never taken hot water in a bath before, and I will not start doing it now."

"Brother Crannach," said Myndil, in an audible whisper, "I know he does not want hot water for the bath, but don't think I can make tea without hot water, not without a miracle, and I'm not sure I can perform one without asking God."

"Hot water for the tea's o' right, lad," Brother Crannach, in an undervoice. "Go."

And Myndil went, muttering to himself the order of how everything was to be brought— "the basin, the cloth, the water, the tea—but hot water for the tea—and then the broth, but should the broth be cold or hot? I don't think hot broth is sinful. I better let it stand just to be sure...", and the rest of the laity, having seen the abbot, took themselves off, with all the natural excuses of caring for the children, to keep them from admitting their guilt at not liking the abbot as they should. Brother Crannach and Brother Vindimir stayed behind, to bring the abbot to his quarters and make sure that all well and to the abbot's liking, though considering his ideas on hot water, they were not so sanguine about everything else.

They came to the room, and how Brother Vindimir did grieve over having to give it up to someone whom he was sure could not deserve it. He said nothing aloud, but his aspect spoke his sorrows as the abbot opened the door. The abbot stood on the threshold, and the many offenses of the orphanage continued: the crimps in the carpet, the breaks in the ceiling, the cracks in the windows, the cobwebbed shadows were new crimes to consider rectifying, but even the lone cabinet in the corner with one of the hinges awry was not half as offensive as the large bed, sitting in the middle of the room, baking under a numinous glow.

"Ack!" the abbot gasped, shielding his eyes with his forearm. "What is that doing here?"

Vindimir and Crannach peered into the room.

"What?" Crannach asked, searching the shadows. "Did ye see the boggart?"

"No. I saw—that!"

The abbot stabbed a finger toward the middle of the room.

"I don't see anything there," said Vindimir.

"The bed!" the abbot cried. "What is it doing here? Why is it dressed so regally? And why is it so large? Get it out of this room immediately!"

Vindimir and Crannach arched brows at each other.

"Sinful nonsense, a bed like this," the abbot went on. "Look at this mattress—it is not even

24

stuffed with straw! Feathers all the way through! And linen sheets— highly iniquitous! Such a thread-count is not fit for abbots to use. Dispose of it! Demonry and devil-worship!"

Vindimir demurred. "It is only a bed."

"And what happens in beds that are comfortable? Sinful dreams are entertained, ease seeps through the body, chastity and goodness are thrown away—nothing good comes of beds! Vile and contentious—"

"But we o' have beds," said Crannach cautiously, "and that one's the best bed of 'em o'."

"What?" The abbot crumbled against the post. "Good God—how can any real prayers be said in such sinful comfort? Straw mats and stone slabs are the best thing for laity. Nothing so good for piety like a back that has learned to sleep on the ground. Makes one feel as dreadful as one should. I've been sleeping on the floor these thirty years, and you see what it has it has done for my person."

"Can Ah ask how auld ye are?" said Crannach.

"Fifty-three. Why?"

A sudden fit of the coughs attacked the Brothers.

"Just wonderin', seein' as how ye're so—" Crannach searched for a kind word, "—ripened an' o'."

Self-impelled religious beauty regiments had worked wonders in turning a fifty-three year old man into a passulated grape. The abbot looked like a rumpled milk skin, his wrinkles bespeaking the age of a caperated cheese rind, the bow of his legs and bight in his back hardly recommending anything, and Crannach and Vindimir looked askance over the destiny of their beds and silently mourned having an abbot who did not believe in the divinity of a good night's sleep.

The abbot inspected the rest of the room, dragging his finger along every surface. "Moderately clean, but that's about as much as I would expect from a place where children are allowed to parade through the halls. Where is the whip?"

"Excuse me," Vindimir exclaimed. "We don't take that approach with the children—"

"No, no, of course not. I meant for me."

The two Brothers shared an awkward glance.

"Nothing so good for a night's rest as a sound flog," the abbot asserted. "Don't you enjoy a good beating, to make you thankful of peaceful times?"

Crannach decided that lying was for the greater good was a charity at present. "Aye?" he hemmed, thinking more of Sister Iarlaith's attempts at making him thankful.

"Hmph! Well, once the abbey is up, I will be sure to have a new whip made." The abbot tutted and shook his head. "I knew I should have brought my own. Well, for now, the bed must go. It won't go to waste, however. The mattress can be torn for kindling, and the frame can be set up as a wrack."

Vindimir turned toward the wall and tried not to cry aloud.

Brother Crannach volunteered his strength, and the bed was lifted and turned and moved out, and Vindimir lamented its passing, until Crannach said, in a low voice, "Ah'm bringin' it to my room fer ye," hauling the frame out of the room. "Ye waited so long, and Ah'm no' gonnae let this go to waste."

Vindimir thanked him from his heart, glad that he should keep his precious mattress but lamenting that he should have to continue in Crannach's room, the sounds of his nightly romps with Sister Iarlaith enough to make him wonder whether he should not sleep on the floor beside the abbot.

The abbot was scrutinizing the patch of ground where the bed had been. "What is this?" He leaned down and took up a small leather pouch. It seemed old, the leather cracked and uncared for. It rattled when he shook it.

"Och, tha's jus' a bag o' teeth, yer laird," said a voice.

The abbot turned and was confronted by two perfectly spherical drupes, both of them larger than his head. He leapt back and fell against Brother Vindimir. "GAH! Don't frighten me like that, you flesh mountain!"

"Sister Iarlaith," said the flesh mountain, with a bob and a smile.

The abbot had never seen so a large woman in his life. She was not merely tall but all encompassing, her circumference determined by her heavy breasts in relation to the size of the room, which had been spacious until a moment ago. Sister Iarlaith brought her own gravity with her; her waist was not planetary, but she had an environmental quality about her, one that ramped into the room like an ice shove, a landmass with two peaks that pointed downward—and they were now pointing at the abbot.

"Belongs tae Myndil's wee pal," said Iarlaith, plucking the pouch from the abbot's hand and nearly hitting the abbot with her vale. "Ah'll bring it tae her. Jus' a few trinkets wha' she's collected o'er the years. Nae bother aboot it." She joggled toward the door and passed away into the hall, her two peaks jossing dangerously under her the fault line of her robes, and the abbot had a moment to breathe.

"Good God!" the abbot exhaled, "a woman with such a curse of femininity so concentrated in one place should be more conscious of her—well, I cannot call them gifts—possessions, yes, that's better. Something so wild ought not to be let loose—GAH!"

A trey was suddenly flung down at the abbot's feet. A large bowl of cooled broth twirled precariously on its edges, a cup of tea thumped down beside it, and just behind it, slumping over the threshold was Myndil, his arrival preceded by the heinous sounds of wood scraping along stone.

"Hrrrn—just—hrrrn—bringing—the basin—" Myndil rasped.

He lurched through the door, dragging the washing basin by a rope tied around his waist, straining with every step.

"Hrrnn—put—the—cold—water—in—hrrrn! There."

The basin flumped over the threshold and landed beside the trey, the cold water sloshing and whipping him in the face.

"Oh, it got my hem," Myndil observed, untying himself. "I shall have to dry it in the sun before the light is gone– oh, the front of my robe is wet too. But your bath is here, which is cold, and your tea is just there, which is hot, and your broth is just there, which somewhere in between."

The delirious smile frightened the abbot somewhat; he had never seen someone so young so sanguine at being asked to perform so laborious task. It would be different if Myndil were not a sensible and thinking young man, but that he was sensible and yet submissive was as worrisome as it was remarkable. Myndil was gawping at him expectantly, though awaiting another order or merely a word of approval.

"Yes, er–thank you, my boy," said the abbot, reaching up to pat Myndil on the head. "Good. Very good."

"I brought the soap too, only I wasn't sure whether you wanted the tallow or the oil." Myndil pulled two ropes from his robes, each of them with a discoloured lump on the end. He held the more pleasant looking lump toward the abbot. "This one is rose scented."

"The tallow, thank you. There will be no sharp scents here–what are you doing?"

"Blowing on your tea for you," said Myndil, taking up the cup and holding it to his mouth. "I wouldn't want it–fffff–to be too hot for you–ffff–and then have you burn yourself–fffff."

The abbot pursed his lips and stared at the wall. Vindimir restrained a laugh.

"There, that should be good enough now–" said Myndil, putting the cup down. "Where has the bed gone? Did Thingunderthebed walk away with it again?"

"It has only gone to be repurposed," said Vindimir.

"Oh, well, no matter, since I slept in Sister Iarlaith's bed last night."

The abbot made a strangled sound. There were many offences, it seemed, that his presence would have to reconcile, the general conduct of the laity being one of them. Commendable are the endeavours of those who believe man is right-minded and has a natural propensity toward good, for though the abbot's mission in remedying the ills of society that had crept into the orphanage was a noble one, trying to mend that which is redundant or faultless is impossible; other people are either one or the other, but Myndil was both at once. He had dried his robes, swept the room, cleaned the abbot's dishes and steamed his clothes all before the bath was done. Vindimir went to find a stone slab for the abbot to sleep upon, and by the time he had returned to the room, the abbot was pressed, dressed, and ready for evening prayers. Crannach returned with a straw mat, and Vindimir lay the slate slab across it.

"Ah, yes," the abbot sighed, lying flat on his bad and looking pained, "absolutely perfect. Nothing so good for a back like a frigid and hard surface. Thank you. You may go."

The Brothers were only too glad to leave, but Myndil, wanting to be useful asked whether there were anything more he could do, to make the abbot's first evening there perfectly uncomfortable.

"That will be all for now," said the abbot, in a languid hue. He charged that Myndil would make sure that his breakfast in the morning was underdone, unsweetened, cold and perfectly tasteless.

He was fascinated by Myndil's compliance; he seemed to operate on a higher plane, one that was fueled by magic, apricity, and an unbending love of the Lord, granting him elation and alacrity untinctured by anything.

"That boy is going to prove very useful to me," the abbot surmised, debating whether to thank god or curse god for sending Myndil his way.

He closed his eyes and prepared to get a perfectly horrible night's sleep, when a tapping at the window roused him. He cracked an eye open.

"Hello! Hello, abbot!" was the familiar cry from without, punctuated by taps on the window pane. "Yes, I was just going to ask whether you should want a glass of water at your bedside—er, mat-side—because you know you might get parched at night. It can be rather dry in the room this time of the year, and with no fey in there with you to remove the dust, you might very well cough in your sleep or wake up with a bad sore throat, which has happened to me on occasion and it is rather unpleasant, so if you like, I can bring some water you. Oh, hello, Sister Iarlaith," speaking to an unseen Sister, just beyond the window. "Oh, is that mat for me? Oh, that is mighty kind of you, though I don't might staying with you again tonight, if you do not mind having me. You are very comfortable as a mattress. You brought a glass of water—that is very well done of you. I suppose the nisser heard me talking about it to myself in the hall and came to tell you—Abbot, here is some water for you. Shall I just leave it here on the sill?"

The abbot closed his eyes, turned away from the window, and prayed to God for a miracle that would either take Myndil's voice away or have him find his vocation at the bottom of an empty well.

"Lad's gonnae be the death o' him," Crannach chuckled, walking away from the abbot's room.

Vindimir scoffed. "Myndil can absolutely suffocate him," said he resentfully, "but not until after the abbey is fully built. I want a new garden."

Crannach simpered. "Angry 'cause he made ye move the bed?"

"Yes. I will pray for my evil thoughts later, but for now, I want to be allowed to be cross." Vindimir sulked and began to stamp down the hall. "Fifteen years I looked forward to Myndil's leaving, thinking it was going to the great joy of my life. Now, however," glancing back toward the room that had been taken from him, "I think very differently."

Crannach could allow for Vindimir's iniquity; all the other Brothers and Sisters were harbouring their own umbrage, and if they were not put out now by the loss of pudding and a comfortable bed, they would be soon. They had nothing to do but look to God and hope for the best—or at least hope that if the abbot were going to be making their lives unpleasant that Myndil would be their means of retribution.

Life happened at the orphanage, the abbot happened to the Brothers and Sisters, but Myndil happened to the abbot, and time would show them whether Myndil or death would be the abbot's end, the former being the likeliest of the two. Evening settled in, the children were put to bed, the laity began their nightly prayers, and Myndil nestled into Sister Iarlaith's shapely crags, his head supported by her ample peaks, flanked by the few fey who wanted nothing to do with the abbot and everything to do with Myndil's saying goodnight to them. Myndil said his prayers, chiming his usual "Goodnight, God!" and drifted off to sleep, his snores carrying down the hall and into the abbot's ear, where they remained, keeping the abbot partially awake until morning.

ChApTeR 3: IN Which MYNDIL hAppeNS TO The ABBOT

The carpenter and his accompanying masons came to the orphanage around mid-morning. They took their measurements and began planning the annex for the dormitory, and after morning prayers and a breakfast of cold pies and thin gruel, the abbot thanked the Lord for the sharp pain in his back, grumbled that there was nothing so nourishing for the soul as a poor night's sleep, and took a more comprehensive view of the grounds. The orphanage was situated on a raised upland, surrounded by the sea, with a sandy bank in front and some woodland behind, but it would soon be an enclosed abbey, a complex to service the greater northeastern area of the isles. Much work was needed to transform the modest anchorage into a thriving community, one that could promote the interests of an abbot who would rather spend his life on his knees thanking god for the cramp he would be nursing all day, and one that would hope to nourish a host of believers, welcoming all those who would leave heathenry behind to dwell under the auspices of the Lord.

There was still the matter of Myndil to consider, however, and the abbot made him gone by making him useful, putting him to work in every corner of the orphanage. He ordered Myndil to go one way after breakfast, and he went another, Myndil's brand of rambling exultation to be deployed on other people whilst the abbot fortified himself with everybody else. A few of the Brothers and Sisters not otherwise engaged with caring for the children, who were kept far away from the abbot rather for his safety than for theirs, accompanied him on his postprandial walk, davering through the peristyle and perlustrating the garden with anxious agitation. The abbot's first evening at the orphanage had not gone well, and his attendees feared saying anything that might offend his ideas of piety, not wanting their remaining enjoyments stripped away. Music was deemed a wholesome practice, as long as it was music that sanctified in the name of god, dancing was only moderately acceptable, to be done in circles with eyes down and arms at the sides, baking and brewing were allowable as a means of subsistence, though the abbot would have everyone practice ritual fasting if he could. They feared for their freedom: they thought they had been following the laws the Good Book laid down, they believed they were rejoicing under His Holy Embrace by caring for one another and looking after His Children whilst sharing in the splendour of the natural world, but the abbot believed they were all sinners, including himself. They must all learn to behave with contrition, to ruminate over their sins with eyes low and head down, they must all acknowledge their faults and befriend their guilt, and they must be sorry and servile every moment of the day to be sure they were living in perfect humiliation. Meekness and mortification were the best recipe for piety.

Of course it was Myndil who asked why.

"But God did give as a voice to speak with, and though we don't all have nice voices—I'm sure mine is not as nice as Brother Vindimir's. His voice sounds like melted cream pooling over porridge—we do use them for good, singing hymns and reciting the Word of God—Oh, should I go and fetch you something warm? You look quite cold."

30

Myndil had just returned from his second set of morning chores and was on hand to point out that they could not very well be spending every moment pleading in penitence; they must eat to remember the bread God gave them, they must sleep to be thankful to God for giving them the Divine Breath of Life, "And after all, it is God who gives us our dreams, and sometimes God gives me amazing ones, when Thingunderthebed is not giving me nightmares."

The abbot stopped walking, unclasped his hands from his back, and let them hang at his sides. "Didn't I tell you to clean the dining hall and wash down the kitchen?"

"I finished a little while ago," Myndil replied, in a glow of pride. "Sister Iarlaith was rather disappointed that I took her job from her, but I told her that you asked me to do it and that she could just enjoy some warm milk and honey whilst I finish her morning chores for her, and she didn't seem to mind much after that. I also swept the halls, turned the cheeses, stirred the vats, milked the cow without her kicking me much, and got the starter out for the evening bread." There was a silence, and Myndil blinked. "Was there something else you wanted me to do?"

"Yes. Yes, there was—hrm... let me see." The abbot seemed pensive and clutched his chin. "Ah! Did you visit the infirmary and help with the bandages?"

"I did, but Brother Crannach said we didn't need any more."

"And what about the laundry—?"

"I boiled and bleached the sheets and sundried the robes before your arrival yesterday."

The abbot almost swore to himself. There must be something for the boy to do—he could not have him pining over his shoulder all day long-- "You can help the carpenter," the abbot declared. "You can make sure his measurements are correct. Run around the proposed glebe, counting the meters, and then bring your result to the carpenter, to be sure he has it right."

"Yes, all right! I will!" Myndil cried, jogging away, but he raced back to ask, "Should I bring a long string, to keep my place as I go round, or shall I make approximations, because I didn't see the carpenter with any sort of device—"

"Just approximate, but do it twice, to be sure you have the right number before going to the carpenter."

"Yes! I will! Twice round!" And away he went, with fists pumping and legs high in a full gallop.

"You realize he's going to be finished in twenty minutes," said Brother Vindimir, sidling the abbot. "What will you have him do after that?"

"Transcribe the first twenty-four volumes in the Good Book. He should practice his hand for ordination."

"But we have many manuscripts—"

"Then this will be another one," said the abbot, with a penetrating look, "one that will remind him of his hard work and me of the silence I enjoyed during the production of it. I will have him copy every book in the library, if it means we can spend a few days together without hearing his voice."

The abbot might not have heard Myndil's voice in the peristyle, but everyone else certainly heard it round the annex. He marched, with steps long and feet high, aspirating every number as he fought for breath. "Fifty-hhfour... Fifty-hhfive... Fifty-hhsix...Oh, hello, Mr Dullahan!" waving to the headless shade as he went round.

"Nurrrrrr...." The Dullahan groaned, marching around the front gate, chasing his blue flaming head across the path.

"I'll see you again on my way back!" Myndil finished his first round of measurements in half an hour, and instead of beginning his second run from where he was and going at it the other way round, he ran back to his original starting point and measured the whole thing again. "I ought to do it slowly this time, to be sure that I've got the right dimensions before telling the carpenter."

The stonemasons watched him from their tent, cleaning their tools and planning their chamfers, spying the curious creature inching along the grass from the corners of the their eyes. "Sixty-one...HrrnSixty-two...HrrrnnSixty-three—maybe I should take quicker steps. It is dreadfully hard keeping my leg up so long—Sixty-four...Hello again, Mr Dullahan!" Myndil accordioned sidelong across the perimeter, putting one foot where the last had been with precise attention, marking his place by the dents in the grass.

"Aw fink thayt one's broken," said one of the masons, nodding toward Myndil. "Looks like 'is 'eads on a bit sideways."

Myndil was opening and closing his legs, trying to judge whether his last step had been a full ninety-one or only three quarters of it.

"A bit barrowed, master said," said a second. "Wheel in the barra down't turn quoite roight."

A third watched Myndil divagate around the tent. "A bit cracked in the acorn, aye."

"Poor lad," said the first mason, shaking his head. "Probably stuck 'ere 'is whole loife, bein' a few corns short of the barley. God bless 'im."

And God did bless him, as far as Myndil was aware: God gave him the wherewithal to do laborious tasks with relatively few pains, and after two hours of measuring and deciphering, he told the carpenter and master mason his findings, was thanked and patted on the head, claimed to be a 'very good lad, only too bad about the lunacy', and returned to the abbot, who was in the midst of his midday prayers.

"I just finished the measurements—oh, sorry to disturb you, but the carpenter told me to tell you that all the dimensions I took were exactly correct and that they have now been done three times, so there is no need at all to send me back to do them again-- and he said to please keep me away from the perimeter unless to do the hauling. The master mason said any loud noises or disruptions near the guild could ruin the dressing, so would you please to be so kind and keep all Brothers and Sisters away from the tent as much during the daytime as possible."

The abbot's eyes winked open. "God is punishing me," he miffled, withering under a raised hand. "What did I do, O Lord, to deserve this? Have I not been your faithful servant these many years?"

"Of course you have," Myndil smilingly assured him. "That's why he entrusted this new abbey to you. He knows you will shepherd his flock."

"If only I could butcher a few."

"What was that?"

"Nothing, boy. Just an afterthought I am going to have to atone for."

Myndil was more than a punishment; he was a veritable curse, plaguing the abbot with ceaseless declarations, his fidgets ruining every prayer, his conversations with God destroying every good Grace. The abbot was forever sending him out on some errand, but twenty minutes later, Myndil would be back again, his coming always foretold by his constant clamour, his verbigeration silenced only by sending Myndil as far away from the abbey as the workmen would allow. If only he could send him farther—there must be a way—and he would think of one, even if he should have to lie to do it. If only Myndil were not half so agreeable—he was so infuriatingly obedient, doing everything the abbot asked exactly when he wanted, and he was so proficient at everything that Myndil left the Brothers and Sisters nothing to do. Calls for the abbot to stop asking Myndil to do work were coming in: he had transcribed every book, cleaned every cabinet, fixed every tile—and all without remonstrance, all without fatigue. The abbot was hoping that Myndil should die from exhaustion, or at least be quieted by it, but the cleric was determined not to have Myndil in the infirmary, as much as every other manager was eager to send Myndil somewhere else.

The abbot sent him away, and everyone else sent him back again, much to the amusement of Brother Crannach, who never minded Myndil much and found the abbot's horror of him particularly entertaining.

"You laugh," said Brother Vindimir quietly, as they were sitting in the newly erected foundations, "but I really think something ought to be done. The abbot is going to throttle him one of these days, and with enough prayer and promised atonement, I really think he'll do it."

"He's warmin' a bit," said Crannach, with timid risibility.

"I somehow doubt that. He has taken away every privilege Myndil has except for talking, and there he has tried. The abbot has does everything short of flog him for his insolence."

Crannach folded his arms and shrugged. "Patience is a virtue an' o'."

A virtue the abbot was rapidly growing thin on.

To make this worse than it already was, the abbot had to accept the other pests living in and about the place: he discovered a boggart when it tried to fit itself under his mat, found the nisser under the dining table, found the wisps hiding amongst the flowerbeds, and discovered a merrow that sat on the shore beyond the gate. There was always something leaping out at him from a corner or a cabinet, something rustling the fescue or gazing his leg, making mindfulness difficult and rest impossible.

"Get out," the abbot spat, trying to move the nissers away from the dairy with a stick. "What do you mean by holing away in here! Go away, and don't touch the butter. It was only just salted!"

"Haw ye," the nisser growled, swatting the stick away with a thwack, "ye only got the butter 'cause o' me. Ah nursed thess cow when she was poorly. Ah'm gettin' me daily milk, and tha's that."

"You've been given more enough milk already, you barbarous wretch," the abbot contended. "Out!"

He swung the stick again, but the nisser caught the end, took it from the abbot's hand with a firm jolt, and snapped it over his knee.

The abbot yelped. "Back, back, you villainous mudlump! Stay far away and don't even think of touching me!"

"That's no' gonnae work," Crannach simpered, lumbering over to them.

"How can you endure these demons? They're insufferable!"

"They're no' demons. They're just God's creatures, same as us."

"Whose God? Surely not ours. The Lord would not create such a tiny felt-wearing dirtmonger that takes a romantic interest in horses and cows."

"Ey! Don't ye be talkin' about me Bessidh like that!" the nisser sibilated, threatening the abbot with a flick of his hat

"Away, away you fiend!" the abbot kicked. "Keep your teeth to yourself! Gah—no! Don't touch my robes!"

"They'll bite," Crannach chuckled. "Ye poke him, an' tha's him pokin' right back."

"Brother Crannach," the abbot flouted, "get that monstrosity out of here immediately."

The nisser gnashed its teeth, and Crannach sighed and shook his head.

"'Mon, Tomte," said Crannach, holding out his hand to the nisser. "Ah've got milk in the pan."

The abbot was all aghast. "That thing has a name? Don't give names to pests. They will be expecting daily meals!"

"They've o' got names, just liek ourselves."

The abbot's face lengthened. "But they're vermin!"

The nisser gave the abbot a vicious look.

Brother Crannach drew himself up, his bearing altering from a soft slouch to a broad and impenetrable double-door barn. "Pardon me, abbot," said he firmly, mantling over him, "but no' everaethin' in this abbey what dosnae agree with ye is evil."

No more was said on the subject. Crannach led the nisser into the kitchen, and the abbot had only to sigh and slump and say nothing, resigning himself to the willful defiance of one whose conduct and character could not be refuted, whose consideration for the feelings of others had never been tried, whose kindness had never faltered, whose faith in what was good and right had never waned.

The construction went on, the season passed, and by midsummer, the abbey, in all its sedimentary splendour, was half finished. The orphanage remained as the western wing of the main building, to the east was the peristyle, the bailey, the kitchen, and the large garden, situated to the south was the abbot's lodgings, and the large dormitory, which was going to take another season at least to finish. The furnishings and ornamentation were not done, but that the construction of the main buildings should have gone up in such good time everyone must acknowledge a miracle.

34

This miracle was called Myndil.

He had hauled much of the stone from the nearby quarry and dragged it back and forth over the sward himself, saving the masons months of work. He followed all their instructions, measured and cut and measured again, made his own litter for pulling the hewn stone uphill, and never rested until the last stone on the main structure was dressed and set.

"Are you going to put all the fittings and grotesques on now?" Myndil asked. "Can there be a chimera? I love chimeras, and I should dearly love to have one at my window—just at the top, there. And can there be a gargoyle? I know you have to put them on anyway to reroute the rain, but can I have one sitting on the gables over my room? And could you make it hang low? Thingunderthebed will be so very pleased to see it—can you make it look like her? Well, not exactly like her, because she's not a gargoyle, but can you use her likeness? I can make a drawing for you."

The stonemasons were tired just listening to him.

Brother Crannach descried the wilting constitutions from across the sward and came to rescue them. "'Mon, lad," said Crannach, gently putting a hand on Myndil's shoulder, "let's help Sister Iarlaith round up the brouneidhs, 'fore they get in the porridge."

"Oh, yes, that would be very bad," Myndil admitted, turning with Crannach back to the abbey. "But what kind of grotesques do you think they will make? I should love to have one above my window to ward off evil."

"Ah doan't think you need a stone carvnin' for that, lad."

Crannach laughed and led Myndil away, and the stonemasons could breathe.

"Lord, that lad down't stop yammerin'," said one. "'E's 'armless, sure as rain, but Aw thought the abbot woulda sent 'im away by now."

"Abbot's been spendin' more and more time in his quarters," said a second. "He says it's fer reflection, but he's probably reflectin' on how to kill hisself. Tsk. Poor aul' codger."

"Aye," a third agreed. "You'd have to be a man of God not to garrote that boy. Gonna do 'im a chimera, if it'll keep the lad quiet."

A few more days passed, and the first harvest of the year was come. Farmers were out in the fields, picking ramps and radishes, taking up the first of the alliums and beets, and Myndil was sent to help, to manage the snails and slugs and keep them off the strawberry beds. This would occupy him until dinnertime, and the abbot dressed it up with all the justifications requisite, that the task was menial but much needed, a necessary part of his training, ordination being half patience and half responsibility, and looking after what God gave them was what every Brother should do when not looking after the children. Myndil made no difficulties: he went very readily, standing and stooping under the sweltering sun, with a hymn in his heart and a "God bless you!" for every farmer he met. The abbot heard Myndil's wretched singing from his lodgings, where he sat writing his letters, and could not stop himself from shouting out his window, "Shut up, shut up, will you! I cannot hear myself think when you twitter on like that! Do your work in silence! Quietness is godliness!"

An echo reached him. "Yes, I will! Sorry—only the strawberries made me think of a song, and I didn't think anyone could hear me from here—oh, hello, grogoch. How are you today? What is it? You want a strawberry? Well, they're not ripe enough yet, but if you wait another month or so, you may come to the kitchen and—"

"No, don't invite any more pests into the abbey, you ill-gotten illegitimate—" The abbot sank in his chair and almost ate his pen. "Damn that boy! He is an abomination." He glanced over at the stained glass window, where an iridescent image of the Lord presided over him. "Don't look at me like that, Lord," said the abbot heatedly, stabbing his pen at the window. "You know the boy is a slight to creation. Yes, I know I am being hard on him. He will never learn any other way. And I will never be at peace until I have scolded him fifty times." He exhaled and returned to his letter. "Why can't I be like other abbots and have armies? Instead I have giant laymen and a bandy-legged barley-child."

Fatigued by Myndil's musings, the abbot remained in his office for the rest of the evening. He spent as many hours as he could in confinement, but he must lead meals and head prayers, and he must be out wrangling the laity and looking in on the orphans a few hours of the day at least. He tried to forget Myndil, but there was always a something to preserve him in his mind: the oppressive hellos, the disgusting jollity—he was entirely pure of heart and therefore a stain on the abbey's congregation. He had the air of a door lintel, a something that hangs about just out of reach, something seen and necessary but uncared for, of little consequence to anybody and keeping out of the way until a foundation falls, and every time Myndil breathed near the abbot, a house came down. He was a continual disturbance, a trial to every one of the abbot's remaining nerves, and inventing more hardships for Myndil to solve, to keep him low and languid, was the abbot's first object.

The bushes rustled outside the abbot's window, and Myndil's head popped up from the sill.

"GAH!" The abbot leapt back, clutching his robes. "By God—what are you doing, creeping about the hedges?"

"Well, I was just on my way in, and I thought why don't I go over to the office, to see how the abbot is getting on with his correspondence, he might like something to eat and drink, because it is very hot today, and I thought I could get it for him—and I decided to take the shortcut through the hedge, only I caught on a branch and—"

"Myndil!" the abbot cried, standing up and wringing his fists. His face crimsoned over with anger, his neck and ears burning in rage. "For God's sake, boy, stop talking! Why must everything be a monologue to you?"

"Well, not everything must be, and I think technically we are having a duologue, since it's the two of us talking, because duo means two persons—"

"Myndil, you know what?"

"What?"

"God has just spoken to me—"

36

"Oh, did he? Please tell him I say hello—Hello, God!" Myndil called into the office. "Thank you for visiting the abbot! I shall speak to you later! But what did God say?"

"Yes. He told me he wants you to go to the forest for a very long time, and while you're there, he wants you to forage and collect wood for kindling."

"Will God meet me there? It will be dark soon, and though I don't mind the dark, sometimes Mr Dullahan gets a bit agitated with his head and begins kicking it, and though his head is always smiling when he comes down to speak to me, he begins shouting my name repeatedly and I have nothing to do but bid him a good day—"

"God will meet you there," said the abbot flatly. "Go, and don't come back until the wood is collected or until God speaks to you, whichever one comes later." He exhaled through his nose and returned to his letters. "And remind me to speak to the carpenter about having this window refitted," he added. "I want it permanently closed like the one in my room."

Myndil was in the wood for sometime, taking up the fallen boughs, and wondering what it was that made the abbot cross. Myndil have never been angry himself and had no idea what could cause someone else to fall into such an unnatural state, but he had collected a good amount of kindling when he sat down on a stump, made a heavy sigh, and raised his eyes to the passing clouds.

"God," he said, addressing the sky, "I think the abbot might be angry with me somehow."

A presence drew near and settled beside Myndil. WHY DOST THOU SAY THAT?

The familiar voice grazed his ear, which was all Myndil's comfort, and Myndil leaned his head against the tree beside him.

"Well, I am doing everything the abbot asks of me, but he somehow seems to be more agitated by my deference. Is there something I am not doing that I am supposed to be doing, something that would make him happy?"

There was a pause. PERHAPS GOD SHOULD NOT ANSWER THAT.

"Yes, you're right. I cannot ask you to tell me the thoughts and feelings of others. That would be taking away their privacy—but it is difficult for me to know what makes others happy sometimes. He does shout at me to be quiet an awful lot of the time. If only I knew how to appease him."

YES. IF ONLY.

"He doesn't seem bothered by the Brothers and Sisters half so much as he does by me. I know this is all just part of my training, and I want to be ordained so very much, and yet I am no closer to being a Brother than I was when he first arrived here. Please advise me, God, on what I should do."

A thin smile browsed the atmosphere. DISOBEY.

"What? But the Good Book says we must obey our elders, and he is certainly much older than me. He has more wrinkles than these hen-of-the-woods and smells like the library." Myndil made a pensive hum. "Maybe his age makes him ornery—but Brother Bouler, when he was still here, was very old, and he was not half so irritated all the time."

BROTHER BOULER WAS DEAF.

"Yes, I suppose that has something to do with it—but he cannot hear the birds in the morning or listen to the children giggle when Brother Crannach tells them stories. Perhaps that's why the abbot is so cross. He doesn't like the children, and whenever they are in the garden and they try to attach themselves to him, he tells them he's going to sell them to the slave markets if they don't leave him alone."

There was a guttural laugh somewhere in the ether. A cough and a hem silenced it.

"But how do I prove myself to him, God?" Myndil implored. "He will never agree to make me a Brother if I cannot please him well enough."

THOU MUST THREATEN HIM.

"Oh, God," said Myndil, with an endearing laugh, "you are so amusing sometimes. You know I would never threaten anybody."

HE HATH GIVEN THEE MANY A TEST. THOU MUST DISSIDENT.

"I don't know that I can, God. I have trouble saying even when I don't like something. I am always generally agreeable and get along with people. If I show myself as willful and go against his word—" Myndil canted his head, and a smile of realization crept over his lips. "Oh, I see what you're doing, God."

YOU DO? ER–DOST THOU?

"Yes. You're testing me yourself, to see whether I will go against your word." Myndil simpered and waggled his finger. "You really had me fooled for a moment, God."

YES. The voice seemed unimpressed. GOD WAS JUST TESTING THEE. GOOD JOB.

"I know you like to work in mysterious ways, so as not to ruin the surprise of what you have in store for us, but it is difficult for me to understand your plan sometimes."

THOU DOST CATCH ON EVENTUALLY, EVEN IF IT TAKES THEE A LONG TIME. A VERY LONG TIME.

"Oh, God," said Myndil demurely, "you're always so conciliating. I love you, God."

GOD LOVES THEE.

Myndil took up the kindling he collected and tripped off to the abbey, leaving the presence behind him. It lilted momentarily, kiting on the wind, the psithurism of the trees drowning out its laughing rale. The wind died away, and the presence went with it, following Myndil back to the abbey before dissipating against the gate, leaving before it could be summoned to bless Myndil's evening meal.

The front room was rather empty that evening: the abbot had remained in his room, claiming illness on account of the headache the heat had given him due to the closed window, the Brothers and Sisters were nursing the children who had come down with a seasonal cough, and Myndil and Sister Iarlaith sat alone at the table, eating their potage of spelt and carrots, a swill that was made a bit more cheerful by the addition of the garlic that was taken in during the afternoon.

"Maybe the food is not bad enough for the abbot," Myndil ruminated, slottering his potage. "He does seem to like things that are pale and tasteless."

"Ah put a bit o' cream in his gruel th'dae," said Sister Iarlaith, with a wink. "He was lookin' a wee bit sicklae, so Ah gave it tae him, to clear his constitution an' o'."

A series of sounds emanated from the nearby latrine, a rapid tubication that echoed down the hall.

"Ah thenk he'll be better by th'morn," Sister Iarlaith nodded. "A bit o' the dairae alwaes does me good."

Myndil soomed his potage, and an idea suddenly struck him. "Sister Iarlaith?"

"Aye, mah duck?"

"Does God speak to you?"

"Sure he does. The Laird speaks tae o' of us, in his own wae."

"That's very true. But does he speak to you whenever you call to him?"

"Most o' the time, aye, and even if he dosnae answer, Ah know he's listenin'. Sometimes he's a wee bit busae, dacin' o' his work, but he alwaes comes tae me when Ah need him most. Sometimes," eyeing Brother Crannach as he entered the room, "when Ah'm a wee bit lonelae, he comes and comforts me of an evenin'."

Here was a sideways glance, and Brother Crannach winked back at her.

"Aye, God comes tae ye," said he eagerly. "Warms yer bed at night."

"Does God visit you too, Brother Crannach?" Myndil asked.

"He doesnae visit me in the same wae he does you, lad, but Ah dae speak to the Lord every night, askin' him tae forgive me o' my sins."

"But what sins can you have to be forgiven for?" Myndil asked. "You are the kindest, most wonderful and selfless person I know."

Crannach took a bowl from the middle of the table and filled it with a quiet agony. "Sometimes, lad," said Crannach, examining his potage, "goodness is no' just action. We gottae be good in thought tae."

"Oh, that I'm sure you are."

"We cannae be o' like yersel', bein' unaffected by the evil in the world. If we were o' like ye, there'd be no devil, Ah'm sure."

They finished their meal and returned to their rooms, Myndil retiring to his original bedroom now that the abbot had got his own quarters, Sister Iarlaith returning to the kitchen, and Brother Crannach returning to the orphanage, where baths and stories occupied him the rest of the evening. At about midnight, when Myndil's snores were suppressing all other sound in the halls, Crannach went to dormitory, passed his room, where Vindimir was sleeping soundly in his lovely bed, and went to comfort himself with Sister Iarlaith. His visit had not been unexpected, and when the door was pulled open, he was pulled into the dark room, to be welcomed by either damsel or devil, falling into her chest in a wave of pleasance, to wipe away the fatigues of the day and take comfort as he could.

Myndil was suddenly awakened by a thumping sound. "Is that you, Thingunderthebed?" he asked, hugging his Good Book pillow.

"Naw, s'not me, boy…" said a slippery voice under the bed frame.

There was a wailing sound caroming through the halls, the intervals between cries rhythmic and recurring, two voices conclamantly calling out in relief and desperation, half pain and half pleasure, the whine of two creatures in distress glad to be so dominated by each other. A sigh slipped down the hall, and the abbey was quiet once more.

"I hope it is not the cow again," said Myndil. "The last time she and the nisser had a disagreement, she lowed for the rest of the season."

Myndil turned over and resumed his snores, but the abbot was still awake, staring at the unfinished ceiling of his room, wondering how he was going to solve the problem of Myndil and reconcile all his woes.

ChAPTER 4: IN Which The ABBESS hAPPENS TO The ABBEY

The smiles of summer brought the foxtail to the distant fields, the bushes bloomed with raspberry and ribe, the bees bombilated across the skeps, and autumn soon arrived. The last harvest of the year was putting in and laying down, and the abbey in all its grandeur was nearly finished. The carpenter went to work on the furnishings for the new infirmary, the masons put the last few touches on the grotesques, and while all this was done with Myndil's help—because he could not very well not help them, since they did put a lovely chimera over his window, which Thingunderthebed was mighty pleased with—the masons and carpenter were industriously trying to get rid of him at every turn, sending him back to the abbot, who spend the chief of his time either hiding in his office or stomping round the sward, shouting at Myndil to do something and begging God for an early death if only to escape the chains of monastic responsibility. Myndil was the most innocent creature, the abbot knew, but his indefatigable ingratiation, his talkativeness, his subrisiveness were a harassment to every one of the abbot's feelings. Myndil had done so much for the abbey during its construction that surely he was deserving of ordination, but to make him a Brother at last would be to secure him at the abbey forever when the abbot would much rather see Myndil a hundred miles off.

Life happened to the almost finished abbey, and with the addition of the new grounds and buildings must naturally come new inhabitants. A mild winter whipped in, and with the colder climes came the news that a party of Northmen were raining the northeastern coast, pillaging any relics and resources, killing or enslaving everyone, and destroying everything else. The abbey was spared any such visits: it was protected on all sides by gates and copses, raised uplands, and then the sea, and while a galley or two might have sculled by, the singular path and entrance to the abbey made it unfavourable for docking and looting. Myndil also made the abbey a particularly undesirable spot, the sound of his voice channering all day long likely to either deafen or deter any raiders nearby, but another abbey, one not far off, only across the sea eastward, was attacked, leaving the incumbent abbess nowhere to go. She had survived along with the children she was looking after, but beyond a few manuscripts and a few small silver pieces, nothing else survived. A message arrived at the abbey from the abbess, begging to be allowed refuge there and to bring the orphaned children with her, and though the abbot was not a compassionate character and would rather have fewer children running about all day than more, he could not say no. A woman of god was imploring him and asking for kindness, and she must be allowed refuge regardless of whether there was room for her and her flock or no. She was written to and invited, and told to bring every one of her followers she could find, hoping she would not be leading any invaders their way.

The abbot gathered everyone at the abbey to the garden to tell them about their latest additions. "The abbess will be here tomorrow," he told them. "She will probably be tired and rather emotional given the circumstances of her visit, so everyone is to be quiet and is not to jumble any nerves."

This was directed at Myndil, who was only too excited immediately. "Oh, thank God she is safe! I'm so glad she is coming and getting away from there. Do you think she can help with me with my ordination? I can practice my oration with her, and of course, if she needs a place to sleep, she is always welcome to my bed."

"She will have her own room," said the abbot, with a pointed look, "and the children she is bringing will be put with the others, at the far end of the orphanage. They will probably be frightened and should not be harassed by any of the stranger inmates we have here."

Sister Iarlaith went to work directly, dressing windows and steaming sheets, preparing new pillows and embroidering little messages of GOD LOVES YOU on all their washcloths. She loved children, and made every child love and mind her within two minutes of meeting them. Crannach and Vindimir helped to prepare new chairs and new places in the front room, and though they had got every spare furnishing they could find, it was not nearly enough: the abbess arrived from headland with a bouquet of little faces swarming about her, all of them much more cheerful than anybody had expected, and all of them relieved to be brought into the main grounds, the sight of Brother Crannach with ready smiles and open arms greeting them in the garden. Small creatures like anything that is agreeable and large, and the children wasted no time in trying to climb Crannach's legs.

"Ah want hem tae carrae me round liek a tree-cat," one of them chimed.

"Why're you so big?" another asked, gawping up at him in wonder.

Crannach lifted her up and hung her round his oaken neck. "So Ah can hold ye like this."

The children immediately made their favourite, clinging to Brother Crannach as he brought them to meet the other children at the abbey, and entering the grounds behind them was the abbess, sore-footed and sorrowing, almost falling on her knees as she came forward, beholden to the abbot for letting her come, and thanking god for having allowed to save so many as she escaped.

Abbess Bhaldruithe, abbess of Ár Siúracha Naofa den Bainne Mór, was younger than anyone could have expected. Her position and writing style had recommended her as a well-educated and middle-aged woman, but she was a young and uncommonly handsome, a blossom in the full bloom of ripened youth, her complexion pale and delicate, her cheeks tinged with the blush of tender mortification at coming upon them all so suddenly. She was an angelic creature, her eyes an azure blue, her nose small and slender, her lips full and flushed and pouting. Her figure was slight, her elegant limbs framed by tight brown robes, her enormous and well-supported breasts her most prominent features, her hands clasped in supplication and pressing them precariously together, making even the abbot look away. She was all loveliness and gratitude, the long hood which partially cloaked her soft brown hair unable to conceal how exquisite she was.

"It's a miracle her attackers spared her," said Vindimir, in a voice of real concern.

Myndil, of course, asked why.

A woman blessed with an abundance of beauty never lasted long under Norse reign, and when the abbess could speak, she told them how much she cherished their charity.

42

"By the Grace of God," said she, in a musical voice, raising her eyes, a shaft of white winter light grazing her cheek. "We come to you so humbled—I am completely overpowered by your ready solicitation—I really cannot thank you enough."

Her voice was restrained by tears, and Sister Iarlaith came forward to cradle her.

"'Tis God's will, dove," said Sister Iarlaith plaintively. "We're o' his children, aye? 'Tis onlae natural we should welcome ye."

"Poor dear Ár Siúracha Naofa den Bainne Mór—" the abbess sobbed, "it's gone... all gone!" She leaned on Sister Iarlaith and relieved her aching heart, crying bitterly over the extent of her loss. "I saw them coming and was able to take all the children and a few of the manuscripts and relics before we fled, but the rest—"

"You are alive and safe," Brother Vindimir insisted, gently placing a hand on her shoulder, not wanting to appear eager, "and the children are perfectly well. Your acting early saved them. Relics are sacred and important to us, of course, but what is the cost of human life?"

"Yes," the abbess sniffed, her chest heaving, "of course, you are right—but I cannot help but feel I should have done more. We had been hearing of raids all along the coast for the past few weeks. I could have prepared sooner—"

"I don't think a raid made by malicious men in the middle of the night is something anyone can prepare amply for. Will you come inside and take water? You will get a headache from crying."

"I will. I just want to thank the abbot properly." She turned and knelt before him, holding her hands together, her forearms throttling her chest. "I thank you, sir," beseeching him, her eyes wide and aspect inviting. "Because you acted quickly in my favour, we were able to come here and be saved. We would still be wandering, had you not agreed to let us join you."

The abbot wondering where an appropriate point for his eyes to settle on was. "Hrm? Oh, yes," recollecting himself, almost blushing. "Er—God's Grace be with you in all things, and His Name be blessed, and so forth." He entreated her to stand, thinking her supplications were all too much, but when she stood, the end of his nose was in line with her chest. He stood back and hemmed. "Yes, well— welcome, Abbess—?"

"Bhaldruithe."

"God bless you," said Myndil.

The abbess almost smiled. "Bhaldruithe is my name."

"Oh." Myndil thought for a moment and made gestures as he tried to spell it out. "V-a-l-d-r-u-h-y-e-h?"

"Not exactly, but you are close."

"If you will show me later how to spell it, I would be most grateful. I'm studying under the abbot and am practicing my orthography along with my script writing. Abbot says my penmanship is really coming along, only I ought to stop drawing in the headers and margins."

A little light established itself over Myndil's head, and the abbess was enchanted by him. "And who are you?"

"Myndil Plodostirr. I'm an orphan—well, I was an orphan—rather, I still am, but only now I'm past the age of adoption. Brother Crannach, Sister Iarlaith, and Brother Vindimir raised me, and—"

"Be quiet, boy," the abbot hissed. "The abbess does not want to hear about your nonsense."

"I don't mind," the abbess assured him. "It's always pleasant to meet cheerful new friends, especially when I've just lost my abbey."

Sorrow came again, and as the tears surfaced, Myndil, without any thought of propriety, moved toward her and hugged her, pressing her chest against his with no idea of immodesty. She returned the embrace, glad to have anyone hold her and console her, and Myndil seemed to vanish in her vale, his thin frame melding between her two bountiful mounds.

The abbot grew angry, though considering Myndil's virtue, he knew not why. He had done with the bestial sounds coming from Brother Crannach's room every other night, and any symptom of affection between the abbess and someone willing to prey upon her plight would not be tolerated. He pulled Myndil away, gave him a sharp look, and ordered him to show the abbess all over the abbey, hoping his incessant talking would deter any ideas of endearment.

He brought her over the grounds, showed her the new annexes and the new dormitory almost done, and when Sister Iarlaith called everyone in for their meal, the abbess was particularly conscious of sitting as close to Myndil as she could. She liked him exceedingly, thought of him as a Child of Light, meant to bring sunshine to the most dismal of views, and even listening to him rattle on about every furnishing and fixture about the abbey made her feel a sense of ease.

The abbot watched them closely, and when she leaned in to listen, he sent Myndil to the kitchen to fetch more milk from the nisser, who was coveting the piggin in the pantry.

"The abbot seems displeased," said the abbess, in a dreadful hush, speaking to the Brothers and Sisters. "Is there something wrong? Do you think my presence here distresses him?"

"Nothin' with ye, luv," said Sister Iarlaith. "'Tis onlae abbot gets a bit fratchae when he hears Myndil blatherin' oan."

"Myndil is a bit of a patience issue," Vindimir explained. "He doesn't think or talk in straight lines, you see. It takes a turn and goes round a bent before the point in anything he says is found, and it fatigues the abbot considerably. The boy talks all day long—he even talks himself to sleep."

"We're used tae it because we raised him," Crannach offered, "but it's been a hard lesson fer the abbot tae learn."

"I find it quite charming," said the abbess, with a sentimental sigh. "At abbey Ár Siúracha Naofa den Bainne Mór, we didn't have any novitiates. It is wonderful to see someone so young so devoted to his duties."

Here was a sagacious look, and the Brothers and Sisters thought her pining commentary was best left to itself.

The evening came, and after the abbess helped bathe the children and put them to bed, she was taken to her room, a small cell around the corner from Sister Iarlaith. She was given a few moments to acquaint herself with the bed and drawers, and Myndil soon came in, to bring her some water and a washcloth.

"I thought you might need this," said he shyly, giving her his Good Book pillow.

She saw the large GOD LOVES YOU stitched across the open pages and made a sanguine sigh.

"Sister Iarlaith made it for me when I first came here, and it's always given me comfort. You lost everything you had when you lost your home, so I thought you might like to sleep with it tonight."

"You are all kindness," she professed, hugging the pillow to her chest. "It does make me feel better, even if only for a moment, probably because it was made with love."

"Sister Iarlaith says God made her for loving things."

"I can believe it," the abbess nodded. "She does seem very maternal. But everyone here is so caring and attentive. I know I do not seem happy to be here, but I am—" She paused, her voice oppressed by sudden tears. "I truly am—I'm so thankful and obliged to you all!"

Myndil sat beside her and awkwardly put her hand on her back. "There, there," he crooned, remembering Sister Iarlaith's words to him when he was distressed, "it's not all bad—oh, what does Sister Iarlaith say when all the children are crying?—oh, yes—Have your cry out now and you'll feel better by morning, would you like a piece of cake?"

The abbess smiled and wiped her tears. "You really are all sunshine, but you see, Myndil, I do feel guilty about something..."

"What is it?"

"Well, when we were running away from the abbey, as the ships were coming toward us, I left some of my Sisters behind—well, I did not leave them, no. I ordered them to come with us, but they would stay behind. They said they wanted to protect the abbey and would distract the raiders so that I could get away with the children. I tried to tell them that it was senseless to stay, but they wouldn't listen, and now—" Her tears surfaced again. "—And now, they are gone. As we were sailing here, I looked back, and there was nothing but fire and ash, and smoke clouding the air..." She hung her head and murmured, "They died so we could escape, and the thought is just too terrible..."

She cried into her hands, and Myndil sat quietly, looking at her and wondering what he should do.

"Whenever I am feeling poorly," said Myndil presently, "I always speak to God. Whenever I appeal to him, he comes quickly, and then I tell him 'Hello, God!' and he tells me how I ought to feel and what I ought to do."

The abbess gave him a poignant look. "God speaks to you?"

"Of course he does. I think he speaks to everyone in the abbey. Doesn't he speak to you?"

"The Lord speaks to everyone in certain ways, but do you mean to say he speaks directly to you?"

"Not all of the time. Sometimes he is busy and only answers later, sometimes he sounds a bit like Brother Vindimir, and sometimes he has a rather gravelly voice and is more of a presence, but he is always sure to come to my aid when I call him."

"Yes," said she, in a softened hue, "we should look to God in times of trial. I will beseech his counsel as I make my prayers." She turned to him and put a hand on his thigh. "Will you stay here with me for a while? I don't want to be alone just yet."

"Of course. I'll stay as long as you w–hrrnn!"

Myndil was being pushed down, her hand pushing against the side of his head, his cheek being pressed into her breast, and she sighed in renewed spirits, holding Myndil's head against her.

"You are amazingly comfortable," he announced. "Sister Iarlaith also has a pillowy chest, only she is much larger than you, and when I lost my room for a while, she let me stay in her bed and–is that you stroking my hair?"

The abbess was petting Myndil's forelock. "Tell me more about your training," she entreated. "I like to hear you talk. It makes me feel less lonely."

"Well," Myndil smiled, all eagerness, "I'm training to be a Brother so I can stay here at the abbey. When it was just the orphanage, they were going to send me away to a nice place, but the abbot came and then I decided I wanted to stay here and live with everybody else–and I've been training for a dreadful long time now. Abbot says I am close to ordination, but now that the builders are almost done with the abbey, and I've copied all our manuscripts twice, and I've helped all the farmers in the neighbouring village with their harvests, I don't know that there is anything more for me to do."

"I can ordain you, if you wish," said the abbess, embracing him about the neck.

Myndil gasped. "You can? Well, of course you can! You're an abbess! I mean–you will? Without me reciting all the Good Book to you by heart or saying all the names of the saints backwards and forwards fifty times? That is very kind of you– but," checking himself, "I should ask the abbot's permission first. I began training under his tutelage, and I should not discount all the lessons he has taught me. It might make him feel badly if I give the honour of ordaining me to someone else. I will ask him in the morning, and we'll see what he has to say about it."

The abbot would have a great deal to say about it, as it turns out: he was walking by the room when Myndil was in the middle of his professions and he stopped to listen. It was bad enough that he was sitting beside the abbess with his face planted against her chest, but it was worse that she was encouraging his whims. The abbot's fists tightened and he stomped away, thinking of what to do now that all his plans of hanging ordination over Myndil's head were thwarted. He could not send him to another abbey; the raids had made that impossible, and though he might like to make Myndil happen to the Northmen–he had it. He knew what he must do to rid of Myndil if not forever then a very long time: he must go on a pilgrimage, one so packaged as so make ordination the prize at the end. He must go out and see what deeds he could do for the heathens of the world, and if the abbot should be so fortunate, and should it be god's will, the Northmen and all the evils of the outside world would happen to Myndil.

CHAPTER 5: IN WHICH MYNDIL IS MADE A MISSIONARY

With more children and more laity inhabiting the abbey, it was natural that the dormitory and the orphanage should be extended, but the carpenter and masons, who had just finished their original job, were missing the necessary resources to extend it even further. They would have to wait until winter was over before anything else could be done; more wood could not be got till early spring at least and more stone would have to be measured and cut, and with ample payment for their efforts, they were paid and sent off, leaving the dormitory in want of a new wing.

"And for all your hard work, my boy," said the abbot, gathering Myndil toward him the following morning, "I have a special reward."

The abbot looked proud of himself, and Myndil was all exultation.

"Is it ordination?" Myndil cried, leaping up and down. "Is it? I was going to ask you about it, because Abbess Bhaldruithe said that she would like to ordain me, but I said I needed to speak to you about it, because I began my training under you and I didn't think it right that anybody else should be allowed to ordain me before you."

"Yes," said the abbot, his features straining to support a smile, "it is ordina–"

"I'M BEING ORDAINED. BROTHER CRANNACH–BROTHER VINDIMIR–SISTER IARLAITH–ABBESS–GOD, DID YOU HEAR? I'M BEING ORDAINED."

Everyone hastened to the garden, hearing the hysterical shouts and wanting to know more.

"Wha's goin' oan?" said Iarlaith, shuffling up to him from the kitchen.

"I'm being ordaaaaaaaaaaaaaaaaaaaaaaaaaaaaaaaaaaaaaaaaaaaaaained!" Myndil raved, frolicking round the garden.

The Brothers and the abbess soon came–even the children's heads lined the windows, all eyes and ears–and everyone was by to witness the historic proclamation.

"I'm being ordained–I'mbeingordainedAbbotsaysI'mbeingordained!" Myndil sang, closing his eyes and leaping up to heaven.

"Aye," said Iarlaith happily, patting him on the shoulder. "Tha's good o' ye, son."

"Wait till I tell God–oh, but he will already know, won't he, because he knows everything."

"Yes, he already does," the abbot asserted. "Because last night, God spoke to me–"

"Oh, hello God!" Myndil cried, waving to the clouds. "Thank you for speaking to the abbot! I have been waiting such a long time–"

"Yes, and God told me that it was time."

"Time for my ordination!"

"Time for one last test of faith."

"I'm going to be ordai–oh? You mean, I have to do one more thing to prove myself?"

"Only a little thing, something that should be relatively simple for you."

"I hope it is easier than building an abbey, because I did not like lifting the stones very much."

"Nothing so arduous, I assure you. No, no–God told me that to end your training and prepare

47

you for ordination, you must go on a pilgrimage."

Myndil's mouth opened and then closed again.

"God wants you to become a missionary—"

"Oh my God!" Myndil squeaked. "I'm so excited!"

"He wants you to travel across Erie and gather as many followers as you can, and they cannot be those who already believe in God's Word—you must convert the heathens, my boy. You must tell them that God loves them and wants to welcome them into his divine embrace, you must relate to them the words of the Good Book, and you must convince them to leave their barbarous faith and embrace God wholly."

Not everyone was as pleased as Myndil at this news. The abbess seemed concerned, and Crannach and Vindimir exchanged chary looks.

"Ah thought onlae the ordained were permitted tae be missionaries," Crannach reminded him.

"Well, I am making the exception here, because God told me to," the abbot rejoined. "The boy's oration is terrible and he has to practice it. What better way to do it than on those who need to hear God's divine message most."

Something was not quite right here—Crannach's feelings told him so—and though he hated deceit of any kind, rank dictated that he could not openly refute him. Myndil seemed elated, and Crannach would allow him to be for now.

"You will use the training you have received over the past year," the abbot continued, "all the studies you've done, and now you must prove you've learned well by imparting God's teaching to others.

"How many followers must I get?" Myndil asked. "How many before I may come back?"

The abbot hurked. "Er—as many as possible."

"And how long must I be gone?"

"As long as it takes to gain a good amount of followers."

"And where should I look? How will I find heathens? How will I know what they look like?"

"Oh, you will know them immediately, my boy," said the abbot, with great horror. "There are ruffians and hooligans strung along the entire coast. You see the road beyond the path, the one you take to visit the farms?"

"Yes?"

"Follow it. Heathens roam along its reaches, as far as the eye can see."

"Oh. Well, that's not very far then—"

"You are going farther than the eye can see."

"Oh. And when am I to go on this pilgrimage?"

"This moment. Sister Iarlaith will outfit you with new robes, you will go and get your book, and I'll proclaim you a missionary before you set out."

A gloom settled over the gathering: Myndil rushed over to Iarlaith, unable to restrain his

48

excitement, but she was all misery, her shoulders wilting, her usually smiling features rapt in a frown. "Mon, pet," she moped, "let's get ye changed." She was always his ready supporter, cheering him on through every trial, but he was being taken away from her just when she had grown used to the idea of his staying there forever, and she could not bear to part with him.

Myndil, however, was only too eager to go. "Do you think I ought to take my pillow with me?" he asked her, as they entered the hall, "I should like to have a reminder of you while I'm gone."

Iarlaith began weeping, and she led him off to dress him in his new linens with a suffering heart, feeling all the anguish of a mother parting with a beloved son, having reaped all the benefits in the connection without having endured any of its hardships.

Vindimir watched them go and folded his arms. "This is not usually how missionaries are made."

"No," Crannach growled, "it's no'."

He marched up to the abbot, his immense shadow preceding him, and with a firm glare, he cornered the abbot by the peristyle, the apparent displeasure making the abbot tuck himself into his robes and sink back against the wall.

"Ah know it's no' mah place tae tell ye how tae run things," Crannach began, his voice rumbling, "but Ah'll just say this so ye know how Ah feel—" He pointed a giant finger at the abbot's nose, "Ah doan't like this."

Crannach mantled over him, and the abbot meeped and whimpered, never understanding how large and indomitable Crannach was until now. It was something of a feat, making the most amiable man in the world angry with him, the blithesome oak becoming a formidable foe, and the abbot almost congratulated himself on riling god's most forgiving creature.

"Myndil might be irritatin' at times, aye, but he's protected here. He was raised without anae knowledge o' the outside world, an' if ye think Ah doan't know what yer daein', ye best think again," Crannach boomed. "Ah'm no' allowed tae go against yer rulin', but Ah'll tell ye this: Ah love that lad like father loves his son, and if anaethin' happens tae him while he's awae, that's on yer head." He leaned down, and said, in a terrible drone, "God's gonnae punish ye."

He thundered back to Vindimir and glunched, and Vindimir looked sincerely impressed.

"I don't think I have ever seen you angry in all my life," said Vindimir, amused. "You are absolutely terrifying when you want to be, and I say that as a tall person myself."

"Ah save it fer when Ah need it," Crannach humphed. "Jus' doan't liek him bein' sent awae this wae. When we were gonnae send him out, we had a place for him tae go. This is aimless. Abbot's lyin' and he's usin' Myndil's desperation against him."

"Is there anything we can do?"

"We can appeal tae the abbess, but she's onlae been here a dae. Well," Crannach huffed, "if God has anaethin' tae sae about it, anaeone who looks at Myndil the wrong wae'll be struck down."

"May your curses reach God's lofty ears," said Vindimir, crossing himself. "Myndil does seem happy to be going at least."

"Onlae because he doesnae know what's out there."

"He does make friends with dullahans and boggarts."

"But he's no' met people," said Crannach grimly.

A worried look was shared between them, and Myndil soon returned, skipping out of the abbey and into the front garden in his new robes, Iarlaith trailing behind in a fit of sobs.

"What do you think?" said Myndil, giving a little flourish. "Do the robes look well? I admit the sleeves are quite long, but I can use them to keep my hands warm, and I can even hide my lunch in them if I need to."

"Here, Myndil, dove," Iarlaith sniffed. "Ah'll tie yer book to yer hip, so ye'll no' lose it."

She fasted a thick rope to his belt and knotted it several times around the cover rig holding his book in place.

"Oh, I could never lose my book," Myndil professed. "This is the very first one I copied, and it has all my illustrations in it, even the one I did with cat holding the little flowers in his mouth."

"Aye," Iarlaith nodded. "Ah remember when we coloured that one, and now look at yis, lookin' o' smart, o' grown up noo..."

She turned and cried on the abbess, who was marveling at Myndil's resplendent robes, thinking he looked rather like a holy man.

"Well, you certainly look the part," the abbot remarked. "And now, I pronounce you missionary to the isles." He made a ceremonious gesture. "May you go out in the name of God and gain many members to his flock, and so on."

Myndil smiled, and his features seemed bathed in golden light, an aurulent spark reaching down from the skies and blessing him.

"Here, Myndil," said Iarlaith, taking a large pouch from her hip. "Ah took this from the kitchen whilst ye were changin'. Bannocks and butter biscuits, to keep yersel' from goin' hungrae along the road."

"No need to worry about that," said the abbot, coming forward with a pouch of his own.

Myndil tied Iarlaith's provisions to his waist and then took the abbot's pouch, which almost brought him to the ground. "What's in here?" Myndil asked, tapping the bottom of the pouch. It made a pleasant jingling sound. He opened it, and inside was a trove of gold coins. "What is all this for?"

"Payment for accommodations," said the abbot. "In the world away from the orphanage, people need to pay for service like lodgings and meals."

"Oh. How much should I give?"

"You'll find out soon enough, I'm sure."

Myndil could not wait to begin his journey, though the sick feelings of apprehension and injustice hung over the heads of all those who loved him. He said his goodbyes to Ozzy the Wight, who was just breaking up the frozen ground in preparation for his new plantation, told the nisser to take care of the cow in his absence, and waved to the children, who were somehow sad to see him go. Sister Iarlaith

50

sobbed on his sleeve, proclaiming she should never be easy until his return, and the abbess held a hand to her heart, looking all the dejection she felt.

"You will be coming back soon, won't you?" said she, with a quiet aspect. "I have lost so many friends, I should not like to lose you too, especially when I have only just begun to know you."

"Oh, yes. I'll come back," said Myndil, nodding eagerly. "I have to come back to be ordain—"

A hand grabbed his and pressed it against the abbess' chest. "Promise me you'll come back," she pleaded, her blue eyes welling.

Myndil was in the midst of promises when two giant arms grabbed him from behind and lifted him in the air. "Brother Crannach—" Myndil coughed, recognizing the excruciating embrace. "I'm not going away long—hhhrrmmm—you'll see—I will need my ribs, however."

Crannach put him on his feet and turned Myndil to face him. "Listen here tae me, son," said he gravely, putting his hands on Myndil's shoulders.

Myndil's eyes sparkled. "I'm listening."

"If anaebody tries tae hurt ye, run away. Doan't try tae fight 'em. Leave yer gold and run, ye hear me?"

"I do, but there's no need to worry, because God will be with me."

Crannach's bitter feelings wanted to remind him that God was not able to help everyone everywhere at once, but instead he kissed Myndil on the forehead and hoped he would be safe, turning away just as the tears began to surface.

Vindimir came forward to say goodbye, and old grievances began to plague him. "I hardly know what to say, now that you are going out into the world except—I will miss you, Myndil. I really will."

"I'll miss you too and think of you every day, because I think of everyone every day, but I won't be lonely, if that's what you're worried about, because God is with me. You always told me that if I was ever feeling alone or frightened, I should speak to God, and God would answer."

"Myndil, about that—" But the abbot was pulling him away, was insisting it was time to go, and Vindimir lost his chance, hoping that by whatever star governed Myndil's happiness, he should still look to god if he felt lonely and that someone somewhere should answer him.

"Goodbye, abbey!" said Myndil, standing on the threshold of the iron gate and waving to everyone. "I love you and I'll be back soon! God bless you!"

He turned, walked through the front gate, and was off, marching down the front path to the tidal crossing with a skip in his step and a hymn in his heart.

Myndil was gone...It was a strange sensation. He went, and took the life in the abbey with him, the sun dimming through the clouds, the snow beginning to tumble down, gloom and greyness settling over the upland. Myndil was gone, and though the abbot might be regaling in the sudden silence, every other heart was grieving.

"Oh, Crannach," Iarlaith cried, gripping his arm, "they're gonnae hurt our poor bairn."

"I'm not sure about that," said Vindimir, watching Myndil prance down the path, singing unmelodically to himself. "Myndil's character might carry him on."

"Ah hope it will," said Crannach, glaring at the abbot with a bold eye.

The abbey felt somehow colder without Myndil in it. The silence bore away the warmth of his smiles, and there was none of the frantic volubility to fill up the gaps in their monastic serenity. There were no incessant questions, no surprise exclamations, and they realized only too late that Myndil was the heart of the abbey, everything else only holding up the frame of slate and stone. Even the children began asking for him, chiming "when's he gonnae come back and tell us storaes an' o'?"

"Soon, and he'll come back with even more storaes," was Crannach's assurance.

"Reallae? Do ye think he'll bring back more pets? Ah want him tae come back wi' a puppy."

"No hounds," said the abbot.

Crannach gave him a dangerous look, and the abbot skulked away, claiming the snow was getting down his robes.

The abbess helped Iarlaith come inside and went with her to the kitchen, to help take her mind off Myndil's absence. "Myndil told me last night that God speaks to him," said she, handing Iarlaith another cloth for her nose.

Iarlaith thanked her and trumpeted into it. "Well, God speaks tae o' of us, in his wae," she snuffled. "Myndil's alwaes had a wee special connexion wi' the O' Mightae, think it mighta been the shock o' havin' his mother die so young and then him bein' abandoned by his father. Poor mite started talkin' tae God 'cause he had naeb'dae else."

The abbess pressed her hand against her breast and sighed, asking that god go with him and bring him back safely, for Iarlaith's sake if not for her own.

God had very different ideas about leaving the abbey. He might have gone with Myndil, but in the newfound silence of the abbot's office, god began to operate on different ideas. The abbot was at his desk, writing his daily letters—it was quiet, actually quiet, even the sound of the children was dampened under the aegis of falling snow—he was humming to himself, thinking that he could hear himself humming to himself, but in the midst of the scratching sounds of quill on pulped paper, a nagging feeling began to surface. In the omission of Myndil's voice, other sounds succeeded, the hiss of boggarts, the whum of wisps, and a voice in the back of his mind: God will punish you... Here was a new sensation, one the abbot could not approve.

He looked up from his page and put down his pen.

God will punish you...

It might have been his own conscience, or the echo of Crannach's wish working on compunction, but the more he tried to dismiss it, the more the voice beleaguered him.

God will punish you...

"The boy had to go," the abbot reasoned with himself, his voice tremulous. "He had been allowed to ruin my peace for far too long!" but there would be no tranquility now. He always told Myndil that suffering was little more than a lesson in tolerance; it was easy to praise god when things were going on well, and the abbot was about to learn just how tolerant he could be.

God will punish you.

CHAPTER 6: IN WHICH PEOPLE HAPPEN TO MYNDIL

It was perfect day for leaving the abbey, the skies brushed over in niveous streaks, the celestial shove pressing eastward, a few flakes falling intermittently down, and everything seemed to line up in Myndil's favour: the tide was low, making the path out of the upland dry, the road was clear from being just passed over by farmers, walking with their drays and heavy carts back and forth from the village a few miles away, and Mr Dullahan was running around the rim of the small island, chasing after his blue flaming head, which had just got away from him again.

"Goodbye, Mr Dullahan!" Myndil called out, waving furiously at him.

The dullahan's head rolled into the near reaches, the blue flame partially doused by the sea at low tide, and the headless body stopped and turned toward Myndil. "Nuuuurrrrrr..."

"Yes! I'll be back soon! Look after everyone while I'm gone!"

"Nuuuuurrrrr..."

The novelty of being on the road, the exuberance of seeing something new, the galaday of meeting new people and telling them about god put a blush over Myndil's journey. It had been many years since he had seen anything other than the abbey and the neighbouring farms, the last time of his being away from the upland islands the first time he had come to the orphanage. His memory of the landscape was infallible, but he had seen the country from the eyes of a five-year-old child, and the depreciation of the fifteen years might have worked its powers on tender recollection. The land had changed a little since then: the studied management of the farms, the plans of villages and towns, the hills and forts of bygone kings had shifted in the last ten years, but the glamour of green under a thin veil of snow was no less exceptional.

Myndil was delighted with everything, the fallow furrows and sweepings knolls, the sheep and horses trotting over the high downs, the ash and rowan garlanding the leavened fields, and every few steps brought on wistful sighs, the ringforts wreathing the distant hills, the dry stone walls following him along the road, the dolemans and standing stones only adding to his appreciation. The waddle and whickerwork of the village farms, the thick thatch on roundhouses, the reserved mounds decorated with clocháns brought an abundance of bucolic views, but Myndil was more occupied with catching the falling snowflakes in his mouth.

"It's all so splendid!" Myndil exclaimed, twirling about, holding his arms out as he spun. "I haven't seen the country in such a long time—well, I help the farmers in the summer, but I haven't been beyond the large well since I was a child." He opened his mouth and inhaled a snowflake. "Imagine all the new places I'll see! Well, I have seen some of the places I'm walking to, but only from afar—the land beyond the stream was never so close before. Isn't it exciting, God?"

A presence hovered above Myndil's shoulder and sat beside his ear. VERY.

"Only think that once there was nothing, and now there is all this—and more, because I know there are more are more islands other than the ones I live on, and then there is the continent—but all the works of Creation are magnificent! Well, at least the land and luminaries are, and the seas are so beautiful, though I haven't swam in one or crossed on in a while—the animals are lovely too, even the hares that Ozzy dislikes, because they get into the garden and dig up his carrots—but even with all this, there are some things you created, God, that I cannot find a reason for. Why did you create wasps? We already have bees, and I like bees, especially the bumble bees when they bumble around the flowers in their little bee way, bumping into everything and getting their little bee fur full of pollen. I don't mean to question your creations, God, or say that some are useless, but whenever I pick the apples at the farms, it is always the wasps that attack me as though I'm going to hurt them, and then I have to run away because I don't like swatting them."

GOD MADE THE WASP TO TEACH THEE ABOUT PAIN.

"But I am pleasant to them, God, keeping away from their nests and leaving them all the apples the farmers do not want. They should be happy in their little wasp village doing wasp things."

THEY ARE HAPPY FULFILLING THEIR PURPOSE. THEY ARE HAPPY HURTING THINGS.

"Oh. I didn't think about it that way before. Is that why they can sting multiple times? Once I accidentally knocked down one of the hives hanging on the eves, and I had to hide in the pig trough until Brother Crannach could shoo them away."

Myndil went on about his saga with the wasps, and the presence seemed to fade and return at various points in the story, divagating around his shoulders, seeming to wonder if he should ever stop to breathe.

"Luckily, I'm not allergic to stings like Sister Iarlaith is," Myndil went on. "Once she found a wasp in her room, and when she tried to let it out, it flew up at her, and she ran out and closed the door behind her, and then had to wait until Brother Crannach could come with one of the cups from the kitchen and take it outside. It did not like being in a cup very much, and just before he could get it into the garden, it crawled out of the cup and onto his hand and stung him on the finger. He didn't feel it much he said, but Brother Crannach is so very strong, I doubt he would feel anything—oh, is that a village?"

Over the next hill, just within view, a few houses dotted the landscape, and dim lights winked from their window. He reached it in due time and waved at everyone passing: some had friendly faces, others rolling eyes, and anytime someone stopped to inspect him, Myndil asked, "Excuse me, but do you know where the heathens are?" He was pointed southward, though one person pointed to the west, which was confusing, and he realized it must be just as the abbot said: there were heathens everywhere, but how to tell them apart from everybody else was the wonder.

He was following the abbot's directions of walking down the eastern coast of Eire. He had never used a horse or cart for travel in his life, not even when he helped on the far away farms, thinking that he could walk everywhere as long as the abbey was somewhere in view. Having no idea how long the country of Erie was, Myndil thought he should be able to walk the whole extent, and by his own estimations, he should reach the southern end of the island in about three hours.

Night came before this happened, however. The moon rose at full pitch, its apricity abashing the stars, and Myndil, having only walked a small fraction of the coast, had no idea where he was. Luckily, the road homeward was straight and easy, and if he ever felt lost, he could always turn around and go back. A few lights up ahead convinced him to keep going, and another half an hour brought him to a small town, one with a market row, several open stalls, and a public house people seemed to be pooling in and out of.

"This must be where all the farmers take their crops after I've picked them," said Myndil, in awe of the prospect. He came to a crossroad, and beside him was a sign, which he read aloud: "UiNeill, west. Ulaid, south. Well, we ought to keep going south, because abbot said the heathens are all along the coastal road." Myndil studied the faces in the market, many of them light-eyed, rosy-cheeked, and topped with dark hair. "Are those heathens, God?"

NO. THEY ARE TOO CLEAN.

"Oh. Well there might be some in that house there. It seems to be some kind of lodging place. Perhaps we ought to stop in and sleep for the night. If there are heathens in there, do you think they will let me read to them?"

THEY WILL LET THEE BEGIN. THEY MAY NOT LET THEE END.

"Well, the Good Book is quite long, so I will pick a short passage to keep them entertained."

YES. ENTERTAINED. HA.

He approached the public house, and at the bottom of the wooden steps was a sign which read: Ulaid Inn: And ye liked it. Modest lodgin's and baths, 'cause we know yer needin' 'em.

"This looks like a good place," said Myndil, "and they have baths, so they must have dirty heathens inside."

A wide grin parted the air at Myndil's side, and the voice was purposefully silent.

Myndil sidestepped a man, who wobbled and reeked when he walked by, and entered, standing over the threshold and greeting everything with vibrant smiles.

"Hallo!" he cried waving to everyone within. "Very pleasant to meet you. I'm Myndil, and I'm a missionary."

The motion in the room seemed to seize. It was a large front room, one with a wooden counter on one side and a band of tables and chairs on the other, the furnishings modest, the trappings abysmal, a few patrons sitting down and looming over full plates. There was a man behind the counter and a woman walking round, bringing a large trey in and out of a small kitchen. The stairs at the back of the room led up to the beds, and fatigued faces peered up from their plates momentarily, to see what the young man in white robes was about and whether or not he could be killed easily. The constant smiles were somewhat unsettling, but he was willowy and unassuming and could probably be thrown a good distance by the right arm.

"How's about ye sit down, lad, and have somethin' to eat instead," said the man behind the counter. "Look like you haven't eaten in th'while."

"Oh, but I have," Myndil announced. "I had some butter biscuits on my way here. Sister Iarlaith made them for me in case I should need something on the road. I didn't eat all of them, and

I still have the bannocks she made me, but she is always trying to get me to eat more, because she says I am very thin for my age."

"Oh, aye?" said the man, in bemusement, eyeing the woman coming out of the kitchen. "Well, how's about ye sit right here and we'll get ye somethin' to warm ye a bit."

"Oh, thank you. That's very kind."

Myndil hopped to the counter and sat at one of the high wooden stools, sitting and waiting obediently with his hands in his lap as though he were at home and waiting for Sister Iarlaith to come round with the gruel.

The man behind the counter poured a steaming amber swill into a tumbler and slid it over to Myndil. "Drink that. Put warmth on yer bones."

"Thank you, my bones are very warm, but I'm sure I will like this." Myndil hung his head over the tumbler and let the steam browse his skin. "It smells delightfully. What is it?"

"Mulled cider. Nothin' but apples and a bit o' spice—"

It was drunk and gone in two seconds, and Myndil slottered and smiled when it was done.

"That was delicious!" he exclaimed. "It tasted almost like the scrumpy the farmers let me have during the apple harvest in the autumn."

"Aye. Probably same apples then. So, ye a farmhand then?"

Myndil's eyes illuminated. "Sometime, but now I'm a missionary."

"Yer sayin' somethin' I can't understand, lad. I got no head fer professions. I'm a publican, I serve the public, and I don't mind sayin' a werd or two elsewise."

The rhetoric passed Myndil by, and he only smiled and nodded and said a pleasant, "That must be nice for you."

"So, yer after havin' a drink. Are ye wantin' somethin' to eat?"

Myndil was told that meals and accommodations were to be sold together, and he therefore agreed to have whatever was serving from the kitchen. He waited and hummed to himself, anxious to ask whether anyone should like to hear him read from his book, and he almost worked himself up to it when he noticed a long leather map rolled out along the wall.

"Mr Publican," Myndil beamed, pointing to the map. "Can you show me where I am, please?"

The man took the map down from the wall and unfurled it over the counter. "That's us, right here," said he, pointing to a pin on the map, stabbed into the northeastern coast. "First town on the coast, last town headin' nort'ward to the sea. Where ye come from, lad? Ye a townie yerself? Yer accent's a bit galánta."

"Oh, that's only because I was taught from a very young age by Brother Vindimir, who was from a very good family, so Sister Iarlaith said. The place where I'm from is here," putting his finger at the most northeastern part of the map. "The islands just off the uplands are missing here, but they are there. The orphanage there is now part of the abbey that was just finished."

"Oh," said the publican, realizing and folding his arms, "so yer wan o' them folk."

"Yes. I'm an orphan."

"Orphan, aye?" The publican spied the book at Myndil's hip. "And they got you wrapped inna all that now?"

"Well, just wrapped in my robes. The abbot had them cleaned and pressed just for me. He told me that I have one last thing to do before I'm ordained and made me a missionary, and off I set, and here I am, ready to tell heathens how much God loves them."

A few chairs scudded across the floor. Plates clatters and spoons were put by, and Myndil suddenly found himself adorned by listeners, none of them solicitous or smiling.

"Are all yer folk a bit soft between the ears, b'y?" a patron growled in his ear.

Myndil pouted and considered this. "I expect so, because brain tissue is rather soft, and whenever Sister Iarlaith used to clean out my ears when I was a child, she always claimed I was cultivating beets and potatoes because of all the dirt she found in there."

The publican laughed and motioned for the other patrons to sit down and finish their meals. Myndil was so painfully endearing; it was impossible to be angry with him long, his features so open and expectant, treating everyone who approached him like a friend, and when he was brought his meal and he looked at the extensive blood pudding without knowing what it was and exclaimed, "It looks frightening but I'm sure it's delicious," the publican smiled and watched Myndil assail his dinner with the zeal of a child.

Myndil was only too full of praise for the meal he received, but when he stood from the counter, to move his legs and ask about the lodgings, a cloud came over the front room.

"'Ere," one of the patrons shouted, "ye gotta pay fer dat!"

He was glaring at Myndil and pointing to his empty plate.

"Oh, yes. I mean to. The abbot told me about paying for things. Will this do?"

He took two pieces of gold from his pouch and placed them on the counter. Eyes widened and hands reached out, and the publican took a mace from under the counter to keep the envious hordes away.

"Ye coddin' me, lad?" the publican asked.

Myndil's eyebrows folded upward. "I don't think so."

"Yer after givin' me two gold."

"Oh. Did I not give you enough for the meal and the lodging? I'm not sure how much that is."

He took another two gold from his pouch and put it on the counter, and the woman who was going back and forth from the kitchen came over. She took up one piece of gold and tried to bite into it. "It's real enough," she claimed, stuffing the coin between her breasts. "Ye a merchant yerself?"

"No, I'm a missionary."

"Dat a job dat gives ye all dat gold?"

"Well, the abbot gave it to me. It really belongs to the abbey, but he told me I should use it for travelling expenses."

"And if I promise meself to yer god, he'll give me some o' dat?"

"Well, if you promise to love God, and follow his teachings—"

"Praise the Lord, then," one of the patrons cried. He clasped the three gold coins left on the counter and ran out the door, the publican immediately running after him with his mace held high.

"Well, that was easy," Myndil exclaimed. "I wonder if all followers will be so eager—"

He turned, and the rest of the patrons were standing behind him, crowding around him and giving him looks of violent asperity.

"Would you like to hear about God?" Myndil asked, in a hopeful accent.

"We'd like to have some of that gold," one of the patrons grunted.

"Oh, well, I'll gladly give you some, if you let me read to you from my book." Myndil took the book from his hip and just as he was about to begin his oration, the publican suddenly returned, the end of his mace spattered with blood, the three golden coins tucked in his hand.

"Any one else thinkin' they're gonna grab what's mine?" the publican bellowed, waving his mace about.

"Oh, but there is no need to covet a few coins," said Myndil. "I have more and will readily share them—"

Fists began flying, the mace swung down and swiped across, and a fight between the publican and patrons ensued, the patrons trying to pry the coins from the publican's hand, and the publican's mace thwacking them all away.

Myndil watched for a moment and then turned to the woman from the kitchen. "May I go upstairs to my room? I have walked an awfully long way and I am a little tired."

THOU SHALT NOT STAY HERE.

Myndil quietly turned aside. "Is it a bad place, God?"

BAD FOR THEE. IF THOU GOEST TO SLEEP, THOU HAST NO GUARANTEE OF WAKING UP.

"Oh."

AVARICE DOTH REND A MAN'S MIND.

"It didn't know these coins carried sin. I suppose that's why the abbot keeps them locked away. I remember Mr Dullahan saying something about that once, how gold made his neck hole itch. I suppose it's my fault for not paying properly. I'll remember only to give one coin next time."

He sighed and quietly slipped away, leaving the public house without any thought of the money he had lost.

Myndil, having little promise of lodgings for the night, continued down the main road. It was a cool and dry evening, and without any notion of bandits or palliards following or attacking him, Myndil thought a well-lit road with a few travelers davering along ought to be safe enough. A good bonfire in a neighbouring field should provide enough warmth and shelter for the night, and he spent the remainder of the evening at a communal fire, sitting beside an old woman, one who asked Myndil to come to her and regretted the invitation ten minutes later.

"Eh?" the old woman creaked, leaning toward him. She was holding a small horn to her ear.

58

"AHEM—I SAID," Myndil shouted into the horn, "WOULD YOU LET ME PRACTICE MY ORATION WITH YOU?"

"Would you let me hatch a nation with you?"

"NO—ORATION." He held up his book. "WOULD YOU LET ME READ TO YOU?"

"If you like."

The old woman weakly held the horn to her ear and Myndil began reading.

"AND LO," Myndil projected, lifting his chest, "IT WAS ON THE FIRST DAY THAT GOD—
"

"Eh?"

"THE FIRST DAY. I'M READING TO YOU ABOUT CREATION."

"You're reading to me about cremation?"

"NO—CREATION. ABOUT HOW GOD CREATED THE WORLD."

"Ah. Does it say when he created back pain?"

"THAT WAS ON THE SIXTH DAY."

He droned on about what god did on the first six days of the world, six days during a time when time was not yet in being, and went through the minutiae of everything that was created on which day only to find the woman suspiciously silent throughout. She had put the horn down; tired of trying to decipher Myndil's proselytization, and fatigued in general, she had made herself deaf and drifted off, her eyes closing voluntarily, falling asleep with a crooked back and bowed head.

Myndil only noticed when he got to the end of the seventh day. "Oh," said he, watching the old woman rock back and forth in her sleep. "Well, at least she didn't run away. Last time I tried to read to the abbot, he threw rocks at me to get me to stop and then sat in his office until dinner." He sighed, helped the old woman to lie down on her straw mat, and tucked himself in beside her.

He wished god a goodnight and fell asleep, the fatigues of the day finally weighing on him. Why anyone should need lodging when they could be asleep outside in the fields was a question he asked himself as he began to doze, and once he was comfortable and unconscious, his usual snores picked up where his voice left off.

He was awake a moment later. The old woman was hitting him in the face.

"Stop makin' that noise!" she rasped, slapping his cheeks. "Sounds like yer pullin' down a cow fence!"

"I'm sorry!"

"Eh?"

"I SAID I'M SORRY. I SNORE VERY LOUDLY AND TALK IN MY SLEEP SOMETIMES."

Myndil was swatted off the mat and away from the fire, the old woman grumbling about young people these days and how they would always make noise when everyone else was trying to rest, and Myndil brushed himself off, straightened his robes, and continued down the road, hoping that he would find some willing heathen followers soon.

Upon the whole, his first day away from the abbey was a pleasant one: a pleasant walk, pleasant people, pleasant conversation, though mostly between God and himself, but he was missing the Brothers and Sisters, missing his bed and his Good Book pillow, missing the abbess' comfortable chest, and even missing the abbot, his strangled reproaches and bitter lamentations sounds he had grown accustomed to hear. On the road leading southward, there was only the sound of his own musings, the occasional boom of god's voice, and distant clamour of the public house, still in upheaval, the publican claiming he should sell the place and retire tomorrow, all by the grace of an unknown god.

CHAPTER 7: IN WHICH GOD HAPPENS TO THE ABBOT

The following morning, the abbot awakened just after dawn and said his morning prayers, thanking god for the pain in his lower back and the want of Myndil's voice in his ear. He sat up from his stone slab, cracked his hips and knees, and feeling perfectly wretched, he waltzed into the garden ready for the day, relishing the studied silence of a Myndil-less life. There was still a nagging sensation in the back of his mind, the commination of Brother Crannach foretelling evil, but considering the prospect of a peaceful and productive day ahead, he could very well acquit himself of guilty feelings.

He waltzed into the front room, sat with his letters and read his reports, glorying in the soothing sounds of winter-- the delicate tinkling of snow, the crepitation from the fire, the alpine tinge in the air-- but the moment the children were brought in for their breakfast, he found he had other difficulties to contend with. The children were given frumenty, because it was Myndil's favourite, and the abbot, upon sooming his usual gruel, found someone had put salt in it.

"I like the gruel thin and unsweetened," said the abbot, eyeing Sister Iarlaith as she sat down, "but I don't think there's a need for it to be flavoured with salt."

"There's nae salt in it," Sister Iarlaith contended. "That's 'cause Ah been cryin' o' mornin'."

She turned away from the abbot and wept into her plate, and Abbess Bhaldruithe, who was sitting by her, made her plaintive airs.

"There, there," the abbess hummed, patting poor Iarlaith on the back. "He'll be back soon, I'm sure."

The abbot exhaled and rolled his eyes, and looked to Brother Vindimir for vindication, but he was busy managing the children and would do anything but acknowledge the abbot's style of grief.

He returned to his papers when Brother Crannach came in. Crannach's prognostications had not been forgotten, but the abbot hoped he would have softened a little, willing to let the disagreement of the previous day pass.

The abbot was wrong, of course.

He looked up from his page, and Crannach thundered by, marching to the opposite side of the table, glaring and growling at him. The abbot whimpered and huddled in his chair, mumbling out a fearful "gmorngmm", watching Brother Crannach take his place at the other end of the table, his aspect changing as he sat and reached for tea and toast. He ate and encouraged the children to do likewise, but they were too much for play and began clambering over his large legs, begging him to lift them up and whorl them round and tell them some new stories.

A child accidentally kicked the table, and the abbot began scolding.

"Sit down and behave yourself," said he firmly. "This is not a time to play--"

Crannach lifted his hand and slammed against the table, the strength of which sent a shock to the other end and made the bowl of gruel in front of the abbot fly up and into his face. Tinkling laughter swelled throughout the room, and the abbot sighed as he felt the gruel travelled down the front of his robes.

"All very amusing, I'm sure," the abbot huffed, wiping himself down. "I don't know that there was a need to—"

He looked up and saw a large shadow along the wall. It was attached to Crannach, but the outline looked as though it belonged to something else, something larger and more sinister. The fire flickered and the shadow expanded, crawling along the ceiling and toward the abbot, the outline reaching outward along the walls. The abbot shrunk in his chair, coiling into a corner and covering his face with his robes. It's not real, he pleaded with himself, it's only your guilty conscience—it's not real! but when he peered up from his collar, he found Crannach staring back at him, his brow low, his eyes shrouded, his glare unwavering. Crannach seemed larger than before, though the abbot told himself it was impossible; fear would find its way into his conscience, however, and the abbot would have brushed off his feelings if not for the glowing eyes.

The abbot started and leaped, his chair almost falling backward. He jumped up, suddenly feeling the need to visit the kitchen and sit with the flour and oats for a while, and ran off, leaving his papers behind, hastening into the pantry, tossing the nisser out of his hiding place and cramming himself under the bottom shelf, murmuring tremulously to himself, trembling over the beast with the golden gaze.

"Get outta there, ye bodach!" the nisser cried, kicking the abbot's shins. "Ah jus took in that milk, and yer gonna warm it!"

"Go away, go away!" the abbot squealed, pushing him with his heel, trying to force himself further into the pantry. "That beast is going to kill me!"

"Brother Crannach," one of the children at the table sang. "Can ye do the funnae growl again?"

"Aye," said another, "last time ye did it, Dimeadh nearly wet hisself."

The children giggled over themselves, and Crannach's features softened into their usual smiles.

"Ye got it once th'dae," said Crannach, his eyes crinkling, "that's it fer now."

The awws of disappointment began, and the flumps and frowns of injustice sulked over the table.

"Nae bellaeachin'," Crannach laughed. "'Mon, now. Finish up, or that's me eatin' yer breakfast."

The children finished what they could, and Vindimir gave the leftovers to Crannach.

"I think you might have overdone it," said Vindimir unassumingly, passing him a bowl of unfinished frumenty.

"Aye, mebbe," said Crannach, with marked indifference, "but it'll give him somethin' tae think about if he ever thinks o' sendin' anae o' the other weeuns awae."

Iarlaith took up the empty bowls and brought them to the scullery, and found the abbot in the pantry, whiffling to himself on the bottom shelf, folded into a square, his head tucked against his thighs, his feet nestled above his head.

"Did you see it—did you see it?" the square squawked.

Iarlaith took up the soap and began boiling the water. "See wha' noo?"

"The beast!" A finger peeled itself from the square and pointed back to the front room. "That thing with the glowing eyes!"

Iarlaith insisted she had no idea what he was talking about.

A cramp settled in the abbot's back, and he slowly unfolded his legs, unfurling from his hiding place and wallowing on the floor. "His eyes…" he muttered. "His eyes have never done that before…"

"He's ne'er been angrae before," said Iarlaith complacently. She humphed and began soaking the plates. "And yer shure it was God what asked ye tae send Myndil awae?"

Here was a sideways glance, and the abbot hardly knew anymore. The idea had come to him from somewhere, and why not god if he is in charge of all good ideas? It was impossible that sending Myndil away was the work of some other forces—and if even if the idea had been his own, it had only been done with right intentions.

The abbot resolved to avoid Crannach wherever possible, the giant oak of a man trundling about the garden and minding the children, but while walking around the back of the abbey to escape his looks was easy enough, he could not avoid every other irritation: Ozzy the Wight was lamenting about there being no loam prepared for his flowerbeds, the wisps were shimmering wretchedly over which tree would be theirs for coming season, and Mr Dullahan had tried to rush the iron gate several times now that he had caught his head again. All of these things would have been rectified had Myndil be there: he was the one who mucked out the sty and ground the bones for Ozzy's beds, he was the one who designated which wisp would shimmer around which tree for the spring, and he was the only one who had spent time with the Dullahan since the specter had lost his horse and his way many years ago. The noise and bustle of Myndil was replaced by other noises now, and while an abbey with Myndil happening to it was a nuisance, an abbey with disconcerted creatures was a horror. The nisser hissed at the abbot when he came near the pantry, the grogoch groaned for cream from the dairy and threatened never to clean the latrine again if he did not get any, and the boggarts in the bedrooms begged for stories to feed their nightly terrors—the sound of Myndil-less abbey was a rage of dissonance, an exsibilation made up of all the little annoyances that Myndil had smoothed away, and now that his voice was no longer drowning out every other clatter, the agony of communal dissent succeeded.

The abbot hid in his office all the rest of the day, even taking his tea and cold porridge at his desk, and though Brother Crannach looked at him through the window and smiled, seeming returned to his usual self, the abbot knew it was only a matter of time before something distressed him, before something tried to walk away with his dinner or tried to kill him in his sleep. He thought of staying with the abbess for a few nights; she had offered him comfort, crooned that it was only a want of rest and worrying about Myndil grating in his nerves, but he thought of the sort of succour she would offer, and while she was given two very prominent and comfortable gifts, the abbot did not know they would not smother him in his sleep the way his luck was going.

He laid down on his mat and stone slab, stared at the unfinished ceiling, and began to bawl.

"God is punishing me," he weked, his voice thin and throat tightening. "O Lord, I did what I had to do and said you did it, and I know you are rebuking me for it!" His own words to Myndil echoed back to him here: suffering is a lesson in tolerance. He would tolerate everything the abbey had to offer for his penance, though he might be dead at the end of it; he had sinned in the name of god and was now weltering in compunction, reaping all the torment his designs so dearly deserved. He clasped his hands together and sobbed to himself. "Thank you, O Lord, for this suffering!" he sniveled. "You know what your humble servant requires!"

He closed his eyes, but the image of two golden eyes mantled by an impenetrable shroud kept him from sleep.

It was a frigid evening. The Brothers and Sisters huddled with the children before the fire and said they would be sleeping in the front room that night, to stave off the chill and keep everyone safe.

"A storm comin'," said Crannach, standing and looking out the window. "Ah'll get more firewood."

The sky was already clouded, any light from the moon and stars extinguished by the brume, and the dampness carried on the wind, bringing Crannach to the small woodland beside the iron gate. He collected wood and kindling, and stood on the brow of the upland, surveying the darkening skies, the celestial quilt billowing in eastward fading from grey to black.

"Ah'm worried," said Crannach, speaking to the dullahan, whose body was running against the gate.

"Nurrrr....." said the dullahan's head, resting at Crannach's feet. "Mynnnnn..."

"Aye, me an' o'." Crannach sighed and tapered his gaze, marking the bad weather pooling in quickly over the horizon. "God," said he, in a half whisper, speaking to the skies, "if yer listenin', Ah know we have tae mind oursel's, bein' in charge o' our own fate, but if ye have anae sae in what happens tae Myndil, please look out fer him. Ah doan't ask ye fer anaethin' because Ah have all Ah need, but Ah'm askin' now, an' Ah'm askin' fer his sake." He paused and felt the tears rush upon him. "Ah've been with people. Ah know what they dae when they find out yer no' liek 'em. They either force ye in wi' the rest, or they try tae stamp ye out." His brow darkened, and his eyes flashed a momentary glint of gold. "Doan't let him be stamped out."

He closed his eyes, a warmth surmounted him, his prayers prevailing and moving along the wind, and he turned back to the abbey, nudging the dullahan's head closer to his body as he crossed the threshold and went inside.

Somewhere in the ether, sailing on the weaving currents, a crack of thunder answered. The brontide bellowed across the easing, convincing the heavy clouds to recede, and the storm decided it would rather leave the upland islands alone and speak to the seas instead.

64

CHAPTER 8: IN WHICH MYNDIL HAPPENS TO THE RABBLE

The refuge of a large tree was Myndil's friend throughout the evening, and he awakened to the brisk scent of morning dew and the remembrance of Sister Iarlaith's bannocks stabbing him in the hip. He ate his bannocks, said a loud, "THANK YOU, SISTER IARLAITH. I LOVE YOU AND I WILL BE BACK SOON," and continued along the road, hoping to meet a few willing novitiates in his way.

It was not long before he met his first band of heathens, and he only knew they were heathens because god told him so.

"Are you sure they're heathens?" Myndil asked, watching the group of plainly dressed men and women flensing fish by a small stream.

GOD IS ALWAYS CERTAIN.

"Yes, of course. What I meant was, how can you tell? They look no different from anyone else I've seen. Do you think they would want to hear about you?"

PROBABLY NOT. THOU WILT DO IT ANYWAY.

"Yes," Myndil sighed, "you're right, only I'm a little nervous."

THERE IS NO NEED TO BE NERVOUS WHEN GOD IS WITH THEE.

Myndil took courage and approached, marching up to the table where the men and women were cleaning and paring their fish.

"Two for a copper," said one of the women.

"Oh, thank you," said Myndil, wearing his brightest smiles, "but I don't want to buy any fish."

YES, YOU DO. GOD WANTS LUNCH.

"Yes, I do want to buy fish," said Myndil mechanically, "but first I would like to ask you something, if you don't mind."

The woman stripped the bones from a large salmon and tossed them into the stream. "Ask away."

"Are you heathens, by any chance?"

The woman fleered and looked up. "Depends who's asking that question."

"Oh. Well, me," Myndil nodded. "I'm asking."

"And what're you supposed to be?" she huffed, marking his resplendent robes.

"A missionary."

Her nose curled. "A whatinary?"

"A missionary. Someone sent on a mission by God to gain followers—"

"Right." She humphed and put her knife down. "What're you sellin'?"

"Nothing. God's love is free for everyone to receive."

The woman glanced back at her friends, and a fulmination of mirth spread across the stream.

"Go'wan outta here with that," the woman cackled, slapping her apron. "Nothin' about the gods is free. They're always askin' for favours. So, how much is your god? What's the buy-in?"

Myndil's smiles began to wilt a little. "I don't think I understand you. Do you mean to say the heathen gods ask you to pay something for their love?"

The woman shrugged. "There's always an offerin' to be made, sometimes a sacrifice, if they're angry enough."

"Oh. Well, I appreciate you telling me. I don't know much about the other gods and have been wondering why everybody does not love their God the way I love mine."

"And your god isn't wantin' any money or sacrifices?"

"He hasn't asked me for any." There was a slight 'YET.' from the back of Myndil's mind. "He only asked me to gain followers for him."

"And how're you supposed to do that?"

"By speaking to people and telling them about how much God loves them."

Another round of laughter, and one of the men came forward to ask, "That's a bit borin', innit? Couldn't you at least threaten us a bit so we could threaten you back?"

"But I don't want to threaten you. God says we must treat one another with compassion—"

The man held his knife up. "I'd rather stab you and take your nice-lookin' robes."

"That would be rude when this is the only clothing I have. And killing is against God—"

"Your god don't allow killin'? Naw, you keep him," said the man, waving Myndil away. "We don't want a god that don't allow us to kill. We need to hunt and fish round here."

"Oh, you are allowed to kill animals," said Myndil eagerly.

"Howsat fair?"

"Because God made the animals for us to care for and eat. We need animals to live, but we need not be cruel about it. There are laws about how animals ought to be treated."

The man folded his arms and canted his head. "What else can't we do under yer god?"

"Well," Myndil hemmed, opening his book to the famed commandments. "Thou shalt not worship other gods before him—"

"So we can worship other gods when he's not lookin'?" the woman asked. "That sounds alright. What else we can't do under your god?"

"No adultery, no stealing—"

"Theys the same thing really," the man interposed. "Why's your god need two commandings or whatsits to say the same thing?"

"For clarity's sake, I suppose."

"What's next on the list?"

"No coveting your neighbours things—"

"But he already says no stealin'," the woman asserted.

"This here god o' yers sounds a bit redundant," said the man. "How's he gonna be a good god if he don't even remember what he just said?"

Myndil turned aside. "He does have a point, God."

GOD IS ALL POWERFUL. THAT DOES NOT MEAN GOD HAS A GOOD MEMORY.

"Wassat?" said the man suspiciously, pointing to the book in Myndil's hand. "That a book of magic yer god gived you?"

"It's the Good Book, an entire book of God's teachings. I copied the whole manuscript word for word from Brother Crannach's and made all the drawings in it too."

Myndil turned the book over and let the man and woman examine it. They would not read it—Myndil had no idea if they could—but they did seem to be impressed with it.

"S' pretty good, 'em drawin's," said the man, remarking the illumination.

"I know the sheep ended up looking like wyrms, but I did a tolerable job on the lettering—and it's not just one book. It's actually twenty-four volumes—"

"But you only got the one book there," said the woman.

"I do, but think of it like a collective work."

"Naw, I don't like best-ofs," said the man, shaking his head. "Theys always leavin' out 'em good bits."

The fishmongers were aimable enough: they stood and listened and asked, and seemed genuinely interested, and Myndil felt brave enough to try for oration.

There was an end to all peace.

"And it was going so well," Myndil sulked, catching his breath, stopping at the end of the stream. "Perhaps I shouldn't have read to them about the great destruction of the two cities."

BUT THAT IS GOD'S FAVOURITE PART. GOD TAKES PRIDE IN HIS WORK.

"I like that bit too, especially with the salt pillar, but it seems to make others angry. I admit that certain portions of your book can be a bit distressing, but I don't know that it warranted that man coming after me with the paring knife." Myndil bent to the side of the stream, to have a drink and wash his face, and lament his poor powers of address. "I was so close," he pined. "The woman in particular seemed interested—if only I did not have to practice my oration—but I need to prove that I have practiced it if I want to be ordained. Perhaps I should just leave off oration for now. If only telling them about how much I love you would get them to follow you..." He sighed and his shoulders sagged. "Why did you make humans so complicated and full of emotions?"

GOD ONLY FORMED THY BODY. GOD WOULD NOT HAVE CREATED MEN IF GOD KNEW THEY CAME WITH OPINIONS.

"But you gave us free will, God. You gave us the ability to seek you out for ourselves and decide whether or not we wanted to love you. Why didn't you just make us love you from the beginning?"

GOD GAVE YOU FREE WILL SO HE COULD PUNISH YOU. IF GOD MADE EVERYONE LOVE HIM, GOD WOULD NOT HAVE A JOB.

"But when you gave us the free will in the holy garden, we sinned, and then you removed us from the garden and wiped us away in the great flood."

YES. GOD REALIZED HE MADE A MISTAKE AND GAVE MEN A BIT OF A REDO.

"It does seem a little unfair to keep letting people choose freely but then punishing them when they don't choose how you want them to. I just wish knowing about how much you love us was enough for them, and really what's better than divine affection?"

MANY THINGS. GOLD. GAINFUL EMPLOYMENT. CARNAL PLEASURES.

Myndil seemed bemused. "But aren't some of those considered to be sinful, God?"

YES, THAT'S WHY THEY'RE BETTER THAN—ER—GOD MEANS THAT'S WHY HEATHENS DO THEM.

Myndil soon came upon another group of heathens, this band of men and women crowded near a small quarry just off the main road. They were chiseling and carving out small pieces of green sedimentary rock, one of them was shaping and sanding them, and another was fastening them to pieces of prettily worked metal. It looked like some sort of lapidary concern, a jewelry making business under the guise of masonry and metalwork, one of the rabble selling all the pieces they made on the side of the road. He watched them for a few minutes, to see whether they were as eager as the fishmongers to skin him and take his robes. He neared and noticed a small sign beside the stall:

Aith Cliath agus An Life ó dheas - Marbal pendance a silvur a peese.

"One of them must have written it," Myndil mused, marking the collection of coals and chalks beside one of the women.

They had many resources, withies and slats, rushes and reeds, even stripped planks of wood and stone. They seemed aimable and busy, carving out pendants and ceremonial pieces, with few customers approaching. These were not the ill-bred men of the public house; here were craftsmen, masters of their own creation, but Myndil still waved at them as though he knew them.

"Hallo!" Myndil cried, from across the road. "Yes, hallo!"

The young men and women looked up from their work and then at one another.

"That boy waving at us?" one of the women asked.

One of the men squinted. "I think so."

"Anyone know a daft lookin' man in white robes?"

They all shook their heads.

"Yes, hello!" Myndil pealed, strolling up to them. "Pleasant morning to you. It is a lovely morning, isn't it?"

"Was till you showed up," said one of the men. "Whatcha want? Lookin' fer a pendant? Need a job done?"

"My name is Myndil—"

"Don't care fer names when I don't ask fer 'em," said the man stoutly. "What's yer business?"

"I'm a missionary."

"A vetinary?"

"He's a god peddler," said one of the women, who was hammering away at a piece of metalwork. "Wan o' them new gods."

"Don't care too much fer gods in general," said the man. "They don't seem to care much about us."

68

"Oh, I'm sorry to hear about that," said Myndil, with genuine displeasure. "My god cares about me. He cares about everyone who loves him."

"Aye, well, gods can love us all they want. That don't mean they're givin' us any money. Does your god give jobs?"

"Well, I am doing a job for God right now."

"Really." The man simpered and slung his hammer over his shoulder. "How much he pay you fer that?"

"Well, when I gain enough followers, I will be ordained, and that will be my payment for the work I do out here."

"Well, ordination's all well and good fer you, boy, but we need money to survive. It's a hard life bein' on the road. To most who pass us by, we're just rabble, people who ply a trade without bein' apprenticed to it. We do good work and we're just wantin' to get by without bein' involved with kings or wars." He flipped his hammer a few times and appraised the smiling and bright-eyed boy before him. "Tell you what. You buy somethin', and I'll have a listen to what yer peddlin'."

"I will and gladly, but I'd rather you listen because you want to, not because I had to buy your attention."

The other men and women in the rabble looked up. The odd man in the splendid robes was taking a pouch from his hip, was holding it out to their carpenter, and the carpenter's face illuminated with an aurulent glow.

"Where'd you get that now?" the carpenter breathed, stepping back and eyeing Myndil suspiciously. "Why're you offerin' me a big bag o' gold?"

"You said you needed money to survive," said Myndil, in a sobering voice. "The abbot gave this to me for food and lodging, but I think he gave me more than I needed, because anyone who knows I have so much seems to be angry about it."

The rest of the rabble came forward, inspecting the gold with grim confusion.

"But you're offerin' it to us," said the metalworker, "just like that?"

"Well, you said you wanted me to buy something before telling you about God. I do want something, but not for myself, probably for Sister Iarlaith, because she gave me food before I went away and is probably worried for me, but I don't want any of you to worry about eating and surviving."

Myndil held the bag out to the carpenter and let him decide how many gold pieces he needed, but the carpenter held back his hand and motioned to the others to do likewise.

"We take money for work, lad," the carpenter told him. "Aye, you mighta got that gold fairly, but we don't know that, and while you're heart's innit, we don't take hapes o' gold aff someone we just met."

One of the stonemasons pushed her way through the small crowd and peered into the bag. "There any more o' that where you come from?"

"Actually, I'm not sure," said Myndil thoughtfully, "but we paid the stonemasons for all the work they did on the new building, so I suppose there must be more, since we need more work done on the abbey."

The carpenter brows arched. "You looking for new builders?"

"Well, the stonemasons said they would be back after the winter, but I know the dormitory needs more rooms, especially if I'm going to be gaining new followers for God, and the byre and dairy could certainly use fixing, because the nisser has been going on about the walls, and the iron work on the front gate is getting a bit–" Myndil paused; every eye was wide and waiting. "Yes, I think we do need more builders."

"And do we have to pledge ourselves to yer god?" the carpenter asked.

Myndil mused a moment. "The stonemasons didn't. I don't think god would ask you to love him, if you were just coming to do work on the abbey."

YES, GOD WOULD, the voice in his ear demanded. YOU ARE SUPPOSED TO BE GAINING FOLLOWERS, NOT CREATING JOBS. GOD LIKES INDENTURED SERVITUDE, NOT PAYING OPPORTUNITIES.

"And there's food at this here abbey o' yers?" said the stonemason.

"Oh, yes. Sister Iarlaith makes all the meals and loves feeding things in general, and there is always plenty of gruel to go round."

"And there's good shelter and that?" asked another.

"The rooms are certainly comfortable, especially the abbess' room, though they might be a little small, if all of you are to stay in one place."

"And there's no chance o' gettin' robbed in the night or gettin' our throats cut?"

"Well, it's never happened the whole time I've been there."

THERE IS ALWAYS A FIRST TIME.

The carpenter held out his hand and offered it to Myndil. "If yer tellin' us you got work fer us, we'll go to yer abbey and do whatever needs doin'. We're just a few friends who had our homes and villages destroyed by the Northmen raids, and we're just lookin' fer an honest way to rebuild what we lost."

Myndil put the gold down and shook the man's hand. "Thank you for not being angry," said Myndil, smiling.

"Thank you fer offerin' us a job," said the carpenter, with a good-humoured laugh. "We'll bring all our tools and supplies with us, 'long as it's not far."

Myndil told them the way, just up the road as far north as they could go, and then follow the path over the tidal crossing to the small island, the one with the iron gate at the front and the small wood beside. He gave them a piece of gold each to start their journey, but when he saw how much they had to pack up and carry with them, he gave them most of the bag, in case they should need to buy a horse or hire a cart along the way.

"Well," said the carpenter, patting the pouch, "we'll consider this payment for the job. This is more'n enough to cover everythin', and we promise not to run off till the job's done."

70

"I trust you," said Myndil, "only mind Mr Dullahan at the gate as you go in. He shouldn't bother you, if he sees the gold you have, but if he has his head on, he might try to chase you round a bit."

They had little idea what Myndil meant by this, but as they had got a job large enough to occupy all of them and they had already been paid, they only said they would be mindful of everyone at the abbey and packed their materials and wares.

"You know," said the carpenter, shaking Myndil's hand again before moving to go, "if you had a job like this fer everyone what's been ruined by these Norse kings, I daresay you'd get everyone to follow yer god."

"Really? But I don't know that the abbey has enough work for everyone."

"Shame, that. Most of us travelling 'long the roads are just plain folk lookin' fer work and a place to go."

"There do seem to be many heathens—though I can't tell them apart from anybody else—and you are aimable enough. I only wish I could do something to get them love God, or at least hear about him."

"There's an easy way," said the stonemason, clinging her tools across her back. "Yer not far from Ath Cliath. If you could go and speak to the king there and show him how much gold yer god has got, he might be willin' to change his mind."

"Aye," said the metalworker. "King's got a head for wars, bein' a servant of Odin and all. I'll tell ye honestly, boy: you won't find many willin' to change the old gods fer new. The Northmen tried to force their gods on us when they took over our ports, but if you can get the king to mind you and change his god for yers, he'll force everyone else to follow him."

"Do you think so? That is—I don't anyone to be forced into loving God. Everyone should seek his holy virtue for its own reward—but if the king would love God freely, he might be able to help me amplify God's message."

"No harm in tryin'," said the carpenter. "You just walk right down this road and follow the signs to Ath Cliath. There're also a lot more people there. You might have better luck gainin' followers that way."

Myndil thanked them from his heart. There were good heathens after all, and though they did not outwardly pledge themselves to god, they promised to go to the abbey and do the work the abbey desperately needed, which was allegiance enough. The rabble went northward, buying a small cart for themselves by the way, and Myndil continued south along the road, his spirits in a flutter, his feet eager to get to Aith Claith, though he had never heard of the place before, and eager to meet everyone living there, though he had no idea the sort of people he should find.

"If only I can get their king to love you, God," said Myndil, skipping past another signpost, "then perhaps he can read to his people and I need never deter anyone with my oration again."

YES, said the voice in his ear, as thought it were stifling a laugh, IF ONLY.

It was only two days since Myndil had been gone, and those who loved him began to grow anxious about hearing news of him. It was rare that any communication beyond the mandatory ecclesiastical notes should come by way of the odd messenger, any writing materials saved for manuscript reproduction or official documents, and finding paper on the road might be difficult. They must settle for news of Myndil in divine terms, through premonitions or messages given to them by god.

Or, in this case, direct visits from those who had met him.

The builders Myndil had entrusted his gold to came to the uplands after travelling for a full day. They came with their cart, their tools, and their supplies to the end—rather the beginning of the road, where the throughfare ended in a vast plateau, veering off to the east in a series of islands gamboling across the sea, and to the west in upland farms, sections of the extensive fields crowned with roundhouses and byres, where most of the livestock remained for the season. A pearlescent gleam of dew blanketed the grass, but it was suspiciously green for late winter, as though the snow were told to retreat from that part of the world and the frost were afraid to approach. They travelled toward the islands, following Myndil's instructions on how to find the abbey, and came to the tidal crossing, made traversable by the low tide. The first small island served as a stepping stone to the second, and the abbey was exactly where Myndil said it should be, the complex of new and old buildings surrounded by a high gate with a small woodland to the side.

"Never knew this was here," said the carpenter, admiring the facade.

"We oughta make a sign about it," said one of the haulers, "else how's anyone else gonna know it's here?"

The building was moderate, the old orphanage now surrounded by the new dormitory, the stonework prettily done with few embellishments to enliven the aspect, the frontage well-dressed, but the annex had cut into the dairy and the few animal enclosures, making the access to the back of the abbey narrow, and the windows and rooms seems smaller than they should have been, either from a want of ready materials or from a want of planned space. They saw the small fire in the front room through the open door and approached the iron gate.

A blue light loomed beside them. It came from the woods, the heavy crunch of feet through the brush nearing them at an alarming rate. They turned and were met with a flaming skull.

"Nurrrrrr..." said the dullahan, noggling up to them.

The rabble drew back behind the cart and raised their tools above their heads.

"Nurrr!" The dullahan reached out, but the moment it heard a certain jingling sound, it stopped and looked at a familiar pouch sitting at the front of the cart. "Mynnn..." the dullahan groaned. Its shoulders stooped and the flaming head seemed somehow sad. It trudged away, the flaming head escaping and rolling away from the gate, its body shambling along behind it.

"What is this place?" the stonemason asked, peering over the cart.

"He did tell us about the dullahan," the carpenter reminded her. "Maybe it's some kind of guard here."

"Then what do you call that?"

The stonemason pointed through the gate to the garden, where Ozzy the Wight stood mixing the mulch with the muck, griping over the atrocious job the abbot had done in trying to make good loam for the roses. "I told him not to put any clay in here," Ozzy's teeth chattered, "but he doesn't listen to a word I say."

The stonemason gaped through the iron bars. "Didn't that lad say this was supposed to be an abbey?"

"It is an abbey," Ozzy replied, hearing the visitors from the gate without any ears to help him. Agitated with the abbot's poor attempt at what Myndil did so well, he stuck his shovel in the ground and marched toward the front gate. "For all his godmongering, he has no idea how to do a proper bed-soil," he grumbled, throwing his gardening gloves aside. "All his praying and good intentions, he is still utterly useless." He sighed a breathless sigh, his bones working out the motions without the lungs to accompany them. He unhooked the latch from the inside and opened the iron gate. "Are you the replacements?" The hollow voice hung in the air, the brow bones bending to mirror muscle motion.

"Replacements fer what?" said the carpenter, with a chary glance.

"For the builders who left not long ago, the ones who were supposed to add to the dormitory and ended up ruining my hedges instead."

The carpenter shrugged. "Suppose so? The lad did say somethin' about 'em quittin' early."

"Oh, come in, then," Ozzy intoned. "I have a garden to plan."

He pulled the gate aside and let them enter with their cart.

"An' that doesn't bother ye?" said the metalworker, pointing to the iron gate.

"No," said Ozzy, with a withered aspect.

"Why'd you have gloves if you don't have skin?"

"I don't like my bones getting dirty. Do you brush your teeth?"

The metalworker had to concede here. "That's a fair point."

"Almost as bad as the children." Ozzy took up his shovel and shook off the blade. "Now, if you'll excuse me, I need to do something that will make me happy and re-dig my grave. Since the winter, the sides have caved in, and the fit has been a bit snug."

He took his leave, marching around the abbey to the small cemetery hidden away at the far eastern corner, leaving the rabble with the abbot, who was running out of his office with his arms flailing.

"Whatisthiswhatisthiswhatisthis!" he cried, in a panic, motioning to their cart. "What is all this? Nonono, you cannot come in here! Go away, and I'm sure I don't care whether you want alms."

"Pardon me, yer lordship?" said the carpenter, not quite knowing how to address an abbot.

"This is the abbey, do I have that right?"

The abbot stopped floundering. "Yes, this is an abbey. What do you mean by the?"

"Well, we met this odd fella on the road. Said his name was Merndyl, or Mendel?"

The abbot paled and felt the warmth fade from his cheeks. "Myndil?" he muttered, almost afraid to say the name.

"That's the one. He told us you were lookin' fer builders to extend some work on yer new dormitory. We were lookin' for a job, and he gave it to us, so here we are, ready to build whatever needs buildin'."

"Nononono, you must be mistaken," said the abbot, shaking his head. "We do not need some ragabash rabble to do anything. We have our own stonemasons who will return eventually, and we do not need anything from you atallrightnoworevergoodday."

"But we comed wit' all der supplies," one of the haulers exclaimed, showing the cart he had just hauled in through the gate. "We even carried all dis woods and stones all der way here."

The commotion rose to such a pitch as to summon Vindimir and Crannach to the garden, and they heard with some surprise that the builders were sent by Myndil.

"That fella came to us and told us about some god you worship," the carpenter continued, "said that you'd provide us with food and shelter, and all we had to do was build new sleepin' quarters for some new followers."

Crannach held his sides in mirth, overjoyed by the news, and Vindimir put his hand to his mouth and tried not to laugh.

"This cannot be happening," the abbot maffled, turning about and looking for help. "This cannot be happening—God, how is this happening? The boy has led some rabble to my abbey!"

Crannach allowed the abbot to wander away and mumble to himself, and he and Vindimir stepped forward to receive their visitors.

"Myndil did tell ye right," said Crannach. "We did need more rooms fer the dormitorae. The masons were gonnae come back after the winter, but if yer here now, ye might as well stae and start work—"

"They cannot stay!" the abbot shouted, from halfway across the garden. "We don't have room!"

"They're going to build the room," Vindimir reminded him.

"We got no trouble sleeping outside on our covers," said the carpenter. "Long as we can have a small fire and somethin' to eat—"

"THEY CANNOT STAY HERE BECAUSE I DON'T WANT THEM HERE."

"But ye told Myndil tae gain followers," said Crannach, trying not to grin. "How're ye gonna know he followed yer orders if he doesnae bring o' his followers back here?"

"What?" said the abbot bleakly, hastening up to him. "What do mean, bring them back here?"

"You told Myndil to gain as many followers as he could and he was not to come back until he did," said Vindimir. "How else is he going to prove himself for his ordination unless he brings his followers here to be counted?"

Crannach made an ominous grin, and the abbot began sweating.

"Nonononono," the abbot cried, hastening over to the cart. He pulled on it and tried to move it, but could not get it to budge. "You cannot stay here—we have no money to pay you for the job, so I guess you'll just have to leave and go build something somewhere else—"

"Myndil already paid us," the carpenter announced.

The abbot stood aghast. "What?"

The carpenter took the bag of gold from the cart and presented it to the abbot. "Paid us fer the job, paid us fer materials, even paid fer this here conveyance cart."

God will punish you... "Yes..." the abbot burbled, staring at the abbey wall, the last vestiges of hope and happiness winking out. "God is punishing me..."

"Well," Crannach laughed, "if Myndil paid ye—"

Myndil's name brought Sister Iarlaith to the front gate. She was just entering the kitchen and caught the word through the open door, and for a moment, under the guise of grief, she was bewitched, thinking Myndil had come back again. She bolted through the kitchen, leapt over the low table in the front room, and jossed out the door, all her flesh following her. Her cheeks were already wrapped in smiles, but when she saw five people she had never seen before instead of Myndil, she stopped, looked them over, and seemed quite embarrassed.

"Oh..." said Iarlaith, all the light in her eyes diminished. "Ah thought Myndil might be—" She hemmed, smoothed her robes, and returned to her matricentric musings. "Did Myndil send ye?"

The craftsmen all nodded.

"Aye, tha's good o' him, that's liek himsel'—is he o' right? Did he look well? Is he cleanin' behind his ears? Is he eatin' an' 'o?"

"Looked just fine to us," said the carpenter. "Clean robes, clean face, his hair a bit disheveled. He does smile a lot though. That normal fer him?"

"Aye," said Iarlaith, with tearful smiles, "that's him right enough. Did he have anae message tae give? Anae word o' where he's goin' or mibbe when he's comin' back?"

No one had any information to give, other than he was continuing south along the coast, and Iarlaith pretended to be happy at this news, smiling while silently wishing Myndil would have followed them home.

The stonemason took something from the cart and approached her. "Are you Sister Iarlaith?"

"Aye," said she apprehensively.

"Myndil mentioned you make all the meals and help care for everyone here."

"Oh, aye?" Iarlaith's eyes brightened, but the effect was momentary, and she composed herself again. "Ah mean—oh, aye. Ah dae tha', aye. How'd ye know mah name?"

"When Myndil gave us the money fer the job, he'd said he wanted to buy somethin' fer you, but he never picked out the piece he wanted. I thought ye might like this one."

The stonemason held out a piece of worked marble. It was a large circular piece with three running hounds etched into it, the outlines all finely worked, the circumference trimmed with silver leaf. The marble pendant was attached to a long silver chain, long enough that it could be draped over a head without needing a clasp. She came forward to put it gently round Iarlaith's neck.

"Oh..." Iarlaith exhaled, her throat clenching. She examined the pendant and could not put it down. "He shouldn'tae dunnit..." she cried weakly. "He shouldnae be spendin' his monae on me."

"He gave us enough money to last a good long while and pay for all our materials," the stonemason explained. "I think his honesty and the trust he gave us to do the job without knowin' us much shows what a good heart he has and how well ye raised him."

Iarlaith sniffed, and her round cheeks luffed. "Aye..." She showed the pendant to Crannach. "Isnae yit lovelae? But if he's bought me this and he's paid o' yous, how's he gonnae get anaethin' tae eat while he's awae?"

"Ah have a feelin' Myndil'll find someone tae feed him," said Crannach, with a good-humoured smile. "He's got a pitiable and friendly look tae him, a wee bit like a lost puppy alwaes waggin' its tail. It's hard tae resist him long. Aye, it's still dangerous on the road, but he's no' been gone two daes, and he's alreadae brought friends back tae us."

The builders began to unpack their cart and canvases, and settle themselves, making their builder's work patch in the garden by the dormitory. Crannach and Vindimir watched them unfurl their tools and set up their materials, while the abbot stood in one corner of the garden, weeping against a willow tree.

"Ah'll tell ye truthfullae," said Crannach, surveying the stonemason as she made her initial measurements, "Ah was worried fer Myndil, bein' out there oan his own, but," eyeing the rabble with a smile, "he did it. He got people—good people—tae listen tae him and come back here."

"I wonder what he said to them," said Vindimir, in a reverie, "I mean before he told them about the abbey needing work. I wonder what his approach was."

"Think it might have tae do with the gold."

Vindimir hummed in agreement. "Greed does motivate."

"Ah think in this case it's desperaetion." Crannach studied the torn clothes and worn shoes of the rabble. "Ah think Myndil might have given 'em hope."

"Do you think he might do it? Do you think he might actually bring hundreds of people here and convince them he's a holy man?"

"It's an amusin' thought," Crannach simpered. "The abbot did send him on a holy pilgrimage as a missionary, which is a holy rite. Aye, o' the saints were mad in a wae, but we've alwaes said Myndil's a wee bit different."

Vindimir watched the abbot melt against the tree and fleered to himself. "If the holy saints all got miracles and hagiographies out of madness and isolation, then why not for Myndil? Only do not call him a saint when he returns. Abbot might throw himself in the sea."

"What's Myndil gonnae be saint o'? Warm hugs?"

"A good a thing as any to be a patron saint for. I think poor abbot could use one right about now."

The abbot was on his knees, leaning forward against the willow, his forehead pressed into the trunk, his body limp, his soul in an agony. "What have I done...?" he feeped, his voice stifled by grief. God was punishing him: he had wanted no noise at the abbey, and now there would be the incessant tinking and thunking of metal on stone all day—and there was not one of them to be doing the work that needed to be done, but five—five voices to be harassing his ears and destroying his nerves, the conclamant cacophony of riotous laughter and wretched construction, paired with the cries of "Ay! Aw jus' found they've got ale here!" and the halloos of jubilation at the possibility of drinking themselves to sleep every night offending his ideas of decency and decorum. "God is punishing me..." he whispered, his hands reaching up and tugging his hair at the sides of his head. "Thank you, O Lord, for this suffering," he moaned, "I have many lessons yet to learn..."

Myndil was happening to the world, and god was happening to the abbot, and if this was but the beginning of Myndil's adventures in missionizing, the abbot did not know whether he should live to see the end of it.

Chapter 10: In Which Myndil Happens to a Healer

With his object in view of seeing the king, Myndil had little doubt of eventual success. He was anxious to present the idea of his god to an authority figure, especially one who was legally permitted to take his head, but he trusted that god would somehow act in his favour, whether to bring him directly to Ath Cliath unharmed or send someone who would assist him there in his way. The road southward soon became tenanted with vegetation, the holly and winterthur crowding the narrowing path, and presently he came to a thicket, the entrance wreathed by high blackthorns, their boughs bending over the trail and meeting in the middle. It was warmer here than it had been in the north, and with the added ground cover, more animals were around, the red squirrels hopping in and out of trees, the stoats and badgers mining the stumps, and crows cawing from the canopies. Two crows in particular stood out to him: they had been following him since the morning, and by mid afternoon, the two of them hand flown overhead and landed on every corner tree he reached.

"Are those your crows, God?" Myndil asked, pointing to the birds.

ALL ARE GOD'S CREATURES, the voice reminded him.

"Oh, yes, but what I mean is are those your messengers? Are you sending them to follow me?"

YES, HA HA. THAT IS EXACTLY WHAT GOD IS DOING. GOOD EYE.

They would not have been remarkable if there had not always been two of them, and the same two, with blue-black wings and grey feathers at their breast. Myndil offered the last crumbs of his biscuits to them, but they waited until he was gone to swoop down and collect their reward.

They followed Myndil to a small gathering away from the nearby woods, a congregation of revelers taking part in some feast day preparations. Stew pobbled in a pot, meat was turning on a spit, bread and butter were going round, and when Myndil approached, they were good enough to share their meal with him, asking nothing in return, even telling Myndil the way to Ath Cliath when he asked. The friendship, however, was short-lived, for the moment Myndil took out his book and asked if they should like to hear about the wonders of god and his creation, the leader of the group stood from the table and said, "I'll thank you to leave my table."

Myndil, of course, said "You're welcome."

A laugh and a few buns thrown at him sent him on his way.

"Thank you for the meal!" Myndil beamed, taking the last bit of gold from his pocket.

They had no interest in his money; they wanted him gone and expelled him with the wish of, "If ye ever come back here, god peddler, we're gonna roast you!"

"Oh, thank you, but I don't know whether I would make a very good dinner. I certainly wouldn't be very nourishing or flavourful without good spices. I would have to be fattened first, if I'm to be made much a dinner of, and Sister Iarlaith has tried to put more meat on me for the last fifteen years–"

A half-eaten leg bone was thrown at his head, and Myndil took his leave, disappointed that he did not get to tell them about god, but grateful that they had allowed him to stay so long.

"And I was going to sing them one of the songs of praise too," said Myndil, as he continued southward. "I thought if oration would not work, a song might. Everybody likes singing."

YES, BUT NOT EVERYONE LIKES YOUR SINGING.

"That's very true, though my singing is much better than my oration. When I sing in the garden to the grogoch, he quite likes it and cleans out the latrine much faster than if I don't." Myndil made a longing backward glance to the gathering in the distance. "They were friendly heathens and did like revelry, though they seemed disappointed I wasn't interested in their grog. Perhaps I should have told them about your holy days."

YOU SHOULD HAVE TOLD THEM ABOUT HOLY WARS.

"But holy days are so much more festive and exciting! And besides, no one should need to go to war to worship you, God."

YES THEY SHOULD.

"Oh, God," Myndil tutting, smiling and shaking his head, "you really are very silly sometimes. I love you, and you see I have never gone to war for you."

YES. THAT IS A PROBLEM.

"There is no need for war when everyone is getting along."

I DO NOT WANT EVERYONE TO GET ALONG.

"I know you are only dour about the heathens not liking you because they said you weren't real and couldn't hurt them if you tried, but I am sure they will come to know you better. If they would only practice a little more patience with me and with one another."

I WOULD RATHER THEY PRACTICE VIOLENCE ON ONE ANOTHER.

"Well, I'm sure we will see those clansmen again," Myndil announced, gaily swinging his arms. "They were very helpful and told me the way to see the king, but—" stopping and pensively lifting a finger to his lips, "—they forgot to give me directions to his palace, or even to tell me if there was a palace—I think they said something about there being a throne somewhere, and they did mention a large river, saying I would have to cross it to get to the king, but that I should know it when I come to it, but it wasn't called the Ath Cliath river, it was called something else, but I couldn't understand them because their mouths were too full. Perhaps I can ask someone along the road about it—oh, there's someone!"

At a crossroads in the near distance, wedged amidst the nemorous lane, was a small cottage, rounded by cobbles and guarded by a stone walkway. It was done in the same style as the roundhouses, but instead of being crowned with a rick of straw and fitted up with hunting accoutrements, it was made of hewn stone and caked in light limewash. The eves were ornamented with bundles of rosemary and lavender, the stone supports for the outer walls bending slightly, the posts wilting under the weight of a fine peat thatch, the top still green and blooming. An amber glow emanated from the windows, the hearth giving life into the small sitting room, the trinkets and memorandums of a hard-earned domestic life garlanded the mantelpiece, the timid and unattended fire breathing upwards, the chimney teeming in ribbons of smoke, the few birds nesting round the rain catch preening themselves against the warm stack. The home seemed empty for the present, any movement from the residents happening just beyond the door, the cramblings of an old woman drawing the querant's eye: she was a fulsome but hardy woman, one who had been used to hard work in her youth and was now bent over a small cooking fire, sitting on low stool before a small cauldron, with a pile of sallies and rushes on one side of her and several bundles of gathered herbs on the other. A wide apron adorned her lap, her feet leaning against the hearthstone, her brow bent, her hands full of business, at once tying herbs over the cauldron and examining the piles of rushes, delineating so many rushes for each of the sallies. She sat in quiet contemplation, her hands moving mechanically, the motions of a lifetime spent foraging done unconsciously now, her worn hands wrapping the bundles and separating the sallies. A few yew shrubs enveloped the front of the house, the rose and buckthorn under the windows serving as a discouragement to anyone who should near the sills, and just beside the small garden behind her was a old whitethorn, its limbs ponderous with age, mantling over the old woman, wending around the trims of cloth and linen left on the tree by visitors long gone. A few cordoned trees were trained along a low fence, rows of newly planted root vegetables dotted the raised beds, and a small milking cow lowed on a small patch of new grass.

Myndil neared and examined the house, the symbol above the lintel catching his eye: it was a stone figure of what he thought was an amphibious creature lying sideways and opening its mouth, but when he narrowed his gaze and looked again, he saw a female figure, one that was crouching and holding open a rather cavernous purse.

He saw a small sign in front of the house which read: TRYD REMEDYS YE'LL RYSE IN TH' NYTE FER.

"I shouldn't like to be up again when I have only just lain down," Myndil mused. "It is so dreadfully hard to get comfortable sometimes, especially without my Good Book pillow with me. When I have just got comfortable, it's a bit of a bother to have to get out of bed and visit the latrine, especially in winter."

There was a pause, and then the voice ventured, DOST THOU NOT KEEP A CHAMBER POT?

"Well, I did when I was younger, but Brother Vindimir said my pot had an odd scent to it in the mornings, and then he made me do all the pots in the orphanage, because he said I was so very loud when I was doing what nature intended. I whistled to keep from everyone hearing me go, but I don't think it helped much." Myndil canted his head and read the sign again. "I wonder if that sign is meant for the undead, though I wonder how many of them are able to read. Ozzy can read, since he was keen on reading before his unlife. It's very kind of her to include wights in her remedies. Not many people think of those like Ozzy—Hallo!" waving and calling out to the old woman, "Yes, hello there!"

She was not so far away as to warrant being hallooed at; she had seen him coming half a mile off, and having marked him out as a bit barmy for skipping down the road by himself, she decided that he was best left to himself. The frantic waves and jovial shouts, however, could not be readily ignored, and she separated the rushes in her hand and grunted, "Hullo yerself, son."

Myndil approached and pointed to the sign in front of the house. "I see you have tried remedies. If they aren't tried by anybody else, I should like try them."

The woman kept her eyes on the work in her lap. "Don't share remedies between patients on account o' the mallacht and that. Look like yer needin' a few remedies yerself, willowy measure o' meadow-water like you."

Myndil investigated the small cottage beside her. "Is this your lovely home?"

"Better be, else what I am doin' here?"

"Oh, yes. I meant rather to ask whether this was an inn or only your shop."

"Neither. This here's my home. I live innit, I heal people what're ailin' innit, and I don't take coin fer the remedies."

"Oh, that's very kind of you. At the abbey, we don't take money for healing people at the infirmary either, though our infirmary is only one bed and Sister Iarlaith with the bandages. Are you a cleric or a holy woman? Do you heal with God's help?"

It was innocently said and inquisitively meant, but the old woman, noting Myndil's robes and his oppressive smiles, felt it as a slight.

"I heal by the power of my patience, son," said she, in a firm hue, glaring up at him, "and you're sure tryin' it, I'll tell ye that fer nothin'."

Myndil was undeterred by this. "I see you have much work to do," said he, sidling her. "May I help you? I'm very good at chores."

The old woman humphed. "If you think you can make yerself useful."

"I can—or at least I am useful when I'm mucking out for the pigs and raking in the mash and, dusting the shelves in the library—" He counted his is many tasks on his fingers and stopped to think. "—And when I'm weeding the garden, and when I'm turning the flower boxes for Ozzy—"

"Aye, son," said the old woman stoutly. "I getcha. No need to have me all by the years." She sighed and murmured to herself, "...About as useful as soot-sullied pan."

"Only my clothes are cleaner," Myndil insisted, "and I can also help with the laundry and the ewery, but the abbot says I do leave streaks on the cups and don't dry the plates as well as I should."

The word 'abbot' caught the old woman's ear, and after another thorough examination of her visitor, she leaned away from him and arched a brow. "Yer wan o' them, aincha?"

Myndil's eyes animated. "One of whom?"

The old woman sighed and turned aside. "Gods' teeth," said she, in a plaintive voice, "everythin's at me this mornin'. First the cow can't be bothered to milk, then it rains on the rushes when I was only after takin' 'em in, and now I got the blow-in's at me. Only fer somethin' should the sky fall down."

Myndil studied the passing clouds. "I don't think the sky would fall. It is called the firmament after all."

The old woman rested her elbows on her knees and glared at him. "You got a purpose to you, or you just aff wandein'?"

"Well, we all have a purpose, even if it is only wandering. God made each of us with a special purpose in mind."

"This here god o' yers give you a name?"

"Myndil. Myndil Plodostirr."

He held out his hand, and the old woman flouted and tapped it with her rushes.

"Brigid's Blessin's and others besides," she offered.

"Oh, Brigid! I know Saint Brigid. She was a holy woman who lived a few hundred years ago and did many miracles, and her father was a chieftain and she turned to God after she was going to be married off and decided she would promise herself to a life in God's service instead."

Here was a sideways glance. "Aye, we'll say it's that Brigid."

"I think she also had something to do with Saint Paudrig—or maybe she was too young to have met him—but I know she was born at sunrise and has her own abbey that she claimed from the Druids—is that her?" pointing to the grotesque above the door. "Is that a depiction of Brigid? It is rather small. And hairless. And it has rather jagged teeth."

The old woman glanced at the figure perched upon the lintel. "That's Sile, son."

"Oh. Is she another saint, or one of the local gods? It looks as though she is bending down and pulling something open—is it two sides of a purse she is holding onto?"

The grotesque had its knees in the air, its arms bending around raised legs, and its fingers coiling around an oval orifice. "Aye," said she dryly, "we'll say that's what it is."

"She must bring you good fortune with such a wide opening. Do you worship her by making offerings and putting them into her—"

"How's about you tell me whatcha came here for, son, 'cause my ears are after achin' with all this here chatterin' yer doin'," the woman demanded.

"Oh, yes. I'm on my way to Ath Cliath and would like to know where the king's throne is, please."

"Which king are you wantin'?" said the old woman, with some derision. "We got a whole collection here."

"The people I met before coming here told me the king of Ath Cliath is named Olaf."

"You mean Amlaíb?"

Myndil blinked. "Is this another one of those orthographic things?"

"Why'd you wanna see him anyhow? He's always fightin' and plunderin' and shoutin' about some nonsense. Just came back from capturin' whatshisname in Limerick. Too sour about losin' the place across the way to the biggun in the south, so he's gotta take over all the other kingdoms, just prove he's worth his salt to everybody else."

"So, is Olaf not a good king, then?" Myndil ventured.

82

The old woman gave him a flat look. "No."

"Oh."

The old woman took another sally and wrapped a bundle of dried rushes around it. "A good king looks after his people, protects the borders, and defends his lands. Only thing Amlaíb mac Gofraid looks after is his pride. His only interest is conquerin', and mallacht take his people besides. He's not really one o' us anyhow. He came from across the pond," motioning eastward, across the sea, "and we just have to live with him, 'cause we don't got a way o' gettin' rid of him. Dunno why you'd want to see him. He's not one fer talkin'."

"The heathens I met yesterday told me that if I wanted to gain many followers for God, I would need to speak to the king. I don't know that I can get him to spread God's teachings, but if I could speak to him—would you like to hear some? There are some really lovely passages, especially at the beginning, and I do need to practice my oration—"

"Better not, son."

"Oh, no? Why not?"

"'Cause I got the god allergy."

"Oh, I'm sorry to hear of it. I've never met anyone who has an allergy to hearing scripture before."

"You'll find there's a lot of us here like that. It's our heritage and such."

"And one of your remedies cannot cure you?"

The old woman murmured something about there being no cure for the spread of 'pig ignorance.'

Myndil wondered about this, but he assured her that the Good Book was "healthsome and rather entertaining," with parts of it being "absolutely riveting, especially about the plagues."

"I know all about that there book you got, son," she assured him. "Sure 'tis a good tale altogether, but my ears are like to fall off if you start readin' it, so better keep yer stories to yerself. I get the itchin' somethin' fierce when all the men in robes start readin' their books at me, and there's a fair lotta yous these days. That all you're doin' here in Ath Cliath? Walkin' around with that there book o' yers, puttin' the stories on people?"

"Yes. I'm a missionary."

"So you're not skilled to a trade, then."

"Well, the reading bit of it certainly is a skill, because it's one I'm not very good at."

"What I meant was, any eejit can do it."

"Yes! Everyone can enjoy reading and sharing the Good Book, and everyone an incur favour with God by doing good deeds—"

"Yer book say somethin' about helpin the elderly to incur favour and such?"

"Oh, yes. There are several sections on the importance of assisting the elderly—"

"Good. You'll help an auld woman and incur favour with yer god by takin' these."

She forced two sallies into his hand and put a bundle of dried rushes into his lap.

"Oh." Myndil took up a few of the rushes. "What do I do with them?"

"Folla me, son. Hold up yer sallies with the one hand," she directed him, holding up her own hand and watching him follow, "and then take yer rushes in the other, and start foldin'. Wend it through one side, fold it over, wend it through again, and fold again. That's it. Once you got the three sides done, hold it here at the openin', turn the whole thing to the right, and start again on that side."

"Oh, I love making crafts!" Myndil reveled, gleefully tapping his feet. "I help the children in the orphanage do their crafts with the Brothers and Sisters whenever I have time after my chores. Abbot says idle hands lead to busy mouths, and if my hands are busy, my mouth stops moving for a while, but not forever, because I still need to breathe."

The old woman somehow doubted that Myndil's lips ever stopped moving; he was one of those who the more you give them to do, the more questions they asked, but he caught on to the method of folding the rushes quickly, and she therefore said nothing. He folded and turned and folded again, tying the rushes at the ends and tucking the sallies into place, and when he was finished, he created a full three-pronged star with a woven triangle in the middle. He was immediately supplied with more rushes and bid to continue.

"This is pleasant—aren't crafts lovely? Why are we making these?" Myndil asked, weaving and folding.

"To honour Brigid. 'Tis her feast day th'morra."

"Oh, that's nice. I had no idea that saints were honoured by having these made for them. I thought they were honoured by having their relics toured and sometimes by having a finger stolen or a shroud removed—"

"Hush yerself now and get to foldin'."

Myndil, having more rushes on his lap than he did for the last one, used them all, packing them together and weaving them round, and when he finished it, he held it up for appraisal. It was slightly deformed, the centre gradually becoming a tragedy as it went on, sunk to one side and overextended on the other.

"Shall I redo this one? I'll just redo this one," Myndil insisted, but the old woman plucked it from his hands and tossed it onto the small pile of three-sided ornaments beside him.

"Go on to the next one," said she, putting more rushes into his lap. "Only six rushes, 'cause the sallies can't be holdin' no more than that."

"Is this a craft your people usually make around this time? Is it like a corn dolly, to ask for a good harvest for the coming year?"

"We ask Brigid to bless 'em and we put 'em on the house for protection against fire."

"Oh. So it's a sort of charm then, a trinket to repel ill luck."

"'Tis so."

"Like the ribbons you have on the tree there?"

He turned toward the whitethorn and marked the many ribbons tied along the boughs.

"Those're for the daoine sidhe, the good folk what mind the land," the old woman explained. "That whitethorn—all whitethorns—belong to the good people, and folk come here to ask 'em for a favours, leavin' 'em somethin' in return."

"Do you ask them for favours?"

She shook her head. "Never. You ask somethin' of the good people when you don't care what yer gettin'. Folk might ask fer a child, and the good people might give one to you, but it might be a changeling, and that's a thing nobody asks fer. No," in a more serious hue, "best avoid askin' 'em fer things if it can be helped, else I'd ask them to help me with the work and take you aff besides."

"Well, I'm glad you didn't ask them, because I like sitting here with you."

Myndil smiled to himself, and the old woman felt a pang at her heart. He was only too good; a shame that he belonged to a foreign god.

"They got the good people where you're from, son?" she asked.

"Of course! Some of them are even my friends, like Thingunderthebed and the nisser and Mr Dullahan."

He finished another three-pronged charm and held it up for the old woman to assess, turning it about and ruminating over the spiraling whorl at the centre.

THOU DOST MAKE AN IMAGE OF EVIL.

"Oh, hallo, God!" Myndil declared, and then, turning to the old woman, "I am just helping this old lady, but we're not making an image of evil, God. It is only the twirly whirly symbol of Saint Brigid."

Someone sighed somewhere. THE TWIRLY WHORLY IS A SYMBOL OF A HEATHEN DEITY. THOU SHALT NOT MAKE FALSE IDOLS.

Myndil held up the charm and studied it. "Am I really making an idol, God, if Brigid is widely known as a holy woman? There is no face or form to venerate."

"Brigid's symbol isn't an idol, son," said the woman, half ignoring Myndil conversation. "It's an offerin'."

"Oh, that's good, because God was speaking to me just now, and he was telling me that this charm for Brigid is an image of evil, but I cannot think how such a small and faceless thing could do any harm to anybody. Hrm...perhaps if I added something to it, God would be happier about it..."

He took up a supernumerary bundle of rushes and began weaving it around the pre-existing prongs.

"What's that you're doin?" the old woman asked, beginning to pay attention.

"I'm just adding one more side to it. It will still have the same whorl in the middle, only now there will be four prongs instead of three, making it look a little more like a cross—there," holding it up. "What do you think?"

Myndil held the cross up to the light, and the old woman flouted.

"Can't be makin' it cross when it's supposed to be three-sided, son."

"But the cross will appease God, and it's so much easier to make a cross straight, and you can plant it anywhere you like. Like this!"

Myndil gently knocked the rush cross into the ground, letting it stand on its own at the top of the garden, making it the aegis of the hedgerow, and the moment he took his hand away, a sudden streak of light broke through the clouds, penetrating the tree behind them, casting a beam of amber light onto the cross. The old woman was about to say something about how tradition dictated that Brigid's symbol was always and only ever done in three-tine fashion, but the beam and the sudden appearance of an aurulent haze around Myndil's head silenced her.

"Do you think this would good enough to venerate Brigid with?" Myndil asked, his features shrouded by golden light.

The old woman narrowed her gaze, looking first at Myndil, then at the cross, and back again. "Hmph. Supposin' we keep it for now," was all her answer. "If yer aff to see the king, best make one fer yerself. I'll dress it with a few sprigs, to keep the wolf and the bog beetle aff you as you go."

"Oh—but do you really think wolves and beetles will be interested in me? Gnats do rather like me for some reason. Brother Vindimir says it's because I taste nicely to them. They are always trying to get into my mouth."

"'Tis what happens when ye never close it."

Myndil fashioned a rush cross for himself, replete with twirly whirly centre, and the old woman separated some springs of rosemary, thyme, lavender, and wolfsbane to fit into the tied ends and nidify the prongs. She went into the house and returned with bunches of dried hazel and lilac. "For added protection," said she, plaiting them together with a few rushes and tying them to Myndil's belt. "Yer aff to see the king, you'll need all the help in the world."

"Oh, thank you. That's very kind of you, but will they really protect me?"

"See that book you got there," said she, pointing to the book at Myndil's hip, "the one you're tryna harass me with?"

"You mean the one you're allergic to?"

"Aye, that one. You think that book's the word o' yer god and therefore it's got special powers and such."

"Well, the book itself is only one I copied from Brother Crannach's manuscript—"

"But you speakin' the words is what you think's gonna give you strength and gain you followers, right?"

Myndil nodded obediently.

"That's what magic is, son. You believin' that yer little book has power and that its protection follas you wherever you go on the road—that's the same as associatin' these herbs and flowers with protection and wearin' 'em," and in an undervoice, she added, "only wolfsbane'll actually keep the wolves away."

She took up the ends of his belt and pinned a sprig of wood sorrel to each one.

THOU SHALT NOT TAKE FOR THYSELF AN AMULET TO BE WORN ON THY—WHAT ARE YOU DOING?

"Trying to smell the lilac," Myndil answered, holding a sprig up to his face. "It's dried out, but I can still get a hint of the scent. I love lilacs, especially in May when the come into full bloom and the bees are buzzing about them—I have a white lilac tree outside my window at the monetary, and in the late spring, the sweet scent comes through the window."

"D'ye ever stop talkin'?" the old woman demanded, sitting down at her cauldron.

"Oh, I don't speak during prayers, because I am too busy speaking to God."

She turned and gave Myndil a conscious look. "I sure don't know what you are, son, but you're company anyway. You stayin' fer dinner, son?"

"I would really like to, because you have such a delightful home and you've been very kind to me, and what you're cooking does smell delightfully, and you are a very good woman to offer rest and healing on the road, but I really must find the king. If you could just tell me the way I should go?"

"That-a way, son," said she, jutting her chin toward the left fork in the road, "but you shouldn't be in such a hurry to lose yer head."

"Do you think I will lose it along the way? I do quite like it where it is now. It's rather practical having it sit between my shoulders, and especially after seeing what Mr Dullahan goes through, I should not like to be looking for it for long."

The old woman made a small sigh. "I can give you somethin' that'll keep someone from takin' it, if yer not mindin' my 'heathen cures and practices' and such."

"Herbs and plants are not heathen—God made them, so they cannot be—we use them at the abbey, mostly for flavouring the ale, but also for fevers and rashes."

"Here, put some colour in yer cheeks." She reached into the cauldron with a large clay cup and drew up a frothing liquid. "Hold that," she bid him, and before Myndil could ask what it was, she took a poker from the small fire and thrust it into the drink, boiling it instantly. "There," she declared, taking the poker out. "Drink that. It'll keep all the sidhe away."

Myndil gave the drink a diffident sniff. "Are they allergic to milk?"

"The iron."

"Oh, yes." Myndil sipped, with hands in supplication and eyes smiling. "Thank you. It's very irony and makes me feel as though I have just swallowed a few coins, but I'm sure it's good for me."

"Well, it'll keep you warm anyway."

She gave him a series of instructions: that if he should be hurt by thorns to find a snail and rub its bottom onto his cuts; that if he caught a sore throat, he should take up one of the lizards by the stream and let it sit on his tongue; and that he should not stand at the crossroads as the sun was going down, lest a fairy funeral meet him on the path.

"Fairies have funerals?" Myndil asked.

"Aye, so they do. Mourners from the other world what run on the wind and cause mischief. Don't get mixed up in their business, son, or that's you done fer."

"Thank you for telling me. I don't believe you told me your name."

"Folk just call me Peig."

"Thank you for all your help and friendly advice, Peig. I do hope we meet again."

"Tell you what, son. If the king don't kill you from the allergy yer about to give him, you come and tell me about it."

It was a promise, one that Myndil was only too happy to make, and with a thousand thanks, Myndil marched off, his freshly made cross dangling from his belt, his newly furnished sprigs swaying with every step.

The old woman stood and watched him go, his light skipping figure vanishing down the road. Two crows fluttered out of a nearby tree and darted after him, the sudden fulmination and pursuit a bit worrisome. "Corbies," she observed. She shook her head and planted her hands on her hips. "Aye, that boy's gonna end up in a ditch."

He has more sense than most, said a voice close by her ear.

Something appeared beside her, the image of a tall figure rippling against the wind, and from the corner of her eye, a billowing outline appeared, one under the glamour of a golden sun, the light emanating from her maternine features, her stately presence preceded by a warm glow, the succour of a soothing spirit pervading the landscape and overtaking the house. The figure glimmered and melded into view, a woman metalizing beside Peig, her countenance at once young and wise, her cheeks framed by a cascade of curls, her frame clothed in a cloak of flame, her aspect indulgent, her eyes attentive and amused.

"Nice lad," said Peig. "Cracked, but nice."

The visitor made a maternal thrum. "Not so different from you, I perceive," said she, with a musical inflection.

They exchanged a conscious look.

"Maybe not," Peig acknowledged, "but I got my head about me. I got the good sense to keep my madness to meself."

The woman in flame bent and took up one of the rush crosses Myndil had made. She examined it in a glow of regard. "This is different."

"Insisted on appeasin' some god what was talkin' to him or somesuch."

"And you did not wish to tell him the truth?"

Peig shrugged. "What for? He'll find out soon enough."

"Indeed."

The woman placed the cross in the window and held her hand over it. A soft golden glow emanated from her fingertips, tinging the surface of the rushes, brizzling them a sunbaked brown. The blessing given, the woman took herself off, vanishing in a sun-soaked blaze, the furole left behind the only evidence of her ever having been there. Peig returned to her cauldron, breaking dried elderflower into the milk and stirring it with her poker, whispering a charm over the brew, asking that Brigid go with the young man, if not to save him from harm then at least to keep his corpse from being robbed.

ChAPTER JI: IN WHICH FRIENDS ARE FORETOLD

The abbey was quiet that evening. The rabble had begun their work on the new rooms for the dormitory, and while they would need more stone for the job, they were able to set up the beginning foundations for the annex. Iarlaith brought them something to eat, the abbess gave them all the ale they wanted, and the builders decided they liked the arrangement, working and eating out of doors, though it was late winter, working at their own pace, safe from any thieves on the road who would come and steal their supplies whilst they slept. The safety was what they liked best, and while they were no closer to pledging themselves to Myndil's god, the comfort of being behind a wall and under the aegis of those who believed they were defend from evil was pleasant enough.

The children enjoyed learning about their tools and crafts, the metalworker especially eager to show them how she worked, and the rabble was more than happy to show them how to amuse themselves, the carpenter showing them whittlework, the stonemason showing them how to carve figures from soapstone, the others displaying their leatherwork to willing learners. The carpenter took some of the firewood drying against the wall and showed the children how to mark it for sculpture.

"Not partic'larly good at it myself," said he, making the penciled marks, "but I can at least show you a bit how it's done."

The Brothers and Sisters supervised their demonstrations, but the children were well-behaved and interested and showed a deference for seeing how something was made. Even the abbot approved; it was something to keep the children quiet, and he had just been reconciling himself to the retribution that god had put him under, repenting with prayer and begging the lord that Myndil should only send them people who would be silent and useful.

The children spent the day watching the rabble, their poor appearances at war with the amount of knowledge they had to convey. The abbess soon came, to give them warmer clothes and thicker socks to wear, and when it was time for dinner, the children were borne away to the front room, and Vindimir and Crannach came to thank them.

"Ah appreciate ye showin' 'em yer work," said Crannach, with grateful smiles. "It's no' often they have the benefit o' learnin' from masters."

The carpenter seemed almost ashamed. "Well, no masters here, really. We all apprenticed somewheres, but none o' us were made masters. Hope the children don't mind that."

"I'm quite sure they don't," said Vindimir.

The carpenter watched the children gather round the table and take their seats, the fights over who was going to sit next to Dimeadh already beginning. "Do the children not go to the farms?" he asked, looking concerned.

"The aulder ones go fer haymakin', aye," said Crannach, "and the farmers let 'em come once in a while tae see the animals, when they've got wool tae give us fer cardin', but we liek tae keep the younger ones close."

The severity with which it was said and the look in Crannach's eye made the carpenter a little fearful.

"Perhaps we are being somewhat overprotective of them," said Vindimir ruefully, "but considering the recent raids and the increase in slave galleys we have seen coming and going off the coast, we prefer to be cautious."

"Does anyone actually come to adopt them?" the carpenter asked. "We didn't even know this place was here until Myndil told us."

"Sometimes, aye, when one o' the farmers is lookin' tae pass on his land or have someone tae help him," said Crannach, "but we mostlae raise 'em till it's time fer 'em tae go out on their own."

"And all these children are left from the raids?"

"Not all, but enough," and with a grim look, Vindimir added, "Too many."

The carpenter nodded and returned to the rabble, glad that they should have been so fortunate to have found Myndil, or he to have found them, the five of them something like orphans themselves, none of them belonging to a living family, anyone else they could have stayed with long passed away.

The abbess was only too glad to have more people to care for. It was pleasant being with Iarlaith and the Brothers and the children, but without someone or something to charm her evening hours, the long winter nights seemed colder and more solitary. The abbot was something of a friend to her, but his sobs of contrition lately had made her believe he would rather be left alone. She approached the builders after dinner, to ask whether they were warm enough and talk to them about their history. Being a refugee herself, her friends taken away and her abbey gone, she thought they might have something in common to talk about, each member of the rabble having been ruined by the Northmen in some way.

They spoke for sometime, talking amiably over warm milk, sharing stories of their survival, when a sound coming at them from a distance made them pause. They turned to the small wood, and the sound came again.

"That's not the dullahan, is it?" asked the carpenter.

The abbess looked toward the gate: the dullahan was running down the path, chasing the head he had just accidentally kicked away. "No..." the abbess breathed, tightly clutched her breast.

They all quieted and waited. A violent roar fulminated, and a long howl hung on the wind.

"What is that?" asked the metalworker, grabbing her tools and holding them defensively.

Sister Iarlaith went to put the children to bed, and Vindimir and Crannach came back to the garden.

A low agonizing howl echoed toward the abbey.

"Is that—a wolf?" said the abbess, grabbing Crannach's arm.

"That's not possible," said Vindimir. "There are no wolves in the uplands."

"There was one once," said Crannach. "It came intae the farms by itsel'. It got awae from its pack, or lost it, and started huntin' the sheep. It didnae last long, bein' aloan, bein' hunted by everaebodae on the farms."

Again the howl reached them, the lowing ululation beckoning anyone who would hear.

Everyone was looking toward the woods, but Crannach was looking southward beyond the tidal crossing and over the sea.

"It sounds closer than it is," said Crannach, his gaze following the clouds. The humidity of the sea and the surrounding mist amplified the sound—he listened again, closing his eyes and concentrating, letting his other senses work out what his ears had misplaced. "There." Crannach walked toward the iron gate and pointed southward across the sea.

In the far distance, there was a small slave ship skimming the water. No one doing anything good did anything at night, and galleys that were sailing under the threat of detection waited for the sun to vanish and the moon to be obscured to make their journey. Vessels leaving from the northeastern coast went only one place, and as their way was due east and the passage not long, the captains of these vessels moved as quickly as possible once their wares were secure. The small ship had one lantern at its bow, several men on its deck, and only one slave aboard. It sailed as quickly as the men rowing would allow, the sound the slave was making forcing them to row faster.

"That's a wallach he's makin'," said Crannach, the tortured yawl carrying across the sea. Crannach shook his head. "That's no' a wolf."

The abbess stared at the ship in horror. "If that's not a wolf, what kind of creature makes a sound like that?" said she, with a mournful air.

"One they will be regretting having captured once they get to shore, I wager," said Vindimir. "Slavers," he sighed. "Always trying to hunt things they shouldn't and sell things they should have left alone."

The oars stopped sculling. Chains clinked, the sounds of bashing and thrashing accompanied the garbled cries, and the howl of something large caromed westward, making repeated cries as though it were calling to someone, someone who was about to happen to Myndil.

chapter 12: in which the faefolk and a friend happen to myndil

"What a lovely old woman," Myndil exclaimed to himself, titupping down the road. "My stomach is absolutely churning from that metallic milk she gave me, but I see no faeries about, so I suppose it's working well enough." He held the sprig of lilac to his nose and gave a hardy sniff. "So kind of her to help me."

SHE WAS A HEATHEN.

"I thought she might be, but are you sure, God? Because I don't think a heathen would have sanctified Brigid so much and adorned me in such pretty flowers."

SHE WAS A WITCH. THOU DOST GARB THYSELF IN WITCHCRAFT.

"Oh, God," said Myndil, with endearment, "I know you're teasing me, because I saw no sacrificial implements in or about her house. If she were a witch, I think she would have tried to kill me and use my entrails to divine the future rather than send me off to see the king."

There was a pause. I DID NOT THINK OF THAT.

"Besides she did warn me about the faeries. They are so very different here than the ones we have at home. I suppose because the ones at the abbey have come to know me and they have become comfortable around me, but that just means all the faeries here are only friends I have not had the chance to make yet, and that's a happy prospect—"

"Watchit, biggun!"

The voice came from below. It was a small voice belonging to a small creature, but became enormous when it opened its mouth, the pitch making a two-foot creature sound ten feet tall. Instinct operating where sense often failed, Myndil immediately leapt out of the way, diving headlong into a nearby hedgerow. He recovered and heard a tiny "humph!" at his feet. He look down and found a tiny man sitting in the middle of the road. He was not terrific or goblin-like, but a shortened version of a perfectly proportionate person, donned in a beaver brown coat, fine shoes, and a woven-grass hat, his ripened face surrounded by more beard than was good for him. He was sitting on a hewn stoven, the small shoots of oak in ivy buttressing his legs, and was languishing over a firkin of whiskey, his hands furnished with two full thimbles, his lips occupied with either managing the drams or keeping his dúidín afloat. He sipped, he soomed, he sucked on the mouth of his clay pipe, and when Myndil loomed and shrouded him in a long shadow, the little man glanced up at him and gowled.

"Fah! Almost wrecked me drink wi' dat..." He placed one of his thimbles down, pulled the cork out of the firkin, and poured a bit of the amber liquid into the thimble, his eyes swimming at the sight of it.

"Hallo, there," Myndil sang, crouching in the middle of the road. "Sorry to have almost stepped on you. I didn't see you when I turned the corner."

"An' hullo yerself, biggun," the little man wheezed. "An' 'tis a fine day when one o' yous townies aren't tryin' to make me a stain on the road."

"I am sorry, but you are rather in the middle of it."

"Aye, an' don't mind if I am," the little man acknowledged, his teeth clacking against his dúidín, "an' 'tis yer job to be goin' round, biggun. Havin' meself a bit of a lie-down at the moment." He rested the thimble onto his stomach and lounged against a mossy rock behind him. "Lyin' down's sure hard work. Need a bit o' the drink to cool me tethers." He sipped from the thimble and let out a slight hic! "So, who's talkin' at me and why's does he not have a drink?" he asked, using the end of his pipe to scratch his ear.

"I'm Myndil," and then, placing a hand over his heart, he added, "friend to all the 'good folk'— well, as much as a friend as I'm allowed to be."

"Are ye now." The little man lifted the thimble and took a swig. "Not fer nothin', b'y, but yer a bit bright-eyed fer the black pool. Not from around these parts—" He leaned forward and sniffed Myndil's toes, "—can't be. Yer too clean. All dem fancy robes and dat. Sure, I could hang you out on the wrack and soak ye with me socks. A bit too rancy-tancy to be gallavantin' with us."

"Well, I do try to keep clean, because cleanliness is godliness— but I'm not from Ath Cliath or any of the surrounding kingdoms."

"Didn't I know it," the little man huffed, pulling on his pipe. "Ye don't smell like the fields."

"I do farm though, among other things. I came from an abbey—"

"Hoo hoo, ana mhaith ar fad!" the little man cried, raising his pipe to him. "Big time, b'y, alignin' yerself with the god-folk. And what do ye do fer dem now? Dey payin' ye wi' all dat gold dey got?"

"Well, I did have some gold, but I'm a missionary."

"A mesentery?"

Here was a pause. "I'm not sure what that is, so I will say possibly. Do you have a name?"

"Too busy fer the names, b'y," the little man chuffed, a ribbon of smoke roiling from the crack in his lips. "We solitaries don't deal in dem. Ye can't hang yer hat on a name."

Myndil wondered if a name could be hung on anything and concluded that if he wrote his name down on vellum, it could probably be hung in the hall or at the end of his bed, as the younger orphans at the orphanage had often done. He did this when he was child, but when Thingunderthebed had moved in, she got hungry one night and decided that if vellum was good enough for Myndil, it was good enough for her. She had been able to report that while Myndil's name had little taste, the vellum he had written it on was very pleasant.

"'Sides, if I had me a name," the little man continued, refilling his thimble, "then I'd have to be givin' it out to every traveller passin', and I want as many friends as I want neighbours."

Myndil blinked. "Many?"

"None, b'y, so I'll drink ye and yer made up name and I'll thank ye fer it."

"Oh." Myndil smiled and nodded. "You're very welcome."

"Sure, yer a man fer keepin' up, b'y. Yer god hasn't taken yer tongue, dat's certain. Here," filling the second thimble, "a bit fer me and a bit fer yerself, and we'll drink to yer bein' a mesentery or whatever ye call yerself."

He gave Myndil the thimble he had just filled and invited him to drink from it, but while the little man took a dram from his own thimble and almost drowned his pipe in it, Myndil held the small silver vessel between his thumb and forefinger and mused over it, the warning the old woman gave him heavy on his conscience.

"Wassamater, b'y?" the little man demanded, wiping his mouth with his sleeve. "Yer god say yer aff the drink for the holy-days an' dat?"

"Is it the Lord's Day today? I don't think so, but since I haven't been doing my daily duties, I can't quite remember the days of the week—"

"Save yer breath fer the candles, b'y. Ye'll have a drink an' dere'll be no bellyachin' about it. On dis here road, yer either enj'yin' the drink or sleepin' it aff, agus sin é."

He relit the bowl of his pipe and tucked it between his teeth, and when he leaned down to wipe the ash from his coat, Myndil noticed a band round the brim of his hat, hung round with sprigs of sweet sorrel. "I think I know what you are," Myndil proclaimed, his eyes aglow with interest. "Are you a leprechaun?"

The little man glared up at him and flouted, thrusting his pipe at him with a pointed pout. "Clurichaun!" he demanded, every feeling offended.

"Oh." Myndil glanced at the thimble in his hand and swished the liquid around. "Is that different, because that does sound quite similar—"

"If I called ye Fyndil, would dat be the same as callin' ye yer real name?"

"I suppose not."

"Then I suppose 'tis not the same, or dat's me a horse's arse."

The vacancies of Myndil's mind tried to work out whether being a horse's rump was closer to being a clurichaun than being a leprechaun, his face wearing the many cogitations in between.

"Leprechaun's me cousin," the clurichaun explained, "yer man what makes the shoes and lives under the cupboards."

"Isn't that the red capped fellow, the one who looks like my friend the nisser?"

"Dat's other cousin, yer man the fear dearg. A bit 'o the codder himself, but he understands hats, so I'll not give out against him."

"If he's your other cousin, why doesn't his name sound like yours?"

"Sure'n ye'll have to be the one to ask him. I can't be lairdin' over him night and day on account o' titles. Don't I got cellars to haunt."

"If you haunt cellars, then what are you doing out here on the road?"

"Waitin' for me troop to wander by."

"I thought you said you were solitary."

"I am dat, but I'm also a shiftless bastard, and if I can get a ride, sure'n I'll take it if it's offerin'. Should be along anytime now, so why not sit yerself down, b'y, and we'll have a bit o' the craic while we're waitin'."

Myndil had little idea what 'the craic' was or how it was to be got, but considering the clurichaun was eager to portion out his drink and offer him good sitting room on his stoven, surely a little craic could do him no harm?

The craic, however, as Myndil soon found out, could do him harm: he sat beside the clurichaun, still holding the thimble in his hand, and thinking Myndil was somehow offended by the shameful amount of drink he had poured out, the clurichaun offered him even more and soon offered him his pipe.

"'Tis a fierce good dúidín, b'y, from the kingdom herself," said the clurichaun, pointing southward. "'Tis just a bit o' the peat moss dried and broken up, but it smokes well."

Myndil politely declined, and the clurichaun shrugged and returned the pipe to the corner of his mouth.

"Suit yerself, b'y," said the clurichaun dismissively. "I'll have me pipe fer the snoke and the drink fer the taste." He took up his thimble and declared, "Yer god's blessings to ye," propinating his thimble with the one in Myndil's hand, "an' may ye never tell yer god I gave ye my blessin's, lest he take his own back!" He raised his thimble to his lips but paused when he realized Myndil was not following. "Wassa matter, b'y? Ye afraid o' the drink?"

"Oh, I'm not afraid of it," Myndil assured him, "only I was reminded that I am suddenly–" he recalled the old woman's justifications, "– allergic–yes, allergic, that's it–I am allergic to fey food."

"Go'wan outta dat now," the clurichaun laughed. "Sure'n dat's just a bit o' the uisce beatha I tanned from yer man in town. No fey food here."

"Oh." Myndil glanced down at his reflection in the surface of the drink. "Well, in that case, I suppose one thimble cannot do me any harm, can it?"

"No harm at all, b'y."

Myndil raised the thimble to his lips, but a sudden suspicion assailed him, and he lowered the thimble again. "Perhaps I'd like to simply appreciate sitting on this stump without a drink to alter the experience."

"Aye, 'tis a fierce good sittin' stump altogether," the clurichaun agreed, patting it.

"It is very nice. Quite comfortable."

"But a drink would make it better, b'y. I see yer eyes, gaggin' fer a whiff. Sure a bit a the drink'll do you all the good in the world. Go'wan, now. Just a drop."

The milk the old healer had given him was still stewing in his stomach, and Myndil reasoned that if he could still taste the metallic aftertaste in his mouth, it ought to still be active. A small sip was all he should resign himself to, but that small sip was enough to roll him off the stump.

"There she cuts!" the clurichaun laughed, with villainous pride, thumping his thighs with his fists.

Myndil wretched and righted himself. "By God—what is that?" he croaked, his eyes welling.

"'Tis the drink of life, b'y. Drinkin' it let's ye know yer alive."

"Is that what the burning in my chest is? It feel as though I've just swallowed a bonfire."

"And ye'll be breathin' the smoke too! Sure'n I can smell the vapours leakin' through yer eyes."

Myndil leaned forward and blinked. "I do believe they're liquifying. What is that odd rushing sound?"

"Dat's the sound o' yer brain dyin' and makin' room fer more o' the drink. Have another."

The thimble was recovered, the drink was poured, and as Myndil mechanically held it to his lips, the flowers and sprigs that the old woman had tied to him for protection began to whither and decay. "Oh. That's unfortunate," he heard himself say, but his arm was being raised, the thimble was being emptied into his mouth, and as he winced and coughed through the delibations, he felt a small hand release his elbow.

"Look'atcha, b'y," the clurichaun said, pouring another thimble full, "all inside out and sideways over it. What to they give ye to drink over at dat god-house o' yers?"

Myndil heard an odd curmurring from below. "Tea and warm milk mostly," said he, his stomach speaking over him.

"Have another, and tell me where yer bound, b'y."

The thimble was thrust into his hand, and as the sprig of lilac on his robe began to chimble, Myndil unconsciously lifted the drink to his lips. "I'm going to speak to the king," said he, resolutely.

"We solitaries dunno from kings. Gotta be more 'pecific."

"Olaf—or Amlaíb I think the old healer called him—"

"Ah, dat fella," the clurichaun grumped, rekindling his pipe. "Sure'n I know him. I've takin' a gander at his cellars and reaved a few o' the casks. Land tax, I call it, paid to me fer walkin' on the land, 'cause didn't we have it first."

Myndil finished another dram and examined the thimble, the stained silver etched with images of horned figures and hunting scenes. "Why do I suddenly feel so compelled to hug you?"

"'Cause we're havin' the craic, b'y."

Myndil was all astonishment. "Are we? I wasn't aware— but when did it happen? I didn't see it."

"The craic doesn't happen, b'y," said the clurichaun seriously. "The craic is a state-o'-mind, and and ye just put yerself in it."

Myndil began to feel his head grow heavy. "The sensation is both wonderful and strange. I feel as though I want to dance and tell you everything about my life all at once," Myndil imparted, in a semi-somnolent tone.

"Well, ye can gab me ear aff it when the troop arrives. If yer bound to see Amlaib and his cellar, I'll ask the troop to take bring ye over, if yer wantin' a ride."

"Oh, yes, that would be very helpful, thank—" A distant voice tried to call out to him, and Myndil's sobriety suddenly revived. "A ride?" he exclaimed.

"Sure 'n don't we faeries ride the horses? When the wind comes through the crossroads, dat's us, gallopin' on the gales. We don't bother travellin' in straight lines, but we always get to where we're goin' in time."

Myndil could feel his stomach beginning a revolt. "A ride would be very pleasant, I think, if your troop won't mind."

"Won't mind at all. Dey'll drag ye along anywhere, if you let 'em."

"When would they be coming?"

"Don't hang by yer teeth, b'y," the clurichaun declared, packing the bowl of his pipe, "they'll be a long in a while. We faeries don't deal in minutes and hours—too dear for us. Time's a thing yer people do. We just wait till somethin' happens and fall in with the course."

Myndil's bowels began to scringe, and the noise they made sounded very much like someone telling him to escape. He should have refused the clurichaun's offer, but the charm of the craic, whatever it was, and the easy manners of his companion made it somehow impossible to refuse. Again, a voice in the back of his mind tried to reach him, a familiarity reaching out and touching that part of him that placed his love of god for his sudden affection for fae. He was under no duress, no glamour but what the few small drinks had afforded; he was just disinclined to go anywhere or do anything that involved legs. "Well, if the wait will be long," he announced, wondering what the sudden ringing in his ear was, "perhaps I had better go myself then. I shouldn't like to put your friends out of their way."

"Suit yerself," the clurichaun shrugged, "I'll not stop ye if yer wantin' to make the journey yerself. I only wanted yer the company th'while longer."

Myndil stood, but not steadily, his legs eager to go but his mind determined to stay. "I would very much like to stay and hug you and tell you all about my time at the orphanage, but I really must be going, though I think the craic would like me to stay."

"Sure'n the craic always wants to stay, b'y, else who's gonna be around to have it? Good luck go with ye, b'y, but if yer goin', a word to the wise," said the clurichaun, taking his pipe from his mouth and holding it to the side of his face, trying to be surreptitious, "keep aff the road, lest the gust overtake ye. Once the wind's gotcha, the troop's gotcha, and dere's little way o' gettin' out again on yer own."

"Oh, thank you, but I think I'm well protected against fae magic—"

"Ha! If ye were, yer not anymore."

He pointed to the wilted sprigs along Myndil's belt, and a dread began to loom.

"But how is that possible?" said Myndil, the desiccated petals crumbling to dust at his touch, "You said what I drank wasn't fairy food."

The clurichaun shook his head. "It wasn't. Just offered ye a bit o' yer own drink, and I'll not be blamed fer what's happened to ye."

"What's happened to me?" Myndil glanced at the empty thimble he left on the stump, the silver figures etched into the surface beginning to warp and move. "Is it because I was in the craic?"

"The craic is fer all folk, b'y, 'tis not divilment." The clurichaun stood, shook out the two thimble and put them in his coat pocket. "Mighta been on account o' the thimbles," he deliberated. "Sure'n dey're only a bit o' silver, but dey belonged to a druid I pinched a few casks a mead from an' he mighta cursed dem a bit."

"Well, cursing a bit is not cursing a lot, so I should be all right—"

The sound of a hunting horn caromed over the adjacent hill, the rataplan of running feet neared from a distance, and the clurichaun stood on his stump.

"Dat'll be the troop," he announced, smoothing out his coat. "Hope the Fear Liath isn't with 'em. His arms and legs are always gettin' in me face, and the smell aff him'd put the cows under." He looked down the western road, and a dome of light was peering over the horizon. "Better go, b'y, if yer not wantin' to get swept up—" but it was too late for escape: a sibilation caught his ear, and Myndil froze.

Who be ye, boy? said a sharp whisper.

Myndil turned, unable to think of moving and looking at the same time—he stopped, one foot beyond the boundary of the crossroad and the other just lifting, and though he saw no one coming over the western rise, he felt a presence watching him. He begged his leg to move in time, but an oppressive silence rushed on him, a blast of wind broke over the crossing, and Myndil was ripped from the road, swept up by an invisible force, carried on a malevolent gale.

The world was a jumble of animation and colour, his body tumbling over itself but never hitting the ground, the sounds and sights of the road flickering in a violent fracas. He was moving, the celeritous pace reminding his stomach of what he had lately put in it, but he was too concerned with being upside down and thrown about to mind gastral rebellion. He looked up—whichever way up was—and saw a dozen feet of all shapes and sizes floating over him, and saw as many undersides sulking in a nebulous haze. He tried to right himself, but because he had no command of his legs, he heaved himself up and over and back down again, his feet waving rampantly in the air as the wind carried him.

The next crossroad came, no nearer to the city proper, a highway serene and subdued. The early spring snowdrops bent in the breeze, the psithurism of the cypresses disturbed the surrounding silence, and from over a knoll, drowning out and frightening off a murder of mantling crows, came the tender sounds of a missionary being hauled along the road by an indistinguishable tempest:

"aaaaaaaaaaaaaaaaAAAAAAAAAAAAAAAAAAAAAAAAAAAAAAAAAAAAAAAAAAAAAAAAaaaaaaaa aaaa..."

It was a chaos of motion, an upset of all agreements of up and down, the bluster and blinter of many small beings moving at imperceptible speed. There was nothing to hold onto, nothing that Myndil might use to pull himself upright and stay there with, but amidst the wreck and confusion of constant dithering, a familiar voice soon called out to him: "I tol' ye to get aff the road, b'y!"

"I tried!" Myndil yelped, being buffeted by the wind. "My feet wouldn't move quickly enough!"

"Well, yer gettin' the ride I offered ye anyway."

Myndil felt a small hand on his belt, and with a firm jolt and a "Hruugghh!", Myndil was righted and floating beside the clurichaun.

"Yer very welcome," he proclaimed, patting Myndil on the shoulder.

Myndil glanced down at his feet; they were dangling, his hems flitting violently in the breeze. They were travelling at an alarming pace, the motions of the cloud of faeries steady within and frenetic without. "How am I moving?" Myndil asked, marveling at his sudden weightlessness.

"Sure'n isn't the troop carryin' ye?"

The clurichaun gestured to the front of the host, and collocated in neat rows were the Golden members of the Unseelie Court, all of them well-dressed and well-pleased, still and serene in conduct but suspicious. Their pearlescent gowns and sideral suits betrayed their rank in faerie society, but the looks and sneers of self-importance told Myndil his presence might not be as wanted as his friend recommended.

"Are you sure I'm very welcome?" Myndil asked, in a half-whisper.

"Ye are to me, an' who cares what the lords and ladies are thinkin'."

"We be thinking about the drink tha' wart supposed to bring us!" one of the grinning fae hissed.

The clurichaun patted the floating firkin beneath him. "Didn't I bring it fer ye as I promised? I got only the two cups, so yous'll have to give me yer own if yer wantin' any o' dis."

"What did ye bring to us, cousin?" said a female faerie, in a guttural accent. "Do it be vermin?"

"Go'wan outta dat. I brought ye a mesentery."

"A missionary," said Myndil.

"Ooh," another small fairy cooed. "Do it be eatable and meatable?"

"Dere's no good eatin' on dis one." The clurichaun tugged at Myndil's belt. "A bit on the lean side."

"Its bones will make good soup…" another faerie remarked, appearing from under Myndil's floating arm. It pulled on Myndil's sleeves and held them up. "It has nice wings…"

A few of the dried lilac petals still stuck in Myndil's robe tumbled out. They grazed the faerie's arm, and the creature drew back, hissing and gnashing its teeth.

"What is this—what is this?" the faerie wrenched. "Tha brings us a beast—a beast!"

"Just a bit o' garnish," said the clurichaun, brushing the lilac dust away. "Pay it no mind at all. Have yerself a drink and don't be so long in the face about it."

The drink was poured and handed round, but every faerie that neared Myndil hissed and wrawled at him, wanting to exact vengeance for spoiling their travelling party but more swayed by what the clurichaun had brought them than they were by a creature who had such a dreadfully small amount of meat. They were hostile to him, if not unpleasant, but the remains of the sprigs that the old woman had laced him with kept them far enough away. Being near so many faeries at once, and in their own environment, produced a strange effect on Myndil: the rush and whir of the scenery was forgotten, though the troop still moved with enchanting celerity, oblivescence was creeping over him, the combination of consciousness and confusion rendering him ripe for domination.

"Excuse me, but by any chance are we going to see the king?" said Myndil, in a voice half-roused, but his query was lost under the cenation of the faeries, who were all drinking and cheering to one another. Without a means to free himself, Myndil feared he might be lost in the cloud of the Court, left without awareness of time or place, but there was always one who could hear and help him, one whose assistance would never fail—as long as he chanced to be nearby. "Oh Lord!" said Myndil, in a reverent accent, "hear my prayer! Please save your devoted and humble serv—hruuurgha!"

A giant hand reached into the travelling troop and grabbed his shoulder, and with a firm jolt, an insuperable strength tore him out of the court. The force of the jolt and the speed that the faeries were travelling at flung Myndil high in the air. He shot up and out, flipping over himself several times, catapulting across the fields, and he was careening toward the dirt with an "aaaaaaaaaaaAA AAAAAAAAAAAAAAAAaaaaaaaaaaaaaaaaa—" when the giant hand appeared again and brought a friend with it, grabbing Myndil just before he hit the ground. He was secured and supported, and put onto his feet, and once Myndil's sight stopped spinning and he felt the ground firm again, he rallied himself, looked up, and found himself besieged by an enormous figure.

"Oh—is that you, God?" he asked. "Thank you for sending your agent to save me."

"I'm not God, but I was glad to save you," said a bellowing voice.

The sonorous tones rippled against Myndil's cheeks. Considering how large the obscured figure was, Myndil might as well be speaking to a mountain rather than a man. He stood back, to get a better view and move into the sun, and when the amber glare of sunlight permeated the view, it revealed the broad shoulders, wide chest, and colossal arms of a man who looked more feral than friendly: muscles clamoured atop one another, his biceps and triceps arguing amongst themselves for good room, an iron neck flexed under the restraint of a golden torc that looked as though it was intimidated by nape holding it, but amongst the insuperable display of might was a gentle face, grey eyes, short black hair, and wide cheeks wreathed in dimpled smiles. At first, Myndil thought it was little more than a walking carpet tacked onto a series of boulders, due to the tufts of thick black hair sprouting up from his chest, but once the features became more distinguishable, he saw a giant man, his looks palpebrous and pleasing, his muscles threatening the stability of his shirt.

"Is it you, God?" said Myndil expectantly. "I didn't think you would be this large or hairy, but you do look very comfortable."

A low and risible sound emanated from a broad smile. "I am not God," the giant man reassured him, "but you might find me comfortable."

The man inclined his head and presented himself. There was a regal air about him, a highborn ease of manner that was lost on Myndil's powers, a studied sovereignty that disguise could never thoroughly do away, his carriage and comportment all unexceptionable, his shoulders straight, his head high, his arms low at his sides; a giant prince trying to make himself seem small and unimportant and failing about it.

"You might be apprehensive of me," said the man, "but there is no need to be alarmed."

100

"I'm not," Myndil beamed.

The man's brows furrowed, and he canted his head slightly. "Aren't you? Are you not able to tell?"

Myndil blinked. "Tell what?"

"Well, if you cannot tell, I should tell you out of courtesy. I am a werewolf."

It was said with such assurance that Myndil simply nodded and smiled. "Oh, that's very interesting. I was wondering about the hair, because it does look a bit like fur, and now I understand why I had the urge to pet it." He paused, remarking the tufts sprouting from the bottom of the man's sleeves. "Oh, it really is everywhere, isn't it—well, not on your face. Your face is perfectly smooth. Luckily it doesn't seem to be crawling up from your back. I can imagine that would be very hot in summer. Is that why you cautioned me? I don't think an overabundance of hair is much frightening, so I'm still not alarmed."

"With how much hair I have, you should be," the man simpered. He smiled, his thick neck muscles flexing. "You do know what a werewolf is."

"Oh, yes. I think I do."

"And you are still not alarmed by me?"

Myndil smiled and shook his head.

"Well, then." The man straightened his back, unfurling to his full height, his immense shoulders rolling out of the way of one another, his chest lifting and pressing outward, his tufts of hair freed from his cape. He had been prodigious before, but he was somehow larger now, a subtle transformation that made him more mystical than man. "I'm glad of it," said he, his resonating baritone relaxing even farther into his throat. "Most people outside of home see me and run off before I can speak to them."

"Oh, that's very rude, not saying hello before they run away."

"Well, considering everyone here knows about me and my kingdom, I cannot hold it against them."

Myndil was suddenly aware that the man was more than three heads taller than him. "You seem amiable enough to me, if not a little wooly."

"Not all werewolves are wooly, as you say. I am one of the good ones—that is, we are all good ones here, not like the werewolves in Francia. We defend our kingdom and protect our people—we don't hunt men for food like they do on the continent."

"That's good to know—but do the ones who eat humans look differently? Will I know them if I see them? Do they look a bit more—" Myndil noted the man's human features, "—wolflike?"

"The Frankish ones do, but there is no relation. They were made werewolves by magic, but we were made wolves by God."

Myndil's eyes brightened. "You mean God turned you into werewolves? You mean my God, Our Lord and Saviour?" Myndil waved his Good Book excitedly about. "Do you follow God's Word?"

"We do, and we love and devote ourselves to His Grace."

"Oh, that's so exciting! God," Myndil exclaimed, addressing the ether, "did you hear what the big wooly wolfman said? The werewolves love you, God!"

GREAT.

"Well," said the werewolf, with some embarrassment, "we do love God, but we aren't sure God feels the same way about us. We opposed God's Word at one time, when Saint Paudrig came and tried to impose his beliefs on us, but because we mocked him, God cursed us. We were turned into wolves for seven years—but that was a long time ago. We've repented since and now devote ourselves to Paudrig's teachings. We're quite accustomed to our wolf forms now, and we use them to defend our kingdom against outsiders."

"May I ask, is it difficult being a werewolf? Is it itchy, because I know if I had to wear fur all the time, I should be always scratching. I also don't like fleas very much."

"Neither do we," the werewolf rumbled, "though we don't seem to attract them in our human forms. The fleas are regrettable, but not constant. Being out in the wild and running through the woods is pleasant, especially in the evenings when there are few people about."

"Are there many God-made werewolves?"

"There are. A whole kingdom full, in fact. I'm from Osraige, but you might know it as Ossory." Myndil gave him a blank look.

"You're not obliged to know it. It's a small kingdom, but a beautiful one, lush with untouched forests and bountiful deer, surrounded on all sides by wide rivers, keeping us well defended against an attack from foreign kings," he intimated, glancing toward the palace of Ath Cliath in the distance. "We stay in our woods, and they stay out of our business."

"Well, if the rest of your people are anything like you, I think you could get any unwanted king gone just by waving your chest hair at them."

"Would that it were that easy. Perhaps if I were transformed, they might feel a little more threatened."

Myndil scrunched his nose. "This is not your wolf form?"

"No," the werewolf laughed. "I can change my form at will. You see, the curse dictates that we're only wolves when we're asleep. Our bodies are dormant, and then our wolf form emerges out of us and—it's difficult to explain."

"Oh, probably," Myndil eagerly agreed, "but I'm very interested to hear about it."

"All you need to know is, if my body suddenly collapses and a wolf leaps out of me, do not be alarmed."

"Oh, I won't be, because I know you know God—but if you're only able to change into a wolf when you sleep, what happens to your body whilst your other form is busy loping?"

"My human form is lying dormant and is entirely vulnerable." The werewolf paused. "I would appreciate if you didn't tell anyone about that."

Myndil, knowing himself and how he could not keep anything in his head from leaking out, made a vague promise and smiled charmingly through it.

"Well," the werewolf continued, folding his arms, resting his shelf of chest muscles on his wrists. "thank God I came along when I did. Had I not taken you from the daoine sidhe that were carrying you off, they might have stolen you away forever."

"Well, I shouldn't have minded, as long as they did not try to eat me, as they had talked of doing. The clurichaun was very friendly and offered me a drink, which may have made me a target for the rest of the faeries, but the time I spent with him was pleasant. I never did get a name from him, but he said solitary faeries don't deal in names—" Myndil realized he had forgot to give the werewolf his. "I'm Myndil."

"I am Aodhgan," said he, with a gallant bow, the background moving around his might.

"It sounded as though you said Ey-gawn, but just for reference, how is that spelled?"

Aodhgan grinned. "Would it matter if I told you? You pronounced it correctly."

"Oh, well. I suppose that's all right then, as long as I never need to write your name."

"Writing materials are scarce enough. I came upon you here because I was on my way to Ath Cliath. If you're going that way, I'd be glad to walk with you."

Myndil was all sanguine expectation. "Oh, I would be delighted— and we could even talk about God along the way! Oh, this is too good! How fortunate that we should meet!"

They began walking, Aodhgan rather leading the way, Myndil seeming not to know which way he should go, and each glad to have company for the little way their road was together at any rate. Not being used to have the company of someone from outside of his kingdom, Aodhgan was pleased to have Myndil to talk to, though Myndil talked most, telling his new companion where he was from and where he was going with eager rapidity.

"Abbot said that if I wanted to be ordained, I had to prove myself," said Myndil, "so I'm going to see the king, to tell him about God and practice my oration on him."

"Really," said Aodhgan incredulously, and then with grim suspicion, "Which king did you want to see?"

"Olaf—or Alaib—or however the orthography deigns it."

"Oh," the werewolf howled in mirth, bending over his knees. "I had best go with you then, at least to the gate. I won't be permitted to enter the palatial grounds. We won't be welcome inside the city in general."

"Because you're a werewolf?" said Myndil, with sympathy.

"No, because of God."

"But God loves and protects us always."

Here was a doubtful look. "I don't mean to comment on your business with Olaf, but if you mean to try to get him to hear the Word of Our Lord, you will need more than love and a book to sway him."

"Do you think I ought to ask God for divine intervention then?" Myndil mused. "Only I know God must be busy, and I don't want to disturb him too much, if he is in the midst of answering other prayers."

Aodhgan stopped to marvel at his companion. "You really are serious about converting Olaf."

"Oh, yes. Abbot says I have to try to tell as many heathens as I can about the Word of God, and I was not to come back to the abbey until I had done it, and I was told by the heathens that the best way to get everyone to follow God was to speak to the king."

A tender glow settled over Myndil. It might have been a trick of the light, the setting sun giving way to the full moon, but there was a numinous aspect about him—the werewolf thought so at least—a faint gloriole bespeaking miracles and disaster, married to smiles of ceaseless exhilaration and a felicity of hope that never slept. A man so young with such blind determination and a willingness to believe in his own invulnerability is the most terrifying thing in the world, and Aodhgan did not know whether he were becoming a little alarmed himself. He would bring Myndil to the city at least, if he could not go any farther, feeling it his duty to assist one so determined to fulfill his purpose though it might end in his demise.

Before they continued on their journey, however, Aodhgan began to scratch the tufts of hair sprouting up from his chest. "I'm sorry to ask this, but would you mind removing that sprig of wolfsbane from your robe," said he, pointing to the withered flowers along Myndil's waist. "It's making my skin itch terribly."

"Oh, yes, very sorry about that," said Myndil, plucking it from his belt and tossing it aside. "I had forgotten it was there. A healer on the road, an old lady named Peig, gave it to me. Do you know her? She said she was putting it on me to ward off—"

Aodhgan began clawing at his neck, scratching the skin under his torc. "Hands really don't do a thorough job," Aodhgan proclaimed. "It's so much easier to scratch in wolf form. The scrape of my claws is so satisfying."

"Is that why hounds are always scratching themselves with their hind legs?"

"One of the pleasures afforded the four-legged." Aodhgan shook himself out and continued leading them on. "How much do you know of Olaf?"

"Very little," Myndil replied. He counted his facts on his fingers. "I know that he is a heathen, and I know he is a king." He held up two fingers. "Oh, oh," adding a third, "and I know he is in Ath Cliath."

"For now," said Aodhgan, raising a brow. "He was not always there so often. In fact, he just returned from a campaign in the south, a place called Limerick, another Norse settlement. He felt threatened by their king and decided to capture him to assert his dominance. Olaf wants to be king of everything without earning a right to it and even calls himself the King of Northumbria, a large settlement across the sea."

"But how can he rule there if he is here? And who rules there when he is gone?"

"Who, indeed. He only came into his kingship a few years ago when his father died. Olaf claims he is still king of Northumbria because his father retained that land, but he recently lost hold of it to his rivals and is anxious to recover it. There have been rumours that he means to launch another campaign as part of his retaliation, but with all his losses from the previous defeat and his campaign in Limerick, I have no idea how—wait."

He held out his arm, and Myndil thought he had walked into an iron wall. Aodhgan paused and listened, his ears perked, his senses everywhere awake. "We're being followed."

"Are you s—" Myndil began. Aodhgan's giant hand clamped against his mouth. "Rrrm yh hre?"

"The wolfsbane you were wearing was interfering with my senses." Aodhgan inhaled, caught hold of a scent, his nose finding the tail-end of a ribbon, and he followed it. He moved behind Myndil and stalked his shadow, giving the ground a few heavy sniffs. He prowled Myndil's feet and pressed his nose against the back of his leg.

"What is it?" Myndil asked. "Do I still smell a bit irony, because the healer asked me to drink her magic poker milk to ward off the—"

"No," Aodhgan growled, leaning down. He indicated something directly at Myndil's heel. "It seems you have a picked up a stowaway."

He made a fist and thrust it into Myndil's shadow, the force of his immense strength cracking the ground. Roads, while often hurt by passing carts and damaged by trading envoys, do not usually respond with an "Oweeee."

"Out of there," Aodhgan demanded, taking hold of the end of Myndil's shadow and peeling up.

"Ow ow ow ow," a voice whinged.

Aodhgan pulled what looked like a slip of lace from the ground, but when he whipped it violently aside, its form dissolved and was replaced by a caliginous brume.

"Why'd ya hafta do thayt?" the wafting shadow wheezed. "Aw woz comfy-like!"

"I don't care whether you were comfortable or not," Aodhgan bellowed. "You inhabited his shadow without asking."

"S' cuz Aw wanted a ride to the palace, dun Aw!"

"What is that?" said Myndil, impressed that his shadow should have become sentient.

"A co-walker, but you might know them by another name. They came here from Alba sometime ago, wandering the isles, travelling between this world and the next—"

"Aye!" the co-walker shouted, hissing delitescently, "An' Aw'm not lost neither! Aw know 'zactly where Aw am, thank yewe, an' 'zactly where Aw'm goin' too."

"And where would that be?" said Aodhgan, standing imposingly.

"Aw wanted a lift to the capitol, me. Jus' fer revengin' purposes, see? 'S wot Aw do, revengin'."

"Are co-walkers particularly harmful?" Myndil asked.

"If you are the one on the receiving end of its 'revenging'."

"Nah, nah, down't got no trouble with thayt won," said the co-walker, a wispy finger pointing at Myndil. "Aw's jus usin' him as a bit o' transportation-like. Aw's just ridin' with the troop and thissun says he's goin' to Aith Claith so Aw thought Aw'd tag on. Aw got folk round there wot Aw need to see, on account o' bizniz. Aw's ownly gonna hang on to him fer a day!"

"Oh, I shouldn't mind that, if it is only going as far as we are. I think we might allow it to come with us, as long as it promises to leave."

"I will make it leave," said Aodhgan, in a threatening hue.

"No need to be punchin' and peelin'," the co-walker insisted. Spectral tendrils reached up and bound in supplication. "Look 'ere, this is me promissin'!"

"And that promise had best be kept, or my evening will be spent hunting you." Aodhgan pointed to his own shadow. "You can stay in there."

"But yewer shadow's too big-like!"

"Find a corner."

"It's also hairy," the co-walker added, in a plaintive tone, "an' Aw down't like hairy."

"You won't be able to feel the hair when you're in there."

"BUT AW'LL KNOW IT'S THERE AN' IT GIVES ME THE WINGLEWANGLES."

Aodhgan raised his fist. "Get in there and be quiet about it," and ask the shadow wafted over, he added, "and do not listen to our conversation."

"AW CAN'T STOP LISTENIN'."

Here was a dangerous look. "Try."

The shadow grumbled and glugged, but it obeyed, and after nestling into a small corner of Aodhgan's shadow, it melded into the space and lay silent for the present.

"My apologies," Aodhgan hemmed, recollecting himself and resuming their walk. "We were talking about Olaf. He has an infamous temper. He never could equal his father's reign, so naturally he has to try and prove himself. His reprisal against his enemies will no doubt be soon, so if you really mean to tell Olaf about the Grace of God, I hope you are going to package it as a way that allows him to see the benefit of being blessed in God's name."

"God did say something about a holy war, but I don't know how anyone could wage war under the Aegis of God. Thou shalt not kill, after all."

"Thou shalt not kill unless in defense of thyself," Aodhgan laughingly reminded him, "and some would take that to mean thou shalt kill thy chosen enemy, because if an enemy has not attacked yet, it does not mean they haven't considered it. Aethelstan knows how to provoke Olaf into an attack, and though you might get Olaf to recognize our God, you will never out-God Aethelstan."

"The king of over-there already loves God?" Myndil asked, his cheeks aglow.

"He is practically married to Our Lord."

Myndil gasped, clutching his book to his chest. "Can one marry God? Nobody told me we were allowed to do that—well, I never asked, but I did not think it was possible—maybe I did hear of the abbess being wedded to God, but I did not know brothers were allowed to marry God too. Why didn't I think of it before? Of course! I would love to marry God—and it does make sense since I love him and devote myself to him already."

GOD DOTH NOT WANT TO MARRY THEE, the voice asserted.

"But I want to pledge myself to you, God, especially if I'm going to be ordained. I can espouse myself to you and make a covenant to speak your holy words always, and then we can be together in this life and the next!"

YOU ARE NOT GOD'S TYPE.

Aodhgan watched Myndil through the whole of this speech, watched how he pleaded to no one and directed his gaze to the sky as though he were really hearing something. "You think you speak to Our Lord directly?" he asked.

"Oh yes! God talks to me all the time. Don't you speak to God?"

"Yes," Aodhgan admitted, somewhat awkwardly, "when in silent prayer or when in the confines of my own den, but Our Lord's answers don't come in so direct a line."

"They do! Perhaps you only cannot hear him—but your hearing his better than mine, with your wolf senses, so you should be able to hear him. He sounds like Brother Vindimir when I'm at home, but since I left the orphanage, he sounds more like a gruff woodcutter with coal in his mouth. He started speaking to me when I was a boy, and he has been my best friend ever since."

WE ARE NOT BEST FRIENDS. THOU ART MY DIVINE SERVANT PERFORMING MY DIVINE BIDDING.

"And that's exactly why we should get married!"

NO.

Myndil laughed and said how God would tease him sometimes, encouraging profanities and putting him in precarious situations, but it was all a test of his endurance of character, he was sure, and he would prevail at last.

Aodhgan could not but laugh here: there was something about Myndil, his peculiarity of character, a willingness to be good in all things that Aodhgan could not but approve. Though Aodhgan was perfectly convinced of Myndil being touched by madness, he liked him exceedingly, admired him for his childlike innocence, found his gratulation and constant excitement endearing, and though Aodhgan must have his doubts about any divine voice really communicating with him- - the invention of his own imagination from being too long alone perhaps—there was no harm in having him think an imaginary friend was encouraging him, though there might be some harm in thinking his imaginary friend ought to do the same for everybody else.

A hour's walk brought Myndil and Aodhgan to the wall of the settlement, and with little difficulty, they had breached the southern entrance and reached Ath Cliath proper before the moon was much. The settlement amounted to little more than a town, bustling under the threat of gloaming, the early evening canopy supporting the stars winking in and out amidst the masts along the port. The sky brushed over in a confusion of hues, the few low clouds condescended to the passing storms, the torches lit about the bank crowning the nearby pool in an ocher haze. The cobbled stone of the main roads was marred by the mud penetrating in from the lanes, pointed turf roofs cut jagged edges against the horizon, and caressing the northern expanse was the Liffey, the river and succeeding estuary issuing from the west, feeding into the pool at the south, the black water rich in minerals merging down from the mountains and escaping into the sea. Wattle walls fenced in stock and cattle, slate tile sat atop shaven timber of taverns, and on the high gravel ridge was the longphort, the naval encampment and domestic quarters atop the promontory commanding a view of the palace below.

Though no ships were sailing out at the loss of the sun and secession of wind, the ports were full of business, goods in sacks and casks being loaded onto ready vessels, large men and hardy women stocking the ships, a few leading a fleet of men and monsters along in chains, filling out the chiurms of the stationary galleys.

"Where are they going?" Myndil asked, watching a few chained men and women be led along.

Here was a grave look from Aodhgan. "You don't know?" said he feelingly.

"Know what?"

"Ath Claith's main export is human flesh."

"Oh, that's distressing," said Myndil, with half a sigh. "Humans are rather gamey and don't have much by way of nutritional value—so the wight at the abbey told me."

Aodhgan seemed bemused. "I meant slavery."

"Oh, well, that's much better."

A short laugh, and Aodhgan clapped his hand over his eyes and shook his head, the novelty of Myndil's ingenuousness astounding him.

"I do not like that there should be slaves," Myndil clarified, "and wish they would all come to the abbey, to be safe and to help with chores, but it is better than being roasted and eaten."

"Some would rather that," said Aodhgan, with a grim aspect. "I came here to find someone who was captured and sold to the markets. I have their scent, but it won't be easy to find them in all this."

Aodhgan surveyed the port, the animation of the crowds and purlieu on the banks beyond attacking his senses.

"How strong is your nose?" Myndil asked.

"What do you smell right now?"

Myndil lifted his nose and took a hearty whiff. "The overall scent is a bit sour really, a something between stale bread and sweat. There is a faint hint of stew and roasting meat coming from some of the windows, and I do smell some firewood burning, but the whole thing is sprinkled over with rotting fish, so it isn't unbearable for me."

"My senses are in an agony, a thousand strong scents all fighting for their right of place." Aodhgan winced. "There is war in my nose."

"Well, I think you might tell it to stop."

Aodhgan had no idea if Myndil were serious. He only smiled and said, "I'll try."

They moved further along the main road, some of the larger brick buildings now coming into view, their way intersected by a bylane, a small road collocated by stalls and brocades, connected by a wattle path, leading eastward along the rivulet to the pool.

"This is Ath Claith," Aodhgan announced, "the foreigner stronghold—foreigners to us, as Olaf might consider us the ones out of place. If you think this is crowded, there were even more of them here before Olaf's recent campaign," and then in a darker hue, "I would have even fewer of them, if I could."

"I've never seen so many people in one place in my life," Myndil exclaimed, waving at passersby and making a gazingstock of himself. "There must be a few thousand at least. And there are so many ships, especially up there," pointing toward the longphort. "Well, there is plenty to see while I'm here. Perhaps I can look about, so I can get a good account. Brother Crannach would have loved to see all this. Where are the monasteries? I am a bit hungry and starting to get cold. We could settle there for the night and set out comfortably in the morning."

"There are none on this side of the river, and you will need to stay here if you want to reach the palace." Aodhgan suddenly became aware of two men, watching them from the southern bank. "It would be unwise to lose this position," he quietly added, "or cross the river."

Myndil's studied the two men who were spying his companion. "Those men are large and hairy. Are they your people?"

"No," said Aodhgan, in a low growl. "We're not welcome here."

"Oh, yes, I remember you saying something about that—But, look, there are other non-human creatures about."

Myndil pointed to a few fey who were managing a stall of teeth and herbal remedies nearby.

"They're either indentured or are being watched, just as we are. Luckily the light is low, and I can move quickly, if need be." Aodhgan tugged on the back of Myndil's robe and held him against his chest. "Stay close to me."

"Are we in any immediate danger?"

"Myndil," said Aodhgan, after a pause, "I like you and I'm glad we've become friends—" Here was a coo and a smile from below, "—but I think you might be painfully unaware of something rather important."

"What's that?"

"People like us who like God are not well-liked."

Aodhgan tried to make Myndil aware of the many eyes following them. Several of the men from the dock stopped and stared, the looks of confusion and then appraisal breaking on the faces of each. The sensible thing would have been to pretend to disregard the incurring assessments and continue with due vigilance, but Myndil, who was delighted to be anywhere that was new, smiled at everybody and waved to everyone.

"Hello! Yes, very nice to see you—lovely town you've made, only a bit dirty—hello! Yes, nice to meet you. Ingenious how you've managed to incorporate so much excrement into your walls—I can almost smell the straw and clay. Hallo! Pleasant evening to you!"

Some gaped in horror, others spat in disgust, but it was the rather large and menacing man who was eyeing Myndil eagerly while sharpening a large paring knife that made Aodhgan move him on.

"I don't mean to tell you what to do," said Aodhgan, in an anxious hush, pushing Myndil down the lane, holding his hands at his sides, "but perhaps we should try to remain inconspicuous."

"But they might like us better if we properly introduce ourselves and tell them we only come to bring them the Word of God. I'm sure they would talk to us and they're only a bit shy. They seem low and lost. We ought to tell them they should smile more."

The idea was just amusing enough, and Aodhgan cherished a small smile in spite of himself. "You know," raising his eyes and shaking his head, "if we both weren't on important errands, I would entertain that idea."

"I'm sure if I read to them, they should be happier. Hearing the Good Book always raises my spirits," Myndil professed.

"They might enjoy the parts about raiding and pillaging."

"We could start by telling that man with the hook for a hand over there—"

"That's a slave trader and we will absolutely not do that," said Aodhgan, redirecting Myndil away from the trading stocks.

They turned briskly down the succeeding lane, walking along the southern wall toward the palace, and once they were out of view and obscured by a trellis and an empty vending stall, Aodhgan surveyed their surroundings and looked at his shadow behind him.

"We're here," said Aodhgan, and then, in a terrifying wrawl, "Get out."

A thin ribbon of smoke roiled off the wall, and an umbral figure filled out, pulling itself from a corner of Aodhgan's shadow. "Aye, aye!" the co-walker huffed. "No need to be silty about it! Aw'n goin', aw'm goin'." The shade seemed to gather itself, collecting every coil from the shadow on the wall. "Gotta git to maw revengin' anyhow."

"Who are you revenging anyway?" Myndil asked.

"A man wot calls himself Risteard. Did one in my acquaintance an injury wot took his life."

Aodhgan arched a wooly brow. "You have an acquaintance?"

"Don't everybody? Got a whole host of 'em, me. Yewe got yewer folk, so Aw got mine, dun Aw.

110

Friend was one wot I used to haunt of an occasion. We became friendly-like, jus' how we's doin' now."

Myndil agreed most eagerly.

"Use to invite me in whenever Aw had a hauntin' to do in town. This Risteard fella ups and does maw friend in, an' Aw'm gonna find him and haunt him till he dies."

"How long does that usually take, speaking in averages?" Myndil asked.

The shadow made a murky shrug. "Couple o' days. 'Bout a week, if he's stubborn-like."

"And where will you go after that? Your friend is gone. Will you visit him in the otherworld, or will you stay here to haunt people?"

"Dunno. Could see him across the planes, could stay about, hauntin' and thayt." The shadow seemed to sink inside of itself. "Haven't really thought about the after bit, honest. Jus' thinkin' 'bout doin' maw job."

"You could come to the abbey," was Myndil's sanguine declaration. A glance from Aodhgan told him he should be cautious. "It's still being built just now, but I'm sure they could use all the help they can get, now that I'm away. You'll be safe there, to haunt and welter in shadows and do as you like, as long as you don't hurt anyone, and I'm sure you will get along well with Thingunderthebed and all the other friends I've made there. If you are very good, you could probably ask abbot to let you haunt a few brothers and sisters on occasion. He does want a friend, and you might sit in his shadow and keep him company at night."

The co-walker raised a tendril to its featureless face and bent in thought. "Might do thayt," it mused, "might take a gander at this abbey, 'long as it's not outta maw way. Whereabouts yew say it was?"

Myndil gave him the general direction—follow the coastline northward until he reached an inlet dotted over with a few fertile islands—and said that he hoped he should see him there upon his return.

"Remember to introduce yourself to the abbot," Myndil reminded him, "or he might think you've come to the abbey to do them harm."

"Aw will," the shadow promised. It moved farther down the lane and durned back to wave a tendril at them before vanishing into the outline of a nearby residence.

"Bye, co-walker!" Myndil exclaimed, waving at nothing before Aodhgan could hold his hand down. "He was very pleasant. Perhaps I should have told him to haunt me again sometime."

"I'm sure it will when you return home," said Aodhgan.

"But you see? They really aren't so bad if you try to befriend them."

Aodhgan was going to remind Myndil that his new friend was going to haunt someone to death, but he checked himself and said only, "I don't think I have the same talent of making creatures like that believe I'm as pure of heart as you are."

"But you must be pure of heart, if you love God half so much as I do."

Aodhgan sighed and his heart sunk for his poor innocent friend. "Myndil," said he, in a more serious hue, "not everyone who claims to love God is good at heart."

Myndil seemed not to understand him.

"Olaf is a fervent follower of his god, and he is far from good, as you will probably soon find out. I don't know what gift God as given you, to always hope for good and act as though everyone is kind-hearted and virtuous, but by whatever means you have this gift, I certainly hope it doesn't get you killed."

"Well, I am mortal," Myndil shrugged, "but I cannot think I will die so easily when I have my faith to defend me. God always comes to my aid, when I need him most."

"But are you sure it's God and not mere coincidence?"

"He sent me you, didn't he?"

There was no way of finding out whether Aodhgan was a means of divine intervention or merely an accidental passerby, but by whatever spirit of generosity and friendliness that guided Myndil and set him off to be the agent of good fortune, Aodhgan sincerely hoped it would preserve him from any evil to come.

CHAPTER 14: IN WHICH MYNDIL AND A WEREWOLF HAPPEN TO OLAF.

They came to the palace, a moderate sized stone building with four hexagonal towers and a ditch built round it, the bank ornamented with palisades, buffeted by a small garden on the western side. The stables and barracks were just beyond the bulwark, and the fires from the cookery and the smokehouse supplanted any of the sights from the smithy at the east end, the bakehouse where a tannery might have been. The king had his preferences, and while the two diverging wings to the west gave the place a cheerfuller aspect, it was still a rudimentary compound, amounting to little more than a town within the four walls, the entrance of which opened to the north, the great iron gate shutting out the view from the road, with the longphort in front and the pool making a natural harbour behind.

Myndil canted his head and made a thorough inspection. "I thought it would be nicer," he mused.

"I admit our palace grounds at home are much more impressive," Aodhgan reckoned.

"I don't mean to comment on Olaf's taste—I'm sure he's doing the best he can with what he has—it must be very difficult to maintain a throne and conquer everything at the same time—but even the orphanage was much nicer than this, and it doesn't even house that many."

They walked around the western side, eyeing the pathetic patch of green sward that pretended to be a garden, wedged between two wings extending toward the bailey. The ditch was somewhat impressive, deep enough to burrow under the walkway leading toward the gate, the chief of the buildings on the promontory, the centre building on the brow of the hill. At the end of the walkway leading to the northern gate were two guards, large and worthy king's men donned in slatternly skins, leather jerkins and boiled breeches, their back-and-breast plates making them look more impressive than they actually were. They were young men, newly-made with golden helms and golden livery, eager to serve and glad to be made important by a king whether a madman or no, and while their spears gave them confidence, their self-assurance shrank by Aodhgan's side, a man who towered over everyone, whose shoulders needed no pauldrons to look menacing, whose hands were large enough to crush any man's skull. Aodhgan wore no armour, to appear civilian though his rolling muscles said otherwise, but still appear dignified without the greaves and bracers his king had issued him; he noted the horn that hung at the soldiers' sides and saw fingers fidget with them as he approached. He stopped and moved back behind Myndil, feigning indifference at the palace.

"We should discuss our plan of entry," said Aodhgan quickly, pulling Myndil toward him.

"We should ask the guards if they'll let us in," was Myndil's hopeful proposal. "If we tell them why we've come, they might be interested in hearing a few passages from the Good Book. There are some really lovely ones later on—"

"Myndil," Aodhgan interrupted him, staring at the guards, who were eyeing them, "while I'm sure a few passages might entertain them, something tells me this might not be the time."

"But, perhaps if we show them we're friendly, they might not be so murderous. We ought to introduce ourselves."

Myndil turned and was about to wave, but an enormous hand clasps both of his hands behind his back.

"Those are gold-helms," Aodhgan reminded him, "the king's personal commanders."

"Oh. Do you think their having golden helmets will impede them from hearing about God? Because I can speak louder, if they should not be able to hear me."

"They can hear you well enough. I suspect they might want to see what's in your bowels first."

"Oh, that's very unsanitary considering I have had a good amount to eat today, including that old lady's poker milk, which will not look very nice."

"They're already suspicious of us. They might know what I am, and my presence will not be tolerated on palatial grounds. Neither will yours, once they know why you're here."

Myndil pouted and deliberated. "I could get purposely captured, and you could come get me out again at nightfall."

"Myndil," said Aodhgan, with a sincere look, "there is no guarantee they will not harm you or that they will even let you see Olaf. They could put you in a hole in the ground and torture you before I reach you."

"Oh, I'm sure that won't happen," Myndil chimed, his eyes sparkling. "God will protect me."

"Not from them."

The guards began marching toward them: they had lingered long enough at the end of the walkway, a young man in white robes with a clean foreign look to him garnering as much suspicious as a towering Gael.

"Oh, hello there!" Myndil called out, his elbows waving now that his hands were being held behind his back. "Yes, hello! Good to see you! Thank you for walking down to us—"

"Halt," one of the guards demanded, thrusting his spear toward them.

"Yes—We're not moving," said Myndil, staring at the spear at the end of his nose. "We stopped walking long before you approached."

The guards made their survey of the visitors: the small and thin one looked stupid enough, harmless enough surely by Aodhgan's side, but the large one—the goliath one, the one they were turning pale about, the one who towered over them, whose chest wider than both of their together, whose arms flexed with iron brawn, whose shadow they were standing in, was beginning to distress them. "Who are you and what is your business here?" one of them demanded.

Aodhgan made his obeisances. Myndil brandished his warmest smiles.

"So good of you to ask, and I'm so excited to tell you!" Myndil announced. "My name is Myndil and I'm a missionary, and well, you see, I was hoping to be ordained as a brother at my abbey, but in order for me to be worthy of ordination, I have to gain as many followers as possible, and I was told by some of your people that in order to convince them that God loves them, I would have to speak

114

to your king and ask him whether he would like me to tell him about God. I just have a book to read to him, you see, and you could listen too, if you like. Would you like to hear some of my favourite passages? I would love to read them to you."

Aodhgan was astonished that the guards had not struck him yet. They seemed more confused than agitated, looking as though they were trying to work out whether this were little more than a lark.

TELL THEM THOU ART MY DIVINE MESSENGER, AN OMEN SENT BY GOD ABOUT THE COMING WAR.

"Yes, I was getting to that, God," said Myndil, opening his book. He licked his finger and flicked through the pages, and Aodhgan stood behind him, with chest out and fists clenching at his sides.

Myndil hemmed and began reading. "AND LO," in a mechanical voice, "IT WAS ON THE THIRD DAY THAT THE LORD SAID UNTO—"

The spears were suddenly at his neck.

"Oh, bother. Why does that always happen when I begin to read? It's my oration again, I am sure of it. If you will let me read it again, I will try a different method. Perhaps it's my tone—"

The spears thrust forward, and Myndil found himself pushed out of the way by Aodhgan's enormous chest.

"He has not hurt you," said Aodhgan, in a low wrawl.

"What do you do here, hound?" one of the guards spat, his spear rather small in front of Aodhgan.

"That's not very pleasant of you to say," Myndil contended. "Aodhgan's not an animal, he's a werewolf, and one made by God, so you ought to be kind to him."

They noted the symbol of Saint Paudrig on his sleeve, the livery of the royal house of Osraige. "We have enough hunting hounds," one of the guards sneered. "When the king needs more, he'll visit your dens."

Aodhgan's eyes tapered. Their words were not nearly as offensive as their breath, which he could smell from ten feet away, and he held his giant hands at his sides, resisting the impulse to crush their heads.

"And you," said the other guard, thrusting his spear at Myndil, "we have all the gods we need. Take your hound and leave."

He thrust his spear downward and slapped the book out of Myndil's hand.

"No!" Myndil cried, quickly collecting manuscript up from the dirt. "This is the book I've had since I was a child! It has all my illustrations in it. I drew on every page, and it took me so incredibly long to colour in all the lines—you've soiled it. I shall have to redo those pages now."

The guards were not listening. Two colossal hands were holding the shafts of their spears.

"There was no need for that," Aodhgan bellowed, plucking their spears away from them.

"Stay back, beast!" one of the guard cried, grabbing for the horn at his side. "Any closer and

I'll sound the ala—"

The horn was pulled out of his hand and crushed, and Aodhgan sprinkled the shards over the threshold, daring the guards to try it again.

"They aren't going to let me in, are they?" said Myndil woefully.

"They could," Aodhgan growled, his eyes narrowing, "if they don't want to see the wolf."

Consternation always operates exactly opposite to how it should: sense would tell the two guards that they ought to escort the smaller of the two men to their king and let him deal with him, but terror reigned in small minds, and the guards, sure that they should win against a seven-and-a-half-foot man with shoulders as wide as a the walkway, decided that they could overpower him because they wanted to. Desire never answers when idiocy is by, and boldness was never so swiftly rewarded: the horn sounded just as a street patrol of eight men were passing by, one of them a commander carrying a large mace, the rest well-armoured and holding spears, and they arrived at the gate in time to see the two gold-helms gaping up at a beast, its shadow encompassing the walkway.

It was a horrorsome sight, its frame twice as large as the man who belonged to it, its head standing at impossible height. The vicious beast formed and flexed in a wreck of fur and muscle, its claws curved and acute, its muzzle notched by fangs. It stood on its hind legs, its limbs weighed down by unconquerable might, its tread heavy, the ground trembling under its padded feet. It raised its nowl and shook its mane, the thick black coat tinged with silver streaks lining the length of its back. Its eyes simmered with rage, the amber glow heightening when it growled. It breathed in sweltering breath, its fumes searing the skin of the men who stood beneath it. It glared at the two gold-helms and flashed its fangs, and a pungent scent filled the air. A roar resounded throughout the docks, turning every head and drawing every eye, the reboation rippling the air and rattling the boats.

The guards froze, their bowels abandoning them. Myndil was all joyous exultation.

"Is that you, Aodhgan?" he exclaimed, smiling profusely. "That's absolutely sensational! I didn't think your wolf form was going to be that atrocious, but it is really terrifying! How did you get so tall?" looking up and craning his neck. "Your features are truly horrid, but don't worry. I'm still not alarmed because I know it's you."

"Good," said the wolf, in a clear but fathomless voice. He turned to the guards and smelled the fear wafting off their heads. "Let him pass."

His breath burned across their faces, and their nates began to quake.

The guards from the dock rushed Aodhgan from behind. His senses knew they were coming, and he turned, greeting them with a deafening roar. The violent sound knocked them to the ground and made Myndil wince.

"That was a bit loud," said Myndil, wiggling his finger in his ear.

"My apologies," said the wolf.

Myndil examined the beast's features. "It still does look like you, in a way, the same bushy black

116

brows, the same kind eyes. If you weren't snarling, you'd actually be quite cuddly. Your fur is very comfortable looking, and you must be very pleasant to sleep next to at night. In certain ways, I think your human form is much more terrifying."

Aodhgan bellowed in bestial mirth, glad to hear someone more afraid of his humanity. The guards tried to attack him from behind, but a sweep of his long tail and a swipe with his claws knocked them back. He was purposely trying not to harm them, but as terror prevailed outside the palace, only more guards were called.

"I will distract them," said Aodhgan. "You will have to run in. Run straight ahead into the palatial grounds and do not stop until you come to Olaf's seat. I will be in after you, if I can."

"Will you be coming in wolf or human form? Speaking of which, where is your human form?"

Myndil looked down, and between the wolf's legs was Aodhgan's body, limp and crumpled at his feet. He bent down and examined Aodhgan's face—he was sleeping, his eyes closed and moving. His arms and legs twitched, moving in time with the motions of his wolf form above him, the dream of one controlling the movement of the other.

"Oh," said Myndil, understanding now. "Well, that is rather inconvenient. Before I go in, I'll move you so you don't get hurt."

The wolf fought off the attacking guards, snapping their weapons and swatting them away, and Myndil bent down and tried to lift Aodhgan's body.

"God, you're heavy," Myndil grunted, pulling upward and not moving him at all. His iron muscles were lead, three-hundred pounds of dead weight in seven-and-a-half feet lying on the ground, and no matter how much Myndil strained and shoved, Aodhgan's body would not budge.

The guards, now robbed of their weapons, began attaching themselves to the wolf's limbs, and Aodhgan, with little effort, tore them from his legs and tossed them toward the river. He was moving away from the palace, giving Myndil a chance to infiltrate, but frustrated with his own want of strength, Myndil did the only thing he could do to protect his friend's body and rolled him toward the ditch.

"If—I—can't—lift—you—" he huffed, shoving Aodhgan's shoulders, "—I'll—just—shift—you—over—"

Aodhgan's heavy frame hung on the bank, Myndil unable to push him any longer. He grabbed the post to the walkway and began kicking him.

"I'm—just—moving—your—body—over—here—so—you'll—be—safe!" The last kick, made with a strong effort, pushed Aodhgan over the bank, and his body rolled into the ditch, tumbling down with a heavy thump. Myndil mantled over the ditch and tried to see the bottom. "I didn't check whether there was water down there. Aodhgan," he shouted into the ditch, "are you all right down there?"

"MY BODY WILL BE FINE," the wolf rumbled, whirling and flinging the guards off his arms. "GO."

Myndil ran up the empty walkway, but a pang struck him and he looked back. He felt an early attachment to Aodhgan, something heavenly and permeant, and did not want to leave him. He shouted the same directions to the abbey that he told the co-walker, anxious they would be separated without a chance of seeing him again. A violent roar told him he was heard, and he ran into the palatial grounds, never stopping until he reached the threshold of the Riverfleet Throne.

The cloud of confusion that followed Myndil gave him the cover he needed. The sound of horns blaring out in the distance and the clamour of the fight outside brought all the guardsmen from inside the palace out. One guard who saw Myndil skulking toward the throne shouting for him to halt, but the cry of possible infiltration, the monstrous roars beyond made Myndil seem unimportant. He garnered a few odd looks from guards running by, but a small man in white robes was nothing compared to the beast at the gate. His book, however, was a much more formidable weapon than whatever Aodhgan's claws could do, and he entered the Riverfleet Throne with his book in hand, his powers of oration ready.

The room was more of a great hall than a stately seat. Fitted up with recent trappings and trinkets from his conquests, a few memorandums from his father, and a large wooden chair at the top of the chamber, Olaf's throne room was a shadow of its former iteration, the previous kings of Ath Cliath having ornamented its walls with prizes now replaced by paltrier views, and standing in the middle of the room was King Olaf himself, king in theory if not in fact, not beloved or accepted by all and knowing it. He was a tall man, his want of might and gravity compensated for in the sword that hung at his side, his hips slender and basculating, his frame lean and shoulders narrow. He was not a handsome man, his wild eyes at war with one another, his jaw jutting and teeth in every direction instead of the right, his bramble of a beard doing features no favours. He was slovenly and scumbered, thinking a regular bath a great enemy, his black leather armour looking as though it had not cleaned since his last campaign. He stood beside a large wooden table, murmuring over his maps, and began to grow agitated upon hearing the clamour outside.

"Odin take those dogs," he swore. "We should have killed them instead of taking them from Limerick." Another roar echoed from the palatial grounds, and Olaf slammed his fist into the table. "What is going on out there?" he bawled, flecks of spit flying from his mouth. "Just skin the dogs and be done with it—" He whipped around to find a young man in white robes standing at the entrance. "Who are you and why aren't you my men?"

Myndil deliberated. "I'm Myndil and I'm not your men because they are busy at the gate."

Olaf examined the infiltrator for any weapons and saw no swords or axes about him. "Heh."

"Are you King Olaf?" Myndil asked, a little disappointed. There was no gold, no silver, no crown to mark his distinction; there was only the stench of pelts the sour feff of old ale lingering around a middle-aged man.

"Am I King Olaf?" the king humphed, in a drunken wail.

"Yes, that is what I asked. Are you King Olaf—or is it Amlaib? Peig said it was a different name. Maybe I've got it wrong. You will have to tell me how you spell your name, so I can learn to say it better."

"O-L-A-F-R. Olafr."

"Oh. That's not Olaf or Amlaib at all."

"My enemies call me Ánláf."

"Oh, that's very confusing. You really will have to choose a name and keep to it, because it is very difficult for your people to remember so many different ones–but if you are King Olaf, I'm glad to see you. I travelled a dreadful long way to see you and give you God's message–"

"Ah, so you've finally come."

Myndil blinked. "You were waiting for me?"

"I was. I was told you'd be coming, or someone like you anyway."

"Oh, then I can begin reading to you right away."

"Is that the message from Constantine?"

Myndil's eyes darted about. "Constantine?"

"Yes. You are his messenger, aren't you? He said he would be sending one to me soon, and you look clean enough."

"Oh, I think you have mistaken me. I came from the north–"

"So you're Owain's messenger then?"

Myndil smiled confusedly. "Who is he?"

The thrunches began. "King of Alt Clut. I've been waiting to hear from him. You said something about a message from God–" Olaf paused and put a hand on his hilt. "Are you're one of Aethelstan's men?"

"I have heard his name before. Aodhgan said he already believes in God, but I'm not–"

Olaf slammed his fist into the table, jostling his cup of ale. "Odin's eye–I'll be damned if I let Aethelstan take me for a fool. What does my enemy say? Hm? Tell me. Thinks he can take more of my land while I'm campaigning elsewhere?"

"Not that I know. I don't really have anything to do with any kings or land–"

The roars without drew closer, and Olaf stared at the entrance, watching his guards fly in the distance, and he drew his sword.

"An infiltrator!" he accused Myndil, marching toward him. "You came with weapons!"

"Me? Oh, no. That's just Aodhgan distracting the guards. He is my friend and will be here any minute to tell you that himself, but your guards would harass him. We did not come to fight–I came to read to you. You see," hemming and holding up his book, "I'm a missionary, and when I spoke to your people about having them accept the word of God, they said I should come speak to you about it, because you controlled which God they believe in, so here I am to tell you that my God, the real God, loves you."

"Your God," Olaf demanded, with wild eyes. "And which God would that be?"

TELL HIM I AM HIS GOD, THE GOD OF WAR AND DECIMATION.

"Oh, God, he will never believe me if I tell you you want him to make Holy Wars–"

"Holy wars?" Olaf was almost shrieking. "So, Aethelstan mocks me, sending me his messenger, trying to get me to accept his gods."

"God," said Myndil helpfully. "There is only one."

Olaf lunched forward. "ARRRGGHHH!" he gurgled, swinging his sword at Myndil.

Myndil ducked and the sword stuck in the wall behind him. "If I could just read to you, I think you might not be so angry—I chose a good passage about the destruction of a heathen city—oh, you're drooling." Olaf was trying to pull his sword out of the wall, and there was a small puddle forming at his feet. "I'll stay over here," said Myndil, moving away. "I have to clean my book as it is because of your guards."

"A peddler of the White God," Olaf seethed, pulling his sword from the wall.

Myndil pouted in confusion. "I don't know that God has a colour. I have never seen him, of course, but I imagine he is more of a green, because of the spring and verdure of renewal—no, please, don't swing at me. I have not read my passage yet."

Olaf lunged and swung at him again. "A spy from Aethelstan! An agent of his White God!"

Myndil insisted god was green. "And I'm not a spy. I only came to speak to you about loving God!"

TELL HIM THAT HE MUST WAR WITH AETHELSTAN. GOD WISHES IT.

"I will not tell him to war with Aethelstan. I came to tell him about you!"

The sword lodged in another wall, and Olaf left it there and grabbed for Myndil instead. He caught him by the back of his robes and held him up to his face. "War with Aethelstan, is it?" he breathed, the foul stench of old ale consuming his prey.

"Oh, that is awful," Myndil grimaced, trying to turn away. "You really ought to brush your teeth. Does Odin not like cleanliness?"

"He likes war, and if Aethelstan or his god sent you to bait me into battle, then I accept, but what he doesn't know is I won't be coming alone." He marched from the back of the hall holding Myndil by the collar, touring him through the palatial grounds toward the black pool at the bottom of the bank.

"I wouldn't kill me, if I were you," Myndil fussed, feeling his hands being tied behind his back. "If Aodhgan finds out you have hurt me, he will probably eat you. His mouth is certainly big enough, though you'll probably taste like moldy bread and old cheese."

"I won't kill you, spy," said Olaf, thrusting Myndil toward the estuary. "I am sending you back to your master with a message." He lifted Myndil up and hissed in his ear, "I come to reclaim what is mine by right, I come with a thousand men, and by Odin I will kill him and parade his head throughout Northumbria, that his subjects will know their rightful king."

"But are you sure the people would like that? That wouldn't be very sanitary—"

A pain struck the back of Myndil's head. The void of unconsciousness consumed him, and he felt himself being put into a small vessel and being released into the water before memory faded and sleep succeeded.

Olaf was shouting for his men to gather, for them to make preparations and make ready for war. A few dissented and disclaimed, claiming they had only just got back from their most recent campaign in the south, and it would be sometime before they could recoup everything that they had lost.

"Get your men ready," Olaf commanded, pulling one of his jarls aside. "We leave at dawn."

"Tomorrow?" the jarl exclaimed. "But our men are still recovering–"

"We will only need a thousand to fulfill our promise to our allies."

"But a thousand is all we have left."

"Enough to deal with Aethelstan's forces." Olaf humphed to himself and watched a small vessel bob out to sea. "And where were you while a spy was infiltrating the palatial grounds?"

The jarl seemed fearful, the remembrance to terrible to relate. "There–there was a giant wolf–a monstrous wolf at the front gate!"

"A wolf," said Olaf doubtingly. "And where is it now? Dead?"

"Gone."

Olaf fleered and swore to himself.

"We were fighting it–" the jarl insisted, "all of us–trying to scale it and bring it down. It must have been as tall as the flagship mast–you must have heard it, those hideous sounds–it's teeth were as long as my arm–A few of the guards even have wounds from its claws–one slash tore through Jari's armour–every guard this side of the river was on the beast, but once it reached the bridge, it just vanished, the men falling out of the sky as though the wolf had never been there..."

"A giant wolf doesn't just disappear," Olaf huffed.

"This one did."

"And where does a giant wolf with dozens of men attacking it go?"

The jarl wished he could say.

CHAPTER IV: IN WHICH A CO-WALKER HAPPENS TO THE ABBEY

Evening came to the abbey, and amidst the prayers and lamentations finishing for the day, the abbot, after having spent the better part of the afternoon telling the Lord how much he hated himself for his sake, and after a firm round of contrition on account of some questionable thoughts regarding the abbess' thighs, it was time for the abbot to enjoy a frigid steep in the basin and a gentle doze on his stone slab. There was nothing so good for the soul as suffering, and as the abbot championed the good in feeling atrocious and recommended misery as good for the health, he could hardly wait to suffer again before bedtime.

The moon nestled in one of the corners of the window, and the abbot exclaimed that God sent the strident nacreous light to plague him even further, which he thanked him for, wincing in the anguish of knowing that God had blessed him with a difficult night of sleep. He settled into the depression in his stone slab, his back already aching, and just was drifting off when a shade passed over his eyes. It was only for a moment, but it was enough to awaken him, the sudden flickering moving in front of the light catching his consciousness more than his attention. He saw nothing but the moon, its full presence bearing down on him, casting an oddly shaped shadow on the floor beside him. He turned and looked, investigating his outline from the corner of his eye, and just as he was about to close his eyes again, a slender black bine reached up from the shadow and touched the end of his nose.

"GAH!" the abbot cried, sitting up and recoiling. "WHAT IS THAT—WHAT IS THAT?"

Two tendrils penetrated the outline—they were pulling something up from the shadow and lifting it from the ground. An amorphous shade peeled itself from the floor, and once had plumed a bit and had taken shape, it made a friendly gesture and waved at him.

"'Awllo, abbot!" said the shade. "Err—it is the abbot, innit?"

It paused, waiting for an answer. The abbot began frothing.

"NO NO NO NO NO," he gnashed, thrashing about. "OUT, OUT, FOUL CREATURE! BEGONE! I CALL UPON GOD TO RID OF YOU!"

He cast his hand outward, calling upon the Infinitude of the Lord to smite the evil intruder, but the co-walker only touched his hand with a murky tendril and emanated a churlish "Hur, hur, hur!"

Brother Vindimir and Brother Crannach were walking in the corridor, having just come in from putting the orphans to bed. The children had begged Crannach for one more—only one more—story before sleep, demanding to hear about how Paudrig had chased all snakes from the island, though there had never been any, and how Brigid had got her cow with the roan ears, when Sister Iarlaith had come in to offer them some warm milk and peach resin, allowing the two brothers to make their escape. They were walking from the children's dormitory to their own bedrooms, admiring the moonlit night and the tranquility it furnished when a gurgling cry echoed toward them from the other end of the hall.

"GET IT OFF ME—GET IT OFF!"

They turned, and under the dim glow of the few rushlights constellating along the walls, they saw the abbot, barreling toward them with arms flailing.

"IT TOUCHED ME! IT'S IN MY SHADOW—GET IT OUT!"

They heard a guttural "Hur hur hur!" and the shadows along the wall danced and thrummed. The abbot flapped and floundered, waving at nothing, and the two brothers hastened over to him only to find him shooing at his own shadow.

"Get off—pff pffffff—" blowing fiercely at his shadow, "Oh, thank God—Did you see it? Did you see that monstrous demon? It attacked me and then it looked as though it flew into my—but I saw it fly off out here."

"What did, abbot?" Crannach asked.

"That THING—That shadow beast! Did you see it? It waved at me and tormented me, and now it's going to haunt me until it is exorcised!"

"Ah, 'tis probablae onlae Ozzy, come in fae the graves again," said Crannach. "Ye know how he is when there's full moon oan. His bones get a wee bit chillae and start clackin' at this time o' the year."

"It was not that godforsaken walking skeleton! It was a shadowy creature with all manner of arms and legs and—IT TOUCHED ME. It put its disgusting tendrils out and waved them at me and touched my nose!"

The abbot, agitated from a kind of suffering he did not like, began sniveling.

The brothers glanced at one another, sharing the same feeling between them but keeping it to themselves. They consoled the abbot, said all that was proper and placating, reconciling him to the notion that whatever it was had probably had its amusement and was already gone, and returned the abbot to his room, tucking him in and cooing at him to 'go to sleep and it will all be better in the morning', but somewhere, in a quiet corner of the abbey, wedged between the mirk and moonlight, the shadows flickered, their animation marked by a fleeting gust and a tenebrous 'hur hur hur', the sound of a one who was glad to have made a new friend and glad to have found a new home, and would certainly not be leaving anytime soon.

chapter 16: in which god happens to myndil

The small currach drifted languidly along, dipping up and over the waves, and though the disagreements of seals and merrows over the ownership of the rocks carried him on the journey, Myndil could not hear them; he was too much rapt in his own musings, his mind in a flurry of colour and sound, the events of the day reiterating themselves many times over, his unconscious mind too busy to make much of his surroundings.

Myndil...

The voice was many voices, one he always attributed to god, and the rest a collation of tones and pitches, one for the abbot, one for each brother and sister at the abbey, one for Aodhgan...

Myndil...

His head fell heavily against the bottom of the currach, something held his hands behind his back, the vague remembrance of the day coming back to him. He croosled to himself, his lips moving, his voice trying to articulate, "mmfmfmfmfmgodisthatymmmm," in the nebulous haze of unconsciousness. He knew he was moving, knew he was bound somehow, knew the back of his head ached—

Myndil!

He thought it was Aodhgan calling to him, trying to wake him out of semi-consciousness and warn him of something. "I'm sorry I kicked you into a ditch..." Myndil tootled. It might be Aodhgan holding him, carrying him and bringing him to safety, but the want of muscles and comfortable fur convinced him otherwise. He was being taken somewhere, his sense of motion told him so, but the saline scent and the swaff of the sea lapping over itself told him where he was.

He wrenched and tried to turn onto his back, and when that failed, he opened his eyes, a thousand stars swarming his view. "Was I hit that hard?" he murmured, staring up at the celestial swirl. At first, he thought he might have lost part of his sight, but he soon realized it was nighttime, his surroundings dark from the lack of sun and new moon, the stars his only marker along the sea. How could I be at sea? I don't remember being put in the water. The rocking is very pleasant, though...

MYNDIL.

He was suddenly awake. "Is that you, God?"

There was no answer. Only the rote of the waves folding over the mirrored stars answered him.

"Did I do it, God? Did I convince Olaf about you?"

NO.

"He didn't see how much I love you?"

HE HEARD GOD'S MESSAGE AND IS DOING AS HE SHOULD

"But will he follow you then, and get all his people to follow likewise?"

HE WILL GET HIS PEOPLE TO FOLLOW HIM INTO BATTLE.

A distant risibility oppressed him, the cachinnations of one far off and yet somehow near persuading Myndil to sleep. A single clicking sound was the last thing he heard, the sound of something sliding into a lock and turning the key, and the presence seemed pleased, gratified to have made something happen, and even more satisfied to have so willing a servant.

Rest was Myndil's only friend at the moment, his currach floating eastward along the water with no oars to steer him and no sails to urge him on. He spent several hours at sea, lying on the bottom of the currach without knowing where he was going and without having any power of stopping himself. To his god and to his apparent plans he must trust, and it was dawn before Myndil was able to sit up and see where he was. The coast eastward lay before him, the sun climbing over the distant peaks, and behind him, the westward strand was gone, the shores of home replaced by the rolling waves.

"God," Myndil pleaded, "where am I going?"

WHITHER THOU SHOULDST.

He looked about him, watching the barm wash over the undulating crests, and, his awareness finally catching up to recollection, he asked, "Where's Aodhgan?"

CHAPTER 17: IN WHICH A WEREWOLF HAPPENS TO THE ABBEY

It was early morning when Aodhgan regained consciousness. The attack on the palace had fatigued him considerably, but he was determined to know what happened and to find Myndil as quickly as possible. He was not obliged to follow Myndil on the rest of his pilgrimage, wherever he should chose to go, but Aodhgan felt a responsibility for him considering he had offered to help him see Olaf, and Myndil had done him the courtesy of defending his human form while the battle was on. The knowledge of Myndil's wellbeing and whereabouts was owed at least, and though Aodhgan could not be ecstatic about having spent the last few hours resting in a ditch, it did a creditable job of hiding him, or making him seem dead at any rate, and he therefore made no complaints. He clambered up the bank and onto the main road, keeping away from the palace, and followed Myndil's faint scent toward the river, asking anyone who would speak to him whether a young bright-eyed man wearing a white robe had come in their way.

The few who would offer him information said that no one of that description had left the palace nor passed them by, and Aodhgan had little else to go on. Myndil's mission was to convert Olaf, and as Olaf was still alive and had not commanded the immediate conversion of all his people, Myndil's mission must have failed—but where had he gone? There was no one hanging in the stocks, no tinge of blood in the air—none that Aodhgan would recognize instantly-- but there was movement at the port, more than the common course of the daily buying and trading: ships were being called down from the longphort, galleys were being manned and stocked, provisions were being secured—a war was coming on, the belligerents and commanders he knew, but whether Myndil was the cause of it, or whether he would be in the middle of it, Aodhgan could only conjecture. I must find him... He could distinguish Myndil's scent anywhere— the distinctive fragrance of smiling innocence and misplaced intrepidity—but the trail ended just beyond the palace, and the few faint hints of it near the pier led to nothing. God would let nothing happen to him—to this, Aodhgan had to trust; by whatever Spirit of Devotion that settled on Myndil's shoulders and whispered in his ear, it had already safeguarded him from the worst, but Aodhgan's conscience plagued him: he was anxious for Myndil, anxious that someone would try to hurt him on the road, even more anxious that Myndil had been put on a ship that was already sailed out and was on its way to the slave markets abroad, but with no trail to follow and all intimation of Myndil ending at the south side of the river, Aodhgan was defeated here. Myndil has friends... He thought of the healer woman whom Myndil had briefly mentioned, but she would only repel him with wolfsbane and tell him to look elsewhere. He had no means of finding the clurichaun Myndil talked of, and though faeries could move over long distances quickly, they could not find anyone on a whim. There was only one place where Aodhgan could go to determine Myndil's fate, and he went the moment he could find passage.

He remembered the directions given to the co-walker the day before, the same directions that

Myndil had shouted at him during the battle: follow the eastern coastline northward until you see an inlet with several large islands, and on the centre island there will be an abbey, populated by many similar creatures and unsuspecting incumbents, and to Aodhgan's surprise, at the end of the northern coastline, where the sea thrashed against jutting crags and the barm lashed basalt columns, there was an archipelago of raised headlands, connected by a sand bridge at the low tide. Aodhgan leaped out of the currach he had secured and walked across the bank, the sand perfectly dry between the outcroppings, and on the centre island, ensconced by calving crags, was a series of large buildings, some looking older than others, the grounds surrounded by a high wall hung round with ivy with a copse of trees on either side. The island was natural, divested from the rest of its sedimentary family by time, but the woodland and issuing grounds were manufactured, supplanted and replanted by human hands, the studied chaos of nature cleared away for the orderliness and decidedness of gardens and a farm. He walked up the main path, admiring the planned approach, and when he got to the main gate, he turned back to glory in the view: the peaks of the far mountains penetrating the sky, the low-lying clouds castling upwards, the clear water watching the world upside down, the issuing bluff caressed by the sea— a splendid prospect, made even more blissful by the want of unwanted people. What equanimity was here before him, his eye following the path along the sand onto the mainland, the road marked out by the white chalk underlying the grass. Did Myndil walk all that way? was another question for Aodhgan to answer to himself. It had taken him only a few hours by boat to get here—how much longer would it have taken him on foot—but distance was nothing to a heart like Myndil's, one that would be eager to travel and travel far, whether the pilgrimage ordered by the abbot or not, the force of friendship making him equal to any journey.

Aodhgan approached the gate, and on the iron door opening up to the main building was a sign that read: A-BEE THES WEY, the word 'abbey' striking out the word 'orphanage', and then in smaller letters, RITTIN BY MEE AN NOT STUPPID DIMEADH.

Who 'me' was, Aodhgan could only guess, but Dimeadh must have been clamouring for the chalk when the sign was put up. He smiled, thinking the sign must have been written by one of the orphans, but when he heard the gentle tones of a grown man shout, "OW. GET OF MY LEG AND DON'T TOUCH MY HAMMER," he peered through the gates to find the builders working on the foundations of an annex to a building. He reached over the gate, pulled the iron latch, and opened the gate to watch, and waited for someone to address him before entering the grounds.

The abbot was just telling Brother Crannach, Brother Vindimir, and Abbess Bhaldruithe of the positively horrid sleep he had suffered due to the newest addition to the abbey, and was still uncertain as to whether he enjoyed it. The horrific visions of shadows strangling him in his sleep he could do without, but as it made him call out to God for help and offered him a supreme test of his faith, he thought he might find some good in being haunted after all. The abbot was just ending his remonstrances as they walked along the peristyle to the front garden, whereupon he spied an enormous man standing just beyond the threshold, his aspect obscured by the iron bars.

"Who is that?" the abbot scowled, craning his neck. "Is it a beggar? I don't like mendicants. Can you see who it is? I don't want to go over there if it's a ruffian. Is it another one of these layabouts?" glancing at the rabble, who were sitting down and eating something. "If he is looking for a bed, tell him we have no more room and he must go and sleep in a drain, and if he does not like it, he can ask God why he was made poor."

"Doesnae liek a beggar," said Crannach, excited to see someone taller and wider at the shoulder than himself. "He looks liek he might be a messenger."

He indicated the symbol of Saint Paudrig emblazoned on Aodhgan's sleeve, and after the abbot indulged in a few sighs and said they might as well see what the stranger wanted, they all marched toward the gate, Crannach the most eager of them to know who would come half so far to see them.

Distance is a great deceiver, and when they neared Aodhgan, they were all shocked to discover just how prodigious he was. From afar, he looked like a hale and hardy young man, if not a little taller than most, but once they were under his shadow, they were impressed and if not a little fearful of his insuperable might: his massive chest threatening to cleave his collar, his biceps challenging the integrity of his sleeves, and even more concerning were the tufts of black hair peeking out of his shirt. They thought at first he was wearing a layer of fur under his tunic, but the muscle definition around his waist made them think differently. His friendly quiet looks, however, smoothed away any agitation, and civil bow he greeted them with recommended his powers of propriety.

"Forgive me for coming here unannounced, but I have an urgent errand I need to speak to you about—if I'm in the right place."

He spoke in a resonant purr, and the abbess felt her thighs tighten.

"Are you the abbot?" Aodhgan asked, leaning down to the small man.

"I am," was the abbot's short reply, straightening himself with feigned dignity. "And who are you?"

"My name is Aodhgan, and I'm a friend of one of the men in your order. I came here to look for him—a young man named Myndil."

"You're one of Myndil's friends?" said the abbess, in a breathless hush.

"How do you know him?" said Vindimir incredulously.

"I befriended him as he was on his way to see King Olaf. I went with him to the palace, but we had some difficulty being admitted. There was a misunderstanding which quickly became a fight-- one which I fought myself—Myndil broke into the palace, but I was incapacitated, and when I awakened, Myndil was nowhere to be found."

The abbot grumbled something to himself about the boy not being dead yet. "I mean—" he hemmed, "by the Grace of God, he's alive, God be praised, the boy lives, and so on."

"I followed his scent down the river, but wasn't able to find him. I thought that if he had fled the city, he might have come back here."

"Followed his scent?" Crannach asked. "Is he no' bathin'? He usuallae smells liek sunflowers, with how clean he lieks tae keep his robes."

128

"Oh," said Aodhgan, somewhat mortified. "Well, I suppose I should tell you out of courtesy. I'm a werewolf."

The abbot turned aside. His fists began rattling. "Another monstrosity the boy has sent back to us," he scolded. "Of course you're a werewolf—you might as well be a plague of locusts, for all I care. God help me—another one to irritate me for the rest of my miserable life. Damn the boy! Damn him to hell and back!"

"Another one?" said Aodhgan, catching the words, looking eagerly at the brothers. "Did another of my kin come here?"

"No, no, son. No' yer kin," Crannach laughed.

Aodhgan arched a brow. "Are you certain? You look as though you might—?"

"No, no' me, but we got quite a collection o' creatures roamin' around." Crannach lifted his hand to screen his mouth from the abbot, though he could still hear him. "Just adopted one o' the shadow folk."

"The co-walker," Aodhgan exclaimed, beginning to smile. "So it did make it here. It followed us for a time. I wanted to rid of it, considering how they haunt people to death, but Myndil promised it would be safe here."

"Of course he did!" the abbot cried, marching off, stamping the short grass underfoot. "The boy promises every ruffian and abomination shelter and security, and then they all come here, to crowd us with their reviling revolting—GAH!" He wrung his fists, thrusting them at the sky. "God is punishing me—he is absolutely punishing me," said he, in a wearied voice, slapping his hand over his eyes. "The boy is my penance forever. I shall never be rid of him and his ridiculous behaviour. He will hound me even in death, I'm sure of it—O cruel, unfeeling God! Why have you condemned me? Have not I repented for my sins against him?"

His lamentations went on, but no one paid much attention while Aodhgan was by.

"The co-walker came," Aodhgan continued, "but Myndil hasn't returned?"

"No, and no word of him either, beyond what the builders have told us," said Brother Vindimir, "but if you saw him and spent time with him, that is some relief. I think you did quite right in coming here. Myndil is sure to be back eventually. He always has a habit of turning up when you least expect."

"I did notice that about him. Circumstances seem to line up in his favour. He was being carried off by a faerie court when I happened to find him and rescue him."

A shout of, "WHY DIDN'T YOU LET THEM DRAG HIM OFF?" echoed in the background. The abbot recollected and excused himself, claiming he was late for a meeting with God about the many facets of penance and admonition, and vanished into the abbey, where wails of mental anguish brought him to his room, leaving the brothers and the abbess to invite their guest inside.

"And you're certain I am welcome here?" Aodhgan asked, stepping diffidently over the threshold.

"And why wouldn't you be?" the abbess asked, sidling him, her heavy breasts flouncing. "You wear the symbol of Saint Paudrig. Do you not follow his teachings?"

Aodhgan paused and looked grave. "I should tell you, before I go further—"

"We alreadae know yer a faoladh, son," Crannach assured him.

"I am also a member of the royal house of Cellaig."

The abbess gasped and began fanning herself.

"Forgive me—I should have formally introduced myself." Aodhgan stood firm and bowed low. "My name is Aodhgan MacCellaig. I'm an emissary for the king of Osraige."

"Ossory?" Vindimir exclaimed. "But have you really come so far?"

"The prince was captured and taken to Ath Cliath. I am my king's huntsman and Lord Protector, and was sent to find him, but just like Myndil, his scent ended at the river. I fear both of them might have been taken across the sea on slave ships, either to be sold or to be made mercenaries in the coming war."

"Another war," the abbess sighed. "The last one displaced so many and brought the raids upon the abbeys, including the one I lost..." She pined and pinned herself to Aodhgan's iron arm.

Aodhgan felt her warm cheek pressed against him, and his complexion deepened. "I'm sorry to hear of it," he said, in a tender drone, putting his enormous hand on her shoulder.

"If Myndil's gone across the sea," said Crannach, "is there anae wae o' findin' him?"

"There is, but I would need to send a message to my king. I cannot leave the island without his permission, and he has spies across the sea who might be better able to help."

"We can furnish you with writing materials," said Vindimir. "Perhaps you might like to stay here until you receive a reply. Myndil might return in that time, if God permits, and as abbot has already reconciled himself to the misery of added company, I'm sure you are welcome to stay as long as you like."

The abbess clasped her hands around her breasts and said a silent prayer, pleading with God to let Aodhgan stay. She liked his attentiveness, his regal air and considerate character recommending him to be as warm and pure of heart as Myndil could be. She liked the abbey, but it was a retired place, far away from the bustle and animation of even a village. No one here was unkind to her, but no one went out of their way to appeal to her particular passions either. There was nothing wrong in two divine servants coming together under one roof or under one blanket— Brother Crannach had Sister Iarlaith, and why should she not have an colossal shape-changing wolfman to warm her bed in the evenings? She frotted against him, the side of her breast delicately grazing his arm, and though Aodhgan said nothing, a slight blush crept up the back of his neck and tinged his ears.

"I accept your generous offer," Aodhgan decided, "but I won't be idle. I promise to make myself useful. I will sleep in whichever room you allow me, and I will keep to wherever you tell me to go."

"Go wherever ye like, son," Crannach insisted. "This used to be onlae an orphanage, but now that it's an abbae, anaebodae can go wherever they liek in the house o' God."

"You're very considerate, but I always prefer asking when I am not at home. My people are used to seeing me, but I understand my presence can be undesirable and somewhat irksome to those who know about our curse. We have long since gained control of our change, so you need not be alarmed."

"We're not," said the three laity, in unison.

Aodhgan could not but laugh. "Now I see where Myndil inherits his fearlessness from."

"Yer no' frightenin', son. Aye, yer a big man," Crannach acknowledged, "but yer no' half as terrifyin' as some o' the others in the collection."

Crannach indicated Ozzy the Wight, who was standing by the graveyard, trimming the bog myrtle and pruning the primroses. He would have waved, but one of the rabble working on the building had trod on his blooming sorrel, and he was currently wondering whether he ought not prune a few feet from one who did not deserve them. Over the neighbouring hedgerow, a flaming blue head bobbed along the top of the fence, and after it trudged Mr Dullahan, his headless body slumping along, with arms outstretched and neck blazing. His head bounced in front of the nisser, who kicked it away for having spoiled the piggin of milk he had just collected, his little red hat flumping and tiny fists writhing in violent anger. There were other peaceable inmates to indicate, but these were enough to convince Aodhgan that his presence here was by no means irregular.

"Are all of them here because of Myndil?" Aodhgan asked.

"Yes and no," said Vindimir. "Many of them came here by themselves, but Myndil kept them here when we would have otherwise expelled them. He simply must make friends with everything—whether that thing is interested in being friends with him is another matter—but if you think this is impressive, you should see what sleeps under Myndil's bed."

"I admit," Aodhgan continued, "I came here partly to learn more about him. He told me he grew up here, and I became curious to know this place better."

"No' much tae know, reallae," said Crannach, shrugging. "Raised Myndil from a lad. He came tae us when he was just a wean, told us his name and all the things he lieked, and hasnae stopped talkin' since."

"But there seems something strange about him, something providential. I'm sure you might know him differently, but to me he seems to be wholly undeterred by anything."

"Aye, that's him," Crannach simpered. "Wouldnae say he's fearless as much as he's just unaware."

"He seems to have no prejudices, no concerns of anything bad happening to him, and he seems completely incapable of seeing evil in anybody else."

"That is simply how he is," said Vindimir. "We thought, when we were first acquainted with him, that he might have been kicked in the head by a pony, but he isn't simple. On the contrary, Myndil is always eager to learn and does everything with a zeal, as long as a friend can be got out of it—but he was always going up to faeries and introducing himself and asking whether they should like to stay for dinner or listen to him as he read his book. From the time he was just a small boy, it was always much the same."

It took Aodhgan a moment to realize: why was Myndil so inured to what most people had been taught to dread? In living among creatures that others would find abhorrent or distressing, he trained himself to accept and was rewarded with infinite forbearance. He became the bastion of friendship because he harboured no presumptions about anybody, and Aodhgan blessed such a place that could produce so devoted a servant, wishing more people would come to the abbey, even if only to see that leniency of character and mutual consideration was possible.

"He told me something..." said Aodhgan, and there was a hesitation as he said it, "He told me that God speaks to him."

Brother Vindimir instantly coloured and turned away.

"He claimed he was speaking to God when I was with him and that God was answering him."

"Was he?" Vindimir asked, genuinely astonished. "But how is that possible? That is—I don't mean to suggest he was lying—I don't think Myndil is even capable of telling falsehoods—but can he really be hearing the Lord?"

"I thought the voice might have been something he imagined, something he invented to keep himself from being lonely on the road, but after spending time with him, I'm not so sure."

"Was he still speaking to God when you left him? What happened when you saw him last?"

Aodhgan gave him a flat look. "He kicked me into a ditch."

Crannach held his sides and laughed. "Yer pullin' our leg, son. Myndil's as weak as a fly. How'd ye let him push a big man like yersel' intae a ditch?"

"Next you will tell us Myndil fought a band of king's men all by himself," Vindimir fleered.

"He did—well, I did," Aodhgan asserted, "but he had to get past them somehow."

He told them the whole as they walked, the two brothers listening but hardly believing a word of the story, and the abbess clutching her breast and attending with speaking solicitation, her features engaged, her disbelief withheld.

"So, if Ah might ask," said Crannach, when Aodhgan had done, "does yer transformation have tae dae with the moon?"

Aodhgan smiled. "No. It can be done at will."

"So, if yer spirit's oot bein' a wolf, what happens to yer bodae?"

"Now you know why Myndil kicked me into the ditch."

They laughed amongst themselves, ready to understand and ask questions, Aodhgan as eager as any of them to fulfil their curiosity, when a familiar sensation suddenly came over him. His senses roused, his instincts fired, and in a blur of motion, he turned and thrust his iron fist at the wall behind him. The building shook, the stone cracked under the force of his might, and from the shadow came a familiar, "OOOWWWEE." A tendril ebbed out of the shade and begged surrender. "S' jus me!"

Aodhgan sighed and retracted his fist. "Why are you in my shadow, co-walker?"

"Jus' came by to say hullo, dun Aw!"

The shade peeled itself from the stone and wafted into shape, making a polite bow, its amorphous head curling in a respectable cue.

"'S me Thistlewraithe," the co-walker announced.

"Thistlewraithe?" said Aodhgan charily.

"Aye, 's right. Gave me a name, so now Aw'm all 'fficial-like." The shade seemed proud of himself. "Aw'm 'fficial haunter o' the abbey, me, an' Aw get to haunt o' them louts what're werkin' on the buildin'." The shadow raised a tendril to where its mouth should have been and wheezed a *hur hur hur!* "Aw already made 'em drop their hammer twice. When they's good and knackered, Aw'm gonna pull their hair and make 'em think all the others did it."

"Well, as long as you are out of my shadow and not hurting anyone." Aodhgan examined the wall. "I will fix that," he promised, running his finger along the crack, "or I'll make you do it."

"Me!" said Thistlewraithe, offended. "Why me?"

"Because you stalked me and made me break it."

"Aw didn't do nuthin'! Yew did thayt yewerself."

Clemency reigned, however, Aodhgan remembering Myndil's lesson of forbearance, and though a creature that could haunt someone to death should be given no quarter, he was inclined to allow a little mercy on behalf of his hosts.

"Very well," said Aodhgan, composing himself, "I will fix it myself and let you go on about your haunting," and then, in a threatening growl, "but stay out of my shadow."

"Aye, aye, go tell the bees," Thistlewraithe moaned, "no need to huff at me all bruzzle-like. Aw'll keep to the rabble and the abbot besides." The shade looked as though it was smiling. "Think he's startin' to like bein' haunted, him. Didn't let him sleep a wink, and he's already thankin' his god for the misery."

Aodhgan said he was glad that the co-walker found a good home and wished him well, watching the tenebrous figure meld into the shadow by the door and vanish. A few short screams down the corridor told them where he went, and they exchanged a few knowing glances before continuing toward the dormitory.

They came to one of the vacant rooms—the one right beside Abbess Bhaldruithe's, and bid Aodhgan to enter. Aodhgan was forced to incline his head, to keep from hitting his forehead against the post, but the ceiling was high enough, and there was only a bed and a desk for his use, giving ample room for him to move about. Vindimir went to fetch some clean linen, and the abbess pretended to be off finding him writing implements for his letters while she was actually standing in the hallway and listening through the door, leaving Crannach to show him round.

"Well, 'tis no' much," said Crannach, surveying the meager furnishings, "but there's a good window and the latrine's no' far."

"It is more than enough," was Aodhgan's indebted assurance. "I hope not to intrude upon you for more than a few days."

"Hopefullae the lad'll be back by then. Ah doan't mind tellin' ye, Ah doan't like that Myndil was sent awae. Ah know he needed tae see the world before bein' ordained, but Ah'll be a wee bit selfish and sae Ah miss him an' doan't want him out there knowin' there's a war comin' oan."

"I hope he does return before anything happens, but I have faith that whatever danger Myndil gets himself into, he will have friends who can get him out of it."

A small smile was exchanged here, and Crannach was about to leave him, to let him settle in, when curiosity came over him. "Er—Ah doan't mean tae pry," said he awkwardly, "but if ye doan't mind me askin', what's yer wolf form look liek?"

Aodhgan seemed pleasantly surprised. "I wouldn't mind showing you." He sat at the edge of the bed and removed his boots. "I will be perfectly conscious when in my other form, so don't be alarmed."

"Ah won't be."

Aodhgan smiled and lay down upon the bed. It was too small for him, like most things were, his large and heavy legs hanging off the bottom end, his shoulders wide enough to fill the whole frame. He clasped his hands across his chest and closed his eyes, and when he exhaled, a transparent outline lifted from him and began to warp, swirling in a numinous haze until a shape formed.

The flickering light from within the room drew the abbess' attention. The suddenly silence within the room touched her curiosity, but when she peered round the door to see the monstrous wolf, her furtiveness was poorly rewarded: she gasped and clutched her breast, the horrious lupine figure towering over Brother Crannach on its hind legs, its claws protracting, its colossal chest heaving, its mouth frothing. It breathed in a low growl, its steps heavy against the stone ground, its long tail sweeping over the bed, its eyes glowing in restrained rage. It straightened, its head grazing the ceiling, and for a moment, its eyes fixed on the abbess, who immediately fled, running down the hall as quickly as her terror would admit. She was sorry to have looked, sorry to have seen so exquisite a specimen transform into so grueful a creature. How can I share a bed with such a beast? was the prevailing question as she escaped into the adjoining hall, and Aodhgan, afraid that he would have terrified someone but glad to have the first shock of it over, retracted his form, withdrawing the physical exhibition and letting the wolf wither and disperse.

"Lord's Light an' o'!" Crannach whistled, rapt by the prospect. "Tha's impressive. If Ah didnae know it was ye behind it, Ah mighta emptied mahsel'."

Aodhgan sat up and simpered. "I hope it did not upset you much." He glanced at the door as he spoke; he knew the abbess would not be coming back anytime soon. "I can control my transformation, but sadly I cannot change what my wolf form looks like. I wish it weren't so monstrous."

"Aye, 'tis good havin' it tha' wae, son. God gave ye tha' form to frighten aff yer enemies and protect yer kin."

Aodhgan supposed Crannach was right: his wolf form had helped Myndil breach the palace, though it could not keep the abbess from running away.

"Er—If Ah might ask," said Crannach, scratching his head, "yer wolf form is even larger than yer human form. Where dae ye put it o'?"

134

"It's a divine manifestation," Aodhgan explained, putting his boots on again. "I release my spirit into the form and concentrate to maintain it."

"So it's a projection' o' yer soul, strengthened by yer heart?"

Aodhgan paused and seemed musing. "I never thought about it that way."

They were interrupted by Brother Vindimir. He returned with new bedclothes and a few firm pillows, and came in asking, "Did something happen? I saw the abbess hastening down the hall. She usually doesn't run for anything that is not the promise of a cuddle."

Aodhgan seemed ashamed, and Crannach realized she must have seen the wolf.

"Was nothin'," said Crannach. "Jus' a spider."

Vindimir sighed and rolled his eyes. "She found one in her vale during prayers and tried to have me excavate it for her. If only she could find prudence in there."

He left to retrieve the writing implements for Aodhgan, as there was little hope of the abbess coming back, and Crannach put a hand on Aodhgan's shoulder.

"Ye know, son," Crannach began, with warm consideration, "Ah doan't know what ye think o' yersel', but just tae tell ye, yer much more terrifyin' in yer human form."

Aodhgan gazed at the ground and smiled fondly to himself. "You're not the first person to tell me that."

"Who was the first then?"

Myndil wended his way toward the eastern shore. He had no oars, no sail, and no free hands to paddle with; he had only his hope and the constant dependence that god would see him safely on shore. The waves made by approaching slave ships helped to move him along, and by midmorning, the currach drifted into the coast and landed on the northern part of the shore, nestling in a bed of raised rocks. There was an estuary to the north, the mouth of a river Myndil did not know, and to the south was a port town, one that dealt in foreign trade, the slave ships from the west and the south lining the shore. Myndil stood from the currach and walked onto the beach, descrying the hundreds of men crowding the stocks. Cries of traders foretold sales and prices, new heads were being ushered in from arriving galleys, and though sense told him to stay far away from the port, his curiosity brought him closer.

Fortunately, no one seemed much interested in him, the business of buying and selling slaves much more important to everyone who landed there, but Myndil would like to know where he was, and more importantly, he would like to know how to get back. He neared enough to hear a conversation, one being shouted between two traders. They were arguing about prices, one for the going rate of mercenaries and the other defending the value of slaves.

"I must be somewhere on the 'over there' island," Myndil determined, "the one where all the slaves in Ath Cliath seem to go. Aodhgan said something about that—" He thoughts turned to Aodhgan, and he hoped he was able to climb out of the ditch. "He must be so worried for me," he moped, watching the chained gangs march down from the ships. "I hope I see him again. His nose can find anyone. I hope he finds me somehow."

He sighed and sulked and kicked the sand, wishing that they had not been separated, when two men came toward him from the port. They were both small men, hardly bigger than himself, each dressed in leather vests and leather breeches, one bald and a bit wider in the middle, and the other narrow and ferret-faced. They did not look particularly dangerous, only a little unpolished, and Myndil thought this was a safe time to make friends.

"Hello!" Myndil called to them. "Yes, hello there! Thank you for coming up to me. You see, I don't think I'm suppose to be here. Someone hit me on the head and put me in a boat, and I drifted here on my own. Can I ask you to untie me, please? These ropes are beginning to chafe."

The two men looked as though they were trying to work out what the word chafe meant.

"Ow, yeh?" one man squinted. "Shame, that."

"Aye," the other nodded, "you look like you belong here, friend."

"I do? Where is 'here' anyway?"

"Alt Clut," the wider one offered, "western coast."

"Or Strath-Clota," said the narrow one, "as we say in the south. Ol' Owain's king o' these lands, but prolly not fa long."

"Aye, war's kickin' up, and guess who's gonna be fightin' innit."

Myndil could hardly guess. "Is it you?"

"No."

"Is it all those men gathering over there?"

"It is, but guess who's joinin' 'em, eh?"

Myndil blinked, and the two men began to groan.

"You!" said the wider one, pointing at Myndil.

"Oh, thank you for the invitation," said Myndil cordially, "but I'm not a soldier."

"That don't matter," said the narrow one. "Long as you look like you can fight, in you go."

"But how would that help a war? Isn't the object of a war to have men who can win?"

The wider one shrugged. "S'just numbers innit, son. Kings need numbers, they send their orders, and we fill 'em."

"Nothin personal, see?" the narrow one nodded. "Jus bissniss."

"Oh, well, in that case." Myndil turned around and wiggled his fingers. "But could I ask you to untie me first?"

"Sure, sure." The wider one came forward and grabbed hold of the ropes. "Before I undo you, could you just breathe into his rag and tell me what it smells like?"

Myndil bent down, and the cloth was pressed hard against his nose. He muffled a bit and waited, but nothing more happened. The cloth was removed from his face and looked at and wondered over.

"How's he not goin' under?" the narrow one asked, scratching his head. "Should smell like mummified remains—" He took a whiff and his eyes watered. "Ow, that is moulderin'!"

"It just smells like strong vinegar really," said Myndil, wriggling his nose.

"Ere—that's prime stuff! That's supposed to knock you out."

"Oh. Well, I've already been knocked out today, so perhaps I've had my allocation of being unconscious for the day."

"Well," said the wider one, jerking him roughly, "we're taking you in."

"Oh, that's very kind of you. I could really use a blanket and something to eat."

"No, son," the narrow one explained. "We're napping you, see? Gonna sell you on the slave markets and that."

"Oh," said Myndil, realizing these men were bandits. "I don't think I should like that very much. Will I still get a blanket and some food?"

"Can't say you will, son."

"Oh, that's rather uncharitable. If you're going to take people prisoner like that, the least you could do is keep them warm and feed them so they're worth more money."

One bandit leaned over to the other and said, in a low voice, "He's got a point."

"'Ere, you reckon we should be takin' this one?" the other bandit asked. "He seems a bit upside in the apple cart."

"He looks right enough. He'll bring in ten silver, if we can pass him off as a mercenary."

"I'm not a mercenary," said Myndil. "I'm a missionary."

"That the same thing, only you just pronouncin' the word funny?" the wider bandit asked.

"No. I'm a mi-shon-eh-ree. Here, I'll show you."

He leaned over and moved his bound hands to the side, reaching for his book with a free finger. The book was a little damp at the corners from being sloshed about the currach, but he was able to turn to a page, and began to read. "AND ON THE THIRD DAY, THE LORD SAID—"

The bandit grabbed the sides of their heads and writhed in pain.

"Argh! What is that?" one cried.

"It's like a chisel in me brain!" whined the other.

Myndil frowned at his book. "Really? Is my reading that painful? No wonder everyone gets so angry when I try to practice my oration."

"I reckon you could kill a man with that. Mercenary, missionary—you could make a man take his own ears off."

Myndil hummed and pursed his lips to one corner of his mouth. "Let me try another way." He hemmed and read the same passage. "AnD oN ThE tHIrD dAY, tHE lOrD sAId," trying a more mechanical tone.

"'Ere," one bandit said to the other, covering his ears, "we gotta make him stop that."

Myndil continued reading in the background, his oration wavering in pitch.

"Maybe we could slit his throat?" the other bandit offered.

"Nah, nah. That might kill him. We won't get money if he's dead. We just gotta find a way to in-co-pa-si-tate him, see?"

"Could bleed him." The bandit shrugged. "Bleedin's natural."

"He'll be too pale, and we won't get good money fer him."

"Could drown him a bit." His friend gave him a look. "Wha? S'only water. Multipurpose and all natural and that."

Myndil went on. "AnD oN ThE FOurTh dAY, tHE lOrD sAId—"

"Sorry, son," the wide bandit said, grabbing his arm and facing him toward the sea. "We're gonna give you a bit of a bath before we sell you."

"The traders don't like dead slaves," said the narrow one, "but they don't mind unconscious ones."

Myndil was in the midst of explaining that he would love a good wash, only did not like the sea much, when they forced him forward onto his knees and plunged his head into the oncoming waves.

"Pbbhthth—I'm not fond of sea water," Myndil coughed. "It's so very cold and bitter—pbththbt— Ungh, it went up my nose, and now it's going to burn me—and it's beginning to burn. When I first came to the orphanage, one of the other children pushed me into the sea, because he was a brute and was angry that I had got a new bed—pbpththth—and Brother Crannach had to come and pluck me out of the water, only pulled me up by my waist and I flumped upside down—pbthtbtht—and all the sea water went into my nose, and I swallowed much of it." Myndil wretched. "It's the most appalling taste, but once the nasal burn stops, my sinal passages are delightfully clear. When we have colds, Sister Iarlaith warms the sea water and makes us put out faces over the steaming pot."

"Gotta bring him in farther to keep his head under," said one of the bandits, lugging Myndil further down the beach. "If he don't go under soon, I'm gonna bury him here and let the tide take him out."

They hauled him into the water, pushing down against the back of his neck, forcing him to take the crest of the wave head on. The water rushed upon him, lashing him in the face, his professions and pleas drowned by plangent rote of the waves, his mouth blowing bubbles in the tide as he talked. They pushed him in farther, keeping his face under the surface, and Myndil told them it was getting dangerously difficult to breathe, but the bubbles only echoed muted sounds, and Myndil felt himself beginning to succumb to the tide.

"God," he entreated, when the water pulled back from the shore momentarily, "please save me from these men. They are rather mean and even though I've told them I don't like sea water, they will make me drink it."

"Shuddup already," one of the bandits grunted, forcing him down at the shoulder. "Never seen a captive what won't drown o' natural causes when we want him to."

"Told you bleedin' was natural," the other argued, "but you wanted to do it the hard way."

They held Myndil down by the back of his head and had almost managed to silence him when a giant hand clasped each of their necks and lifted them into the air. They were hurled toward the shore, the faint "AAAAaaaaaaaaa—" echoing down the coast, and Myndil felt himself being lifted out of the sea. It was the same iron grip, the same insuperable strength holding him up and smacking against his back, getting him to cough out the water he swallowed. He was dazed for a moment, his view clouded by a confusion of sea water and sound, his mouth drooling out the overpowering saline taste.

"Are you all right?" he heard someone ask.

It was a familiar voice, the same resonant purl, only slightly higher in pitch, more blithesome and less severe.

"Let me tend to these two first," said the voice, lowering to a menacing growl.

Myndil was put down well away from the water and was given a moment to regain himself. He shook his head, blew a strand of kelp out of his nose, and tapped the sides of his head to clear the water from his ears. The sound of two heavy fists pounding flesh and cracking bones drew his attention, and in the muddle of consciousness, he saw a familiar hulking outline. He was about to call out, "Aodhgan?" when he found himself face to face with a not-exactly-Aodhgan.

"You're safe now, but you've swallowed a fair amount of water," said the not-exactly-Aodhgan. "Lean forward and try to bring up as much as you can."

The colossal hand on his back felt like Aodhgan's, but there was a gentleness missing, a tender awareness of his own insurmountable strength that was wanting here. The hand slapped him on the back, and Myndil coughed out a bit more water. "Just as unpleasant as I remember," Myndil grimaced, slottering at the lingering taste.

"I'm not aware that being drowned is ever pleasant," the not-exactly-Aodhgan simpered.

Myndil was righted and the symbol of Saint Paudrig came into view, the vibrant three-leaf sorrel embroidered onto a dark blue sleeve. It could not be Aodhgan, but he had the same grey eyes, the same square maw, the same soaring height, the same muscular arms—it must be someone in the same family—or was it the same pack, Myndil thought to himself, because they are all werewolves, but I suppose it would depend on which form each favoured more... His hair was a bit lighter than Aodhgan's, more of a dark brown than black flecked with hints of silver. He seemed younger, the smile more self-assured and the character more cordial, and though his stature was gargantuan, he was still not as tall as Aodhgan. He was busy twisting the arms and legs of the bandits around each other and doing it with little apparent effort, the joints and bones snapping with a mere turn of his wrist.

"Forgive me for not reaching you sooner," said the possible-relation of Aodhgan. "I was hiding amongst the rocks and was waiting for the traders to move farther off." He stood at full height and rolled his shoulders, the screams of agony from the two bandits well satisfying him. He lifted the two twisted forms and tossed them into the sea, their gurgling shrieks muted by the waves, and then turned his attention toward the tie holding Myndil's hands behind his back. "Are you much hurt?" he asked, ripping the rope apart and freeing him.

"I'm not hurt at all really," said Myndil, smiling up at him. "The taste in my mouth is regrettable, but no cuts or bruises, I think. Thank you for ridding of those men, though I don't think they will be much able to swim with their arms and legs tied about one another."

Myndil's saviour made a charming grin. "I sincerely hope not."

He was a handsomer iteration of Aodhgan, one unaltered by the anxiety of responsibility and age. There was a regal air about him, the same noble sensibility that Aodhgan cherished, only unlike Aodhgan his stateliness could not be concealed, his head high, his chest lifted, his aspect proud and blithesome.

The saviour introduced himself with a gallant bow. "My name is Eochaid," said he, performing the same motions as Aodhgan, the world warping around his immense shoulders.

Myndil listened to the name and felt his ears break. "Can you repeat that, please? I thought I heard you say yo-khudz—or was it yo-kheth?"

"Yo-khudz is how I say it, but you may use whichever is easier for you."

"And how is that spelled?"

He rumbled in rolling mirth. "I see you've learned not to trust our names. Now you know how we confuse the Northmen: we give them names to choke on, and they stay out of our kingdom. And what is your name, if I may know it?"

"Myndil—but Y and then I, and not mine-dil, but minn-duhll."

"Myndil," Eochaid repeated, with a gratified nod. "I'm very pleased to rescue you."

140

"I am glad to be rescued, thank you."

"We both came from across the sea, so I hope I can return you safely home. I must return to Erie, to let my father know I'm alive. I was captured by slavers who invaded our woods and brought me here to be sold either as a slave or a mercenary at a high price. I'm quite impressed with how much one of the slavers was willing to pay for me. I never thought myself worth as much as ten cattle and several weights of silver, but I will have to bear that in mind if I ever wish to auction myself."

"I don't think I was being talked of as worth half so much," said Myndil, a little disappointed.

Eochaid gave his shoulder a hardy pat, and Myndil almost collapsed.

"Be grateful they thought you worthy enough not to kill you," said Eochaid, righting him. "Had you been deemed worthless, they would have killed you before I could reach you. It is nothing to compare yourself to. I am only worth so much because of what I am." He paused and made half a sigh. "I don't mean to alarm you, but I should tell you out of courtesy–"

"That you're from Osraige and you've been cursed by Saint Paudrig and you're a werewolf," said Myndil, smiling.

Eochaid seemed only too astonished. "How did you know that?"

"Aodhgan told me."

He gripped Myndil's robes and held him up. "You know my cousin?" Eochaid exclaimed, in an ecstasy. "How do you know him? Did he send you?"

"Yes–well, no–well, God sent me to you–rather God sent him to me–I think he was looking for you, and he found me instead, and we went to Ath Cliath, he to search for you and me to speak to Olaf, to try to get to him to hear about God and listen to me read from my book, which he was very rude about–but Olaf accused me of being a spy and said he was going to bring his men to reclaim his land, and then he put me in a boat and sent me across the sea, but Aodhgan got left behind and I'm not sure of what happened to him, though I'm sure he's all right, because he is so large and it hurts to walk into him. He showed me his wolf form and then fought all the king's guard, biting and gnashing at them and striking them with his great and terrible claws, and then I kicked his body into a ditch."

Eochaid put his hands on his knees and bent over, succumbing with mirth. "It is so wonderful it must be true," said he, wiping the tears from his eyes. "I cannot wait to mock him for this. Out of all the hunts and fights my cousin and I have shared together, I have never once kicked him into a ditch."

"Well, it was more of a friendly foot nudge really–he is so incredibly heavy, I could not lift him at all, not even his shoulders! Are all the men in your family afflicted with shoulders wider than doorways?"

"Some of us are," Eochaid smiled, displaying his iron might.

"I told him I needed to speak to Olaf, or I should never be ordained, and then he told me Olaf would never listen to me about God, because he had his own God and didn't want to follow the God of his enemies, but then he told me about Aethelstan and how Olaf hated him for taking over his lands here, which we are standing in now, I imagine, and that Olaf wanted to reclaim the land but was not able to because he just returned from a campaign to the south and captured a king and lost many of his men doing it, but as I enraged him, and God told me that Olaf would be punished for not believing in him, Olaf is taking all the rest of his men and is going to be invading in the next few days."

"That's why there are so many slaves being sold as mercenaries." Eochaid gazed down the shoreline, his eyes unconsciously counting the hundred of heads crowding round the stocks. "Olaf will not have enough men to win without either mercenaries or a truce between the other kings, and I don't know that any of them would want to ally themselves with him just now. I heard a few of the slavers speaking about a meeting between the kings on this island. I suppose the kings' men are buying every able body and presenting them as part of their forces. I was brought here yesterday and was able to gather some information while I was in captivity. I escaped at night and have been hiding amongst the rocks, waiting for my cousin or one of my father's agents to come, but Aodhgan has sent me you," smiling down at Myndil, "and you seemed to be on a mission."

"I have to speak to Aethelstan and tell him that Olaf is coming sooner than he expects."

"Why would you wish to tell him? Do you think you can stop the war? The battle has been a long time coming. I'm surprised it has not happened yet."

"Olaf was fighting someone in the south—another king, Aodhgan said—and Olaf had only just come back from capturing him. Aodhgan says Aethelstan is a man of God. Perhaps if I tell him God does not want him to fight, he will not go to war."

BUT GOD DOES WANT THIS WAR. GOD WANTS ALL THE KINGS OF THE ISLANDS TO WAR WITH EACH OTHER. KING OLAF COMES WITH A THOUSAND TROOPS, AND THOU HAST MADE IT SO.

"Oh, hello God!" Myndil chimed, waving to the ether. "Thank you for sending Eochaid to help me. That was very kind of you."

YES. GOD SENT HIM TO THEE OUT OF MERCY. OF COURSE. AHEM.

"But God, surely in your benevolence and great clemency, you would rather not have people die when they would come to you willingly?"

IF THEY ARE DEAD, THEIR SOULS COME TO ME REGARDLESS. WIN-WIN FOR GOD.

"But there will be so much bloodshed, God, and would not you prefer your subjects to come to you in peace, only after they have lived a goodly life in service of the Lord?"

PRIVATION AND PENURY NOURISH ME. GOD WANTS DISTRUCTION AND CHAOS TO WEED OUT THE NON-BELIEVERS. SEEK OUT AETHELSTAN AND SPEAK UNTO HIM: YE, THE LORD HATH CHOSEN THEE TO LEAD THE DOMINION.

"You don't know Aethelstan," said Eochaid, interrupting. "He calls himself the Lord's Right Hand and thinks he's a divine agent meant to conquer every kingdom from here to Erie. He believes God speaks to him."

"But God speaks to all of us," was Myndil's plaintive reply.

"And we all speak to God when we want to ask for His Divine Grace, but when many kings claim they are the chosen by the Lord, there can only be one victor there, Myndil. Aethelstan believes God has chosen him to be High King of the Isles." Eochaid folded his arms and looked across the sea. "Belief is well and good when there is no pride involved, but rulers should not declare themselves divine under God. My father never claimed to be chosen by God when he took his throne. He is blessed to be King of Osraige, but he knows that is a privilege that can be taken away should he fail to protect his people."

Myndil blinked. "Your father is the king?"

"He is, and I am prince, and my cousin is my father's royal huntsman and Lord Protector."

"Oh."

There was an awkward pause, Eochaid sensing some misunderstanding in Myndil's looks.

"I don't think it's wise to speak to Aethelstan, but we cannot stay here," Eochaid continued, spying another two galleys coming in over the horizon. "If you want to try to convince the kings of this island not to have this war, I will take you to them."

"You will?" said Myndil, his eyes brightening.

"I know they are meeting northeast of here, in a place called Scone, the seat of the kings of Alba."

"Well, it is little wonder they should have the royal seat there. Scones are delicious, especially with jam and the clotted cream. Brother Crannach is originally from Alba, and just to make him feel at home, Sister Iarlaith does scones for him every holy day, and they really are perfect the way she does them, not dry, beautifully crisp on the bottom, and golden on the top."

"I wish we would be promised scones by going there," Eochaid laughed, "but Scone is just the coronation seat of the king. Alba is quite large, and the king never remains in one place long." He turned eastward and scanned the rambling expanse. "It will be a long distance to run. I don't know if we will make it time to meet them, but we must try. If I can get you close to them, what will you say to them to get them to hear you?"

"I can tell them I have news from Olaf. Olaf already accused me of being a spy for Aethelstan, so perhaps if I pretend to be a spy after all, Aethelstan might let me explain things to him, as long as I offer him information about how many men Olaf is coming with."

"That's quite clever. Are you sure you're not really a spy?" Eochaid sniffed Myndil's hair. "You don't smell like one."

"If I am a spy, I certainly have no idea of it. And I should be a very poor spy, getting captured and being almost drowned by bandits."

"But perhaps that was your plan all along," said Eochaid wryly. "Perhaps that was a trick, made to lure me from the rocks. You might want to tell your informants the whereabouts of a missing prince."

"I really don't think I do."

Eochaid could not but laugh here. "Whatever we do here on this island, Myndil, we should stay together. We might not want to be near the shore when the landing party arrives, but we should remain close to each other until my cousin comes."

"I hope Aodhgan does come," said Myndil wistfully. "I desperately want to see him again and tell him I am sorry about kicking him."

"I am sure he didn't mind. I've done much worse, though nothing so amusing."

"But if Aodhgan doesn't come, how will we get back across the sea?"

"We could hide until nightfall and steal one of the currachs along the jetty," said Eochaid, pointing to a line of boats in the distance. "It will be hard going, but you made it here in a small currach. There is no need to worry— I know my cousin. He will never stop searching until he has found us. He is my father's huntsman for a reason. He has my scent, and I'm sure he has yours if you've spent much time with him, and once he finds a trail, he never lets it go. Here, let's help him." Eochaid grabbed the embroidered emblem on his sleeve and tore it off with a sharp jolt. "I will leave this here for him to find," said he, placing the corner of the cloth under a rock. "You should leave something of yours."

Myndil only had his robe and his book, and while he liked Aodhgan and would do everything to assist him, he could not bring himself to rip the robes he had taken such good care of. They had been so difficult to keep clean—but his belt could be left, and he untied it from his hips and put it with Eochaid's sleeve.

"And just in case," said Myndil. He rubbed his hands together until they were warm, opened them and blew across his palms, trying to spread his scent along the shore.

Eochaid almost choked with mirth. "I never thought about leaving a scent that way. That should be enough, as long as we keep out of any woods and there is no heavy rain to wash away our scent. Come, let's be off for Scone before those galleys reach the shore."

Myndil was still rather disappointed about there being no scones in Scone—why should scones be named after a place that did not have them? "But if it's quite far and you said the kings are meeting presently, how are we to travel there so quickly?"

"I will carry us," said Eochaid, sitting down. "I am the fastest out of all the wolves in my family, and I never tire of running."

"But I cannot run half as fast as you, I'm sure. How will I get to Scone?"

"You're going to ride me."

Myndil looked quite blank. "In your wolf form?"

"Yes," Eochaid laughed, "although I could easily carry you on my shoulders."

"But you will leave your human form behind if you change."

"That's where you are going to help me."

"Oh, I love helping!" Myndil clapped. "What am I going do?"

"You are going to cradle me. Sit behind me. I am going to lean my back against yours, and all you have to do is hook your arms round with mine and make certain I don't fall."

"I hope I'll be able to," said Myndil, sitting down behind him, their backs touching. "You are rather heavy."

"If you cannot hold me, I can always carry my human form in my mouth, but I won't be able to run as quickly, having to think about not biting myself."

Myndil inched closer and reached behind himself, Eochaid linking his enormous arms in his. Myndil knew they must look ridiculous, he being thin and wiry, struggling to hook his arms around and trying to prop himself against a man who must have carried two hundred pounds of muscle at least.

"There—" Myndil grunted, trying to hold his arms together, locking Eochaid's elbows at his sides.

"Good. I'm going to change. My body will fall against yours, so lean more against me."

Myndil pressed his feet into the ground and pushed his back against Eochaid's, thinking this would be enough to support him, but he was so much larger than him, Eochaid's shoulders well above Myndil's head, that once Eochaid began to relinquish his human form, the weight of his body was overpowering, Myndil having to dig his heels into the ground for leverage to keep himself from being crushed.

"I can hold you," Myndil wrenched, desperately working his legs, "but I don't know for how long."

"You won't be struggling long," said Eochaid, his voice deepening. "Don't be alarmed."

"I—won't—be," Myndil heaved.

He felt Eochaid's body slump, and Myndil immediately pushed back against him, trying to get his human form to fall forward and relieve him of the excruciating weight. He was soon relieved of the weight, however, when he found himself suddenly sitting on a broad and burly back. It was tunneling under his legs, it was rising and lifting him up, and Myndil instinctively grabbed whatever he could to steady himself. He caught a thick tuft of bruneous fur in each hand.

"There should be a comfortable sitting place in the middle of my back," said Eochaid's voice, in a resonant growl.

Eochaid raised his nowl, and Myndil slipped downward, settling into the groove in his lower back.

"Oh, that is quite comfortable," Myndil exclaimed, his legs disappearing into the three coats of fur. "Your wolf looks a bit different from Aodhgan's."

The features were not half so horrific as those of his cousin: his large eyes seemed rounder and less sinister, his teeth and claws were shorter, and his ears though longer were much softer. Where Aodhgan fur patterns were black and white, Eochaid's were brown and black, Aodhgan's soft gradient contrasting with Eochaid's stark stripes, his fur longer and more unkempt but lush and inviting. Myndil could not help pushing his fingers through it repeatedly.

"Is it wrong that I want to continuously pet you and tell you that you are a very good boy?"

145

Myndil asked, combing his fingers through his coat.

"Please do," Eochaid panted. "No one else does. While you're up there, if you could pull apart my mats, I'd be grateful." Eochaid shook out his extensive mane. "I'm shedding my undercoat, and it's beginning to itch."

Myndil did what he could while his arms were still linked around Eochaid's unconscious human form, his fingers picking through the thick coats and tugging at the matted roots.

"That feels incredibly pleasant," Eochaid crooned, his hind leg reaching up to scratch behind his ears.

"I am very good at back scratching," Myndil proclaimed. "Brother Crannach says I have fingernails like daggers. He often asks me to scratch his back, especially in the winter, when he's been sitting by the fire and his skin becomes dry. He's nearly as tall as you are, but not half so hairy."

"You won't find many who rival us in hair, Aodhgan especially." Eochaid gave his haunches a stretch. "Hold tight to me."

"Where shall I hold you so I don't pull on YYYYYOOOOOUUUUUUUUUUUUUUUUUUUU UU—"

A burst of alacrity set the world in motion, Eochaid's lope so quick and powerful that Myndil's legs were almost taken out from under him. They left the coast in a blaze of speed, the violent pattering of Eochaid's paws thundering away, the giant brown wolf dashing across open fields, the wind lashing at Myndil's face, his cheeks fluttering in the wind, his eyes narrow and watering.

"Am I going too quickly for you?" Eochaid bayed, his tongue lolling from the side of his mouth.

Myndil felt the flesh from his eyelids begin to burn. "A little!"

Eochaid measured his pace, still darting across the open fields, but slowing enough that Myndil could sit comfortably on his back while balancing his unconscious form, without needing to clamber for purchase very much. They tore along the main road, the pounding of Eochaid's paws caroming across the moors, the ground surrendering to his stride, the peaks of nearby mountains trembling, the valleys answering the echoes with timid fremescence, the lupine prince dominating the landscape, while his human form made a somnorine snore.

The world blew by in a brush of colour, the towns and villages painted over in a stroke of speed, the defined outlines of rocks and trees fading, but Myndil was beginning to enjoy the sensation, the undulating of the wolf's back, the exhilaration of false flight, the gnats and midges buffeting him and dying against his face. "Is this how you travel at home?" he asked, picking a midge from his teeth.

"This is how we travel on our hunts," Eochaid replied, his fangs gleaming in lupine glee. "My cousin doesn't like to run free as a wolf as much as I do. He says it leaves our bodies vulnerable."

Feeling the weight of Eochaid's human form pressing down on him from behind, Myndil must agree. "I didn't know that Aodhgan was your royal huntsman and that he was looking for a prince."

Eochaid whined subrisively. "I'm sure he was eager to keep it a secret. He cannot tell everyone

146

he meets that he is searching for a kidnapped prince. He's protective of me—he has to be—he's my guardian, appointed by my father when I was born."

He told Myndil of how they grew up together, of how Aodhgan, though twelve years older than him, was made Lord Protector of the royal line from an early age. Aodhgan was the only child of the king's younger brother, and when Aodhgan's father was killed in a sudden attack, his mother having died shortly after he was born, the king adopted him and raised him as his own, hoping that he would be a companion for Eochaid, teach him right principles and keep him from getting into scrapes. Eochaid was born from a late marriage, and he grew to be a good-hearted and loving boy, if not a little impulsive and foolhardy, but under Aodhgan's governance, he became a respectable prince, if not fit for rule just yet than to be molded into prudence in time. The king ordered that there should be no difference between the prince and his cousin, Eochaid learning and obeying all the same rules that any one from the lower ranks would have done, Aodhgan serving as a check to all his instincts, his towering height and indomitable strength always at hand to restrain him. They trained together, wrestling and playing with each other in the woods, the favourite game of all the cousins being 'hide and hunt', all the siblings going to hide and then challenging Aodhgan to find them. Even when Aodhgan was younger, his talent at hunting was renowned, so strong were his senses that he could find anyone miles away even in his human form. Aodhgan always won—even during their monthly hunts, but he would never kill; even from a child, from the first time he had discovered his lupine form, Aodhgan found it difficult to strike something that was smaller and weaker than himself. Killing is what keeps us apart from the wolves, was the lesson the king had taught Aodhgan, and the lesson Aodhgan had taught Eochaid, wanting him to remember that while wolves were noble creatures, they were royal servants of God and not the monstrous abominations that their family curse suggested. Eochaid rarely strayed from Aodhgan's side, honouring his place as guardian and only tormenting him by hunting alone some of the time. He admired his cousin, esteemed his abilities and wished he was more like him: the treasure of Osraige, the beloved fondling of the king, respected by everyone who knew him, feared by many, hailed as the greatest huntsman in the realm—but even with all the advantages of birth and situation, he had few friends and fewer confidants; his position alienated him, his rank impeded him, and his wolf form was so notoriously terrific that despite every honour he had earned, he received no invitations from prospective admirers. Eochaid enjoyed the attention and solicitations from anyone eager to know a young prince, but Aodhgan would rather keep to his obligations, looking after his little cousin, shadowing the crowned prince, making sure all was safe and secure in the kingdom. They were more like brothers than cousins, Eochaid spending every day with Aodhgan, though he was closer in age with his other siblings, but no one could chide him so much or pin him so well, the only person in the kingdom—other than the king—who could tell him what to do and have him listen, who could paw him down whenever he got too bold. Their strength seemed to come from the shared part of the family, the king and his brother also being mountainous men, but no one could hope to equal Aodhgan's senses, gifted to him by his mother's side of the family, herself an excellent tracker before a short illness took her off. From a young age, Aodhgan was told that to be afflicted with the curse of Ossory was to be alone, everyone carrying the curse having to accept it in their own way, some choosing to remain by themselves to keep from passing it on. Those outside the kingdom who knew their secret either shunned them or hunted them, some of the more foolish clans believing that they could become wolves themselves if they caught and killed one of the royal family and paraded about in their hides. This was a myth, of course, circulated by the low and licentious, but did not stop them from killing Aodhgan's father or trying to steal the prince away, hunters looking to either gain the powers of the curse for themselves or gain a fortune by it.

"I was captured by foreign hunters who crossed into our woods," said Eochaid, bounding over a stream. "I went hunting alone against Aodhgan's wishes and got careless. Because he's my guardian and is always supposed to be at my side, I know Aodhgan feels responsible for what happened, though it's entirely my fault. I always enjoy teasing him like that, but this time my japes came back to me, and now my father is in a panic and Aodhgan is away from the kingdom, searching for me everywhere. I know he feels responsible, and I feel terribly about it, but," and there was a glint in his eye, "I wanted to hunt something myself for my betrothed."

"You're getting married?" Myndil exclaimed, clasping his hands together and then quickly grabbing at Eochaid's fur to keep himself from falling. "Oh, that's wonderful! I'm so excited for you!"

"Well," said Eochaid uneasily, "it's an arranged marriage. We had only just met, but I like her and wanted to impress her. She's not from our kingdom and I'm concerned she has no idea what she's getting herself into. I don't know if she likes me as much, but our union will make an alliance between the upper and lower kingdoms. I can only hope she will not 'mind the wolf', as we say."

"I daresay she should like you—she certainly will if you take her travelling this way, only perhaps building yourself a seat for your body, so she doesn't have to carry you might be helpful—and you are very warm and snuggly, and your fur is mighty comfortable. I'm sure that would win anyone's heart on a cold night."

Eochaid yipped in a laugh. "Would that potential wives be as easy and forgiving as you."

"And what about Aodhgan? Is he getting married too?"

"My cousin, though he is much beloved, especially by me and my father, has had no success with suitors."

"But Aodhgan is so delightful and wooly," Myndil contented.

"He is, but there a few difficulties in his way: his not inheriting the throne, his age, his strength, his formidable size, and there is always the wolf. Many who see his wolf form are frightened away by it."

"I'm not afraid of it, and I love Aodhgan—not as much as I love God, of course—but how can anyone not love him once they get to know him?"

"He has no confidence when it comes to approaching women." Eochaid leaped through a series of standing stones and through an issuing meadow. "I will tell you about one instance if you promise never to tell him I told you."

"I swear it never to tell him you told me," Myndil vowed, placing his hand on his book, "though I can't promise I won't hint at it and tell him I feel badly for him about it."

Eochaid brayed and howled, and slowed as they came to a sparse copse. "When a family of nobles from lower Osraige were visiting," Eochaid began, negotiating his path between the trees, "my father asked me to take an interest in them, the two daughters especially. They were of age, and my father thought I might as well get along with them. One of them left the party to look in on her room. She was wandering through the palace by herself—this was all well and good, until she was confronted by my cousin. Aodhgan can distinguish everyone by their footsteps. He didn't recognize hers and thought she might have been an intruder. He did what you think he did."

"Did he introduce himself in his perfectly handsome way?"

"He did that after he showed her the wolf."

"Oh."

"She was horrified, and the look on her face has haunted him since. He did apologize in his handsome way."

"And he does apologize very handsomely," Myndil noted.

"He even recovered it a bit by saving her from a wolf attack during the hunt we had in honour of their visit, but she was always fearful of him and carried wolfsbane with her just to keep him away. He's been hesitant about approaching anyone ever since. My father and I even thought of finding him someone from the continent, someone who didn't know about our curse. I told Aodhgan not to say anything about the wolf, but he refused. He said he could not lie and did not care if he had to be alone forever, but would not marry on the bonds of dishonesty."

"I would marry him," Myndil firmly professed, "if that's what he wanted, of course. I'm not afraid of him, even in his wolf form."

"Wait till he stalks you from the shadows and leaps at you in the middle of the night."

"Is that a game the two of you play?"

"It is one I thought would be fun to play when I was younger, but that ended in me never wanting to roam the woods at night ever again. When we are at home, while his body sleeps, he sends the wolf to patrol our borders. You can sometimes hear the screams of bandits in the distance."

"Seems unfair that he should be alone," Myndil demurred. Eochaid's unconscious body began to crush him from behind. "Perhaps if your people came in smaller sizes—"

Eochaid bounded higher along an approaching hill and shifted his human form down along his back, easing Myndil's burden.

"If only we had a large rope, I could tie your body to you," Myndil observed. "Is everyone in your family so large?"

"No. My sisters are no bigger than you, but my father is a large man, and Aodhgan is the largest among the siblings and cousins."

"How many of you are there?"

"I hope we live long enough for me to show you one day." Eochaid banked and loped down the rambling knolls, the glint in his eye dancing. "Have you ever made love to by a pack of werewomen?"

"No, but I rather imagine it is like being coddled by Sister Iarlaith or Abbess Bhaldruithe."

Eochaid's ears perked. "Are they substantial women?"

"Sister Iarlaith says she is big boned and made for comfort, which Brother Crannach always agrees to, but Abbess Bhaldruithe is quite small everywhere else except her chest. She's amazingly comfortable for head rests, like leaning back on two very large pillows."

"And you did this at an abbey with no repercussion?" Eochaid yapped.

"Of course. She had just been turned out of her own abbey by a raid, and she said she was in want of comfort. She asked me to do it, and you know it is very rude to say no to a woman of God when she is distressed."

Eochaid realized Myndil was entirely serious and was suddenly very interested in a pilgrimage. "I would see this abbey of yours."

Myndil was glad he should be so eager to visit—he would have all his friends come to the abbey, if he could—and as they passed the remains of a hermitage, he began to feel heartsick for home, glad to be on so important a mission in the name of God, but wishing that he did not have to hold Eochaid's body much longer.

CHAPTER 19: IN WHICH A WEREWOLF HAPPENS TO A VERY WILLING ABBESS

Night came to the abbey, the sun taking refuge behind the eastern wall, the golden blush of the late winter blooms diminished under the fading light, the sky nebulated by the approaching squall. It was many hours since Aodhgan had sent his message to the king, and he had yet received no reply. He knew a day must pass before a return message could be expected, but it was impossible waiting, his anxiety playing against his patience; he wanted to be doing something and wished Myndil were by, his liveliness and volubility filling up the time, the happy star that followed him sure to breed more adventure if not more trouble. He felt like patrolling the perimeter of the grounds, prowling the shoreline in search of bandits, but the tide was in, and being not at home in Osraige, Aodhgan could do nothing but wait.

He was invited to eat with everyone, a modest meal of boiled oats and brined meat, but it was warm and filling, and he thanked Sister Iarlaith for having done her best with the little they had. He was used to eating more, or going out to hunt if there was not enough, but he understood that he was a guest in the house of God, their meager portions wracking him with compunction that he should be grateful to have anything to eat at all. Gladly would he have submitted to hunt to feed them, but their woods were small and had little game, the few deer wandering about at this time of the year hardly worth catching. With such moderate portions, Aodhgan wondered how Brother Crannach could be so large—until he saw how Crannach readily disposed of whatever the children did not finish.

"Waste no' an' o'," Crannach said, offering Aodhgan a half eaten bowl of oats.

Aodhgan smiled and accepted, and enjoyed the epulary chat that came with it. The dining hall was confined, but there was a seat for everyone—even the rabble made a place for themselves, sitting on shelves and decorating the window sills, much to the abbot's vexation. He heard the many prayers of the abbot, all said in an audible whisper, "God give me strength not to commit sins against You—visit upon me the patience to wring the table cloth instead of their necks—Almighty, Blessed He, who makes them choke on their spoons." The abbot lived in a state of continuous toleration, enduring existence rather than regaling in it, looking as though he could not wait to ascend to the open arms of his god, but, like Myndil, he chose to accept everything as a test, and with so many new inhabitants at the abbey, the abbot did not know whether his faith was worth the relief that failure would furnish. One of the pagan rabble flung oats across the table, much to the delight of the children, but it landed in the abbot's lap, and that was enough to bring all the maledictions out.

"That is the end—the very end!" the abbot disclaimed, standing from the table, his hands clasping his robes. "I'm sure I don't care if you are building the dormitory for nothing—you are in the house of God—"

"Ya mean we're buildin' tha house o' God," one reminded him.

The abbot's fingers dug into his palms. He hated everybody. "Damn you—damn you into oblivion! May God smite you where you sit—"

"If he does that, then we can't finish buildin' his house."

"GAH!"

The abbot flung his fists in the air and stomped away, proclaiming that he was very sure he did not care whether it was a sin to wish evil upon others but hoped God would forgive him for wishing a very swift damnation upon them all.

Aodhgan had no idea whether he should laugh, but Brother Crannach chuckled and claimed another unfinished bowl of oats for himself.

"Nae bother, son. He does this at least twice a dae since he came here," Crannach explained. "'Mon, time fer the best part of the evenin'."

He brought Aodhgan into the old orphanage, and now that the children had aet their dinner, it was time for their postprandial play. The nisser living in the dairy came to join them, Sister Iarlaith was entreated for songs whilst Crannach was begged for stories, because he always 'did the voices' and chased after them if there were any monster parts to be acted out, and they sat before a noble fire, some of the children looking eagerly at Aodhgan, wondering what he could do to entertain them.

"Ye wanted tae know where Myndil grew up," said Crannach, motioning round the little sitting room. "Here it is. Nothin' special."

"I disagree," was Aodhgan's smiling reply.

He saw how happy the children were, how much they loved and minded their caretakers, how Sister Iarlaith kissed their bruises and wrapped their cuts, how Brother Vindimir brought them their toys and played with them, how they were clamouring for Crannach to pick them up and swing them about—the tinkling risibility, the fabricated tears, the joys and tragedies of a normal childhood, one afforded to so few who lose their parents so young.

"My uncle made me his ward when my parents passed on," said Aodhgan quietly. "I was fortunate to have a loving guardian who treated me like a son."

"Aye," Crannach replied, "tha's what guardians are suppose tae dae."

"Adoption is a difficult thing to discuss among the royal clans, especially when there is a throne and a curse involved. May I ask how you came here, Brother? Were you brought up here?"

Crannach hemmed and averted his gaze. "Ah came when Ah was a bit aulder. Nae faimlae tae look after me when mah Ma was taken away—but 'tis a long storae, son, one many year gone now. Here's where mah faimlae is. Myndil's a bit o' bother atimes, aye, but he's faimlae tae, just liek the rest o' the weeuns. Naebodae comes tae adoapt 'em here, bein' so far from everaethin', so they stay with us till they're readae tae go on, but they're alwaes welcome back."

Crannach seemed hesitant to tell him something; it was at his tongue's end, Aodhgan noticed, the sudden blush of timidity when he spoke about his own childhood, but Aodhgan let it pass, hoping that Crannach would be more willing to talk when they were alone.

152

"'Aye, 'mon," Crannach called to the children, "one storae and then we're shuttin' eyes."

There was a collective aww at this.

"Nae bellyachin'. Yer up late anaewae because we have a visitor."

"Can he tell us a story?" one of the children chimed.

Aodhgan felt twenty pairs of eyes suddenly upon him. "I can tell you the story about the Wolves of Ossory," he offered, "but I'm not as skilled at storytelling as Brother Crannach is."

Here was a conscious look. "Aye, aye, Ah'll dae the tellin'," said Crannach, resigning himself. He told the version of the story that he knew, being sure to leave Aodhgan's personal portion out of it, recounting about Saint Paudrig and how he had come to the kingdom offering them the Word of God, and the children listened with wide eyes and open mouths, their attention claimed by depictions of the wolves who populated ancient Kingdom of Osraige. Even Aodhgan was enthralled, wanting to set him right where the story went wrong, but he left it to imagination to entertain the children. The story was soon over, and the children were full of questions, instantly wanting to know whether the wolves were still there and why they never saw them.

"If the wolves are good," one child asked, "why don't they come and protect us from monsters?"

Here was a glance at Aodhgan. "Because they must protect the children in their own kingdom," was his solemn reply. "Wolves are also not well liked in some places."

"But these wolves are good," the child insisted.

"They are, but sometimes it can be difficult to tell."

"Brother Crannach," one of the younger children sang, "I want the wolves to come and play with us."

"Aye, they will," Crannach promised, "if ye 'mon tae yer bed and sleep now."

The awwws rung out again, and Crannach began collecting all the children to their beds. Aodhgan watched him lumber through the room, the children latching onto him and scaling his limbs— there was something about him, of this Aodhgan was sure; his senses told him so, his nose was on fire with speculation, telling him that something about Crannach was not quite right. There were many non-humans at the abbey, and one of them might be confusing his senses—Thistlewraithe hopping in and out of everyone's shadows, Ozzy the Wight tucking himself into his mound of dirt for the night and lamenting that the daffodils should not be in yet, Mr Dullahan's head bobbing along the top of the fence—but regardless of what Crannach might be, the children loved him, and he treated them with all the fondness and concern of a devoted parent. There was a reverence here, a hallowed appreciation for care and cultivation which Aodhgan must acknowledge, a healthy place for children to grow and the abandoned to seek refuge. It felt very much like home, though the palace in Osraige had no boggarts or nissers to furnish its halls, and Aodhgan felt he knew the secret to all Myndil's odd ways, his infallible good humour and his belief that everyone was his friend attributed to the sympathy he received when he was young.

The children were put to bed by the Brothers and Sisters, and Aodhgan was bid a goodnight, told he was free to go about the grounds as he liked, but he was tired from the long day and would rather try to rest. His conscience also plagued him, his mind running toward his cousin and his king the moment he was alone. He wondered whether he ought not defy the king's orders and cross the sea immediately, feeling that even spending one night idle was valuable time lost, but his wolf form, though swift, could not fly, and he convinced himself that there was nothing more to do but worry quietly in his room and wait till morning. He flumped onto the bed, his legs and arms hanging over the frame, and fell soundly asleep, his dreams only momentarily haunted by the boggart under the bed before it realized who and what was in it.

The snow soon came, nothing extraordinary or impassable, but it blanketed the abbey, and while the abbot lay on his stone slab, thanking god for another snowfall nobody needed— one he would be making Crannach or Aodhgan clear away— the abbey was rapt in frost, making the inhabitants take refuge in each other's beds when there was no fire to warm themselves by. Sister Iarlaith found her way into Brother Crannach's arms, Brother Vindimir went to sleep in the sitting room to avoid being sought out, and Abbess Bhaldruithe went to fetch more firewood, the small cinders in her room having already died away, her fingers clumpst with cold. Her room was beside Aodhgan's, and though her sense told her his bed would be the warmest in the abbey, she avoided it, the image of the monstrous wolf still distressing her. She went to the intermural stack of wood just outside the dormitory door, but it was empty, depleted probably by the rabble, who were taking up much of their supplies as of late. She returned to the hall and passed Aodhgan's room, hastening by to evade any sighting of the wolf, but presently, as she was about to reenter her bedchamber, she stopped and turned back, her ear caught by a particular sound: someone was snoring, the violent stertoration so loud it was shaking the walls. She thought she might peek in to Aodhgan's room, to see if anything could be done about it, else she would never get to sleep, and she stepped over the threshold only to be stopped by the sight of giant wolf sleeping on the floor. It dozed in front of a dormant fireplace, Aodhgan's body still on the bed, his human form making the noise.

The wolf slottered in its sleep, its teeth gnashing unconsciously, and the abbess gasped, clasped her hand over her mouth, and froze, not knowing what to do. The wolf was as tall lying down as she was standing up, its enormity expatiated by the heavy breaths making its immense torso rise and fall. It made a few somniloquent whines and stretched, moving along with its master, Aodhgan turning onto his side, and the wolf following. It rolled and extended its legs, its giant paws landing directly atop the abbess' feet. She was caught, and the only way she could move without waking either one of them was down. She sank silently to the floor, but as she suddenly felt warmer, being beside the nine-foot beast, she made no complaints. She had the sudden urge to push the rough pads on the bottom of the wolf's feet, but she refrained, fearing it might provoke the wolf and have it suddenly wake.

A few minutes passed, and the wolf finally moved, rolling back onto its stomach, but when the abbess was freed, she did not immediately leave the room: the wolf seemed somehow less frightening than before, its flicking ears and languid tongue making it seem more like a giant hound than an abomination. Its fur seemed softer by moonlight, the cerulescent sheen scintillating over its thick coat. She moved to the beast's side and gently caressed it, her fingers disappearing in a profusion of fur, the lush undercoat begging to be touched. The wolf stopped whining, but the abbess hardly noticed; she was too busy weltering in the comfort of a full winter coat. She knelt to the wolf's side and leaned her back against it, sinking into the black and white abyss, the solacious sensation pulling her in and keeping her there. She quickly succumbed to sleep, her body fully embraced and supported—and an eye opened, the consciousness of one only half awake investigating, descrying the abbess lying in his mantle, watching her doze against him. He knew she was there—he must know, the wolf being his eyes and ears even when his body was asleep—and he pretended not to notice, hoping some of her fears would be allayed, and she wish to know him better. To learn that the wolf could only be a friend to her is what he had to trust—he liked her there, the pleasance of having someone beside him, a novelty afforded him so seldom, and with the hope that she should remain for the night, he wrapped his long tail around her, mantling her in a cloak of sable and silver, and wished that by whatever providence had brought him to this abbey he should be so fortunate to have her stay with him till morning.

The buntings and jackdaws summoned the sun, their aubades welcoming the early frost, and before the white light of morning whelmed the abbey, the abbess awakened to find herself on the floor. A hazy remembrance of the night before roused her, the distinct sensation of warmth and comfort reviving her, but she was not cold, nor was she alone: the wolf was gone, and its is place was a large blanket clasped around her by two enormous arms. She looked up and found Aodhgan sitting behind her, his eyes closed, his aspect tranquil, his heavy chest supporting her head. She knew she ought to move, but she had no inclination, and she nestled against him, a little relieved the wolf was gone and happy to be pressed in the royal huntsman's crushing embrace.

Aodhgan knew she was awake, the same one eye open and looking down at the top of her head, spying his prospects before reacting: she did not seem to dislike where she was, and he left it up to her whether she would move or not. Humiliation soon came over her, however; she began to like her position too well, her back leaning against the wall of iron, her cheeks grazing his chest. His breathing slowed and he was becoming nervous, afraid of liking where she was too well. He moved out of respect, shifting his body away from her, and the abbess was immediately up, embarrassed and affecting not to show it.

"I apologize for intruding," said she, with an anxious laugh, "but it was absolutely frigid last night—I had no firewood—there wasn't any left—and it was so cold—and you seemed quite warm—and really it was so dark—I thought if I could just warm myself for a moment—"

"There is no need to apologize," said Aodhgan softly, putting the blanket aside. "I was glad you came in." He stood and moved into the light, his smiling features in full view. "I want to be useful while I'm here. I am pleased I could offer you comfort."

The abbess was already thinking of several uses for him: he offered to chop and stack more firewood, but she deemed that unnecessary when they might save a few trees and she might gain a new bedfellow. She tripped off to say her morning prayers, and Aodhgan could breathe, his conscience and sense of propriety holding back what his loneliness would betray. He had forgotten about his king and cousin momentarily; his mind was in raptures over the evening: a woman had spent the night sleeping against him, and whether she liked him or the wolf better as a bed, Aodhgan should not mind it. He closed his eyes and thanked his god, offering a humble prayer to his grace, beholden to Myndil for having sent him here, and though Aodhgan still could not be sure that Myndil was really a divine agent, that he should be the one responsible for such an evening was a small miracle at least.

His exultation was short-lived, however: a message soon arrived at the abbey, it bore the king's seal and came from Osraige. Aodhgan tore through the seal and read the letter to himself whilst everyone else was at breakfast. It was a short letter, but gave him the information he wanted: he was being given permission to cross the sea, he was being allowed to travel wherever he might to find his cousin, and he was not to come back until the prince was recovered.

"Tell him we want none of your other kinsmen here," the abbot humphed, assuming the contents of the letter. "You're shedding everywhere." The abbot pulled a large tuft of black fur from his hem and tossed onto the floor.

"My apologies," said Aodhgan. He closed his letter and stood from the table. "I must go."

The abbot pretended to be sad about his leaving and failed miserably.

"But are you to leave directly," said Brother Vindimir, "with no provisions or preparations of any kind? It is quite dangerous across the sea. I do not mean to suggest you cannot take care of yourself—considering your abilities, I have no doubt that you would do better than most—but there are countless wars that go on across the way. How will you even find your cousin?"

"First, I will follow the route of the slave ships. There is one main port that accepts all the ships from Ath Cliath, and there is a trading stock not far from the pier. I doubt Myndil and my cousin are still there, but once I'm here, I will find my king's spies and ask if they have heard anything. They will want to know of my arrival anyway. Once they give me a direction, I hope to be able to pick up a scent. Once I have that, finding Myndil and my cousin will be easy, as long as they have not gotten into any further trouble."

"And if ye cannae get a scent?" Crannach asked.

Aodhgan almost smiled. "I will follow the trail of destruction and the shouts of those who claim they have just run a rather cheerful and avid missionary out of their towns."

The children begged that he would stay, even if only for one day more, that he might help them climb the oak tree beyond the garden, but he must beg their forgiveness and must be gone his moment.

"When I return," he told the children, kneeling down to meet their pouting faces, "I will bring the wolves back with me."

"That's ye promisin'!" one child shouted. "Nae fibs!"

"No fibs," Aodhgan laughed. "Here."

He pried the seal from the king's letter and showed it to the child. "The emblem of the royal house of Osraige, the three running wolves, hunting together and holding one another's tails." He took the child's hand and put the seal in his palm. "I give this to you, as a member of the royal house, making you my steward at the abbey."

"Whoa…" the child breathed, gaping at the seal, treasuring it up in both hands.

"You have duties to fulfill in the meantime, and must look after your siblings until I return."

"Ah will, as long as Ah still get to tell Dimeadh he smells funnae."

Aodhgan bellowed in a rolling laugh. "Be kind to those younger and smaller than you," said Aodhgan, patting the child on the head. "They look to you for guidance, though you may not know it, and how you act and what you say are always being watched."

The child glanced at the seal in his hand and then looked mindfully at Aodhgan. "Even when Ah'm bathin' an' o'?"

Aodhgan smiled from his heart. "Maybe not then, and maybe not while you're sleeping, but at all other times."

"They'll say whatever comes tae mind," said Crannach, speaking low and standing close beside him. "God go with ye, son. We'll be waitin' for yer return."

A conscious look and a touch of the arm, and Aodhgan nodded his thanks. He moved toward the door when the abbess approached, her eyes low and lips almost frowning.

"Must you go now?" she asked, in a plaintive voice, her demure features downcast and chest sinking. "You have only just come."

She seemed disquieted, her previous apprehension of him giving way to all the disappointment that partiality supplies. He felt her unquietness, wished to assure her he would return in good time, but the quivering lip silenced him for a time. He stood close with her, his towering stature clothing her in his long shadow.

"I am grateful that I've been accepted here," said Aodhgan, in a delicate purr, "but I must go. I came to wait for word from my king, and now I must fulfill my obligation," and then, in a serious hue, "I promise to return, and I will return with Myndil when I do."

She looked up, her eyes twinkling with tears. "It will be cold at night, while you're gone…"

Aodhgan felt a pang at heart. "I will fill your room with firewood before I leave."

Her features almost lifted into a smile, but an iron arm blazing past her made her start. His massive fist sailed beside her head and landed against the wall behind her, splitting the stone. A familiar "Owweee" seeped out, and Aodhgan clamped his iron hand around the co-walker's throat.

"Do not haunt the abbess while I'm gone," Aodhgan demanded, pulling the shadow toward him.

"Aw wown't! Aw's jus' listenin' to the goodbyes!" the co-walker cried, flailing its tendrils about. "No hauntin'—honest-like!" The shade wafted its tenebrous coils at him and sniffed. "Jus' enjoy a good cry, me. Jus' 'cause Aw am wha' Aw am down't mean Aw down't like a bit o' romancin'."

Aodhgan hauled the shadow to the door and hurled it across the garden. "Go haunt the dullahan."

"Aye, aye!" the shade luffed, bobbing across the primrose beds. "S' jus' Aw wanna see the miss happy, dun Aw!"

Aodhgan exhaled, his chest heaving. "My apologies," said he, bowing graciously to the abbess, "I didn't mean to frighten you."

She hemmed and turned aside, her heart all aflutter. "I was not frightened at all," she murmured, with half a smile.

Aodhgan marched to the building site where the rabble had collected their supplies, and he took all the firewood they had taken from the stack the day before. He placed half in the abbess' room and half in his own, that she might not be over-encumbered with too much, letting her use his room for any auxiliary stores. He trundled over to the rabble, who were lounging beside the dormitory, and began stalking them, and when they quieted upon seeing his giant frame blot out the sun and fill their view, he said, with a terrific gowl, "DO NOT."

He pointed to the intermural stack where the firewood was supposed to stay, and the rabble froze and gaped at him in silence.

"Aye," said the hauler presently, nodding and scampering back. "Aye."

He growled and thundered away, the ground trembling under his heavy steps, and said his last goodbyes, ignoring the wry calls from the abbot to 'leave the boy out there and let god deal with him'. He stood at the iron gate and waved, the brothers and sisters and the children waving from the door, and he went toward his currach, leaving the abbey with uncertain feelings. He was eager as ever to find Myndil and his cousin as soon as possible and return them safely home, but something had happened to him in the smaller hours, a something between affection and acceptance, a something discovered in the vales of a doting admirer that made him want to stay. The compunction of leaving them all, though he had no responsibility to them and every duty to his king, besieged him. It made little sense that he should have an attachment to a place after spending only one day there, but he was missing Osraige, the hiraeth of home tinting his prospects—And yet why should I not want to stay? was the prevailing notion as he leapt into the currach and pushed away from shore. He remembered his promise to the child, the lovelorn look on the abbess as he left her, and the conversation he had with Crannach: they had made him one of them, a family of foundlings, adding one to their great number and glad to have him, the magic of friendly attachment that made him believe he belonged there.

The currach drifted out to sea, Aodhgan sailing with the current, the calm water reflecting the abbey as he passed it by. His muscles worked the grips, his arms sculling in broad sweeps, the blades of the oars slicing through the water in a violent flurry. In the rippling image, he saw a familiar figure standing on the shoreline, and he looked up to find the abbess just beyond the iron gate, her hands in supplication, her eyes raised to the sky. He stopped and waved to her, but she was too rapt in prayer to notice, asking god to follow him wherever he should go and to watch over him, that she might have another chance to be out of firewood for the night.

A good passage brought him quickly to the western coast of Alt Clut, the catchment of the Clyde awaiting his arrival. He brought his boat to shore, staying away from the trade stocks and the main port, and stationed it by reinforcing the hull with a few heavy stones.

Someone instantly came to see whether they could lift them.

A spindly shifting figure slithered down from the slave galleys, and just as Aodhgan turned his back, the rogue slipped in for a trial, fitting his fingers under the boulders and trying to pry them up. He grunted and heaved, and suddenly found himself ten feet in the air.

Aodhgan jolted the rogue by his collar and turned him around, the tips of their noses almost touching, the rogue's legs thrashing away, clambering for purchase and running on air. "You cannot lift those stones," Aodhgan bellowed, his sonorous voice rippling across the rogue's face. He caught him by the front of his shirt and breathed down his neck, "Leave my currach alone."

"Aye, big man," the rogue whimpered, his legs quivering. "Ah will tha', aye."

Aodhgan dug a hole in the wet sand with his foot and threw the rogue into it. The rogue sniveled and cowered, fearing the giant would crush him, but Aodhgan only put the wet sand back over him and let the swelling water seal it shut. The rogue popped his head out of the sand and thanked the enormous man for his great kindness in letting him live.

"Stay there and guard my currach if you want to do something useful," Aodhgan rumbled.

He left the rogue in the sand and marched toward the main port, his senses everywhere awake to the bustle of the trading post. A few galleys were coming in, the chiurms of slaves being led off under the governance of new masters, and Aodhgan scanned the rows, searching for the symbols that would give away one of his king's spies.

One of the slave traders soon spied him, however, and after taking mental measurements of his size and strength, he approached. "You look like a strong—"

"I don't think I do," Aodhgan warned him, with a firm glare.

He straightened to full height and flexed his enormous chest, and the slaver began to rethink his appraisal.

"Right you are," the slaver announced, moving along.

Aodhgan sighed and examined the crowds. "Any longer and I will have to start wringing them out," he said to himself. He wondered what it was about himself that seemed ripe for unwanted solicitation. He was aimable, but he had learned that to keep from frightening off friends, he would have to stoop his shoulders and make unassuming smiles. He carried no weapon—he needed none—had little money, wore no jewels, and his incomparable stature should have been enough to deter anyone, but some men would be splendidly stupid and take his strength as a personal attack. Fortunately, a few flexes took many rivals off, but one soon approached who wanted to see Aodhgan, who was glad to see him, and even more had been waiting to point him in the right direction.

"Lord Protector," said the approaching figure. He was a moderate-sized man with neat appearance, and had the same dark hair and grey eyes as Aodhgan, only a bit more hair around the jaw. He wore a tunic and long cloak, but the clasp bore the emblem of Osraige, and Aodhgan allowed him to draw near. He omitted the bows and kept his voice low.

"Tell me I'm not too late," said Aodhgan, in a fevered hush. "Tell me you have seen him or heard of him."

"I have, lord. I received word that our prince landed here two days ago. He remained here for sometime, probably waiting for a chance to return home, but something happened. He found someone, another like himself who had been stranded ashore. He saved him from being killed by slavers."

"Who was it?"

"I have no name, lord, but my informant said it was a holy man, a young novitiate with brown hair to his shoulders, wearing a white robe and carrying a large manuscript. My informant said he didn't know why but the holy man would not stop talking."

The broadest smiles overspread Aodhgan's face. "Myndil."

"My informant saw them further down the coast, but by the time they came to report the news to me and I arrived here to confirm it, they were gone."

Aodhgan was too overjoyed to listen longer. He thanked the informant, told him to send word to their king that he had located the prince, and barreled down the coast, passing the rogue in the sand who was dutifully watching his currach. He narrowed his gaze and studied the shore, inspecting the rocks at the estuary tumbling onto the sands, and just northward, where the firth of the Clyde met the sea, was a small currach, washed against the rocks without oars or seat blocks. He hastened toward it, and the moment he was within range, his senses were firing, the two familiar scents drawing a trail along the coast and over the neighbouring downs.

"Eochaid," he said, taking hold of his cousin's scent.

He followed it toward the rocks, and Myndil's scent began to interfere. The ribbons of each aroma coiled around one another, Aodhgan allowing his nose to lead the way, and just where the whitewash crashed against the firth, the black rocks bathing in saline barm, Aodhgan found a familiar patch of cloth lying beside a familiar belt. He took them up and gave them a hardy sniff.

"Thank God," he exclaimed, his heart a little relieved.

The closed his eyes and concentrated, drowning out the sounds and scents from the sea, allowing the familiar fragrances to form a path. His feet began moving, his legs following his cousin's strides, the burst of smells assailing him. He found the moment of transformation, the musk of Eochaid's wolf form leading him on, his senses tracing the line of travel along the high downs. He had it: the thread of excitement, the lingering aroma of woodland and rain, the fur and petrichor of many seasons, the lupine outline concentrated and clear, the scented strand racing northeast—and Aodhgan was gone, running over the rocks and across the moors with fervid haste, his legs moving as quickly as his human form would allow. He would have left his body at the shore and continued as the wolf, assured of reaching Myndil and his cousin even sooner, but he feared the slavers might try to imprison him and drag him off, and he was already late in recovering his cousin. He held his cousin's cloth and Myndil's belt and hurtled through the sparse vegetation, the birch catkins blowing off the trees as he rushed by. He had no map to go by, no vision of the landscape ahead; he had only the redolent lead to follow, and it was perfectly straight and thankfully strong.

CHAPTER 20: IN WHICH MYNDIL AND A WEREWOLF HAPPEN TO THE KINGS

It was only a few hours before Eochaid brought Myndil to their destination, but Myndil was somewhat sorry that the journey should have been over so soon; he had never been to this part of the isles before, and the country was particularly lovely: the blissful dales, the niveous peaks, the spruce and gorse wearing their brightest greens. Eochaid went around the few forests they passed, keeping their scent from crossing the woodland line, and went north along the Clyde, running the brim of the valley, their way eastward marked by Loch Lomond. They paused to admire, the sunwake streaming along the surface, the surrounding hills carved by ice, the summits wearing their gowns of glaciation in chiseled streaks, the small islands marking out the path through the tarn and dotting the placid canvas, and east of the scene, lording over the loch, was Ben Lomond, the beacon of the highlands, the versant belloch crowning the lentic divide, the issuing path drawing the way eastward in glens and braes, the road wending around sprouting trees, garlanded on each side by heather, the sharp alpine scent garlanding the air.

"We will pass by again on our way back," said Eochaid, bounding along the road, breaking into a charge again.

"It's so beautiful," said Myndil, marveling at the mountains in the distance.

"It is, the mountains particularly so. We don't have slopes this high at home."

They soon crossed from Alt Clut into Alba, leaving the straths and rivers behind, racing past villages and hunting lodges, the few women who were out waulking their wool at the hour hardly believing what they saw when Eochaid and Myndil darted by. Reports of a giant wolf mounted by a rider in white with a dead man on his back began circulating, but the story was too fanciful to be true, and anyone who saw them either claimed madness or fatigue, thinking they were working too much to be seeing a werewolf lope by. Eochaid ran at full speed, never stopping for anything, his legs in want of a good run, his stride indefatigable and free, his tongue flapping in the wind, his human form undulating against Myndil's back. Myndil would have complained of being crushed more often than he should like, but the scene was unexceptionable, the country in every direction beset with verdure, the nearby birds and bucks claiming his attention, the feeling of riding at such alacrity exhilarating to him. If he were a judge, he should say being a wolf, or a werewolf, at anytime was more a blessing than a curse; to be allowed the command of so fine a place, to race at liberty over rambling downs, knowing nothing could catch you—except hunters and their bows, but even that seemed impossible here. Myndil would have given much to be able to travel like this at any time, and he felt sad that Aodhgan should not like it so well.

They soon arrived at a crossroads, one overcome by marching legions, the rows of mercenaries marking out their way forward. Eochaid followed the advance away from the main road, scanning the gathering horde, watching them collect toward a high knoll. He followed the knoll upward and came to the summit, the hill overlooking an embankment, and at the bottom were nearly a thousand men, all of them either mercenaries or royal legions, the best of whom were collected around two men, both important-looking and stately, though one featuring more prominently then the other.

"This is it," said Eochaid, panting heavily, pacing the top of the hill. "It seems we have come in time."

"You ran very fast," Myndil commended him, patting him on the head. "We were only travelling a few hours—but are you sure this is Scone? I saw only one sign quite a way back along the road, and this doesn't look like an altogether kingly place."

"This is Scone." Eochaid jutted his muzzle at a strange looking stone situated between the two men. "There is the king's seat, and these men are probably coming to be counted among the soldiers."

They were coming to be portioned out, as Eochaid suspected, and standing in the middle of all the milling mercenaries and spiritless solders were King Constantine II and King Owain, the former an older man with long dark hair and a grave countenance, and the latter a little man, round and bucculent and somewhat preoccupied. Constantine stood with a missive in his hand and was reckoning up their resources while Owain was very interested in the dirt he had got under his fingernails on the ride in.

"That's one, two, three hundred for you," said Constantine, "and five for me."

Owain began to nod, but the calculations did not add up and began fumbling over themselves in his head. "Why do you get five?"

"Because my land is larger and is under greater threat of invasion."

"Oh. But what about my land?"

"Nobody cares about it, not even you."

"Oh." Owain sniffed and glanced about. "Is Hywel coming?"

Constantine clutched his missive and looked pained. "Hywel is a dip. He has already accepted Aethelstan's lordship and refused my invitation."

"Did you send flowers with it this time? You know how he appreciates flowers."

"I should have sent a ballista and a very angry dog."

"I liked Hywel," said Owain, in a discomfited hue. "Why did he have to side with Aethelstan?"

"Because he is a ninny and wanted to use Aethelstan's mint to put his face on his own silver pennies," Constantine gave a short humph. "Hardly like a king at all."

They went on amongst themselves, Constantine counting and adding the soldiers he liked to his great number while Owain considered what he ought to have for his dinner when all this battle business was over. Eochaid and Myndil peered down at them from their place on the hill.

"We are either late or early," Eochaid mused. "I don't see Aethelstan."

"How do you know those are not him?"

"The smaller one is Owain of Alt Clut," said Eochaid, his nowl pointing toward the rounder man, "and the taller one is Constantine the Second."

162

"What happened to the First?" Myndil asked.

Eochaid simpered and shook his mane. "He is King of Alba, and he's been ruling here for many years. They have either just parted from the other kings or are meeting here without them. This is Constantine's seat, which means he might have the say in what happens at this gathering."

"Do they believe in God?"

"Constantine certainly does." Eochaid marked the large gold cross around Constantine's neck. "He is known for making everyone under his dominion accept God's judgement."

"I should be able to speak to him then, but what shall I say? He and his people already love God."

Eochaid rumbled in deliberation. "Perhaps I can help you here."

"Really? What are you going to DOOOOOOOOOOOOOOOOOOOO–?"

Eochaid suddenly lunged forward and loped down the embankment, Myndil plunging along on his back, his hands gripping Eochaid's fur, holding tight as Eochaid leapt from the hill onto the plateau where the two kings stood.

A wave of exclamations rippled over the crowds of men, the sight of an enormous werewolf thundering down from above and stalking their kings bringing their hands to their weapons. Constantine stepped back and reached for his sword, but Owain, glad to have anything to look at that was not the war accounts, smiled and put out his hand.

"And who's this nice boy?" Owain cooed, reaching out to touch Eochaid's nose. "Is he a good boy?" He began clapping his pockets. "I don't think I have any treats on me–"

"Mother of God," Constantine cried, clutching his golden cross, "what is the meaning of this?"

To Owain's instant dismay, the wolf vanished, and in its place stood Eochaid, his human form a pageant of power, his mass of muscles contracting, his stature still alarming, towering high above both kings, but Myndil's smiling features and a formal introduction helped smooth the business.

"Forgive the intrusion, Your Grace," said Eochaid, with reverence, speaking mainly to King Constantine. He bowed low and presented himself. "Prince Eochaid MacCellaig of Ossory, son of King Donnchadh."

"Ah," said Constantine, with marked indifference, "the cursed kingdom. Yes, I know your father. A good man, if not a little reclusive. You stay out of important affairs, but you breed excellent mercenaries, I understand. And who is your companion?"

"Myndil, missionary and man of our Lord, hailing from the abbey of–?"

He glanced at Myndil, waiting for him to fill up the gaps in his knowledge.

"Oh, I think they're working on the name just now," Myndil replied, "but it's along the northern coast of Erin, and is a delightful place. It was an orphanage before and I grew–ppb thrhpmh."

A large hand covered Myndil's mouth, and Eochaid pushed Myndil's knees from behind, forcing him to make his obeisences to the reigning king. Owain was looking about for the wolf and did not attend, while Constantine was contemplating, examining the exhibition of brawn before him and wondering how such a small kingdom could produce something so striking.

"Gentlemen, whatever your reason for interrupting this counsel, I bid you welcome," said Constantine, folding his missive and tucking it away, "but we have little time. We are on the short end of business, but you come here in so hurried a style, you must have important news to tell. Tell it quickly. I'm old and hungry and have not had my tea."

Eochaid nodded and pushed Myndil forward, encouraging him to speak.

"Your Majesty," Myndil began, trying for reverence, "I have just come from Ath Cliath and have met with King Olaf."

"Olaf?" said Owain, beginning to be interested. "Did he send you?"

The deference was gone out of Myndil's air, and he relaxed into his usual state. "Yes—Well, no—well, God sent me, but Olaf did send me across the sea, but he thought I was a spy, so he told me his plan of coming to war with Aethelstan, and he said he would be here by morning, and that he was coming with a thousand men to take back what lands were rightfully his."

"Oh, goodie," said Constantine, with affected unconcern. "We can have our war and be done with it by luncheon."

Eochaid seemed bemused. "You mean to fight with Olaf, Your Grace? Has he invaded your lands?"

"No, but Aethelstan has invaded mine. You see, gentlemen, we have this morning met with Aethelstan, who says I have violated some treaty or other we made after he took Northumbria. He marched across my borders proudly as he pleased, and when he was asked to leave, he said God told him that he was to be king of all the English, whatever that means, and that he was destined to 'unite' all our lands and rule over us as High King. A few sorrysops have already bent to his will, but I refused, on the grounds of being forced to accept that my people must be called 'English' under his dominion."

"What does that mean?" asked Myndil. "Who are the English?"

"A new creation," Constantine sighed, rolling his eyes. "I abominate new creations, especially those that are trying to threaten me into relinquishing my lands and titles. Aethelstan is a dunderhead. He was once a brilliant young man, but taking Olaf's lands has given him a taste for conquering, and now the man can never do anything without pomp. Anyway, we refused his ungenerous offer to allow ourselves to be taken in by him, my fellow Scots liking our own identity best."

"Am I a Scot then, if you're all Scots now?" Owain asked.

"No."

"What am I then?"

"You are Cumbrian and a duffart."

"Oh."

Owain went back to wondering where the wolf went, and Constantine gave Eochaid and Myndil a flat look.

164

"I am not overly fond of Olaf," Constantine continued, with half a sigh. "He's impulsive and foolhardy and smells like potted ham."

Myndil had thought his throne room did smell a bit like a brining bin, but he thought that had been the fault of the pigs outside.

"But I like Aethelstan even less, and though Olaf is a wretched heathen, he is willing to help me defend my borders in exchange for my help in defeating Aethelstan."

"So you're going to fight against him?" said Myndil.

"Yes. Aethelstan already has the place picked out, a lovely spot south of here, Dún Brunde, but he calls it Brunanburh, another new creation of his. He says there is to be one fight, one High King of England under God, and so on. God should tell him to govern his own people and not pester mine. He is mad, roping his younger brother Edmund into his madness, proclaiming them to both to be King of the English, when really he is just using poor Edmund as a steward."

"And do you have the means to defeat him, Your Grace?" Eochaid asked.

"I do, if Olaf makes good on his promise, as you have just told me he will. I know that even with Olaf's men, I won't be guaranteed a victory, but for the sake of my people and for the sake of making Aethelstan look like a fool, I will ride out and do what I can."

"Forgive me for remarking, Your Grace, but you are an older man."

"I know," said Constantine coolly. "I am grown tired of this," touching his brow and sinking all his agony in a sigh. "I always thought my retirement would consist of dying young, but I have lived and succeeded as a king in spite of myself, and now I must do what kings do and die on the field."

Owain suddenly looked up. "Will I die on the field?"

"For your sake and mine, I certainly hope so. Do not look for me in the afterlife. I shall beat you."

Owain sank in deflated expectation and pouted at his shoes.

"Well, messenger," said Constantine, "you have done your duty, and now you may go. If Olaf will meet us at the shore, I must finish counting my men. I am famished and therefore have done with this conversation."

"You know," said Myndil, "it is rather a shame there aren't any scones here. Why is this place called Scone if there aren't any?"

Constantine had no idea whether Myndil were being serious or not. "This is our esteemed capital," said he, with unanswerable dignity, "not a place for bannocks and breakfast."

"It really ought to be, because scones are delicious, especially with jam and clotted cream, and a bit of salted butter."

"He's right," said Owain eagerly. "I could do with a scone right about—"

A folded missive swatted him on the head. Owain murped, tucked his head between his shoulders, and looked down in silence.

"The capital," said Constantine indignantly, "is named after our honourable seat, the Stone of Scone, stone of destiny, where we have crowned the kings of Alba."

He gestured toward the small seat beside him. Myndil was expecting something grander, but he saw only a low stone stool, fitting round with brass rings.

"That doesn't look very comfortable," he observed. "It is rather small. All the kings before you must have been very tiny."

Constantine began grinding his teeth. "We kneel on the stone and are anointed on it. We don't sit there forever."

"Oh. You must have rather well padded shins, to kneel on something so hard."

"We manage." Constantine exhaled and rubbed his temples. "Well, gentlemen, I must prepare for war. So, holy man," turning to Myndil, "if you will give me God's blessing for success in the coming battle..."

He looked at Myndil expectantly, and Owain instantly jutted in.

"What about me?" Owain demanded. "I'd like a blessing too, if you please!"

Myndil glanced at Eochaid, hardly knowing what to do. "I would like to give them God's blessing, only," he said, in a audible whisper, "I'm not yet ordained, so I don't think my blessings will count for very much."

"You are a man of God, Myndil," Eochaid kindly reminded him. "Your devotion and love for the Lord counts for something."

He pushed Myndil forward, and both kings supplicated themselves, holding their hands around their crosses and closing their eyes.

"Erm," said Myndil, taking up his book. "I, Myndil Plodostirr, under the governance of this Realm, which I think is Alba, by the Grace of God–" he waited for an objection, but no voice interposed, "--offer you blessings for the coming battle," and then quickly added, "and I hope everyone has a pleasant time and finds the action mighty delightful and goes home without getting hurt."

CONSIDER THEM BLESSED, the voice fulminated. THAT DOES NOT MEAN GOD WILL LET THEM WIN OR ANYTHING.

Myndil made a joyless smile. "God says you are blessed."

Constantine nodded and thrummed to himself. "Unorthodox, but tolerable as benedictions go. You have my thanks, holy man."

There was a strange sensation, the feeling of something ominous clicking into place, the sound of something sinister singing Myndil's praises. The curmurring in his stomach told him something was wrong, and Myndil asked, in a frantic voice, "Where did you say the battle was taking place?"

Constantine gave him the direction: a large field not far from where they landed at the shore, only farther south, under the firth of the Clyde and well beyond the port, marked out by an ancient artesian spring.

"I expect we shall see you there," said Constantine, turning to his men. "We could use a wolf of Ossory on our side, should you be inclined to participate."

"I thank you, Your Grace," said Eochaid, with due genuflection, "but I must return home to my father as soon as possible."

"Of course," said Constantine, with a languishing look. "It is never the ones who should be left to fight who do. Come," speaking to Owain, "let's have something to eat while we wait for the heathen wastrel and his men."

Owain followed him down the walk, lamenting that he should not have seen the wolf once more, and Constantine bid his messengers goodbye, saying quietly to himself as he walked away, "When this is all over, I am joining an abbey far away from everyone and telling absolutely nobody."

Eochaid carried Myndil off, seeing he was agitated and wishing to appease him. "Myndil," said he softly, bringing him to the base of the embankment, "Are you all right? You seem faint."

"I felt something..." said Myndil, looking discomfited. "Something—something lamentable and horrible."

"And you are certain it was not just your stomach telling you you're hungry?"

Myndil clutched his stomach. It made a few violent wambles. "It might be."

"Come," said Eochaid, lifting Myndil onto his shoulders, "we will find something for you to eat along the way."

"But will speaking to Aethelstan do anything now that they are all bent on fighting one another?"

"We will soon find out."

A few minutes spent in the nearby village brought Myndil out of distress and into gaiety again. He felt like a small child riding on Eochaid's shoulders, the feeling putting him in mind of when he was a boy and being carried about by Brother Crannach, who would dandle him about for hours on end, the delightful sensation of being taken about the orphanage enough to secure his happiness. A few scones were purchased, given to them by a old woman who thought they looked like "twa gud lads, no' liek mah lazae bastart wha' sets at hoam and dosnae left a finger o' dae," and Myndil began to feel like himself again, the fresh butyraceous scent of fresh bread smoothed over with jam and clotted cream reviving his spirits, though the sound of someone laughing maniacally in the background was concerning.

It was fair country all round, the highlands gliding in quietly from the background, the splendid rustication of uplands and lowlands, the brontide of far off storms silenced by tramontane views, the peaks piercing the langourous clouds, and Aodhgan was going at a good pace, his feet following his desperation, keeping the patch of his cousin's sleeve and Myndil's belt in hand. The scent remained strong well into his journey, wending away from the scattered woods, Eochaid having done exactly as Aodhgan always instructed him, and though there were plenty of men along the road, some marching toward the fields below, some moving slowly along the highway in want of better trade from farther towns, the trail was never lost. He garnered a few nervous glances as he barreled down the bylane, some desirous of knowing where so enormous a creature was going in such a hurry, some merely interested in him as a foreigner, but Aodhgan never stopped, despite the calls from women to have him help them bring in their wool or the shouts from passing recruiters to have him join the king's ranks.

He would not stop until he reached the trussocks on the highland divide, having passed Ben Lomond without admiring it, his attention on finding his cousin and Myndil before the scenery could be missed. The glen cutting eastward bore the scent he was searching for, but as he was about to follow, cutting through the mountains to the north and south, another scent cut to the southwest. He paused and concentrated, his senses straining, his eyes low and ears listening, his instincts firing on all fronts. It was the same two scents, the same musk of familiar fur and starched sunflowers, only the trail leading southward was stronger. He looked down to see how it was, his eyes retracing the his cousin's steps, the few large pawprints off the main road moving in one direction and then scattered over in another. He was sure they went eastward, but then must have turned around and come back, the ribbons of aroma growing more robust the further south they went. They cannot be far, Aodhgan reasoned, examining the way southward, feeling it in all his senses and all his impulses. His feet turned along the road and he was off once more, running beside the highway, his eye catching an occasional pawprint as he went.

The increase of men on the road became concerning. Standards and flags of Cumbria and Alba lined the lanes, men in leather armour trudged in jagged rows, the swords of soldiers and axes of farmers furnishing every other hand, and the sight of longbows and full quivers told him where these men were bound. Myndil, what have you got Eochaid into? was the repeating question, Aodhgan measuring his stride to assess the number of gathering hordes. He heard the raillery of the marching lines, a few of the men marking him and wondering whether he would join them, one of the older and smaller men calling him out.

"Ah, big yin," said the older soldier, posting up to Aodhgan and trying to keep pace, "come tae fight wi' us?"

Aodhgan eyed the thickening crowds. "I had not planned on it."

"Lookin' fae yer faimlae? Got yersel' a brither fightin' in the war?"

"I sincerely hope not."

"Well, nae bother, lad. Battle's probablae awreadae started. Kings went oan ahead wi' their big yins, strammentraw lads. We're jus' bringin' up the rear."

Aodhgan began to run faster, racing through the passing dales. He was soon back at the firth, only standing on the hill overlooking the rocks, the coastline in view but farther off. He need not worry about following scents any longer; the path was etched and notched by bobbling heads, men pooling into the path in front of him, thousands of mercenaries pouring out of galleys and onto the shore. Here were not the hardened men of the highlands; these were men who had seen countless conquest and were grown weary of it, the fatigue of persistence on their faces, the studied monotony of emotional detachment, the languidness that only meaningless massacre supplies—and then he saw him.

"Olaf," Aodhgan rumbled, his grip tightening around Myndil's belt.

The king of Ath Cliath stood on the shore, his flagship having just arrived, his sword brandished, his beard wild, his aspect jeering. He was only too glad to be going to war, probably thinking he could take his land back in a trice, but his men were already tired, having prepared for battle and rowed across the sea in only a day's time, having brought little to eat and only the promise of an early return home to sustain them. It was evident that he expected the battle to be short, but by the grumblings of his already trundling men that the campaign might not successful on his side. He marched down the shore, captious and ill-mannered, fixing his pelts and pauldrons into place, and walked ahead of his men, slamming his sword against his shield and calling out his battle cry, trying to invigorate them and succeeding in nothing.

I could have it done now, Aodhgan thought to himself, moving farther off, crouching as he ran, concealing himself in the tall white heather beyond the rocks, I could finish what we started in Ath Cliath, I could render him useless and convince his men to return home, and this war would never need to happen, but Aodhgan knew better than to interfere with the designs of villainous men. Why Olaf was here now, he would not ask, but who he meant to fight he would soon find out. That he came to reclaim his lands, this Aodhgan had suspected, but what the men from Cumbria and Alba were doing amongst the hordes from Erin he would soon find out. He thought Myndil only wanted to convert kings not have them fight each other, and while he had no idea that Myndil had been to see Constantine and Owain, he conjectured that part of whatever this velitation was about was somehow Myndil's fault. A war for the dominion in the north must happen, and if a few more kings should join the fray, in hopes of retaining their lands and gaining a mountain or two besides, Aodhgan would have no share in their fight. He would get his cousin and his friend and get out, and nothing the passing legions could tell him would change his mind.

He allowed Olaf and his superior soldiers to pass him, pausing only to let them march by, the bowmen and shieldbearers following, providing cover upon his entrance into the field, and as Aodhgan stooped and hid between the furze, he saw an old woman, standing on the side of the road, offering food and drink to anyone who wanted. The sight was not uncommon in times of war; many women who were left at home would offer favours or memorandums to men marching off, wishing them good fortune or a good death at least, but this woman was offering poultices and potions, handing out sprigs of lilac and seamrog, and in return the men offered a strip of cloth or a ribbon to be tied around a tree. She stood beside a whitethorn and tied each ribbon around a different bough, the longest of which upheld a series of rush crosses, most of them three-sided, but there was one tied round with four. She loomed over a cauldron and stirred its contents with an iron ladle.

A feeling told Aodhgan that she was a Cailleach, come down from the highlands to revel in the time of year, but she was too slight and unpretending to be made much of, the men undeterred by her, many seeking out her company and cures.

She gathered her skirts and sat at her cauldron. "Whatcha doin' here, b'y?"

Aodhgan made her no answer, uncertain as to whether she were addressing him.

She put down her sprigs and glared in his direction. "Don't belong here yerself."

Something within him stirred, and he felt caught. He offered a polite bow. "None of us do," said Aodhgan gravely.

"Aye, well." The old woman sniffed. "Who let you outta the kingdom? Sure'n yous never come outta yer woods."

Aodhgan raised a brow. "You know what I am?"

"B'y," said she stoutly, "yer the biggest thing on the isles. They got mountains here smaller 'n you. Think I can't tell wan o' yis by lookin' atcha? Go'wan outta that now. I can smell yer pack miles aff when it rains."

A conscious look was exchanged. She glowered at him for sometime, the eye of grim judgement assailing him, and Aodhgan noticed the wolfsbane lining her belt. He stood back, his senses beginning to be hampered by it, and the scene in the background diminished, the movement of the soldiers slowing to a crawl, the vibrancy of banners and standards waning, the rataplan of marching feet fading under the aegis of her regard. She was older than her appearance admitted; his senses told him so, the wikes and wrines of a grandeval guise serving to conceal something something even older. He remembered a name, one Myndil had told him when they first met, belonging to an old healer he had met along the road, and he was about to ask her what she was doing on this side of the sea when she nodded toward the southeast.

"Saw yer other wan runnin' down the path," said she, "gallopin' the turf under him and takin' the sky down with him."

Aodhgan's eye widened, and he was gone, hastening down the highway, his mass and might moving at full speed, bowling over any solider who got in his way.

The old woman humphed and shook her head. "Faoladh. Always puttin' 'emselves in it."

A presence descended and rested on the whitethorn beside her, its awareness watching Aodhgan fade from view. *Are you not doing the same?*

The old woman knew that she was, but would never own to it.

170

CHAPTER 22: IN WHICH GOD AND AETHELSTAN HAPPEN TO EVERYONE ELSE

The horses had been standing for hours, and the armoured men sitting atop the horses were beginning to grow restless. They had been given the promise of a swift battle followed by a glorious cenation, but as it was they were grown tired of waiting and were very much in want of a good walk. They were waiting at the bottom of a valley, a large gorge with a river on one side and a forest on raised ground on the other, and sitting on his horse at the front of the lines was Aethelstan, his beard trimmed, his hair moulded, his armour spruce and shining. The birds chirruped in the surrounding trees, a fog began to roll in, and the Wessex forces waited on the south bank, gazing upward at the top of the gorge, waiting for men to begin riding down any moment now. The men clutched their swords and axes in languid expectation, the time of excitement long died away, but Aethelstan, situated beside his younger brother Edmund, who was fidgeting with his pony's bridle, still looked triumphant, his countenance speaking all the grandeur he felt on being God's champion.

He was really waiting for Olaf, though he had no idea whether he was coming, suspecting in part that Constantine and Owain might have asked the lumbering heathen to join their little velitation, but he would be ready no matter the opponent, having cut down all his rivals over the last few years. Constantine would provide a tolerable challenge—and Owain nobody thinks for—their shared faith a point of contention, Constantine too believing in god, or believing he believed in god, or believing that god believed in him, but regardless of what the king of Alba believed, god would be on the side of Wessex because Aethelstan wanted him to be, knowing that he was the rightful chosen of all Englishmen, whether anybody else knew what Englishmen were yet or not.

Aethelstan adjusted his golden crown, careful not to spoil his hair, and seemed proud of himself, having draped his limbs in his finest attire beneath his armour, ready to be lauded when he should win and to look resplendent while doing it. He made a few valiant poses, to practice for when the battle should begin, and held his large golden cross to the waning sun, the aurulent sheen casting a glare over his men behind him.

The horses whickered uneasily, and the line of earls began eyeing one another.

"Do you think they're coming, lord?" one of the earls asked.

"Of course they're coming," Aethelstan replied, with unanswerable dignity. "Cannot you hear them, man?"

The earl leaned forward on his horse and listened with his hand cupped around his ear. He eyed his peers for confirmation. "No, lord. I hear nothing."

"That is not nothing, man! That is the sound of anticipation!"

"Is it? Sounds like the birds are havin' a go at each other." The earl pointed to two crows on the nearby pines, squabbling with one another in the boughs.

"A sign from God," Aethelstan avowed. "One for sorrow, two for joy—and there are two, which

171

means we are to have the joy of victory very soon."

The earl demurred. "I think that's magpies, lord."

This, of course, went unheeded. "The smaller bird is meant to represent our enemy," Aethelstan insisted, "and the larger bird is meant to be us, crushing our enemy underfoot."

"They got beaks, not feet, yer lord," said another earl. "And I don't think they're fightin'. They look like they're f–"

Here was a sharp glare. Aethelstan flashed his golden cross, and the men quieted.

"Right you are, lord," the earls nodded.

Another round of anticipation began. The horses pawed the ground, swords were put down and axes slung over shoulders, and the silence was broken through by Edmund, who had displeased his pony by pulling his mouth and was growing tired of waiting without having anything else to play with.

"Aethel," the young boy chanted through his nose, "I'm cold and I want to go home."

"We will go home after we kill all our enemies in the name of God," said Aethelstan sweetly.

"May I have a biscuit when we get home?"

"Yes, after we win, my cherish."

A sound drew the men's attention to the top of the valley. A brontide neared them from the entrance to the gorge, foretelling the appearance of something large and ominous, the rataplan of heavy feet pulling up the ground, the pounding echoing on the gossamer frame of the mist.

"Here they come!" Aethelstan cried out, raising his cross. "Prepare yourselves!"

The earls raised their weapons and fixed their shields, but the sound of deflated expectation soon filled the front line. Racing down the gorge was a giant wolf, its arms and legs pumping away, its tongue out and muscles surging, and mounted on its back, seated against what appeared to be a large body, was a holy rider, his aspect wild, his head blessed by an inscanescent crown.

"Ah, look there. You see, men?" Aethelstan pointed. "God sends us his holy messenger, to bless the field before we spill first blood! Let it be known that on this day, in nine-thirty-seven of our Lord's nativity, God sent his holy herald to me, riding in on his–" The messenger neared, and what was clouded by mist was now becoming clear. "–On a giant horrific beast?"

"Good God, what is that thing?" one of the earls cried, raising his sword. "It has human arms and giant claws!"

"Quiet." Aethelstan sniffed. "It is a sign from God, and I won't have you besmirching a holy messenger before the battle. I didn't think God would send me a prophet on a lupine monstrosity, but I accept God's will as it is and so will you, and that is all."

Eochaid loped down the gorge, enjoying the wind whipping through his thick coat, and Myndil was holding on as if for life, the tears pooling away from his eyes.

"I'm assuming the man in the crown holding the cross is Aethelstan," Myndil surmised. "Why is his horse also wearing a crown? They look as though they have the same hairstyle."

"I told you he is mad," Eochaid panted. "He thinks he does everything to magnify the Lord's grace when he's really just doing things to please himself."

"How did you first come to know him?"

Eochaid leaped over a large boulder at the bottom of the valley. "He was once invited to celebrate the holy days in Osraige. My father would not have invited him, but he is powerful and many insisted my father have a good understanding with him. Instead of coming himself, Aethelstan sent an emissary, because, as the emissary told us, 'his lordship wanted to see whether we were really God's servants or a kingdom of braying hounds'."

"Oh, that's so rude," Myndil asserted. "And even if you should have been hounds, it was very kind of you to invite him from such a long way." He pouted and looked offended. "I would have come, had you invited me."

"I know you would," Eochaid yipped, "and when this is over, you will be invited to Osraige for my wedding, if there still is to be one."

Myndil gasped and instinctively clutched his heart, almost falling backward. "Really? Oh, I'm so excited! You will have to tell me what kind of wedding present werewolves like. Should you like a nice big bristly brush?"

"I certainly would."

Eochaid pounded toward the front line, the dust from the field trailing behind him. He thundered across the field, and when the line of earls approached, he skidded to a halt, Myndil almost flying off back, only weighed down by Eochaid's human form trailing behind him. The earls raised their shields, suddenly aware of wolf's size, but Aethelstan came forward when the dust cleared and greeted them.

"There you are, holy messenger," said Aethelstan, greeting them. "You are woefully behindhand, but I daresay you come precisely when God meant you to. Does my enemy come? Do tell me they come soon. My leg is getting the cramp."

Eochaid sat on his haunches to let Myndil down, and every weapon was raised and pointing, the men who held them shaking in trepidation, the sight of gleaming fangs and unmitigated might hardly what they were expecting. Eochaid scratched behind his ear and shook his mane.

"Aethel," Edmund croosled, "there's a big bad wolf looking at me."

"Yes, my treasure," said his brother, snoaching, "but a big wolf from God, so there is no need to worry."

"I don't like it looking at me. Make it stop."

To make everyone easy, the wolf disappeared, and standing before them was an immense young man, bowing in form and sidling Myndil. Eochaid would have offered civilities and an introduction, but he knew Aethelstan cared for no one but himself, and though the king of Wessex might not recognize a prince of Erie, his earls certainly did. They lowered their weapons and inclined their heads, knowing not whether to be amazed or confused.

"And where are my opponents?" said Aethelstan, examining the gorge behind them. "Have they run home already?"

Eochaid pushed Myndil forward, urging him to speak. "Well, you see, Your Grace," Myndil began, "we just came from meeting with them—meeting with Constantine and Owain, that is. They were counting their men, and though their hair was not as beautiful as yours, they said they had met with you and that you had decided on this place for the battle, and then Constantine, who already loves God, told me he has enough forces to defeat you if Olaf should make good on his promise, which he has done, and he said you said there was to be one fight, one High King of England under God, because there was something about a violated treaty, but now Olaf has sided with him, in the hopes of reclaiming his land here, and he is coming with a thousand men—"

"A thousand heathens," Aethelstan corrected him, with a pompous laugh, "nothing I regard. We have hardened men of God to bolster our ranks. There is nothing to fear. I fully intend to rout them all."

"But we came all the way here to warn you that Olaf is going to join Constantine and Owain, and you cannot take on three armies by yourself."

Aethelstan glanced at his men, and the lines swelled in mirth.

"Of course I can. My men can take on any foe that stands before us, and we will cut them down with equal fervour. Great is God to have sent you to me, to give me such a warning, but have no fears. I was hoping Olaf would join us, and whatever challenge our enemies put in our way, we will triumph over all."

He raised his voice and his cross, and the front line echoed his wish, the roar of conceit undulating through the ranks.

"And with you granting me the lord's blessing," Aethelstan continued, holding out his cross to Myndil, "there can be no doubt of the victor here. God sent you here to bless me, did not he?"

Myndil stared at the heavy golden cross. "Well, yes—but, no—well, he did send me, but not exactly in the way you think—I'm a missionary, not a messenger, and you already love God and don't want to hear my oration just now—I'm here by accident, or by providence, if you want to think God brought me here—but I came to ask you not to fight this war because so many people will die."

"You mean they will die, which is just what God intended."

Aethelstan looked about him with smiles of maniacal glee, and Myndil began to feel afraid of something.

"But the Good Book says: thou shalt not kill—"

"Thou shalt not kill unlawfully," said Aethelstan firmly. "We have arranged the battle, and as the only one who is doing any unlawful killing is Olaf, God will grant me leave to kill him and as many others as I like."

Myndil was caught. Aodhgan had been right in saying no one could out-God Aethelstan, reason and sense falling against an impenetrable wall of dismissive airs. God had told Myndil he wanted Aethelstan to win and Olaf to fight, and to have them stop now would be to go against divine predilection. How do I stop them from killing each other? but Myndil knew the answer, though he suspected his entreaties would be ignored.

174

"You know, Your Grace," said Myndil, staring at the gold cross. "God just spoke to me, and he told me that he is very proud of you and that you have done such great work in gathering all your men here, that you have won by default, and says you are High King in His Name, and that everyone should go home and have a nice tea to celebrate."

THOU DOST TELL LIES, the voice in his ear bellowed.

Myndil flinched.

GOD SAID NO SUCH THING. THOU SHALT TELL HIM THAT GOD WANTS HIM TO GO TO WAR AND WIN. DO NOT PUT WORDS IN GOD'S MOUTH—ER, IN THY HEAD.

Myndil's heart beat quick, the sick feeling of deceit consuming him.

"Yes, God has just told me," Myndil went on, his bowels curmurring, "that everybody must go home right away before anyone shows up, or your kingdom will fall to ruin."

"Nonsense," Aethelstan cackled. "God has told me every day for the last three years that I must war to rule all of England. Wales has already accepted my ascendancy, and now the north must submit."

"But God spoke to me—"

"But God spoke to me and told me that I must rule the island as High King under one divine banner," Aethelstan hissed, pointing the golden cross at Myndil's neck. "I'm sure you must have misheard him."

The vicious flout, the fragile forbearance—Aethelstan would not be denied, and Myndil would have to obey and accept. The sound of men marching down from the gorge drew ever nearer, Eochaid standing close to Myndil, ready to pull him away at any moment, the earls with their hands on their hilts—it was all a confusion, all misery, all resignation now.

"And now, with your blessing," said Aethelstan, pushing the cross against Myndil's chest, "we will get on with it."

Myndil took the cross and examined it, its weight in gold, its fitted garnets seemed all at war with his plain robes and goodwill.

"Bless me now, please," Aethelstan sang, watching men begin to pour into the valley. "I want to have this done before my enemy forms their lines, thank you."

Myndil held up the cross and Aethelstan inclined his head.

"I have no way of knowing whether this is right," said Myndil, putting the cross down, "but God wants you to win, though that does not mean you will win—and you will still have to do the fighting—and you might very well die in battle, though I hope nobody dies really—and you are perfectly happy with killing thousands of men just to prove that you are right?"

"If God wants it," said Aethelstan, smiling. "These are not my people. They make themselves willing sacrifices for my holy cause."

Myndil held up the cross and put it down again. Why, God? He grimaced. You are the spirit of love and kindness—why do you want him to kill these men?

BECAUSE THAT IS WHAT IS SUPPOSED TO HAPPEN.

But he's going to hurt people!

BUT AETHELSTAN IS MY FAVOURITE BECAUSE HE LIKES MURDER.

But you're not supposed to play favourites.

GOD DOES IT ALL THE TIME. I CHOOSE PROPHETS. I CHOSE YOU.

But I'm just a missionary.

YOU ARE A HOLY MESSENGER, SENT BY ME TO ENSURE DIVINE DEVISTATION.

Myndil held up the cross again and held his breath.

"Give me the blessing," said Aethelstan, through his teeth. "You have no choice. God does not give you free will, and neither do I."

Here was a dangerous look, and Myndil conceded, reconciling himself to a murmured, "Godb lessesyouunderthe boughsofheavenandsuchamen," and returned the cross.

Something somewhere clicked, the nothingness of cogitation slipping into place, a doubt in the back of Myndil's mind drew up, and a mirth rose from the ether, a stifling risibility championing all that must be and silencing all that could be no longer.

Aethelstan lifted the cross high in the air and turned toward his men. "God has blessed us this day! We will have the Great War, we'll all rejoice and magnify his grace as English men, and I will be High King of England!"

A fulmination of cheers caromed down the valley, and Myndil felt ill, disliking this style of divine providence, very much wanting to be held by Eochaid and be taken home.

"And here they come!" Aethelstan pointed to the top of the gorge, where King Constantine and King Owain appeared, the former already seeming disenchanted with the business, and the latter only too delighted to see so many prettily barded horses.

Eochaid put a hand on Myndil's shoulder. "We should leave," said he quietly.

"You will go nowhere, sirs, until I have won," Aethelstan demanded.

The earls raised their weapons, pointing them at Myndil, and Eochaid made a threatening growl.

"Stop doing that," Edmund whinged. "I don't like when hounds show their teeth."

Eochaid would have done more than that, had Edmund been older. It was really the only thing anyone needed to know to prove Aethelstan's zealotry: he had brought a child to battle and expected him to watch him win the war.

Constantine was hardly surprised to see Edmund in full regalia. It was like Aethelstan to include his family in his affairs, especially if the business of the day was death.

"You brought the boy," said Constantine, with half a sigh, riding up to him. "Charming."

Owain rode in behind him, smiling and nodding most emphatically.

"And where is your son, Constantine?" Aethelstan asked.

"On the ridge, ready to risk his life for your nonsense."

"My nonsense is God's will," Aethelstan insisted.

He pointed to Myndil, who was huddling under Eochaid's heavy arm.

"Well, the divine messenger has finally reached his destination," said Constantine. "I hope Aethelstan did not harm you in anyway."

"I don't like him!" Myndil cried. "Aethelstan's mean!"

"That's 'the High King is mean' to you."

"Not yet it isn't," Eochaid simmered.

There was a pause, all important men giving one another all insidious stares—except Owain, who recognized Eochaid and trotted close to him.

"Hello again, my friend," Owain waved at him, his round body jostling in the saddle. "Tell me, is your marvelous riding wolf somewhere here? I remembered to bring the treats this time." He fumbled through his leather armour and produced a small pouch. "Dried venison and salmon slices."

Eochaid's eyes widened with interest. "I like those."

"Oh, jolly good. I hope you will give them to him for me and tell him what I good boy I think he is, and the next time I see him, I hope you will let me ride him and rub his ears."

The pouch was given over whilst Constantine and Aethelstan settled the accounts.

"How many men did you bring for the reckoning?" said Aethelstan. "Tell my man, that he might write a poem about it later."

A man with a script in hand was brought over, and Constantine enumerated how many men came from each side. It was all business, the tally of mercenaries and soldiers offered in peace, the list of their names, their family houses all accounted for—when suddenly, in the middle of Constantine asking Owain how many of his men had got lost or ill along the way, a whizzing sound and a thunk! scattered some of the horses. Everyone looked down: a long arrow stuck into the ground. They looked up, and at the top of the gorge stood Olaf, his shieldbearers charging down, his archers preparing another volley.

"Oh, that imbecile," Constantine tutted. "He knows absolutely nothing about civility."

Aethelstan raised his cross and cried, "IT STARTS," riding round in an ecstasy, his horse galloping along the front line. "ONE UNITED KINGSHIP UNDER WESSEX, BY THE GRACE OF GOD."

Eochaid moved immediately, grabbing Myndil and running toward trees.

"I couldn't make him stop," Myndil cried out, clinging to Eochaid. "I even tried to lie—lying feels awful! How can anybody do it? Does this mean God really wants this war?"

"No, Myndil. It means they want this war, and they will have it by whatever means. If they had listened to you—"

Eochaid's senses fired, his ears twitched, a sound reaching him before they was aware. He lifted Myndil and threw him out of the way—a ballista bolt sailed down from the top of the valley and burst against the ground, the head sticking into the field where Myndil had stood, the shaft splintering from impact and glancing off Eochaid's chest.

Myndil landed and rolled to safety, but was instantly up, watching the waves of horses and weapons collide, the conclamant sounds of steal and iron ringing in his ears. Men charged with their shields, opposite forces stabbed with their spears, and it was a calamity of conflict, three forces fighting one from all sides, arrows streaming down from above, torches raining in fiery streaks, darts and bolts whistling and landing every which way. Horses reared and fell, men were trampled under the stampede, and Myndil seemed to be miraculously unharmed, all the soldiers inundating the ravine passing him by. He saw Eochaid half way across the field being charged by the shieldbearers, the full armoured men half his size threatened by his presence. One blow bowled them over, Eochaid's full swings swiping them easily away.

"Don't touch my friend!" Myndil shouted, running toward Eochaid. "He is not one of them— No!"

Someone dove for Myndil with a dagger in his hand, and Myndil dodged and slapped him on the head with his book.

"Stop that," Myndil demanded, hitting anyone who came close to him with the back cover.

Eochaid was getting irritated with the amount of men charging him and started punching them in the chest, every single one struck sinking to their knees, their ribs shattered, their bodies instantly broken. He picked up one of the men at his feet and started using him as a cudgel, holding him by legs and bashing anyone in his way.

As terrible as the battle was, Myndil enjoyed watching Eochaid use soldiers in inventive ways, holding them as shields, using them as battering rams, skewering them with their own weapons. He evaded every strike, his lupine reflexes doing well against the waves of untrained soldiers. He made his way to Myndil and was almost within reach when Olaf suddenly appeared.

The Norse king, delirious and frothing, swung his sword in all directions, hardly caring who he struck—until he saw a familiar face from the corner of his eye. He turned to Myndil and almost choked with rage. "YOU," he raled, stabbing his sword at him.

Myndil hit someone out of the way with his book and looked up. "Oh, hallo, Olaf!" he chimed, waving at him from ten feet away. "I forgive you for sending me over here in that boat. Because you bound me and sent me here, I met Eochaid."

There was a violent roar somewhere behind Olaf and a dozen men flew into the opposite lines.

"There he is! His cousin helped me get into your palace. I don't know that I'm glad to see you, but I did tell you that I wasn't a spy, and you didn't listen, though I don't think it matters now, but if you had believed me and only let me tell you about God, you wouldn't be over here losing the battle—no!" leaping away from Olaf's sword. "Don't swing at me!"

"This is your doing!" Olaf teemed, heaving his sword at Myndil. "You made me come here before I was prepared!"

"You did that yourself—no, don't slash my robes!" Myndil cried, evading and pulling his robes around him. "I have taken very good care of them and it is so dreadful hard keeping them clean, and I won't let you get blood on them because that will never come out—" Olaf slashed at him, but Myndil ducked. "And not my hair, please, because my hair is short enough and has a hard time growing—No! Don't make me ask God to smite you! God, stop him from hurting me, please!"

"Odin take you!" Olaf bellowed, lifting his sword above his head, but as the sword came down, Myndil was gone. The sword struck down and stuck in the ground with no one under it.

Eochaid had just lifted two men, bashed their heads together, and threw them aside, and was reaching for Myndil when he suddenly vanished. He had not evaded or quit the field; he was simply gone as though he had never been there. Both Eochaid and Olaf stood in wonder, examining the patch of ground where Myndil was a moment before. They eyed the ground and then one another. Eochaid bellowed and charged, and Olaf was swept away by a large bolt.

Myndil had closed his eyes when Olaf raised his sword. A few swats of his book should not stop a two-handed sword from cutting into him, but divine intervention was a safer method of escape. He expected to be either injured or saved—Eochaid was almost within reach—but when he opened his eyes, he saw nothing and was nowhere. The battlefield was gone, the landscape entirely missing, the world around him devoid of any distinguishing features. He took a few steps—he heard no footfalls and felt nothing pressing back against his feet. There was silence, but it was constructed silence, contrived by magic or artifice—a realm with no rules, but a realm with nothing, the absence of everything but himself. He spoke, "Hallo?" and there was an echo, one that seemed to ripple on forever in every direction. There was no colour—the world was painted in varying shades of grey, but there was no top and no bottom, only grey leading into a dark grey as it went on. He followed it, looking for anything or anyone to tell him where he was. "God?" No voice answered, but a sound reached him from something that seemed like a hall.

Someone was there—he could tell by the odd clapping sound. It was a gradual ovation, the sound of someone either impressed or overly agitated. Myndil followed it, the sound getting closer though the hall seemed farther away. The grey of nothingness faded into black, two sconces appeared on bottomless walls, and standing under the glow of dim light was a small one-eyed man, his skin red, his limbs wiry and wan, his body slight, his feet hooved, his head horned. He smiled at Myndil, his mouth wicked and wide, and applauded him as he approached.

"Well done, Myndil," the little man crooned. "Well done indeed."

Myndil instantly recognized the voice. "Is that you, God?"

"It is, my missionary. Or perhaps I should say my minion."

Myndil seemed doubtful. "I don't mean to question you, God, but can it really be you? Or perhaps it's a manifestation of what my mind thinks you ought to look like, just like that burning bush business the one time so very long ago. If it is really you, I did think you would be taller, considering the booming and terrible voice."

"Well," the man sniffed, "I am a god."

"But are you my god, God?"

"I am. You prayed to me, and I heard you, and I answered in your hour of need. Is that not the definition of being your god?"

"Well, there is supposed to be an amount of belief, a dash of faith, and that sort of thing, but if it really was you and you really did help me—but did you bring me here, God?"

"Of course. You asked me to save you, and here you are."

"But where are we?"

"Underground, in my home, well away from the battlefield, where no one can hurt you."

"Oh, I'm so excited to be in your home, God! Should I remove my shoes? Am I supposed to be on my knees? The floor seems clean and I should not like to tarnish it. My robe has got a bit of dirt on it from the field."

"There is no need for any ceremony. It is I who am glad to welcome you here. You have fulfilled your purpose, my minion. You did everything I asked, whether you wanted to or not. You are my incumbent agent of chaos, the harbinger of inevitability, the delicious child of ill-fortune." His eye boggled, and a grin overspread his lips. "And to think you just came in my way."

"What do you mean, God? I have been praying to you and you have been speaking to me since I was a child."

"Poor affectionate little creature," the man pined. "I am your god, but I am not that god," pointing to the book in Myndil's hand. "There are many gods in the realms of infinity, and I am but one of many."

Myndil blinked and recoiled. "But there is only one true God, God. My God."

"Then that is me," said the little red man, presenting himself with a flourish.

"But I mean God who wrote the Good Book—" Myndil realized what this was all about and began laughing to himself. "I see what you're about, God," he giggled, waggling a finger at him. "I understand. It took me a moment-- you're testing me. You're testing my faith once again, since I did not trust your judgement about the war. It's because I questioned you and because I told a lie—yes, I see. This is all a trial of my faith. Oh, God," smiling affectionately. "I know it is you, God. I know your voice and your presence, and fully understand. THANK YOU, O LORD," calling out against the nothingness, "I ACCEPT YOUR TRIAL AND ASK THAT YOU GRANT ME—"

The little man gestured, and Myndil's mouth was shut.

"It is no test of faith," the man assured him. "I am really a god. To prove it, I will even tell you my name."

Myndil clapped his hands over his ears. "But the holy name of God will make my ears bleed if I ever hear it or take it in vain. Brother Vindimir said it would."

"I wish my name had that ability, but it doesn't and you are perfectly safe. I am Velinas, God of Disorder. I chose you to be my disciple, and I chose well. I wanted you to cause this war, and you have. I had a bet going with Odin that I could make Olaf go to war and lose his kingship, and now I have won. You helped me win. You went to speak to the rabble on my orders, you went to speak to Olaf, you blessed the warring nations, you brought devastation and calamity immeasurable, and I could not be more proud of you."

Myndil was bemused. "Is that why you wanted them to fight? You had a bet with a heathen god? But Aethelstan says it was a holy war, one that God told him to fight, to take over all of England.

Was that you, God? Did you speak to him too?"

"That was probably that God," said Velinas, pointing to Myndil's book. "I don't deal in holy wars, only heathen affairs, but heathen or holy—these are just words you use to define gods you like and gods you don't. I am a god, I am not a holy god, but unlike holy gods, I listen to prayers and make things happen. Every time you have called out to me, I have answered you, and where was the holy god when you called?"

"So," said Myndil slowly, trying to decipher, "in my room, when I didn't want to leave the abbey, that was you?"

"No, that wasn't me, but every other time it was me."

"So, that time, in my room, it was God."

"No," said Velinas, his frustration growing. "That was Brother Vindimir, pretending to be your god because he wanted you to leave the abbey."

"And before I came to the abbey, was that you too?"

"That was your imagination. You were a boy, and you imagined that God was speaking to you, like a little imaginary friend."

"And every night, when I said goodnight to you—?"

"THAT WAS NOT ME, NOR WAS IT YOUR GOD," Velinas smouldered, his eyes flaming in sudden rage. "YOUR GOD HAS NEVER SPOKEN TO YOU. YOUR GOD HAS NEVER ANSWERED YOU. YOUR GOD DOES NOT CARE ABOUT YOU."

"But those times when I asked for help and you didn't answer, but God sent help anyway—"

"THAT WAS COINSICENCE."

"But Both Aodhgan and Eochaid believe in God—"

"And yet their god cursed them and their line for eternity. How can you reconcile that to holiness?" Velinas took a deep breath and exhaled. "Was I not kind to you, Myndil?" he entreated him, with asperity. "Did I not save you and put you on the path for greatness? You were nothing when you left the abbey, and now have the ear of kings. You brought down the ruler of Ath Cliath and made Aethelstan holy ruler of his isle—you have power, you have meaning. Is that not what you want?"

Myndil was silent for a moment, his mind tumbling over itself, trying to catch at sense and succeeding ill. "I...I just wanted to love God..." His shoulders withered, hardly knowing what to believe. Was it true? Did he imagine God where there was no God? Was it all a ruse invented by fancy and run on the wings of evil? He held his book to his chest and pressed it to his heart, his lips touching the leather biding, his head beginning to ache.

"What do you want?" said Velinas, in a compassionate hue. "As a god, as your god, tell me. You did my bidding, and I shall reward you. Whatever you would like."

Myndil's eyes lighted, the sanguine glow rekindling. "I want to practice my oration with you. No one but God will hear me, and if I could just read to you, so you could put me right--"

He began flipping through the pages, eagerly hunting down a particular passage, and Velinas marched away into the murk.

"If I could just practice this one part—" Myndil called after him.

"You understand nothing about divinity," Velinas languished. "My time as your prayer piece is over, and I no longer need to listen to your constant drawl."

"But, God—or not my god—if you are truly a god—if you are not the God, the God from the Good Book, the one I have been praying to all this time, why did you answer me so much?"

Velinas turned back and made a pitiful look. "Because out of all the minions have I spoken to and recruited to do my bidding, you were the only one who talked back."

A sigh of ash and brimstone escaped him, a look of understanding was shared, and then he was gone, melding into oblivion, his forked tail vanishing along with the light. Myndil felt a pang at his heart and could not tell why.

YOU HAVE SERVED YOUR PURPOSE, said the voice in his mind. NOW GO AWAY, SO I CAN TELL ODIN HE LOST.

Many questions prickled Myndil's mind, the barm of recognition finally coming to a boil, and he wanted to ask them all—did he really cause the battle or was that only Velinas' instigation? Did he have other followers? Why choose him when he could have had anyone? Or perhaps was he one of the many faces of god?—but the moment he opened his mouth, the smell of blood tinged the air, a world of colour whirled upon him, the clang and clatter of metal rung in his ears, he was back on the battlefield, and a sword was swinging at his head.

CHAPTER 23: IN WHICH FRIENDS AND FAMILY HAPPEN TO EACH OTHER

"God, please save me!" Myndil cried out, ducking in time to miss the blow. "I'm sorry I said I thought you should be taller!" He leapt out of the way and into another sword. He jumped back, the blade just grazing his robes. "Please, God! If that really was you, I didn't mean to offend you! I really did like your underground cave!"

No voice answered him.

He waited, feeling that his belief had wavered and was therefore working against him. He held his book to his heart and raised his eyes to the sky. "I believe, God! I always have! You were my first and very best friend! I love you!"

There was no answer, and Myndil dove out of the way of spear thrusts and a torrent of arrows, refusing to surrender to despair.

A few swipes glanced off his sleeves, but a soldier with a face baked in blood soon charged him, the blind vehemence of a killing blow driving his sword onward. Myndil tried to scamper away, but there was nowhere to run, the rising wall of the valley behind him. He would have to duck in the middle of the charge and roll through his assailant's legs if he wanted to get away.

"God, please don't let this man hurt me," Myndil murmured, holding his book against his heart. He closed his eyes and prepared to dive. "Please—I want to see my friends again!"

He opened his eyes and lunged forward, but the soldier and the sword were gone. They were lobbed into the air and were currently sailing across the field at different altitudes, the sword landing near the raised forest, and the soldier landing on a spearhead halfway across the field. Myndil was watching their course, trying to work out how they could have flown so far, and did not see the axe. He looked down, watched the axe swing at his chest, and felt himself being swiftly jerked back by something, someone pulling him or pulling back on his robes. The axe was gone too, the screams of its wielder carrying over the field, and Myndil felt himself being lifted up, being raised from his collar. He was taken off his feet, and a giant hand turned him around.

"Aodhgan!"

The familiar features were life to Myndil, the smiling eyes, the luxuriant brows, the insuperable muscles of the friendly mountain encompassing his view. His legs kicked in exultation, and Myndil fell on his friend's neck, embracing him with unmitigated joy.

"Aodhgan!" he cooed, hugging his iron chest, failing to get his arms around him. "I am so glad to see you!"

"And I you," Aodhgan purred, holding his friend against him with one hand. "Even more glad that you're alive and I was not too late."

Someone tried to get in the way of their reunion, a bold man with a two-handed axe, but Aodhgan's arm got in the way of his face. The man broke his nose against a giant elbow and crumpled to the ground.

"Aodhgan! Oh, Aodhgan—we've been waiting for you! We were waiting on the shore, but Eochaid said—Oh, I found your cousin! Rather, he found me—and he saved me from bandits after I landed ashore, and he said he had been hiding in the rocks waiting for you—and I knew straight away it was your cousin, because the two of you look so much alike, only he is a little smaller than you, but not by much, because he also has impossible shoulders and frightening arms—" Aodhgan swung his arm back and sent another bold assailant flying. "But Eochaid is here—rather, he is somewhere—I was with him the whole time here, and he let me ride on his back, but I had to carry his human form, which I think gave me a bit of the backache—" Another soldier fell against an iron leg and careened into the facing wall. "—but Eochaid helped me speak to Constantine and to Owain, though that didn't help much in the end—but we did try to convince everyone not to fight, but they all ended up fighting anyway—and I was so worried about you and that you might not find us—but here you are—and you never told me the person you were looking for was a prince and that you were the king's huntsman!"

"My apologies," said Aodhgan sincerely, holding out his arm and letting soldiers hurt themselves against it. "I did not know whether I should have told you. I did not want to endanger you any further."

"I know now, so it doesn't matter— and Eochaid is really lovely. He asked me to comb out his mats and to come to his wedding!"

Aodhgan simpered. "Of course he did." He punched through someone's shield and gripped the bearer's neck. "I think we should go."

"Yes, I would like to, please."

Aodhgan tossed the shieldbearer into the crowd and created a path across the field. "Let's find my cousin first."

"He was fighting near the forest when I was—" Myndil paused and thought whether he should tell him he had been whisked away by god-but-not-God. "I think something important is supposed to be happening here," he added. "There are so many men being killed, but God wanted it to happen, or at least that is what God told me—"

"This is the work of foolish kings and no one else." Aodhgan put Myndil on his feet and scanned the fatiguing hordes, looking for signs of soaring soldiers and broken bones. "Come," marching toward the raised forest, "we will all return to the abbey together. Everyone is waiting for you."

"Waiting for me? Did you go to the abbey?" Myndil exclaimed, hopping on his toes.

"I did. I went there looking for you, not knowing what happened to you after you saw Olaf."

"Did you say hello to everyone? Did you meet Brother Crannach and Brother Vindimir and Sister Iarlaith—"

"I met them all, and now understand why you are the way you are." Aodhgan smiled sagaciously and let out a reobating roar: "EOCHAID."

The name rippled across the field, making many men turn to see the gargantuan huntsman enter the field. A crowd of men nearby flew into the air, their weapons flying and arms flailing, and under the mound of felled earls Eochaid appeared, smiling and throttling a soldier under each arm. His eyes brightened at the sight of his cousin. "Aodhgan!" he cried, tossing his victims aside.

The two giant men barreled toward one another, everyone between them lunging out of the way. They ran toward each other with open arms, their thunderous strides cracking the ground. The two cousins met with a thunderous crash, the force of which pushed anyone near them away. They held each other close, their foreheads pressing together and noses touching, Aodhgan excessively relieved, and Eochaid overwhelmed with happiness. Chaos happened around them, swords stabbed and men still fell, but few dared to interfere with their reunion. Everyone on the field still living and fighting must know what they were, and as neither of them had any wounds and were accompanied by the king's holy messenger, it was best not to attack them.

Eochaid held his cousin tightly, enjoying the embarrassed affection wrinkling Aodhgan's eyes. "I knew you should find us," said Eochaid. He punched someone who charged them without even looking down. "I knew you would come, if our father would allow you to leave."

Aodhgan pressed his forehead hard against Eochaid's. "I see I didn't need to hurry." He glanced down at Myndil, who was standing close at his side. "You were in good company."

"I rescued him from the slave traders."

"You mean he rescued you from yourself."

Eochaid smiled. "That's not untrue." He marked a streak of silver in at the sides of Aodhgan's head. "You've aged, cousin."

"Like milk or wine?"

"Like cheese really." Eochaid felt a tap on his shoulder. He turned and blew away a severed finger than had landed near his neck. "Seems we are both getting a bit of a rind."

"We will need a good hard bread to sit on very soon."

They shared a short laugh, and Aodhgan suddenly grew severe.

"That is what happens when you almost lose your family," said he, giving Eochaid a grave look, and then, with a parental dispatch, he added, "Never disobey me again."

"I promise I won't do it on purpose."

"Come," said Aodhgan, turning and repelling a charging soldier, "our father is waiting and wants to hear news of you."

"Can we finish the battle first? It has been so long since I've been allowed to fight and I'm having a pleasant time."

A look of reproach here, and Eochaid groaned and followed his cousin away from the field.

"This is not our war," Aodhgan reminded him, plucking a ballista bolt from the ground and using it to clear their way. "Our people are used enough as mercenaries. We should not be fighting here."

"I wasn't taking sides, cousin," Eochaid promised. "I was merely attacking anyone who came to attack me first."

"And you were doing a lovely job," Myndil beamed.

"You weren't doing too terribly yourself. How did you disappear like that, when Olaf came to attack you?"

A pang of guilt wracked Myndil's heart. "I asked God to please not let him hurt me..." was all his answer.

Aodhgan saw Myndil's anxiety and put his hand on his back. "There is nothing wrong with asking for miracles and then feeling unworthy when they happen," said he, swatting a sailing volley of arrows overhead. "We are suppose to look to God in times of danger, but we should never feel ashamed to receive his rewards."

Myndil was hardly listening: an intimation of maniacal laughter permeated the ether, the same laughter he had heard when he blessed the warring kings. He looked back as they ascended the path out of the gorge, and the sound of Velinas' voice plagued Myndil's mind: the valley and issuing downs were strewn with bodies, severed limbs and rolling heads decorated the field, the adjacent river red with blood, the tributaries littered with broken weapons. His conscience was in a torment, the voice of God still silent, so rapt in his own consternation that he missed the dead pony in his way and tripped over its legs.

God was not there to save him from falling, but Aodhgan was, the might and fidelity of friends better than what any dissident deity could promise. A hand held him back from the ground, but to make sure he would not fall again, Aodhgan lifted Myndil over his shoulder and carried him out of the valley, leaving the wreck of errant kings behind them, Aodhgan and Eochaid focused on the prospect ahead, though Myndil was watching ruin behind them.

chapter 24: IN which myndil and the werewolves journey home

Having found his friend and recovered his cousin, Aodhgan was very ready to leave this island. He had done with all the imprudence of willful kings, and though Eochaid would have stayed for remainder of the battle, his only wish was to return to the abbey and visit a very willing abbess again. He marched up the main road, Eochaid at his side and Myndil slung over his shoulder, though he could have carried him in one hand, mindful of those still running toward the battle as he was of those running away. Eochaid had thoroughly enjoyed himself, however, having been allowed to exhibit his abilities and exercise his strength for the first time since his abduction. There were no hunters or poachers to fear on a battlefield; there was only the clash of swords and axes, and the roar of Aodhgan, defender of his crown and terror of his kingdom, stifling every other sound. It was delightful to him, to see his cousin use his powers in either form, watching the men scatter in trepidation, desperate to escape his crushing might, his iron arms and giant fists cudgeling everyone who got in his way. It would be a story to tell their father, one he should listen to and luxuriate in many times over, but Myndil, though glad to be borne away from the battle, was cherishing different thoughts. He was glad to be rid of Olaf and Aethelstan, glad to be coddled by Aodhgan, but he quit the field with very disquieting feelings, the message of the Velinas uppermost in his mind. He had called Myndil the agent of chaos, had accused him bringing about the war, and though part of Myndil was still convinced it was only god teasing him, he could not help but wonder whether he had caused the Great War after all. How much had been put to chance and how much was the consequence of his asking for divine intervention? The question plagued him, and though he quietly called for god to relieve him of his fears, no one responded. His mind was suspiciously silent; there was only the comfort of Aodhgan's hand taking him from his shoulder and putting on his feet, and the warm smiles of two werewolves asking him whether he was all right.

"Oh, yes," said Myndil, a little muddled. "I'm always well, especially when you're both with me, only--" He paused and lowered his gaze, "I cannot help it, but--do you think I caused the battle by trying to talk to Olaf about God?"

"Olaf's a madman," Eochaid huffed instantly. "Even with Constantine and Owain's help, he came here with few men to reclaim a land his father had trouble keeping hold of."

"But do you think he would have come now, if I had not riled him about it? I know you said that everyone was expecting a war, but considering his conquest at home, do you think he would have come at all but for me?"

Aodhgan folded his arms and eyed Myndil suspiciously. "Why would you think any of this was your doing?"

Myndil shrugged and was hesitant to say. "I'm a bit worried that God is somehow angry with me."

Aodhgan and Eochaid erupted in mirth.

"That's impossible," Aodhgan exclaimed. "You were sent out to bring God's message to those who would hear it."

"But perhaps God is disappointed that I did not gain many followers. The ruffians were quite pleasant, but perhaps, if I had practiced my oration more, the message might have carried farther— but God did want me to talk an awful lot about holy wars and divine retribution, and I thought he was only testing me at the time—perhaps if I had said something different, to make God's love seem more appealing—"

Two giant hands touched Myndil's shoulders, and the faces of his friends, leaning down and smiling at him, crowded his view.

"We're here," Eochaid reminded him. "We might already follow the Lord and Saint Paudrig's teachings, but you gained us in your travels."

"Whether you succeeded in having others come to know and love God as you do is really up to those who want to know him," said Aodhgan, in a fathomless purr. "You could say Olaf is being punished for expelling you, but whether that is your fault or not has only to do with him. Everyone who believes in God's Grace or chooses another way must be left to themselves to believe what they will. You can only tell others about your beliefs, you cannot force them to follow you, nor would you want to—that is why Saint Paudrig failed in our kingdom on his visit. We were cursed as a result of running him out, but had he left us to come to know and understand God on our own terms, he might have been more successful. There are many ways in which people celebrate divine consciousness, and whether others do right or wrong in this world, Myndil, you can only be responsible for you."

Aodhgan pointed to him, and Myndil looked down at the giant finger touching the centre of his chest.

"If you are kind and treat others with compassion," said Aodhgan, lifting Myndil's chin and raising his eyes, "then you have done all that is asked of you. Living in the midst of war and uncertainty is difficult enough. The burden of belief should be added to no one's concerns."

"But I'm sure God must be displeased somehow— he so very silent now, and he had always answered me before—not always in voice, but—"

"He's probably busy dealing with all the death," said Eochaid, thumbing toward the battle they left behind.

Myndil deliberated, Aodhgan's conciliating pats on the top of his head quelling his qualms. "So," said he presently, fidgeting with his fingers, "you don't think I could be the incumbent agent of chaos then, do you?"

Aodhgan arched a brow. "I don't think you would be purposely."

"But, as things have turned out with Olaf and with the heathens and now with the war, I don't think the abbot will ordain me."

"Is that what you really want?" said Eochaid, with a sagacious smile. "I don't think it is."

Myndil pouted. "What do you mean?"

"How many friends does this abbot have?"

Myndil began counting on his fingers and then stopped when the number did not go above zero. "Well, he certainly knows everybody, but I think God is really his only friend, and even then, I think he believes God is more as a figure of authority than of love, meant to keep him respectable and teach him humility at all times. He says he likes to be punished by God because it is teaches him important lessons about the exhilaration of suffering."

"And how many friends do you have?"

Myndil held up both hands and began count. "Well, there's Brother Crannach, Brother Vindimir, Sister Iarlaith–though they raised me, and even if they should not think themselves my friends, I certainly do think them my friends–then there are all the children in the orphanage, and then there is Thingunderthebed, Mr Dullahan–"

"The point I wanted to make," said Eochaid, smiling and holding Myndil's hand down, "was that while not everyone likes a holy man, everyone certainly likes you. You don't have to be ordained to have friends."

"But if I'm not ordained, I cannot stay at the abbey."

Aodhgan narrowed his gaze. "Who told you that?"

"Well, abbot said–"

"Did he." Aodhgan's chest muscles flexed over themselves. "Well, we will return to the abbey with you, and you can tell him we are your followers."

"Really?" said Myndil, his eyes glimmering. "But you have already been there, Aodhgan. He knows that we are friends already."

"And we can add Eochaid to your list. The abbot was not exactly fond of having one werewolf in the abbey. I'm sure he will be overjoyed with two."

Eochaid grinned, and Myndil's spirits seemed lifted for a time.

"Now that you mention it," said Myndil, after a pause, "I have really made so many friends on my way, perhaps I should not like to stay at the abbey all the time. I was so happy at the orphanage– when it was just an orphanage–I never thought I could be half as happy anywhere else..." His voice trailed though his mind was active, busy working out the benefits of having spent time roaming the country.

He was quiet for sometime–quiet for Myndil, at any rate–silently asking God for guidance, which no voice would give. They continued along the road, and the prospect opened, the highland range coming into view, the clouds glowering over the distant peaks, the blue borage coming in, the trillium rousing in the renewed warmth. Eochaid was about to propose they change into wolves and run back to the shore, being not far away, eager to be nearer to home sooner and eager to cheer Myndil a little, but the sight of an old friend brought back all of Myndil's natural cheerfulness and volubility.

"Oh, hallo, Peig!" he cried, waving furiously. "Look, Aodhgan– it's Peig! The healer woman I told you about who gave me the flowers."

The old woman had just stood from her cauldron, having boiled down some figwort for wounds, when the familiar voice reached her. "Gods teeth," she grumped, sinking in agitation, "If 'tisn't the rain, 'tis the plague at me." She turned and put her hands on her hips, Myndil running to her as though he meant to embrace her. He stopped before the cauldron, beaming in high glee, and her eye naturally descried the two goliaths walking up behind him. "Beannachtaí abhaile," she sighed, eyeing Eochaid. "'Tis not everyday I got the prince o' wolves at me."

Eochaid was amused and offered a slight bow.

"Well," said Peig, speaking to Aodhgan, "you found him so, and good may he do you. Didn't end up in a ditch anyhow."

"No, I didn't," Myndil sang, "but Aodhgan did, which I am still very sorry about."

Aodhgan looked his full approbation.

"Aye, well, there's still time," the old woman sniffed. "War's not over yet."

"I think it is," said Eochaid, indicating a few stragglers who were running for the shore.

Myndil noticed the tied rush cross on the tree behind her. "Oh, you saved the crosses we made! I hope Brigid liked them. And did you have a nice feast day for her? But what are you doing over here? Your home is on the road to Ath Cliath."

"Same thing you're doin' here, lad," was all her answer.

"Would you like us to take you home again? Aodhgan came in a currach and is going to take us back across the sea. I'm sure it would be no trouble to bring you along."

She gave Aodhgan a hard look. "Think I'll stay here th'while, lad," said she, studying Aodhgan's stature and impossible might. "Sure'n they'll be men comin' up from the field what'll need healin'."

Myndil would have her come with them but he would not press her, and as she was determined to offer her services where they were wanted most, he only said he wished her well and hoped he would see her again at her home soon. He knew she would not come to the abbey, though the invitation almost escaped him; he would have her be safe and comfortable at her own house. He gave her a hug, which surprised her, but she did not dislike it, smiling in spite of herself and saying, "There's somethin' wrong with that b'y," as he skipped away.

The nods from Aodhgan and Eochaid were mutually exchanged, and they went westward to the shoreline, Peig watching the two wolves negotiate who was going to be running and who was going to be carrying.

Do not hold it against them, said a voice, with maternal consolation. A presence wafted from the tree and toward the old woman, settling somewhere in the air beside her. They were desperate to end the curse put upon them.

"They're still arrachtach, after all that forgiveness their god promised 'em. Sure'n what'd forgettin' the Gods an' our own ways get 'em?"

The presence swayed and canted, watching Eochaid change, Aodhgan hold his cousin's his human form and pick up Myndil on the way. Perhaps a good friend.

The ride was short but pleasant, the sea spray pobbling in with the tide, Eochaid loping blissfully along the wet sands, Aodhgan doing the work of holding his cousin's human form, and Myndil enjoying the unencumbered romp, happy in the prospect of going home and of possibly being there by evening. God was still silent, but he had his friends to reassure him that he had done his best to fulfill his obligation, and of the rest he must acquit himself, leaving god's mercy and forgiveness to time. They passed the port, the few mercenaries who had quit the field looking for a quick passage home, and they found Aodhgan's curragh, situated beside the rocks, exactly where he had left it, the weight of the boulder still holding it down, and the rogue he had left to guard it still wedged in the sand.

"Hello, head in the sand!" Myndil pealed, jumping down from Eochaid's back.

The rogue looked up, saw the gargantuan wolf sail toward him, and flinched. "H-h-hullo!" the rogue whimpered, spitting out the sand from his mouth.

Aodhgan looked over his curragh and removed the stone, dropping it beside the rogue's head.

"Ah-Ah watched it fer ye, aye!" said the rogue, in a hopeful accent. "Ah made sure naebodae touched it, jus' how ye asked—please don't kill me!"

"I won't," said Aodhgan, stepping over him.

Eochaid folded his arms and laughed. "It always amuses me that everyone assumes Aodhgan is the murderous one just because of his size," he simpered, speaking mostly to Myndil. "He won't even kill rabbits when we're out on hunts."

"They are small and have little nutrition," was Aodhgan's excuse.

Aodhgan threaded the oars and prepared the currach, and Eochaid reached into the sand, plucking the rogue from the hole and shaking him off. He put him on his feet, dusted his shirt, and gave him a hardy pat on the back. "There you are," he happily announced. "You're free to go."

"Ah'm free tae go?" said the rogue, in almost a wounded tone. "But wha'm Ah gonnae dae wi' mah lyfe? If it's no' stealin' boats, wha' is it then, aye? Ah thought tha's me oot with the tide, an' Ah'm still here."

Eochaid glanced back at the road. "You could always go pick the battlefield clean and bury the unclaimed dead, so their spirits don't haunt the island forever."

"Aye," the rogue nodded, his throat bobbling, "Ah will tha'."

The spindly figure scampered away, running toward the battlefield with newfound fervor, the prospect of trinkets and treasures pried from the piled dead enough to sooth his ideas of a meaningless life.

"Did you make him sit there this whole time?" Eochaid laughed, watching the rogue run down the road.

"I told him if he wanted to do something useful with his life, he could guard my currach instead of steal it," said Aodhgan, sitting in the high seat.

"And where did you get this currach from?"

"I borrowed it."

"From Olaf, I hope."

"Of course."

Aodhgan gestured for them to join him and sit down, and once Eochaid and Myndil were secure, Eochaid having to put Myndil on his lap, the legs of the two giant men taking up much of the room, they were off, Aodhgan scudding away from the shore in a violent flurry, his iron muscles working away, the oars tearing through the water, the force of his sculling propelling them into the sea with speed.

There were not far from shore when a familiar figure appeared on the beach: it was running toward the port, it was grappling along the jetty, it was fumbling with the moors and ropes—cries of agony rang out, a large man crumbled to the ground, sinking to his knees and raising his eyes, screaming the blasphemies of many gods and many follies.

Myndil peering around Eochaid and looked back at the shore. He coiled his hand around his eye and peered through the pinhole. "Is that Olaf?" he asked.

Eochaid turned and tapered his gaze. "Certainly looks like him. He does seem to be relieved of his weapons, half his armour, and a few fingers though."

"And one currach," Aodhgan added.

Olaf was crambling onto his flagship, moving as quickly as a shattered knee and broken limbs would allow. Blood and a missing eye made reeling in the moorings difficult, but even more difficult was trying to get his ship to move without the galley of men to man it. A few of the jarls who had accompanied him to battle followed onto the ship, but they were just as wounded, just as suffering and sore-footed, missing limbs and missing eyes, and it was a struggle even to lift the sails. The agony of his loss besieged him, the battle he had foolishly wanted and just as foolishly thought he could win, his pride and complacence acting on his vanity, convincing him that he ought to defeat Aethelstan because he wanted to, and though Aethelstan had not been without casualties, Olaf's losses were far too great. He had arrived unprepared and undaunted, and he would leave the battle the loser of the isles, his dominion permanently diminished, a failure of kingship, a ruler of ruin. He noggled to the prow of his ship, and clung to the stempost, crying out to his gods, "He cursed me! That wretched spy! That abomination of god! He cursed me! He made me do it! By Odin, he made me do it!" He raised his bleeding fists to the sky, and Myndil's name caromed over the sea, the echo rippling over the gentle waves, making its way to Myndil's heart.

He would have stood from his place in the currach and waved, Olaf certainly not a friend, yet Myndil always thought it best to acknowledge acquaintances no matter how evil, because it was the right thing to do, but it might be salt in the wound for Olaf just now, and Myndil kindly left off. He would see him some other time, probably in Ath Cliath when this was all over, to make his apologies as he could, for ruining his kingship or for saving the people of Erie from it, to tell him that though he had meant to be friendly with him, god it seemed had other ideas. Whether god had meant for Olaf to lose and all his men to die, Myndil had no way of knowing: the voice was still silent, the presence still absent, and Myndil nestled in the bend of Eochaid's arm, the iron strength and fraternal kindness a much-needed restorative to his nerves.

Aodhgan rowed west until the shores of Erie were in view, and once the coastline began to curve, he turned and followed it northward, making for the abbey and Myndil's way home. A familiar sight soon charmed Myndil's imagination: it was the first image he had gained of the land beyond the abbey, the same remnants of ring forts and roundhouses, the same waddle and wickerwork, the homes and hills dotted with clochauns, the dry stone walls divagating over fields and drawing his eye toward the uplands—he was coming home, he was coming home with friends, and never was he more excited.

"Oh, I can see the island!" Myndil exclaimed, pointing to a dot in the far distance. "I cannot wait to see everyone and tell them everything that's happened—and I will get to see the new additions to the abbey. Aodhgan, you've already seen them, so don't tell me. I should like to be surprised when we arrive."

"I have no reference of what to tell you," said Aodhgan, with smiling eyes. "I saw your home for the first time and don't know what has changed since you left."

"That's very true—but Eochaid hasn't seen anything yet, so don't tell him either. I cannot wait to introduce you to everyone. I'm sure none of them will be frightened of you—no one was frightened by Aodhgan—" Aodhgan said nothing here. "—and I'm sure everyone will love and mind you, especially Abbess Bhaldruithe."

Eochaid winced and thought he had misheard. "What did you say her name was?"

Myndil repeated the name, and Eochaid was astonished.

"We must remember that one, cousin," Eochaid laughed. "Another name the Northmen can choke on."

Aodhgan would be remembering her name for other reasons, and as glad as he was to see Eochaid safe, he was even more avid to fulfill his promise of returning to the abbey and bringing Myndil home.

"When we get to the abbey, we can make sure you send a message to your king right away," Myndil continued. "I don't know that we have many birds that understand wolf at the abbey, but we do have crows and the occasional magpie, and they might be able to convey your message back to Ossory."

Eochaid and Aodhgan shared a bemused look.

"What to you mean?" Eochaid asked.

"I wrote a message to my king when I was at the abbey," said Aodhgan, almost laughing. "Brother Vindimir gave me writing implements to use. I didn't whisper to the crows."

Myndil seemed disappointed. "You mean you cannot talk to animals when you're in your wolf form?"

"No," they both replied.

"Oh."

"We can speak to you in our wolf form," Eochaid reminded him, "but animals won't understand us. Can wolves speak to fish or to bees?"

"They might be able to and I just not know it."

They could not argue with Myndil here.

"We can't even talk to other wolves," Eochaid added. "We're a different species altogether. The only communication we share is growling at one other."

"But you don't howl at the moon?"

"Not on purpose," said Aodhgan. "Neither do wolves."

"Oh." Myndil fidgeted. "I always assumed they did it for their little wolf religion."

Aodhgan stopped rowing to laugh. "Do wolves have gods?"

"Well, I don't know that they have the ability to believe, but I should like to think they have some form of deity who loves them. I know it is not every creature's providence, but everyone ought to be loved by a being in charge of their creation, if they can be."

Aodhgan began rowing again, his heart full, and Eochaid put his hand on Myndil's shoulder, thinking him the purest and most beloved being in the world.

It was only a few hours before they reached the islands off the northeast coast of Erie. The day gave way to evening, and the stars began to loom the gradient of gloaming when Aodhgan docked the boat. Myndil and Eochaid went ashore, Myndil almost running up the tidal crossing to the abbey, and Aodhgan tied the currach to a budding ash, certain no one would take it but wanting to leave it for Eochaid's use should he need it on his return journey home. Myndil almost tripped over himself, flailing and racing up the path, calling out toward the iron gate with a, "HALLO! YES, HALLO! IT'S ME! I'M HOME! WAIT TILL YOU SEE WHO I'VE BROUGHT WITH ME!" with delirious elation. He leaped up the bank and fell over, his eagerness getting in the way of his steps, but as he plummeted to the ground, he suddenly found himself suspended in the air, his face an inch away from the floor.

A giant hand lifted him by the back of his robes. "Careful," Eochaid laughed, putting Myndil on his feet. "You don't want to have survived a war only to be hurt by the road," but Myndil was too in raptures, too happy to be home, too eager to see every friendly face. Homesickness had not visited him often during his time away, but he felt a something like tender reminiscence to be able to return to those who loved him best.

"HALLO! YES, IT'S ME! COME AND SEE WHO IS HERE WITH ME!"

Somewhere, in the frigid silent of the prayer room, the groans of anguish began. The abbot was sitting in tranquil despondence, on his knees with hands in supplication, and was in the midst of thanking God for the day fraught with travails and torments, when the familiar voice reached his ear. His soul withered, and his lip began quivering. "O, Lord," he whimpered, raising his eyes and holding out his arms, "why dost thou hate me so? Please commend my soul unto thee instead of forcing me to see that boy again." He implored the sky and waited for death, but nothing happened; only the sound of a loud and long "HALLLOOOOOOOOOOOOOOOOOOOOOOOOO OOOOOOOOOOOOOOOOOOOOOOOOOOOO!" penetrated the window and struck his spirit,

194

killing all further will to live.

Myndil burst through the iron gate and stood in the glory of his home, thinking how lovely it was, seeing it under the glamour of a short absence, thinking it was much changed when there was only one new building and adjoining hall he had already seen before he left, and a small extension to the dormitory that had not yet been finished. "Oh, isn't it beautiful!" he exclaimed, clapping his hands and kicking up his heels. "Oh, halloo heathens!" waving to the rabble, who were busy with work. "I'm so glad to see you made it here and that you've already finished so much of the foundations! Everyone has done such exquisite work—"

"Don't tread on the thyme," Ozzy the Wight lamented, shambling by, nudging Myndil with the handle of his shovel. "I only just put in the new patches."

"Ozzy!" Myndil cried, almost hugging his bones. "Hallo, Ozzy! I'm so glad to see you! I'm sorry I wasn't here to do the mulch, but I'm back now and can help you if you need it. The daffodils are coming in, and they look absolutely lovely!"

Ozzy would have smiled, if he had muscles to spend, but his jaw looked as though it was happy and was glad for the compliment.

"Oh, look how they've added to the new building!" Myndil shouted to Aodhgan and Eochaid, who were leisurely coming up the walk. "And they even redid some of the dressing the stonemasons did. They made the chimera on my window look positively frightening! We should have them do a few werewolves for you. I'm sure they wouldn't mind taking your likeness. The moulding is very well done—and they even put Peig's little god figure with the open purse above the door!"

The rabble came from their working station, a little fearful to see Aodhgan again, and to see him with another almost as large as himself. They glanced up at the stone figure Myndil was pointing to, the one mounting the post above the entrance to the front room, her fingers prying open a cavern between open legs. "Aye, we'll say that's what it is," said the carpenter.

"Hallo, heathens!" said Myndil, embracing them awkwardly. "I'm ever so glad to see you. Do you have everything you need to finish the job?"

"Mostly," said the stonemason. "We'll need a fair bit o' stone once the rest o' the foundation is up, but it's a good work and good bein' here. The meals are reg'lur and the sleepin' accommodation's nice."

"You have done an amazing job—I hardly recognize the old part of the dormitory from the new now."

"Thanks," said the rabble, with a collective blush.

"I'm sure everyone must be delighted. I know I am, and I haven't even seen inside yet. Brother Vindimir must be overjoyed. Once you're finished, he will have a large room to himself now and never have to share Brother Crannach's room again."

Aodhgan approached and inspected the intermural stack of firewood he had told them not to touch. Every stick of firewood was still in place, and he gave the rabble a look of grim approbation.

"Kept every piece there, like you said, sor," said the carpenter, the rabble nodding eagerly amongst themselves.

Aodhgan narrowed his gaze and growled. "Good."

They trembled and looked away.

"I see you've already made your mark, cousin," Eochaid observed.

"Rest o' the building should be done in a few weeks, 'long as we can get good stone," said the stonemason, with eyes low.

"This is the best we could do with what we had, yer reverence," said the metalworker, speaking to Myndil, "—er whatever you go by now, that is."

"I am not a reverence," Myndil insisted. "I am your friend, and so I shall always be."

"Er—sure. We'll say friend, aye."

"And you are my abbey-mate now. We will get to spend more time together, and I can read more of my book to you, if the Brothers and Sisters haven't been doing that already—Hallo, Abbess Bhal—"

Myndil was suddenly muffled by two overwhelmingly large breasts, and the abbess' arms crumpled him from behind, her slight frame surprisingly strong when she was pressing someone into her chest.

"Oh, you are home!" the abbess sobbed, burying Myndil in her deep vale. "Thank God, you are home!"

"Mff gldmb to snn ytmm," Myndil muttered, suffocating slightly.

She was singing her acclamations to God when a long and familiar shadow surmounted her. She gasped, threw Myndil aside, and ran up to Aodhgan with arms open and chest flouncing. "You brought him back," she cried, grabbing Aodhgan and pressing herself against him, her features buried against his iron waist, all ready appreciation.

Aodhgan smiled down at her, never happier to receive such a welcome, and carefully caressed the top of her back. "I promised I would," he thrummed, kneeling down. "I said I would return, and I have kept my oath, by the Grace of God."

"You did," she sniffed, her delicate fingers taking his hand and holding it to her heart. "You have. By the Grace of God."

Her tears were real, her red eyes and flushing cheeks told him so, her hand pressing against his, betraying the chief of her feelings: she was pleased to have Myndil home but grateful to have Aodhgan back again, the beginnings of their acquaintance garnishing all her prayers over the last few days. She felt indebted to god for returning him here, unwilling to settle for anything else now that she had a royal wolf of Osraige as a bed, and she gratulated in her praises to heaven, thanking god again and again for his safe return, her tearful smiles speaking all the relief and exultation she felt. He held her close and browsed her cheeks with his thumb, wiping the tears that tinged her complexion, the tributaries that a variety of feelings produced warming her face. She craned her neck and parted her lips, eager and expectant of something, and he leaned down, his features meeting hers— when Myndil suddenly cried out, "But you have never introduced Eochaid yet!"

196

They pulled back from one another, the abbess hemming and turning aside, and Aodhgan standing and looking a little ashamed, but he still held her hand, still brought her forward as Myndil was pulling Eochaid toward them, and still held to her as he made their introduction.

"This is my cousin Eochaid," said Aodhgan, "prince of Osraige."

A similar long shadow suppressed her, the same features smiling down at her and bowing low, only younger and more arch, and her eyes sparkled, feeling that to have two such men on either side of her a blessing from god, to be sure.

"I'm pleased to meet you–" Eochaid began, but the cries emanating from the abbey of "NO, NO, NO, NO, NO–NOT ANOTHER ONE–I FORBID IT–I ABSOLUTELY FORBID–" made everyone turn to the abbey.

The abbot was marching toward them, his fists flying in a fury, his features already flouting, and Myndil made it worse by trying to hug him.

"Abbot!" he cried, hanging off his arms. "I'm so pleased to see you! Aren't you glad that I'm back and that I've brought you some new friends? Look, there is another wolf from Ossory who believes in God."

The abbot would not say he was glad; the sight of two werewolves and the thought of the amount of fur they would be shedding on his floors was not a thing to make him happy at anytime. He stewed in silence, his fists gripping his robes at his sides, his teeth clattering.

Eochaid now saw what his cousin had meant and laughed to himself. "I am honoured to be welcomed here," said he, with a sagacious smile. "Not to worry, abbot. We will not be staying long."

"Oh," the abbot grumped.

"We would never intrude upon your kindness without sending word first. We will write to my father, to tell him that we are safe here, and we will be gone by morning."

"But you are welcome to stay longer," said the abbess, in a faltering voice. "Surely, you must be tired and in want of a long rest."

"We do, but my father is eager to have us home, and I will not make him wait longer than he needs to."

"Yes..." she whispered, her eyes downcast and colour heightening, "I–I am very sure your father will be pleased that Aodhgan has found you...And...And of course... you must be eager to journey home. How happy he will be..."

She turned away, almost grabbing Myndil's shoulder to cry on, when a hand on her arm gently brought her back around.

"He won't be, when I tell him I mean to stay for a while," said Aodhgan attentively.

She looked up to see how it was, and his aspect was as sincere as his words. "Do you–do you mean to stay for a long while?"

"I do," and eyeing Myndil, Aodhgan added, "at Myndil's request."

Myndil was all happy gratulation. "Really?" He leaped with joy. "Oh, I'm so excited! I don't remember asking you, but maybe I did when we were running away from the battle—if I didn't, I certainly would have, because I love you and should like nothing more than for you to stay forever—" the abbot began gnashing, "—but of course you may stay as long as you like! I'm sure Crannach and Vindimir and Iarlaith and all the children cannot wait to see you!"

Myndil ran off to fetch them and to tell them the news, leaving the abbot to welter in silent wrath, and Eochaid quietly took his cousin aside to ask him what he meant.

"Do you really mean to stay longer?" said Eochaid.

Aodhgan nodded. "At least until the new work on the abbey is finished." He gestured toward the abbess, who was coddling the abbot and asking if he should like some tea and a lie-down. "What do you think of her, cousin?"

"Myndil mentioned her as willing." Eochaid made an appraisal of her. "God has given her many gifts."

"He has, which I hope to enjoy after I write to our father." Here was a conscious look. "She has seen the wolf and does not mind it."

Eochaid, beginning to understand, broke into a broad smile. "Cousin," he exclaimed, overjoyed for him. "Is it true? Then of course you must stay."

"I will—to convince the abbot to ordain Myndil at least, and if he won't, to torment him about it for a while."

"Father will not like having you away," Eochaid mused. "You know how he is when you leave the kingdom—but if you tell him you have found someone, he might be more eager to lend you out."

They shared a brotherly embrace, pressing their foreheads together, Aodhgan kissing his cousin on the top of his head, and Eochaid patting him on the back.

"I could not be happier for you," said Eochaid, his heart full, "but you will come home to visit."

"Of course—certainly for your wedding."

"If my betrothed still waits for me. She might not want a prince who was captured by slavers."

The abbess was just taking the abbot back inside, to give him a nice warm dish of nourishing gruel, when he broke away from her, flying at the cousins in a violent rage.

"Nobody is staying here!" he cried, his fists flailing at them. "Nobody is sharing anyone's bed or thanking God for returning anybody home—everyone is leaving and I have absolutely done with all manner of nonsense in this abbey and I am asking God to smite every last one of you!"

His fist accidentally landed against Eochaid's stomach. Eochaid looked down, having felt nothing, and laughed about it. The abbot pulled his hand back and cradled it, wincing in agony.

"You would dare strike a prince?" Aodhgan demanded, with mock complacence.

"Gah!" the abbot moaned, having forgot he had royalty in his midst. "It was not consciously done! I was angry and I'm still angry and I only want to be left alone to wallow in punishment for the rest of my life!"

"I think you will enjoy being punished by allowing my royal representative to stay here as your guest," said Eochaid, with a stately air, his chest muscles peaking. "My father will be very pleased to know you sheltered us in our time of need and I'm sure he will want to reward you well for your kindness."

The abbot hemmed, and his face lengthened. "Well, if His Majesty means to be charitable..."

"We have little gold in our kingdom, but we do have excellent hunting grounds and plenty of wood, and I'm sure my father will make you many presents of game to stock your larder and feed your orphans with."

The children suddenly poured out of the abbey, following Myndil to the front garden, and remembering Aodhgan and glad to see him standing beside another enormous creature, they raced toward him and attached themselves to his legs.

"He's back! He's back!" the children cried.

"As I told you I would be," said Aodhgan, watching them scale his limbs, "no fibs."

"Aye, nae fibs," one huffed, "but now ye huftae let us ride ye!"

Aodhgan humphed. "Do I."

"Aye! Abbess said if ye came back, we'd get to see yer wolf."

"Aye, and we'd get tae pet ye and take ye fer walks an' o'."

"What about you?" one of the children asked Eochaid, gaping up at him. "You look wooly. You got a wolf too?"

"I do," Eochaid nodded.

"Can we see it? Please? Pleeeeeeeeeeeeeeeeeeeeeease? Ah'm practicin' my pleases, 'cause Brother Vindimir says Ah'm rude."

"Aodhgan will show you his," Eochaid offered, his smiles unabated. "I am not staying long."

"Aww," the children whined.

"But we need moar wolves, 'cause we needs ye tae use yer noses and tells us who let one go in the bedroom."

"Aye! Ah sae it was Dimeadh!"

"No, it was Aoife!"

"It wasn't me! It was Paudrig!"

Aodhgan was appealed to for his abilities. He sniffed each child and concluded, "It was Dimeadh."

"See! Ah telt yis!"

"They find new uses for you, cousin," Eochaid laughed.

Aodhgan smiled and shook his head. "Why would I be our father's royal huntsman when I could be detecting more ventuous prey."

Eochaid turned away and laughed into his hand, and Crannach came to greet them, glad to hear the verdict of the nose that knew no lies and pleased to have discovered himself innocent of any crimes.

"Welcome back, lad," said Crannach, offering his hand to Aodhgan.

They shook hands and patted arms, and Aodhgan invited Eochaid to meet him, certain he should notice the same thing he did upon seeing Crannach for the first time. Eochaid glanced at Crannach, then at Aodhgan, then at Crannach again. "I'm pleased to meet you," said Eochaid, giving his cousin a conscious look.

Crannach shared his sentiments, introduced Vindimir, who had come up behind him, and then set about wrangling the children to bed. It was getting late, baths must be taken and teeth must be brushed, and once he had corralled them toward the abbey again, Eochaid pulled his cousin aside.

"Can he be—?" Eochaid whispered.

"I was sure he was, but he told me I was mistaken," Aodhgan replied. "But there are many curious things at this abbey," giving a glance to the two crows perching in the ash tree beside them. "Wait till you see what lives under the bed."

Crannach, having seen Myndil with the children and wanting to give everyone else the first rights of gratulation, came forward to welcome Myndil home. He wanted to be the last, knowing that Iarlaith had been the most anxious for him and ought to have the privilege of seeing him first, but his heart was too much besieged to hold back much longer.

"Brother Crannach has always been that big," Myndil was telling Eochaid. "Even when I was a child and he used to make bear noises when he told us stories, we—"

Two immense arms grabbed him from behind and lifted him up, crushing him against a warm and familiar chest.

"Brother Crannach!" was Myndil's restrained exclamation, rubbing the back of his head against the side of Crannach's face. "I was just telling Eochaid about all the growling sounds you used to do when telling stories."

Crannach was silent for a moment, his voice oppressed by an abundance of tears, his heart too much in the exultation and relief of having Myndil back safe. He bent his head into Myndil nape and pressed his nose into his shoulder, his tears dampening Myndil's robes. He turned him around, held him up by his arms, and said faltering, "Ah missed ye, son..."

"I missed you too, Brother Crannach," said Myndil, with genuine feeling.

The instinctive questions of 'are you all right' and 'did you eat anything' came to mind, but Crannach would leave those for Iarlaith, and instead he put Myndil on his feet and said only, "Yer wolf friend told us a bit o' what happened while you were awae."

"Oh, but he has not told you about the battle!"

Crannach simpered through his tears. "Mibbe we better no' tell Iarlaith about that, aye?"

"Oh, but I was not hurt, and God was there to look after me—or at least I think it was God, and Eochaid would not let anyone hurt me, and Aodhgan came to save us both—well, save me really, because Eochaid was enjoying hurting the bad people."

Eochaid tightened his fists, and his shoulder muscles flexed.

"Ah see ye caused quite a commotion while ye were out," Crannach laughed. "But Ah'm glad ye made friends and had a pleasant time."

200

"Oh, yes, very pleasant. Everyone was so kind—well, most people—and it is a shame Peig didn't come back with us, because I think she would have liked it here. But when I go out again, whenever that will be, I'll invite her here and hope she'll come so everyone can try her magic poker milk."

Crannach was glad to hear Myndil's emphatic recantations again, though he had little idea what he meant, and he patted him on the shoulder. "Well, let's hope ye'll no' go out again fer a while, aye? 'Mon, Iarlaith'll want to see ye."

And she did want to see him. She had heard the signs of his return from her place in the kitchen, and she was just preparing the soup for dinner and the bones for Ozzy when Myndil's emphatic cries reached her. "Mah bairn's back! Mah wee bairn's back!" she began raming, hastening through the plates. She took the pot off the small clay range, opened the bread oven door, and threw everything else aside, hearing Myndil voice just beyond the front room.

"I'm sure we have enough to feed everyone," Myndil was saying to their guests. "Sister Iarlaith always—mnpmhffmpfpf."

He was tackled by a wall of flesh cloaked in woolen robes, and Myndil held his arms out to embrace Sister Iarlaith as she crumpled him against her chest.

"Mah bairn," she cried, holding him against her, "my wee Myndil!"

Myndil was shoved so far into her breast he could not find his way out. His voice mumbled something, but the sound was lost in her robes. Eochaid helped Myndil peel himself back, and Iarlaith's necklace was stuck to his face.

"Look at ye," Iarlaith wept, cradling Myndil's face in her hands, "ye huvnae eaten. Ah know it."

"Well," said Myndil, his cheeks pressing inward against themselves, "I dih ferghet to eat the las few days, buh tha's on'y becauseth I was riding a werewolf much ov the time, and there were no scones when we goh t' Scone."

Iarlaith had no idea what he meant; she only knew that he looked thin and in need of nourishment that only her brand of coddling could provide. "Tha's nice, son," said she sweetly, releasing his cheeks.

"Did you see how many friends I made when I was away?"

"Aye, Ah did." She showed him the necklace and marble pendant and thanked him from her heart.

Myndil suddenly remembered. "Oh, yes! I had entirely forgot about it when I sent the builders here. I had wanted to buy you one. I wasn't sure which one you would like, but I'm glad you chose that one, with all the little hounds running about on it. It reminds me of Eochaid—oh, I'll introduce you!"

Myndil pulled her out of the front room and into the garden, and Iarlaith was immediately standing in Eochaid's shadow. She looked up and found not one giant hirsute man but two.

"Oh, my," said Iarlaith musically, impressed with Eochaid's size. Had Aodhgan and Eochaid not both been smiling, she might have been a little fearful of them. "Are there more o' yous?" she asked, craning her neck and shielding her eyes, trying to see Eochaid's face from the shadow.

"Quite a few," said Eochaid, with a friendly bow.

"My God. What dae they feed yous in Osraige? Ah been tryin' tae get Myndil that size o' his life, and nae matter how much he eats, he's as wispae as a willow."

They talked on, Eochaid glad to meet the woman who had trained up his friend, and Vindimir, who was standing with the children and telling them not to climb their visitors' legs, took the opportunity to welcome Myndil home.

He gave Myndil an assenting nod. "You did well," was all his approbation.

Myndil smiled so sanguinely, but Vindimir felt the guilt of fifteen years hang upon him. He wanted to say more to Myndil, wanted to tell him the truth about the voice of God at the abbey, but he would leave his compunction for another hour: Myndil was back, and Vindimir thanked by whatever grace of god that followed him on his journey that he was safe and sound.

The first joys of his return belonged to the family he had left behind, any of them somewhat glad that he had gone now hoping he should never leave again—except the abbot, whose happiness had quit him long ago, and whose remorse was all returning. He was back at the willow tree in the corner of the garden, he was leaning against the bark, and he was thanking god, either for Myndil's safe return or for his suffering—both were much the same—and he wondered if he should ever know peace and quiet again with so many new lessons in suffering at the abbey.

Everyone was invited to take the evening meal in the front room, Iarlaith professing that she had made more than enough gruel to go round, and having had little to eat in many days, Myndil was only too happy to dress the table. Aodhgan offered to help while Eochaid asked whether he might avail them of writing implements, if it was not too much trouble. He should pay for everything or replace what he used, not wanting to take anything away from his hosts that they might need, but Vindimir assured him they had enough to write on, and gave him whatever he needed, Eochaid sitting by the fire to make his message and only stopping when he saw the nisser trot by.

Eochaid glared instinctively, his senses following the nisser across the room.

"Wrap tha' starin', biggun," the nisser humphed, putting the piggin of milk down at the table. "Ay'm here by invitation, same as yis."

The nisser returned to the kitchen, and Eochaid's gaze followed, wondering what else was wandering about the pantry.

"It's interesting here," said Aodhgan, smiling.

Eochaid watched a few wisps gather round the garden. "I'm surprised they all live together. We can't even get along with the wolves at home. Is there anything malicious that lives here?"

"You saw the wight outside, but he seems only interested in his flowerbeds, and there's the dullahan, but he just wanders around the gate following his head." Aodhgan suddenly turned and raised his fist, holding it up to the shadow flickering along the wall behind him. "Don't do that."

"Aw'm not doin' nuffin'!" said a voice.

Eochaid turned toward the shadow and felt his ears itch. "I was wondering what that was."

"Get out of there," Aodhgan growled.

"Wha'! Aw'm not hauntin' yew! Aw's just welterin'!" A few tendrils raised from the shadow, and the co-walker pulled itself from the wall. "Aw, no!" Thistlewraithe cried, spying Eochaid. "Now we got two o' yews!"

"Co-walker!" Myndil exclaimed, leaping toward him. He tried to embrace his tenebrous limbs and grasped at nothing, passing through his vaporous form. "Aodhgan told me you were here!"

"Aye, Aw'll bet he tol' yew."

"And how do you like it here? Are there enough shadows here for you to jump through?"

"Aye, when Aw'm not bein' hounded by werewolves what wouldn't know a good hauntin' if it leapt up and smacked 'em in the fangs."

"Do not think of haunting my cousin," Aodhgan warned him, "and you had better have left the abbess alone."

"Aye, Aw'm leavin' yer biddy alone. Got the rabble to haunt now, dun' Aw."

"They have work to do, though. I hope you haven't been haunting them this whole time," said Myndil.

"Weeeeeell, Aw gotta make it werth the haunt, see? If they down't drop a hammer on a toe or scream murder when they fall off the ladder, is it really werth the werk? Hauntin' tough bissniss."

"I'm sure it is, and by the looks on their faces, I'm sure you make their lives positively miserable."

"Aye, 's a good pairin', me 'n 'em." Thistlewraithe raised a tendril to his spectral mouth and looked as though he were pretending to whisper behind it. "Yer abbot's no fun to haunt, mind. 'Tween yew and me, yeh?" sinking his voice, "Aw think he's cracked."

The abbess put the abbot down in his seat at the head of the table, and he sat mumbling to himself, looking deplorably.

"Talks to hisself barmy-like," Thistlewraithe continued, "sayin' all manner o' lunatical jabber, about god punishin' him and thayt fer sendin' yew away."

"Oh, he need not worry about that," said Myndil. "I have had such a lovely time away—most of the time, which I'm going to tell everyone about once we sit down."

"Aw think thayt's what yer abbot's afraid of."

"You're welcome to join us, of course. I know co-walkers don't eat gruel, but there are plenty of shadows for you to hop in and out of with all the candles along the wall."

"Stay out of the children's shadows," said Aodhgan, the hair on his chest fruzzling.

"Aye, aye. Aw know better than to try fer it. Aw'm stayin' sunward, me."

Aodhgan was conscious of cracks in the wall he had made upon his first visit to the abbey. The rabble had made nominal repairs, but he would honour his promise and mend them as soon as time should allow. Eochaid wrote and finished his letter while the tea was in preparation, Iarlaith came in with the bowls of gruel and fresh fried bread, and once the children were ushered to the table, they all sat down together, to hear the story of Myndil's adventures, whether everyone wanted to hear the whole of them or not. The abbot's nerves were soothed by tea, but not for long, Myndil's theatrical retelling involving many gestures and many voices, him imitating the many meetings and acting out the many encounters along the way, Aodhgan and Eochaid being applied to for their parts, filling in the gaps wherever they could, Aodhgan agreeing to be Olaf and Eochaid showing his wolf form when Myndil mentioned the ride across Alt Clut and Alba. The children were delighted, captivated by every moment, so engrossed by the wolf and by Thistlewraithe's shadow puppetry on the wall behind that they forgot about the gruel, gladly letting their dinner cool, happy to be entertained by such a long story whether all of it were true or not. He came to the battle, talked about all the different kings and made sure to tell them it was wrong to kill even, if in the name of God, leaving out the part about meeting Velinas, still uncertain about whether he had been saved him or been swindled into sin, and wound up the whole with, "And then we sailed back here, and here we are, glad to be home but glad to have gone away, so you need not worry about feeling badly about sending me," speaking to the abbot, who was staring at the wall, trying to fantasize a life that involved Myndil losing his voice.

He still spoke through dinner, the children asking questions and Myndil answering, Aodhgan happy to sit beside the abbess, her thigh pressing eagerly against his, whilst Crannach urged everyone to finish their bowls before he started on them.

Eochaid was still hungry after eating, disheartened to see such a meager spread—not on his account, however; if he wanted more, he could always go out and hunt for his meals, but he sincerely hoped the children had more to eat than gruel through the long northern winters. "Cousin," said he quietly, leaning over to Aodhgan, "tell me you will hunt for them while you are here. They need more than groats and warm milk to sustain them."

Aodhgan pushed his bowl toward his cousin and urged him to eat what was left. "There is more bread—"

"No," said Eochaid, with quiet humility. "We came upon them suddenly, and they had no time to prepare anything for us. It is not their fault that we are accustomed to more." A pang struck his heart, and he gave the rest of his meal to the nisser, who came in to offer him more milk for his gruel.

"If they are poor," said Aodhgan, "they don't seem to notice."

He gently indicated Brother Vindimir, who was busy untangling hair and fixing nightgowns while the children reiterated their favourite parts in Myndil's story, pretending to be valiant kings and princely wolves, making each other laugh or cry, asking Myndil to tell the story again before bedtime, Sister Iarlaith collecting empty place and playfully dotting little noses with touches of gruel, the girls giggling and recoiling, the boys roaring in high revel, claiming they were wolves and would hunt anything in their way.

The picture was not the perfect happiness Eochaid would have liked; he should like to see a roast goose on the table for the children and good amount of root vegetables and fragrant herbs ornamenting their plates, but they seemed satisfied, warm and sheltered, loved and looked after, and Eochaid must be contented with a small abbey far away from any large farm.

"We are not a rich kingdom," said Eochaid, his heart still sinking, "but we must do something for them."

"We will," Aodhgan promised, "though I don't know that they would have it any other way."

"The abbot certainly would."

The abbot was muttering to himself, his aspect blank and eyes bleary, Myndil talking at him and not stopping until he reached the subject of ordination.

"And even though I have only got a few people to love God," said Myndil, "I was wondering if that were really enough for me to be ordained. You had said that I should get a great many followers to join us, and I know you didn't mean that they should come to live at the abbey, only come to be converted and tell you how much they love God, but I thought I should ask, even though I'm not sure if I ought be ordained. I didn't know where I was going when I left the orphanage here, but I did put my faith in God and listened to him whenever he answered me—if it really was God—and I think even God might be disappointed in me, but I have gained so many friends I don't think I can be sad about not being ordained."

"Well," said the abbot, rousing himself, when he realized Myndil was no longer speaking, "I did say you needed followers to qualify for ordination. The rabble haven't pledged themselves to God, and the two werewolves you brought have already accepted God's Grace, so you will just have to go out again and—"

"You will ordain him," Aodhgan demanded, his shadow somehow increasing.

His immense chest arched and swelled, and the abbess pressed her legs together.

Aodhgan straightened and rolled his shoulders. "He completed his pilgrimage. He brought people to help you build your abbey. He helped me recover my cousin. He blessed three kings of the islands." He mantled over the table, his shadow threatening the abbot. "You will ordain him."

The abbot whimpered and hid behind his chair. Crannach chuckled on Vindimir's shoulder, but Sister Iarlaith, who came in from the kitchen to bring out more bread, suddenly looked strange, staring out the window of the front room, as if she could not believe what she saw.

"I will—I will ordain him!" the abbot cried, shielding himself with his chair. "I'll do it! Please— by the Grace of God, don't break me!"

"But you like suffering," Myndil reminded him. "I thought you said you like when God punishes you, because it teaches you lessons about forbearance."

"I lied—I lied!" the abbot wailed. "By God, I lied! I sent you away because I couldn't bear to listen to you anymore and wanted God to deal with you!"

"Well," said Myndil gleefully, understanding in part, "God did deal with me, and then he brought me back here, and I am really all the better for it, but I don't know that I want to be ordained immediately. Eochaid said that you are ordained and have no friends, and though I wanted to be ordained so I could stay here, I think I want to have friends more than I want to be ordained. If I am installed here, I won't really be allowed to go out much if I need to help care for the children."

"I don't want you to have more friends!" the abbot miffled, gripping the front of Myndil's robes. "I don't want you to speak to anybody about God and I don't want you to bring them back here! I'll ordain you if you promise never to make another friend again!"

"Oh, well, then I certainly don't want to be ordained. I like friends and I want them to know about God and everyone to love him as much as I do—but I got so few followers on my first pilgrimage—"

"Then who're they?" said Sister Iarlaith, pointing out the window.

Everyone turned and craned their necks. She was pointing to the iron gate: a steady stream of people lined the path, a hundred heads at least leading the way down to the coast. Everyone came from the table to look, crowding the front window, looking in disbelief and then amazement. A light breached the low clouds, a numinous beam illuminated the path from the shore, and somewhere a chorus thrummed a melodious chord.

"What..." the abbot breathed, completely at a loss.

"There's a lot o' people oot there, abbot," Sister Iarlaith urged. "An 'undred at least."

The abbot's jaw hung, and the pit in his stomach deepened. "He did it..." he whiffled, "The boy did it..."

"I did it?" said Myndil doubtingly. "But I don't think I did anything. How could I have? I don't know any of those people."

Eochaid's eyes narrowed. "That's King Constantine," pointing just beyond the iron gate.

"What!" the abbot cried, huddling under the window sill. "Does he mean to invade us? You—wolf prince or whatever you are—change with your big ox of a cousin and defend us!"

Aodhgan came closer to look. He studied the heads and faces of the meandering crowd. "He has no armour or weapons, and he's walking with women and children."

"And King Owain," Eochaid added.

"WHAT." The abbot grabbed Myndil by the front of his robe and gave him a firm shake. "What did you do? Why are there kings coming here?"

"They're refugees," said Aodhgan, in a somber hue.

He immediately went out, and though the abbot begged that he should not let them in for fear of being taken by surprise and raided, there was nothing he could do to stop him: Aodhgan was going to the gate, Eochaid was following, and everyone in the abbey soon joined them, eager to meet the two kings and hear why they had come.

A small ship was moored against the coast, the stream of people wreathed the breadth of the shore, a sea of features and faces wearied from the journey, all of them frigid and fatigued, seeking nothing beyond the binds of sympathy for their loss. Standing at the head of the stream was King Constantine, his regal air quite gone, his robes and armour changed for a white linen gown, his age revealing itself, his aspect old and worn. He had been humbled by the shame of defeat, the flag of Alba on his ship low and torn, and he came forward with eyes low and head bowed. King Owain, however, was much the same, his round face wreathed in a smile, his plump fingers waving at Eochaid. He saw Aodhgan beside him, marked the thick hair on his chest and arms, and wondered if the nice riding wolf he had met had a little friend.

"So," said Constantine, meeting them, "this is where you skulked off to." His eye followed the outline of the abbey behind them. "A tolerable place, as constructions go. You will have to fortify this gate, if you mean to keep out the Northmen, but a solid building upon the whole."

There was a sorrow in his voice, and Myndil came forward to greet him.

"I'm glad to see you again," said Myndil cautiously, "and you, Owain, though I'm afraid of what seeing you here means."

Eochaid and Aodhgan bowed when acknowledged, and Constantine waved them off.

"No," said he, with a solemn sigh, "I am not a king anymore. I have done with all the formalities of sovereignty. My duty now is to everyone else ruined by my recklessness."

"You lost the war," said Myndil sadly, "even with God on your side—the real God?"

"God deemed it that Aethelstan should win, and that my son should die." Constantine looked grave. "Why God chose to let Aethelstan kill so many of my men is something I will never understand. They were good men, many of them I knew for much of their lives. I lost my dignity, but even more importantly, I lost my lineage and my kingdom."

"I'm sorry to hear of it," said Eochaid, "and sorry we could not do more."

"It was not your doing," said Constantine, shaking his head, "and it was not your place to fight a war that had nothing to do with you or your kingdom. I made an agreement with Olaf, thinking we could win against Aethelstan, that I would be rid of a nuisance and he would get is wretched land back. I had not counted on his idiocy and ill-prepared men. I am my own demise. I bring to you all those whose lives I have utterly destroyed, the wives and children of my men who died in battle," presenting the sea of sorrowing faces behind him. "Their lands were claimed by Aethelstan, and I refused to leave them behind, to be ruled by that madman."

"As any good leader would do," said Aodhgan.

"A leader, yes, but whether I was good or not must be left up to time, I expect. I come here to beg you to shelter them. I have nothing to give you in compensation but the Grace of God that only heaven carries."

"Of course we will give them shelter," said Myndil. "That's what we're supposed to do—right, abbot?" Myndil turned around. "Abbot?"

The abbot was walking into the water, the dismal wreck of his own reflection gawping back at him, his aspect crowned by a loom of stars, the moon mocking him. He walked in up to his waist and stopped, gaping despondently across the sea. "He did it..." he mumbled. "Damn the boy... he did it..."

"And what of the rest of your kingdom?" Eochaid continued.

"A fate left to the one who will replace me," said Constantine. "My cousin Máel Coluim, a young man and hopefully less foolhardy to trust to the whims of lunatics. My line, as it is, is ended. I buried my child in the name of God and I gave my kingship to one who might use it better. I promised that I would retire to an abbey, and here I am. I mean to be ordained, and I mean to be your a disciple," turning to Myndil, "if you will have me."

Myndil started at the appeal. "Me? But I cannot ordain you—I can't even teach you. I'm not an abbot. I'm not even a brother."

"But God chose you," said Constantine, almost overwhelmed by grief. "He gave you the sense to try to stop me from going to war, and he took you from the field before the battle was done. Yes," standing close and marking Myndil's features, "God follows you. I do not know by what grace he does, but he follows you, and so I will follow you, and so will they."

He knelt down and lowered his head, and his people followed, the ripple of genuflection waving over the crowd. Owain was looking at the carrageen that had just washed up near his foot and forgot to kneel until Constantine slapped his arm and pulled him down. The image of a hundred people pledging to devote themselves to Myndil and his god was not lost on his friends: Vindimir stood in silent astonishment, Crannach and Iarlaith smiled knowingly at one another, the abbess clutched her breast and cried on Aodhgan, and Eochaid grinned at the abbot, who was weeping and disclaiming to the sky.

This was all too much for one who had hardly thought himself deserving of so many supporters, and Myndil drew Constantine to his feet and urged everyone else to follow. "I think," said he, glancing over his shoulder and speaking low, "you had better learn from the abbot instead. The two of you are nearly the same age and seem to dislike similar things, which is always helpful, and," spying the abbot in the water, "I think he really needs a friend."

The abbot's shoulders shook as he wailed. "I give up, God! I give up! You win..." sobbing and holding out his arms, "...you win. I give myself unto you, O Lord, and ask that you take me into your embrace..."

He sank back onto the bank, his legs in the water, his features raised and eyes closed, waiting for absolution or death. Something touched his shoulder, and he shuddered. He thought it might have been God, coming to claim him at last, but it felt too much like a hand. He opened his eyes and looked up, and found Myndil standing over him with Constantine at his side.

"He would like to be ordained," said Myndil gently.

"Oh." The abbot moved out of the water and hemmed. "Yes."

Myndil moved farther off, to help everyone gather the refugees into the abbey, and the two men stood on the shore for sometime, each looking at the other, humbled and chastened, one ruined by vanity, the other ruined by indignation, both humbled by a young man armed with a book.

"You absolutely hate this boy, don't you?" asks Constantine, with a faint smile.

The abbot sighed, his heart almost broke. "With all my soul."

Constantine put a hand on his shoulder, and the abbot sobbed out his woes. He was forced to admit that he had been the cause of his own misery: had he accepted Myndil as he was and ordained him when he asked, he never would have left the abbey, but his own intolerance had set Myndil on the path of righteousness, and if Myndil was now the chosen instrument of God, that was his doing too.

Constantine wrapped his arm around the abbot's shoulders. "I had to deal with Owain for most of my life," was his commiseration. "Come," turning toward the abbey, "We will have much to talk about."

The Brothers and Sisters were busy finding accommodations for their new visitors when Owain sidled Eochaid and asked whether he had seen the wolf again.

"I hope you gave him his treats and told him what a good boy he is," said Owain.

"I actually still have them," said Eochaid, taking the pouch from his pocket.

"Oh. Well, perhaps, when I see the wolf again...?"

Eochaid gave Aodhgan a conscious look and changed into the wolf, Aodhgan holding his cousin's human form and Owain clapping giddily.

"This is all I've wanted ever since I first saw him," Owain happily exclaimed. "Isn't he lovely? His coat is so thick and lustrous. And would he like a treat?" He opened the pouch and Eochaid instantly sat on his haunches, his nowl high above Owain's head. His tongue reached down, submerging Owain's hand, and Owain was never more delighted.

"Oh, there's a good boy! Who wants another treat? Yes, I know you do. You're a very good—

oh, would you like to play? If I throw a treat, will you fetch it? There!" tossing a treat across gate. "My, you jump so high and run so quickly—I was almost blown back! Would you like another? Oh, you want your belly rubbed." Owain knelt down and scratched Eochaid's stomach.

Aodhgan was thoroughly amused. "If only all our guests in Osraige were so willing to see our wolves," he simpered.

"How many are there?" Owain asked, rolling in the grass beside Eochaid. "Are they all different sizes and different colours?"

"We're all different. My cousin will be on his way back to our kingdom. Perhaps you would like to accompany him."

"Oh, may I? Please? I have no more kingdom to rule. I have left it all to my son to deal with. I should like to go, if you'll let me."

"Yes, please take him," said Constantine, with a withering look, walking by with the abbot. "I have had to rule with him at my heels for forty-three years. Take him away with you, and let me have my retirement in peace."

Myndil was portioning out part of his room for their guests and telling Thingunderthebed that as glad as he was to see her, she was to be a very good girl and not give anyone any nightmares.

"Ah promyse," said the horrible voice, under the mattress, "but onleh if Ah can give yeh nyghtmares latehr on."

"Of course you can," said Myndil. "You know how much I love your demonic murmuring. Nothing else puts me to sleep so quickly."

He gave his Good Book pillow to some of the children, dressed his blankets around the older women, and furnished everyone with tea who wanted it. He found Brother Vindimir's glass on the nightstand and went to put it in his room when he suddenly stopped and said to himself, "I should refill it first. I'm sure he will be thirsty after such a day, and he will need some water to splash onto Thingunderthebed if she frightens him." He turned and went into the hall, and standing before him was Brother Vindimir, looking somewhat bewildered and forlorn. "Oh, there you are, Brother Vindimir. I found your glass beside the bed," Myndil told him. "I'm going to refill it. Would you like cold water or warm?"

Brother Vindimir, with a very good grace, took the glass and held it, looking it over for a while. "Myndil," said he, with great contrition, "I owe you an apology."

"What? But why? You haven't done anything wrong, and certainly never done anything wrong to me."

"But I have, Myndil, and my conscience is preying upon me about it, and it cannot rest with me. You see—" Vindimir paused to consider. "I know it might seem futile to say it now, but—" He hesitated, his eyes downcast and shoulders stooping. "I did not always like you, Myndil, and as such did not treat you with as much compassion as you deserved. When you first came to us—we thought—I thought you had been hurt and neglected by parents, and indulged you almost as much as everyone else did. You were so small and so immensely thoughtful, especially for a child so

210

young, but you spoke to yourself very often, so much so that we began to wonder about you."

"But I am always talking to myself, Brother Vindimir, because I often talk to God."

"Yes, and that is precisely what I mean to tell you." Vindimir sighed. "Did not you find, Myndil, that when God sometimes spoke to you, he sounded a bit like me?"

"Oh, yes, but God has many different voices."

Vindimir recalled Aodhgan telling him that God spoke to Myndil on the road. "He does? But are you quite sure about that?"

"Of course. When God speaks to you in the privacy of your own mind, doesn't God sometimes sound like you?"

"No, Myndil."

"Oh."

"Myndil, I am trying to tell you that ever since you came here, it was me pretending to be the voice of God. I began doing it because I didn't want you to feel lonely. You came to us in such a state, my heart was broken for you, watching you ask God all these questions all the time and nobody answering, I wanted someone to talk back to you. I began pretending to be God every night when you said your prayers, and then, because of my guilt, I kept doing it, hoping you would grow out of it, but you didn't. I wanted to stop and felt I could no longer deceive you, but I couldn't bear for you to know the truth. I began to grow agitated—really, with myself-- I was tired of sharing a room with Crannach and wanted a room to myself. I acted selfishly and deceitfully, and while I do not deserve your forgiveness, I hope that in time—"

"There's nothing to forgive," said Myndil, his eyes shining. "If you did it then I'm sure God wanted you to do it, and you know it was not your voice I heard all the time. God spoke to me before I came to the abbey too."

"What?" Vindimir paled. "What do you mean before you came to the abbey?"

"Oh, yes. God spoke to me long before I met you, and he spoke to me after I left too. He was with me all the time while I was on my journey."

Vindimir gave him a curious look. "How many voices does God have?"

"Well, if I have to count, at least five."

"And whose voice was it before you came here?"

"Sometimes it was my voice, sometimes my father's, though I can't really remember his voice now, but sometimes it was no voice at all and more of a feeling. If you were the voice of God for me for a little while, I'm sure you only advised me to do good things, because I only like doing good things, and you have raised so many children here, and we learned about loving and minding God from you."

"I hope," said Vindimir, his voice faltering, "I taught you right lessons to live by."

"You must have, because look how many people there are living here now."

Vindimir half smiled. "Yes. And my nonsense about wanting my own room seems so foolish. I wanted to ask you, Myndil, ever since the builders arrived: what did you tell people when you went out? How did you get them to listen to you?"

"I told them what you always told me," Myndil declared, with a glowing aspect. "I told them that God loves them."

Myndil smiled and skipped away, off to find pillows and cushions for those who were sleeping on the floor, and Vindimir sank against the wall, his compunction tyrannizing him. Myndil was only too good, too kind, and too forbearing, abilities that though he had taught them to Myndil were missing in himself. He cried without knowing why, beleaguered by his own failings, feeling undeserving of Myndil's unconditional love.

Crannach soon found him, to tell him they were going to need his room and every room just to house a hundred on top of the inmates they already had, and gave him a cloth to blow his nose into. "Are ye sad about losin' the bedroom again?" Crannach asked.

"How..." said Vindimir, his voice oppressed by tears, "how can he forgive me?"

Crannach shrugged. "That's our Myndil. That's how he's alwaes been, and Ah doan't think he'll ever change."

Vindimir dried his eyes, folded the cloth, and returned it. "Do you think God really does speak to him?"

"Mebbe, but Ah dona't think it matters. If he thinks God talks tae him, he's no' hurtin' anaebodae by it. His real power is no' in his belief in God but in his own abilitae to make friends, and if we gave him the confidence to love everaebodae, then Ah doan't think we did badlae by him."

Warm milk was bringing round for the new children, Iarlaith proving herself to be grand matron of the abbey, an office always of interest to her, and now that she had over a hundred heads to manage, she was happier than ever. The abbot sat with Constantine in the front room, trading stories of their younger days, remarking how much they despised their positions and questioned god, and were glad to be getting to know one another, commiserating over large cups of tea and the crepitation of the large fire, though several of Constantine's people now slept near their feet. It was a mild evening but still cool enough to warrant a lit hearth, the rabble sleeping amongst the masonry outside enjoying their own fire, Thistlewraithe dozing in their shadows, and Ozzy grumbling over Mr Dullahan's head, which he would let bobble into the bulb beds no matter how many times he asked him wrangle his limbs. Crannach brought Vindimir back to his room, sorry to have him back in the bed he had been waiting so long to leave, and as Sister Iarlaith would be joining them, her own room relinquished to the many women who came to stay with them, Vindimir could only sigh and say he would cover his ears when the time for cuddling came.

Myndil went to sleep in Aodhgan's room, along with Eochaid and Owain, having little room even to step around people on the floor of his bedroom. He came in and found Aodhgan lifting the bed and putting it against the wall.

"There will be more room if we all sleep on the floor," Aodhgan insisted.

"But I think there is good room for two in that bed—oh, yes, I see what you mean."

Eochaid put his body in a corner and closed his eyes, Aodhgan did the same, and the two giant

212

werewolves stretched out along the ground, their colossal limbs and long tails curling around one another. Owain took his blanket and snudged against Eochaid.

"It is not every day I can say I got to sleep amongst the pack," Owain exclaimed, nestling down, luxuriating in Eochaid's comfortable coat.

"Well, where shall I sleep?" said Myndil, glancing around at an empty corner.

"On me," said Aodhgan, pointing to his back with his nose.

"Are you sure? You are much bigger than the bed, but I do kick sometimes."

"I probably won't feel it."

"And I do snore, which is why Thingunderthebed likes giving me nightmares."

"Try not to snore in my ears," was Aodhgan's only condition. "My hearing in this form is much more sensitive."

"I'll try not to snarl, in case your instincts think I'm a rival."

Myndil crawled atop the werewolf's back and flumped down, sinking into a sea of fur, the tufts of black lifting up around his outline, the delicious decumbency and warmth from the wolf beneath one Myndil never wanted to sit up from.

"You are amazing comfortable, Aodhgan," Myndil proclaimed, the wisps of wayward fur attacking his mouth.

"I'm also shedding." Aodhgan rested his chin on his forearms. "Your robes might be black tomorrow."

"Well, that is really no trouble. I'll comb it off and give it to Iarlaith so she can make sweaters out of it."

Aodhgan was glad to be useful, even if by default, and the four of them huddled together, resting in a pile, Owain charmed by being raised and lowered against Eochaid's ribs, and Myndil falling asleep almost immediately, his snores so violent Aodhgan muffled them with the end of his tail. It was just after midnight when Abbess Bhaldruithe came to join them. She had given up her own room to accommodate others, and spent five minutes in Crannach and Iarlaith's room before skulking away to Aodhgan's, the remembrance of their night together making her long for that night again. She stood on the threshold, a little fearful at first of the sight of two giant wolves, but Owain's blissful smiles and Myndil's snores convinced her that she was certainly most welcome. Ears flicked and perked, an eye opened, and the abbess took her place at Aodhgan's side, burrowing into the penetrable coats, sinking into the wealth of comfort, an iron arm providing her with ample cover, a muzzle turning to rest in her lap.

Under the veil of serene security, the abbey and all its inhabitants slept undisturbed until morning. The early hours saw the abbot and Constantine awake, each having fallen asleep in their chairs, Sister Iarlaith up before anybody, to bake the bread and boil water, and Myndil, in the confusion of cubicular comfort, was warmed over by the morning sun. He was awake but not willingly, his eyes still closed, the indulgence of a lupine cradle carrying him in and out of consciousness.

MYNDIL.

The voice roused him, but Myndil's eyes remained closed. "Mmmf?"

MYNDIL.

The voice grew louder but not more ardent.

Myndil tootled to himself. "Is that you, Thingunderthebed? It doesn't sound like you..."

His head sank back onto the bed of thick fur and he began to drift again.

MYNDIL. IT IS TIME TO RISE.

"Is it? But Aodhgan's wooliness is so lovely..."

THOU HAST DUTIES.

He did; now that Myndil was back at the abbey, he had his daily chores to do and prayers to perform, and the particular voice roused him slightly. "Is that you, God?"

YES, CHILD.

"Oh, hello, God!" he yawned, making his pandiculations with his eyes closed. "I missed hearing you. Does this mean you aren't angry with me anymore? I am sorry about the war and all, but you did tell me to speak to the kings—" Myndil realized and was up in a moment. "Hallo, God!" sitting up and opening his eyes. "I'm awake and ready to do the morning pr—"

He blinked and saw several faces staring at him.

"Myndil," said Eochaid, standing over him in human form, "are you all right?"

"Oh, yes, perfectly well. God just came to say hello. Did you hear him?"

Aodhgan gently rolled Myndil off his back and pressed his nose against him. "I think you were dreaming."

"Oh. But was I? Because God sounded like Brother Vindimir again, and he is sleeping all the way on the other side of the abbey."

Aodhgan changed into his human form and came to stand Myndil on his feet. "I think you might be feeling some concern about everything that's happened."

"Oh. Well, we'd better start helping Sister Iarlaith. She will have many breakfasts to make."

He hoped they all had a pleasant sleep and left the room, his smiles fading slightly, his conscience now aware of Vindimir's roll in playing god—but it could not have been him—or was it Velinas, back to tell him about more bets with heathen deities?

THOU HAST NO NEED TO WORRY.

The voice spoke in solace and rose from the back of Myndil's mind.

GOD LOVES YOU.

The assurance was all Myndil needed to carry the day, and he continued down the hall, all the chores and all the work that must be done seeming trivial compared with the joy in his heart. He had been the agent of chaos, he had helped bring down three kingdoms at least, and he entered the kitchen with a smile for Iarlaith, feeling himself acquitted of any qualms, glad that God should love him, regardless of whether it was really god or not.

CHAPTER 26: IN WHICH LIFE HAPPENS TO THE ABBEY

Breakfast was better than everyone had expected, the vat of boiled oats and brined meat serving everyone at the abbey, and the several large bucks that Aodhgan and Eochaid brought in later in the morning would more than feed them all, making the abbot not half so irritated that they had left clumps of hair all along the halls.

Baths and clothes were provided for everyone who wanted them, Myndil apologizing to their many guests that they had not something better to offer. The abbess and Iarlaith promised that they should start work right away on new outfits for the children, and Constantine for his part went about looking to resettle his people, claiming that Alba had allies in Ulaid and might be willing to have help on the farms once the height of spring should come around. Eochaid offered everyone a place in Osraige, claiming, "Though it's a small kingdom, we have more than enough room for everyone. The journey is long, but everyone is welcome, as long as you don't mind our wolves."

Few could refute so generous an offer, but they would wait and see what their king could do for them before leaving him behind.

The letter from Osraige soon came to beckon Eochaid home. He had told his father that Aodhgan would be staying behind and worried that their father might dissent.

"He gives you leave only to stay until the wedding," said Eochaid, reading the letter to him, "and then he wants you home. He cannot bear to be without you so long. I think he loves you more than he loves me. He doesn't mention how happy he is to have me return."

Aodhgan laughed and gave his cousin's shoulder an affectionate press. "Because he is going to scold you for hunting by yourself at night and getting captured. It's your fault that I was away."

Eochaid smiled and read on. "He says that when you do come home, you are more than welcome to bring her." He glanced at the abbess, who was fitting wool caps on all the smallest children. "Father is overjoyed for you."

"I will need a companion when you are married," said Aodhgan, in a fond hue. "You will have your own insolent children to chase soon enough."

Eochaid had not thought that far ahead and pleaded, "Let me marry first. We will see if she wants wolves to raise."

They locked in a warm embrace, pressing their foreheads together, Aodhgan saying he should miss him dreadfully, and asking only that he should write to him when he was safe at home.

"I will, and I will send it with plenty of stock for the larder here," Eochaid assured him, "however much they need to last the winter. There are many people here now, and there are likely to be more coming."

"I will hunt and provide for them."

"Even rabbits, cousin?"

Aodhgan grimaced. "If I have no other choice."

Eochaid prepared to leave the abbey, thanked the abbot and all of his hosts for their great kindness in accommodating him, and everyone gathered at the front gate to see him off. He turned to Myndil, who came forward with a hug, and Eochaid lifted him off his feet, crushed him affectionately, and put him down again.

"I never would have believed someone as fortunate as you existed if we had not met," said Eochaid, putting a hand on Myndil's shoulder. "Werewolves have few friends outside our kingdom, and I am grateful that God has given me you as a friend. As prince of Osraige, I extend every invitation of hospitality to you, Myndil, and as you mean to go out again and gain more followers, I ask that you make your way to Osraige and visit us anytime. My father's house is always open to you. My only request is that when you come, you won't bring any wars with you."

Myndil and Aodhgan laughed. Constantine, who was within hearing, made a sepulchering sigh.

"You will come with Aodhgan for the wedding, and when the abbot ordains you," said Eochaid, giving the abbot a sharp look, "I'll convince my father to let you do the ceremony."

"Really?" Myndil cried, leaping up and down, "I can marry you? I mean—I can marry you and your betrothed, but I would marry you too, if you asked me, because between you and Aodhgan, I could sleep on either one of you every night."

"You might have competition there," Eochaid rumbled in mirth, "but I appreciate your offer." He glanced at the back of the crowd. "Your Grace, are you ready?"

"Yes, yes, just coming!" the little man joggled, noggling up to him. "I was fashioning a little harness, something for me to hold onto that would fit comfortably under your arms." He held up a series of leather straps. "It will wrap about your body and let your undercarriage support you, though it might not be comfortable. We will have to look about for a good riding seat. May we try it out on the way? I don't want the wolf to run all that way-- it will be soon tired—but if we could do just a teensy little RIIIIIIIIIIIIIIIIIIIIIIIDE—"

The wolf was under him in a moment, and in another moment, he was looping his legs through the harness and around his human form, and was off, bounding away down the path and across the low tide, Owain whooping and flopping on his back, having the time of his civilian life. Aodhgan watched him go, with happy lips and sad eyes, but a touch on his arm soon lifted his smiles. He looked down and found Abbess Bhaldruithe at his side, the comfort of her presence softening the pain of parting. He took her hand and pressed it, holding it tight against his side, his immense frame obstructing their display of attachment from the abbot, who would be sure to lament the howls and yawls coming from their room every night.

A few weeks saw the end of the construction at the abbey: the builders were able to secure more stone from a nearby quarry beyond the farms, and with a little gold to persuade them, the farmers conveyed all the materials they needed to finish their job. They even followed Constantine's instruction and fortified the iron gate, the metalworker securing the latch and making entry impossible except from the inside. Everyone was asked to offer their appraisal of the work, and when the new rooms in the dormitory were deemed worthy and everyone was satisfied with the annex, the abbey was declared complete for now. Before the rabble took their leave, as the snowdrops of late

216

winter were sprouting from the flowerbeds, the abbey was named and a sign saying "YEW AR VERY WELLCOM TO THE ROGHA AN DA DHIOGHA ABBEY" was erected just beyond the tidal crossing, inviting anyone who was looking for refuge and a warm meal to enter, the sign reminding them in small letters to "MYND THE DULLAHAN."

A new life happened at the abbey, and at the instigation of Aodhgan and the resignation of Myndil, the abbot conceded to ordain him, though Myndil was not being made a Brother. He would remain a holy man, as Vindimir jokingly called him, one to whom everyone could look for prayers and songs, hope and interest, an avatar of what godliness should be, a right model of happiness, someone to perform ceremonies and gain followers, and go or stay at the abbey as he liked. Myndil would stay for a while, eager to see what the rest if the islands had to offer but wanting to be home just now, glad to see the abbey flourish and eager to help with so many followers to manage. He assisted the refugees Constantine had brought with him, helping to rehouse them at the farms not far off, the letters Constantine had written to his connexions in Ulaid thoroughly answering, the abdicated king having more allies than he previously believed. A few more weeks saw the chief of the refugees comfortably resettled, some staying on to study at the abbey, and Constantine remaining with them to be ordained. After some study and much commiseration under the abbot, Constantine became a Brother, happy to enjoy the simple pleasures of warm gruel and raising children, the weight of managing a kingdom traded for the responsibility of spiritual consummation, and though he was glad to be relieved of Owain, he did miss him. He was a someone to speak to, a someone to sympathize with throughout the whole of his reign, though their conversations consisted mostly of Constantine's complaints. He gained a new friend in the abbot, who was softening as to his ideas of suffering being wholesome, Constantine providing him with a different perspective on comfort and devotion, each lamenting on the other's trials, and Constantine bearing the abbot away whenever Myndil was by.

Myndil had happened to many people, but in the case of Aodhgan, this was reckoned a good thing. He had been the pride of Osraige, the fondling of the king and right hand of the royal family, appointed guardian to the heir of the ancient throne, but here Aodhgan's only duty was to be useful, and his only obligation was to fill the larder every night. He spent his evenings hunting, spent his early mornings patrolling the woods and the coastal line, and spent much of the day with the children, who did not mind the wolf as long as it played with them and gave them rides. He loved their attention, letting them pull his ears and climb all over him, and though the abbot had told the children no hounds, he said nothing about werewolves. The abbot made his plaintive airs over the amount of fur he found on the carpet before the fire, but any time he complained, Crannach was good to remind him that if the abbot had never sent Myndil away, Aodhgan would never have come back with him. Aodhgan was sure to help everyone, conveying anything that needed to be carried, aiding the children in their lessons, always ready to man the infirmary, helping to sniff out lost toys and missing books, telling Dimeadh to bathe after smelling him across the garden, and warming the bed of one who always wanted him and never minded the wolf.

Abbess Bhaldruithe was perfectly fulfilled at the abbey. She was only too happy to have

217

so many new people to care for, glad to take up the duty she had once had at her own abbey, and ready to help everyone ruined by war regain what they had lost. She served and smiled, preparing all the baths for the new children, drying them off and dressing their limbs, providing everyone with linens and furs—the latter fashioned from the many tufts she found in her room—and making sure everyone always had the succour and support they needed, filling every hand with tea and offering everyone a bed. She spent her afternoons marching across the peristyle, with the brace and buckets strapped across her shoulders, going to and from the large well many times over. At the end of a day, the buckets were often too much for her to lift, her strength having its limits, but there was one whose strength never faltered, whose unconquerable brawn never failed. She filled the buckets to the top and stooped under the brace, her back beginning to ache from carrying them all day, but a giant hand descended and relieved her of her duties, lifting the brace from her shoulders and carrying them off with little effort. She looked up and saw Aodhgan walking ahead of her, carrying the brace in one hand as though they weighed nothing, taking them across the garden, putting them down beside the kitchen door, and walking away without turning round, not evening stopping to be thanked. She would thank him later, of course, with parted thighs and writhing supplications, her fervent calls to god, offered either on her back or on her knees, Aodhgan gladly receiving them and returning them, praising their lord for giving her so much compassion and endowing her with two very prominent gifts he would always appreciate.

Myndil became the emissary for the Rogha an dá Dhíogha abbey, his once-little orphanage now the pride of the northeastern coast, boasting the residence of kings, master builders, lord protectors, faefolk and werewolves, the beacon of hope and salvation, a sanctuary for anyone who needed it. The small upland island had been the saving of him when he was young, and now he was glad to give it over to others, to share in Sister Iarlaith's meals, in Brother Crannach's affection, in Brother Vindimir's sense, and in the abbot's sufferings. His greatest happiness in life was to see everyone else happy likewise, and if he had been the means of showing someone the effect of acceptance and unconditional love, he was satisfied and asked nothing more. Myndil had happened to the world, though it liked him in general, it still gave him back just in case. He still talked on, still spoke to god every morning and night, and though he had learned about the origin of two of the voices, he still spoke to god because he could not help it; God had always been his closest friend, his greatest supporter, one whom Myndil could tell everything whether there was anyone really listening or not, one whom Myndil was always willing to love because he must love everybody. He was goodness itself, made more so by his spirit than his situation, his divinity arising more from the goodwill of others than the lessons to be learned in his book. His oration was still horrendous, but he would practice, though he had proven it was better to gain followers by showing them kindness than by telling them of it. Even if his idea of god was not what everyone else's was, it had defended him against the cruelties of life and allowed him to make the most wonderful friends, everyone who loved him agreeing that even if he was not particularly divine, he was most certainly pure of heart.

218

Fate of the Norns: Ragnarok
SAGA - FAFNIR'S TREASURE

Fate of the Norns: Ragnarok
CORE RULEBOOK

CHILDREN OF ERIU

Fate of the Norns: Ragnarok
LORDS OF THE ASH

PENDELHAVEN PUBLISHING